TO
Scotland
FOR LOVE

Other Titles by Lizbeth Selvig

The Heirs of Craigwarren
Never and Forever Scotland

Seven Brides for Seven Cowboys
The Bride Wore Denim
The Bride Wore Red Boots
The Bride Wore Starlight
Betting On Paradise
Heating Up Paradise

Love From Kennison Falls
The Rancher and the Rock Star
Rescued by a Stranger
Beauty and the Brit
Good Guys Wear Black

Chandler County
Missing By a Heartbeat
Missing One Angel

Anthologies
Love in the Land of Lakes – What's Up Dock?
Festivals of Love – Bun Wars
Wild Deadwood Tales – Gotta Have Faith

TO
Scotland
FOR LOVE

An Heirs of Craigwarren Novel

LIZBETH
SELVIG

Webster Publishing

To Scotland For Love

ISBN: 978-0-9988564-9-0

DEDICATION

To Robin

You were always the most amazing cheerleader, supporter, reader, encourager, and believer-in-me. I cannot believe you won't be beside me at launches and book signings, making swag with me until all hours, and quilting up a storm, but I'll forever hold you in my heart and feel you watching over me with your angel wings.
Thank you, my beloved sister. I will miss you. I will love you always.

CHAPTER ONE

"It looks more like a gargoyle than a god," Bridget said.

Noah Portman glanced at his sister, squatting beside him on the century-old ballroom floor next to a prone wooden figure. He couldn't argue with her. The four-foot-long oak sculpture billed as a statue of Jupiter, stared at them with half a face and had, to use the kindest terms, seen better days.

"He does," he said. "The old head of the Roman gods here has had a tough fifty years."

"'*Head* of the gods?' Noah, did you make a pun?" Bridget's green eyes always shone with fun but never more so than when she teased him. "I'm speechless!"

"That'll be the day," he muttered.

He flexed his shoulders and raised his eyes, taking in the huge, ruined ballroom of the Broadburn Hotel. Over the years, Minneapolis city planners had systematically razed most of the derelict business buildings left from the early twentieth century, but the long-abandoned Broadburn had miraculously avoided the wrecking ball. Courtesy of an entrepreneur with more zeroes on his bank balance than Noah could fathom, the hundred-year-old hotel was about to get a second chance at life. He was here to meet the man, and make a bid for taking on this room's renovation.

The sheer scale of the job, however, had Noah thinking twice. If he hadn't needed the commission more than he wanted to admit, he'd have thought more than twice.

Bridget patted the statue's one solid cheek. "Poor Jupiter. It'll take a master carver to repair him. Or a magician."

"Of which I am neither."

"Oooh, I call B.S." She swirled her index finger at him. "You wouldn't be one of only two people Frederickson is considering if you weren't a magician—with wood, at least."

Noah adored his sister, but she'd been prone to Pollyanna syndrome since the day of her birth. If she wasn't telling people they needed more happiness and magic in their lives, she was showing them how to find it—a sometimes valuable but often highly annoying trait.

"At first glance, this is a much bigger job than I imagined, Bridge. Don't oversell my abilities."

"I couldn't oversell you. This is the kind of opportunity you've been dreaming about."

He couldn't argue with that, either. Carefully, he picked at the ruined half of Jupiter's face, gauging the depth of damage. Several splinters of oak crumbled away. He stood, stretching quads that burned from squatting too long. Bridget bounced up with him.

"So?" she said. "It'll be a fun challenge to fix him, right?"

"That can't be fixed. It has to be replaced."

She waved a hand. "Easy-peasy."

He stared as if she wasn't a living, breathing master's degree candidate. "Do you actually know the meaning of 'easy-peasy'?"

"Sure. It means, give it to Noah Portman."

A long sigh eased from his chest. He shouldn't be surprised; over-the-top enthusiasm was her thing. Besides, Bridget had given up a precious morning free of classes to accompany him. He should appreciate her passion and her unwavering faith.

His feet left a circle in the thick dust on the floor as he turned to take in more from fifty years of neglect. The hundred-year-old ballroom had once been a stunning showpiece, that much he could glean. All that was stunning about it now, however, was the size of the task it would be to restore order.

"Look at this place!" Bridget gestured as if it were a roomful of treasure and not trashed walls and fixtures. "It's incredible."

"I carve animals and make furniture. I'm not sure I renovate vintage ballrooms."

"You carve very realistic animals, and you make furniture that puts all other woodworkers to shame." Bridget grabbed his hand and tugged. "Come on, Gloomy Gus. I'm Leonard Frederickson. Tell me how you start in here."

She all but danced him through the sea of fallen crown molding pieces littering the broken parquet flooring, her Tigger to his Eeyore. Bounce to caution. Optimist to pessimist. The way they'd always been. Flutters of what was, maybe, early excitement stirred deep within him. Leonard Frederickson of the overflowing bank account, had warned this would be a big project, but Noah hadn't lied. This was more than he'd expected. Even so, appreciation swelled in his artisan's heart. Renovating this space would be a once-in-a-lifetime project.

"The wainscoting would have to be first. It's impressive mahogany, but see here?" He ran his fingers down a section of dull, red-brown wood. "All the cracks? They show how dry and warped the wood has become. And across the room there's water damage on that whole wall—that's not salvageable. I would remove it, see what could be repurposed, and replace it with a sustainable wood— American cherry or even oak. This room is probably eighty-by-forty; the mahogany in here probably cleared acres of rain forest."

"See, you're brilliant!"

"Hardly. That's your easy-peasy part." Noah pushed aside several pieces of wood on the floor with his toe, studying them before bending to pick one up. "This is all crown molding, hand carved back in the day. To replace this exactly would be impossible. I don't know what Frederickson wants, but I hope it wouldn't be to have someone carve two hundred and fifty feet of classical Greek molding."

"You could do it."

"Bridget, stop." He turned her by her shoulders to face him. "You aren't here to be impractical, only to encourage."

She smiled and saluted. "I know, I know, but if I don't get all excited, who will?"

"Nobody else will need to."

"Then I'll have done my duty."

He pointed to the three soaring windows on the outside wall of the room, two topped with massive wooden valance boxes, covered in carved grapevines and flowers. "Those need complete refurbishing, assuming the wood is in good enough shape, and a third needs to be built and carved from scratch. I suppose that's easy-peasy too."

Her eyes softened and she placed a hand on each of his forearms. "Look, I'm sorry. I know full well this is anything but easy. I happen to think it's an amazing, worthwhile project. It's like raising the *Titanic* and fixing it up."

"Really? The *Titanic*?"

Bridget pointed at him. "Right, there it is, your skeptical hermit face. I'm serious, Noah. If the art of this doesn't excite you, then look at the practical. You've said yourself if you don't get some bigger commissions, you'll be selling carvings and furniture from underneath a freeway bridge. Well, brother of mine, commissions don't come any bigger than this."

There it was: stark reality.

The letter had come from his landlord last week, informing him the garage apartment where he lived and worked was being sold. He had six weeks to find a new place. The timeline seemed generous enough on the surface, but Noah would never find a space as affordable as where he was. Without a fresh source of income, he might well find himself between a workshop and an overpass.

Bridget was wrong, however, that the art of this project didn't excite him. Despite his Eeyore-ish streak, the ballroom renovation fed completely into his dedication to craftsmanship. Eeyore thrived within him not because he didn't appreciate beauty, but because he knew better than to count on things or people until he was sure they'd be around long enough to deserve an outpouring of emotion.

"Once upon a time, this place was big and bold and filled with partying people," Bridget said, eclipsing his thoughts. "Reclaiming it would be a massive undertaking, sure, but it *would* be like repairing the *Titanic*, and wouldn't that be wonderful?"

"It's not the *Titanic*. It's a crumbling hotel."

"A hundred-year-*old*, crumbling hotel they want to place on the historic register."

He finally allowed a smile at her exuberance. She really was hopeless.

The phone in his pocket buzzed and his smile faded. He did business through his modest website and a landline. Only important clients and family members had the cell's number.

"Maybe Frederickson is running late?" He pulled out the phone, but his brother's name flashed on the screen. "Strange. It's Ewan."

They talked on Saturday afternoons, regularly as clockwork, Ewan from his new home in Scotland, Noah from his small apartment. This was Monday.

"So, answer," Bridget said.

"I'll call him back. Frederickson is due any second, and I don't want to tell Ewan about this until it's a done deal."

He started to put the phone back in his pocket, but Bridget grabbed it. "If he's calling at an odd time like this, it must be important."

Noah narrowed his eyes in reproach, and she huffed at him.

"For crying out loud, Noah." She answered and lifted the phone to her ear. "Hey, Ewan! How's bonnie Scotland?" She paused, her whole face lighting up as she laughed. "Does it ever *not* rain? … Yes, he's here, looking at a lot of dust. That's why I answered…" She squinted around the room. "Well? As a matter of fact, there's something potentially very big up. Why? Is your Spidey-sense tingling again? … Wait, seriously? I was kidding."

She stared at Noah and pointed to the phone, her eyes widening. He understood her amazement. Ewan never failed to know when something was happening, good or bad, big or small. He had a scary gift—like a freaking psychic.

"No, no, it's no bother, I'll grab him," Bridget said. "Say hi to Ainslie, okay? Love you!"

Noah hesitated when she held out the phone again. She leaned toward him, and her dark chestnut hair framed her face, accentuating those green eyes, making her look like an exasperated cat.

"You might be the most wonderful recluse I know," she whispered, "but I *also* know you require regular advice on how to get out of your cave and grab the world by the tail. You'd do everything on your own if we let you, but Ewan could give you good advice."

He took the phone and turned away, knowing his irritation was unreasonable. She was right again. He did guard his reputation as a minor recluse, but only because it offered him some control over his interactions with others. People were perfectly fine; he simply preferred they avoid crowding or clinging or adjusting his schedule. He put the phone to his ear.

"Whaddya want?" he said, dispensing with a real greeting. "You're bothering me at work."

Ewan's warm laugh eased Noah's tetchiness. His brother was only a year older, but he'd always been Noah's champion, even since moving away.

"Glad to hear there's work to interrupt, but I told Bridget you could call me back."

"It does no good to tell Bridget anything. What's wrong?"

"Nothing. Tell me you're really in the middle of some huge decision. I'll know I'm right, and let you go."

"Right about…?"

"A premonition."

"You and your weird-ass premonitions. I'm bidding on a job, that's all."

"A big job?"

"That old Broadburn Hotel near St. Anthony. Guy named Frederickson from some investment firm is renovating the place and he's looking for someone to work on the ballroom."

"It's a great opportunity." Ewan wasn't asking a question, and the hairs on the back of Noah's neck stood in prickly attention.

"You know that somehow?"

"I usually know a good deal from a bad. Vibes, man."

"You are a frightening person." The goose bumps he got from Ewan's weird woo-woo dissipated. "I'm meeting the guy any minute. I'll let you know if he convinces me it's great."

"You should take the job."

Noah sighed. "There's another guy in the running. I know him, and he's damn good. He's also got a partner, and that could mean he'd get the job done faster than I could."

"You're a better choice. My advice? Bid fair, don't try to lowball because you think you're some kind of rookie at this. Impress this guy with your skill and fairness. I think you'll get it."

As if Ewan knew anything about bidding contracting work. He was an advertising guy, like their father. However, he did know people.

"Yeah, yeah. Thanks, I'll wow the hell out of him. Now tell me what you really called about."

A beat of silence verified that he'd caught out his brother.

"Told you…I had a feeling."

"Nope. That's a cover. If that were all, you'd have called me later tonight and asked *why* you'd had this feeling."

"You keep thinking and go meet your developer. Call you later is exactly what I'm gonna do." His voice was overly cheery and upbeat.

"Ewan, it's me. Knock it off. What do you want?"

"Your help saving my ass. But it's a long story. I'll tell you when you're done."

Concern landed like a dead weight in Noah's gut. Suddenly, he wasn't sure his brother's 'feeling' had anything to do with him. "Okay, I'm serious. What's wrong?"

"Nobody's dying." Ewan's voice breezed over the words. "I've got a housing inspector breathing down my neck, and I need your expertise. That's it."

Seconds earlier he'd said he wanted "help saving my ass." This brush-off was too casual. Ewan had been a complicated mix of big brother, father figure, and best friend since he'd been five and Noah four, and their mother had lost her battle with leukemia. There was little the two hadn't and didn't share, and Noah knew his brother better than he knew himself. Ewan's requests for help were rare.

"As long as nobody's dying," he deadpanned.

"No humans. There's a goat here that might die soon."

"Uhhh, you've officially been there too long, dude. What?"

"No lie, there's a goat. Lives in the barn, slightly crazy, her newest skill is opening the gate to let the chickens out. She's a pain in the rear."

"No wonder you need your ass saved. You haven't got nearly enough to do."

Ewan's chuckle flowed across the miles again. "Oh, man. I wish that were even remotely true. Text me when you're home. I'll let you go now."

"Yeah, okay." Noah hesitated. "You're sure everything's okay?"

"I am. Talk soon."

They disconnected and Noah stood, staring at the phone. Ewan needed his advice. No big deal. Why, then, did it feel more like a seismic event was hovering beneath him waiting to shift the earth?

Ridiculous. Things were up in the air, and even minor emotions were off-kilter. Noah wanted this commission. He needed it. He wasn't at all sure he could land it. Having Ewan call with some enigmatic problem only played into the stress. There were no seismic shifts.

He shook off the phone call and focused back on his surroundings. Bridget stood fifty feet away next to a large bundle on the floor. He followed her zig-zag path through the dust, and when he reached her she held out a piece of fallen crown molding covered in intricate filigree swirls.

"What if you carved something fancy for the corners and maybe the middle of each wall, then machine worked the rest with simple, classic lines?"

He scratched one cheek. "That could work."

He could make anything work when it came to wood. In truth, he understood wood far better than he did people. Wood was more malleable, more forgiving, even longer lasting given the proper care. Still, carving massive, intricate, grape-vined window cornices and Roman gods in large-statue form?

"It's all doable," he said quietly. "Daunting, though."

She waved a dismissive hand and pointed past the scaffold to the top of the room. "Only because of the time it will take. Imagine those faded floral murals on the ceiling. Picture it with the crown molding done, those light fixture frames rebuilt and the painting refurbished."

"You aren't going to compare it to the Sistine Chapel, are you?"

She laughed softly, all teasing gone from her voice. "No, Eeyore. I'm telling you I know this isn't simply remodeling a room. *This* is a legacy."

A fresh thrill of anticipation swept him.

"Yeah, yeah." He downplayed his blossoming eagerness and focused on the bundle under the scaffold. "What's this?"

He squatted again and pulled on the corner of what looked like faded gold brocade draperies. After careful unwrapping, he revealed the treasure with a long, low whistle. Bridget let out a gasp. In front of them lay another statue, this one in far better shape than the first.

"This guy makes what's left of Jupiter over there not even count as a carving." Bridget said.

The new statue also lay face up. Its oak finish had dulled with time, but a few golden-brown patches, still polished to the warm, original patina, survived. The figure bore a wide fool's grin, a four-foot-long, curly beard, and a cherubic-body with its arms surrounding a large, round vessel, tilted to allow free-flowing wine.

"I'd say we've found Bacchus," Noah said. "He was one of the four statues Frederickson said originally stood in the corners."

"Dude's clearly ready to party." Bridget laughed.

This version of the Roman god of wine was a cross between classic depictions of a fat, gluttonous drunk and kinder images of a leaner, slightly inebriated younger man. The finely carved features, the intricate curls in the beard, and the cheerful flow of the carver's strokes mesmerized

Noah. On inspection, he found one hand, one foot, and a few beard curls missing, and there were significant cracks in the wine vessel and the statue's torso. Even so, it was the best-preserved thing in the room.

"Michelangelo is turning green with envy from the grave," Bridget said, giving Bacchus's cheek a deferential stroke.

Noah pursed his lips in amusement. "This is a nice carving, but I think old Mike already did the definitive Bacchus."

"Nah, they hated his sculpture back in his day. And this carving *nice*? It's gorgeous. And they want you to repair it and carve three more from scratch to go with him. I am so proud of you."

"I haven't been chosen yet. But it would be an opportunity."

Her exasperated cat surfaced again. "You are the most understated man in the history of men. An understater's understater. This is career-making, Noah. This would mean it doesn't matter that your arse of a landlord is evicting you. You can find your bliss—the way Ewan did."

His heart twisted slightly. Their brother had found his *bliss* all right, four-thousand miles away with a woman who was in the process of turning him into a skirt-wearing Scotsman as well as, in four months, her husband. It all made a nice, tidy story on the surface, since their late mother had been born and raised in the Highlands of Scotland and, by virtue of her birthright, left her three children with the three-hundred-acre homestead in Glencoe where Ewan now lived. Still, the inheritance—and his future sister-in-law, Ainslie— had spirited Ewan away making yet another person as good as gone from his life.

"'Bliss' is no more than one of your romance novel words. And 'arse'? Really?"

"Practicing Scot-speak. Ewan used it when he came home to visit, and it's much funnier than 'ass.' I'll need it when we go for his wedding. And you should read a few romances to soften up. You're a curmudgeon at age thirty-three." She patted his cheek.

He shook away thoughts of Ewan getting married in a kilt and scowled at Bridget. His life situation wasn't ideal or romantic. He lived and worked out of a remodeled garage. Still, he managed. He sold a few carvings on consignment here and there, and got enough custom woodworking jobs to keep himself clothed and eating. Moonlighting with Curt Robinson Contracting, an old friend's construction business, paid most utilities. However, since neither his landlord nor Robinson, ancient school friendship aside, were princes among men, Noah didn't need romance. He didn't need bliss. He needed security.

Out of the corner of his eye, he saw the door to the ballroom open and he nudged Bridget.

"Frederickson," he whispered.

A rich bass voice filled the room ahead of the man who possessed it. "Noah! You made it. Sorry I'm late."

Leonard Frederickson covered the ground between them rapidly, his short stature at odds with the thespian-worthy voice. He stood half a foot below Noah's six-one, but his build was twice as muscular. Noah knew the celebrated entrepreneur and philanthropist was in his late fifties, but the only hint of his age were the threads of silver in his neat black beard and at his temples. His youthful face, as rich a brown as Bacchus's burnished oak, exuded conviviality and perfect confidence. His jeans and untucked light-blue polo shirt made him as approachable as someone's really cool dad.

"I'm very happy to meet you in person at last," he said.

"Mr. Frederickson." Noah grasped the man's outstretched hand. "Likewise."

"What do you think of my project? Pretty amazing, isn't it?"

"I don't think you did it justice when we spoke."

"It's hard to describe." He turned to Bridget. "Hello. I'm Leonard Frederickson."

"I'm Bridget Portman. This is an amazing room. An amazing building."

"It is. It'll be a great asset to the city when it's completed. That's the plan, anyway. And you two...?" He waggled a finger between her and Noah.

"He's my brother," she said. "I'm here to help him navigate the social aspects of this meeting. He's the talent. I'm the extrovert."

"I see. Temperamental artist, eh?"

"Far from temperamental," she said. "Calmest person you'll ever meet."

Noah *was* rarely flustered, but he wanted to gag his chatty sister. People didn't need to have this much information about him or his personality. His work should speak for itself. Frederickson only smiled and turned to Noah.

"What's your first impression?"

"It's a monumental job, but it's doable."

"Exactly what I thought when *I* first saw it. In my opinion, this is the most important room in the renovation plan. It doesn't have the most damage, but it has the most precious damage. It's doable, you say?"

"There's more research to do. Some of this wood will be hard to match. And I'd like to know what new woods you're willing to use and what you expect for the statues."

Frederickson smiled and nodded. "I appreciate that you aren't cocky at this stage."

"Noah won't be cocky at any stage," Bridget said. "Confident, but never overly so."

He shot her a that's-enough-talking glare and turned back to Frederickson.

"This isn't a project to take for granted. There's nothing easy about it, although the challenge is intriguing."

Frederickson nodded. "I've been upfront that I'm considering two bids for this job. One thing I like about your resume is your construction experience in addition to your carving skills. The other candidate concentrates almost exclusively on artwork and sculpting."

"I know him," Noah said. "He's talented."

And more gregarious, a faster worker with a looser style, and possessed of a decent-sized ego. But undeniably talented.

Bridget clapped her hands, nearly dancing in place. "I'm sorry, Mr. Frederickson. But I have to brag a little bit about Noah because he won't."

"Don't…" Noah warned, his voice a throaty growl.

"Yes. Do." Frederickson nodded.

Bridget turned a sweet, victorious smile on Noah. "The other artist might be talented, but my brother has a magic touch with wood. It's a gift from his ancestors."

"Oh, for the love," Noah muttered. Bridget and her obsession with a heritage they knew little about. She'd always been the one sibling fascinated by Scotland and now, with Ewan living there, she'd grown obsessed.

"Ancestors?" Frederickson quirked a brow.

"Scottish," she said. "Our mother was born there and our brother now lives near Glencoe in the Highlands. Believe me, there's magic in the genes, and you'll see it in Noah's work."

"That's it." Noah reached for his sister's upper arm and dragged her gently to stand behind him. "Stop talking now, Bridget. I'm sorry, Mr. Frederickson. If I'd known she wouldn't behave, I'd never have brought her along."

Leonard Frederickson laughed. "Don't apologize for her. A person needs a bit of magic to pull off crazy plans like mine, too. A sense of adventure and wonder now and then is a good thing. Also, you know the original builder of this place was Scottish. *Broadburn*—a wide stream, is what they told me."

"See!" Bridget popped from where Noah had stashed her. "This is *fate!*"

Frederickson held out his hand again. "I'm glad to have met you both. Please, call me Leo. Are you an artist, too, Bridget?"

"Sadly, no. That entire pot of gold went to Noah. I'm a student. Finishing my master's in anthropology."

"Sounds fascinating."

"To a history nerd, yes." She laughed. "I definitely find this *room* fascinating. It might not be ancient, but it's a wonderful starting point for a study of people."

Leo studied them. "You two make a unique team." He rubbed his palms together. "Let's take a quick spin around the room. Give me your thoughts."

Twenty minutes later, after sharing his observations, with Bridget burbling alongside like a stream they were navigating, Noah stood beside the door with a thoughtful but still-effusive Leo Frederickson.

"Thank you for all your insights, Noah. I'm looking forward to your sketches and your bid."

"I'll get it all to you in a couple of days."

"We're already starting on other parts of the hotel. This room is the final piece. I'd like to make a decision and then have whomever I choose get going as soon as possible."

"I'll look forward to hearing from you."

With that, the man was gone as quickly as he'd appeared, leaving a tiny swirl of dust settling from where he scuffed the floor on his way out.

"Ohmygosh, he's amazing!" Bridget said. "Noah, you've got this. He likes you."

Noah sighed. "He likes *you*. He's one of your alien-race, weird, chirpy people. Annoying as it is, you made good points. It's the only reason I'm not mad as hell at you. Big mouth."

"You're never mad at me. I'm too wonderful."

Noah ignored her and let his gaze roam the room a final time. "It's a hell of a lot of responsibility. It would be far too easy to eff up."

"Yup. But you won't."

He gave up the last of his reticence in the face of her tornadic spirit. If he was honest, carving tools and the art that sprang from them populated his comfort zone. People he could ignore unless they were part of his sphere. Like Bridget. Like Ewan, whose in-person companionship he missed like a lost limb. But, pesky as she was, Bridget had helped him navigate the people part of this project. He owed her.

"Fine. I won't eff up. And I'll text Ewan. He can rag on me, too."

"The job will be yours. I sense it."

He wasn't as confident. Frederickson had wanted a few things Noah had been honest about not having in his wheelhouse. He could find people who did but that would have to up the bid…

"I've seen enough," he said. "Time to take you back to the world of eggheads."

"Don't you owe me lunch first?" She batted her lashes.

"Maybe at a drive-through where nobody can hear you talk."

"Free food. I'll take it any way I can get it."

In the hallway outside the ballroom, Noah knocked off a quick text to his brother.

Meeting went fine. Feeding Bridget then going home. Can call in 45.

They weren't out of the building when a reply pinged through.

When does the job start?

Noah laughed. "Jeez, you two," he said, sliding a look to his sister and thumbing a response. *Soon, IF it happens.*

This time the reply took a few minutes. They were at the car by the time it came through, and the words stopped Noah in his tracks. He frowned and handed the phone to Bridget. "What the hell does this mean?"

I need you first. Come to Scotland. Save my ass. THEN start your new job. Call when you get home.

Even the garrulous Bridget was rendered nearly speechless. "I have no idea."

CHAPTER TWO

Mairi MacDonald smiled at the rainbow-colored sign on her classroom door. "Welcome to Mrs. MacDonald's Fourth Year Class" read the curlicued letters. It was the first personalization she'd made to the space, and the simple touch lifted her heart, even though it still hurt that she'd been forced to take this new job at all.

Blast her brother, the worthless waste of air, who'd seen to the demise of her teaching position in Glasgow—a job she'd loved for the past six years. Scandal had always bloomed in that man's wake like mushrooms in manure.

When Aiden had dragged his lifelong drug problems directly back into her life two months ago, her school's parent council had requested she be asked to take a leave of absence—no matter how false or atrocious the lies he'd made about her being involved with his addiction had been.

Mairi's nature had never been to run from a fight, and underneath the sting of injustice burned the resentment of hiding away. The truth was, however, she could no longer afford to be the fiery crusader of her uni days. She was a teacher of young souls and, more importantly, a mother. Her primal instinct was to protect her daughter—her darling, imaginative Ella—and when this new job, eighty-five blessed miles from Glasgow, had come to her, Mairi hadn't hesitated.

She took in the empty classroom one more time, finalizing a mental list of what she needed to fill it with fun tools and tantalizing learning spaces. She had plenty of ideas from her years of experience, but teaching in a small Highland town would require different sensibilities than teaching in eclectic, working-class Glasgow.

With her mind overflowing, she flipped off the lights. School start was four weeks away, but the head teacher had allowed her to visit the room and get a sense of the space. She'd imagined Westmuir Primary to be a hole-in-the-mountainside, backward place, but she should have known better. The school was a lovely old brick building nestled near Glencoe, with a picturesque view of Loch Leven from its schoolyard. The atmosphere inside the building was equally friendly. It would be cozy and bustling when filled with children.

After waving to the groundskeeper, she climbed into the little white Vauxhall she'd borrowed while her own car was in the service shop, and checked her mobile. She had a bit of coverage so scrolled to Ainslie's number and tapped the screen. Her friend answered in two rings.

"Mairi! Tell me. It was charming wasn't it, the classroom?"

"It was. As you promised."

"We aren't as sophisticated as you city folk, but we manage." The sweet Highland brogue rolled off her tongue, a softer, rounder accent than Mairi's own crisp native Glaswegian.

"I was showing my prejudice." Mairi laughed. "I'm sorry."

"Nothin' to apologize for. Listen. I have news. I just heard that the house is empty and cleaned. Do you want to go see it?"

Mairi's heart danced into excitement. "You sure you have time, Ains? I know how busy you are."

"Plenty of time—I want to see it, too."

"Have I told you how grateful I am that you opened up your life and home for us?" Mairi said. "You've done so much."

"You have, and no need to thank me anymore. We've loved having you at Craigwarren, and Ella is a little living fairy girl I'm considering keeping even when you move into town."

"You know full well there are days you can have her," Mairi laughed. "I assume she hasn't gone wandering off this morning?"

"So far she's stayed right here with me. She does love the loch, though."

"Gah…" Mairi rolled her eyes though she was alone in the car. "That girl and her imagination. Talkin' to the kelpie for pity's sake."

"I have to say, if half of what Ella claims the water horse says is true, he's quite the insightful creature. On the other hand, if it's all made up, your daughter is scary brilliant."

"I don't know where she got it from. I'm too much of a realist, and James had as much magic in his soul as a politician."

"I know."

Mairi gritted her teeth, embarrassed. Lately, every conversation managed to include her long-gone ex-husband and her brother. One was absent from his daughter's life, the other a drug-addled tosser. That needed to stop. She'd moved from Glasgow to get away from the toxic males in her life.

"Sorry. I don't mean to go on about old problems when good things are about to happen."

"Och, who else do you have to vent to? You need to get it all out before you can move on."

"I love you, you know that. When shall we go to the house?"

"Ella and I can leave now and meet you. We can go for a treat afterward. I love spoiling her and making her love me best."

"I don't think you need to bribe her for that. Where is your beautiful man as we speak?"

"Ewan has a video call this afternoon if he can keep the Wi-Fi working long enough. At the moment he's with Innis, fixing the fence where the stupid goat got through again. She doesn't run off, but the chickens and donkeys get out."

The weight lifted from Mairi's chest. Craigwarren was the most wonderful place she'd ever visited. The homestead had passed through generations of Stewarts and Camerons, and contained its own loch, its own beautiful craig, and endless legends attached to it all. Craigwarren had belonged to Ainslie's godmother, Catrione Kerr, but she'd recently passed stewardship of the lands and home to the next heir, her great-nephew Ewan Portman. Ainslie had fallen hard for the American, as he had for her. Now they were living with Catrione and her husband, Innis, making repairs to the property, *and* planning a winter wedding. Her friend was the happiest Mairi had ever known her to be.

She had no idea how Ainslie and Ewan kept such amazing humor with their crazy schedules and a deadline, now a mere five weeks away, for refurbishing an old groundskeeper's cottage behind the main house. They wanted to start a bed and breakfast and they'd fallen into a big booking for the cottage—if they could ready it by mid-September.

Meanwhile, barmy animals, endless hiking paths, and buildings full of history all added to Craigwarren's charm. As excited as Mairi was to move into her own space, she would miss the warmth of the old house, and Ella would hate leaving.

"I will miss your crazy place," Mairi said. "You're all a wee bit mad up there. Or at least the animals are."

"No argument from me, but you'll only be seven miles away. We'll be together often. Believe me, you won't miss it come winter."

"Maybe not. All right, I'll meet you at the house in, what, twenty minutes?"

"Perfect. See you then."

Excited to show the pretty rental house to her seven-year-old, who'd get to have her own room, Mairi snapped her seat belt and turned the key, but as soon as the engine came to life, a gunshot-sharp knock on her driver's side window made her jump. With her hand on her chest, she opened the window and greeted Westmuir's head teacher.

"Christina! I didn't know you were here or I'd have stopped by to talk with you."

"I was away from the office until a few moments ago." Christina Sullivan, an attractive woman in her early forties, perpetually wore her long black hair, threaded with slender gray strands, in a tight pony tail. She didn't smile easily under the best of circumstances, and the worry grooves between her brows always seemed permanent. But her love for the children in her school had been obvious from the first meeting.

"You visited the room?" she asked.

"I did. It's a lovely space."

The head teacher hesitated, crossing her arms in front of her chest in a gesture that seemed almost nervous. "I'm glad I caught you before you left."

Mairi frowned. "Is everything all right?"

"I spoke this morning with the headmaster at your former school in Glasgow."

"Paul Taylor?"

"It seems he received a call from someone in your family. I understand you didn't tell them you were moving."

"No, I didn't." Mairi closed her grip more tightly on the steering wheel. "I'm not close with either my mother or my brother. As I've told you, I prefer my brother in particular not know where my daughter and I are."

Her stomach began churning with a dread she hadn't experienced in weeks. She'd been honest with Christina about leaving Glasgow because of family problems. She hadn't, however, revealed details. There'd been no legal reason to do so.

"I recall, but I wasn't aware you'd kept your move a complete secret."

Judging by the firm set of Christina's mouth, it was obvious this was more than curiosity.

"To be frank, my brother is a convicted drug addict. I don't advertise that personal family information, but there you have it. The fact is, I want to keep my whereabouts from my brother a secret for as long as possible because he'd been harassing us. Can I ask who in my family called Paul?"

The answer was oblique but revealing. "You also didn't tell Ella's father where she was going."

Mairi stared at the woman whose questions suddenly sounded like interrogations from a television police drama.

"What, exactly, is this about?" she asked, her voice clipped now.

"Evidently, James MacDonald is concerned about allegations brought against you by your brother."

"*James* is concerned?"

Not possible. Her ex-husband had long ago decided making travel blogs was more important than pretty much anything else, including fatherhood. Inconsistent child support was all she ever heard from him.

As for her brother, Aiden lived in their mother's house since leaving a halfway home for drug rehabilitation. He'd undertaken a vendetta against Mairi in the past months, but he didn't know where she was.

"My ex-husband couldn't possibly have anything to do with this, and there have never been any charges against me."

"But I understand the police *are* investigating you over drug dealings in your former home?"

"Excuse me? What?"

Even while it beat double-time in fury, her heart plummeted to her stomach. What malevolence was Aiden spawning now? After spending a year in prison and another six months in rehab, he'd been angry with Mairi because she'd given police the information that had gotten him arrested. Two months ago, he'd carefully planted a rumor with Paul Taylor and a few prominent school families, that Mairi had not only allowed him and his "colleagues" into her home over the years, but was the main person involved with drugs and dealing. She had turned him in to save herself, so the allegation went.

The idea was ridiculous, and the police had agreed once they'd asked a few in-depth questions. The rumor had planted seeds of doubt, however, and in the minds of two influential school council members, Aiden's contention that Mairi knew about drug deals had been too concerning. What Aiden wanted now was money and, ever devious, he was apparently not above causing more damage to extract it from her.

"You deny your home in Glasgow was the scene of drug deals? And you deny knowing anything about an investigation?" Christina asked.

"I absolutely can and do deny both of those things. I have never been involved in anything illegal, nor was my home ever the scene of criminal activity."

"But you were let go from your last position because of similar allegations."

"Is that exactly what Paul Taylor told you?"

Paul had always been her biggest champion and she knew he trusted her. He'd done what he'd had to do, but he wouldn't betray her personal secrets.

"He said he asked you to take a leave so you could address personal family issues."

"That's *right*." Mairi worked to keep the edge of anger out of her voice. "A few parents heard false rumors that I once knew about drug deals out of my home, and of course they were concerned. *Anytime* drugs and primary students are mentioned together it should be concerning. I agreed to a leave to protect the school and brought Ella here until this all gets sorted."

Christina's eyes narrowed just enough to be noticeable. "And you didn't think it would involve my school?"

"Christina, there's nothing for this school to be 'involved' in. I came here to be away from my family's influence on my daughter, not to hide from a scandal."

For the first time, Christina Sullivan's face softened into a semblance of sympathy. "I want to trust all of this is true,

Mairi. Mr. Taylor made it clear he believes you're an exceptional teacher, and I shouldn't be concerned. The police contacted him and he contacted me because he thought I knew the situation. He also insisted he hasn't revealed your whereabouts, and that was my red flag."

It was small comfort to know Paul still kept her whereabouts secret, and she wondered with annoyance why he hadn't contacted her first—especially if he'd heard from James.

"It shouldn't be a red flag," she said. "This is all happening far from here, and I'm working to solve the situation."

Christina's features hardened back into authoritative sternness. "My problem is, I feel blindsided. I'm left to wonder what else I don't know."

"I understand, but I told you everything I legally needed to tell you. My reasons for leaving out personal details were important, and I did it to protect you as well as me."

"Then you'll understand that my first priority is to protect this school."

Mairi's head swam with disbelief but, suddenly, the only thought in her head was that this was the bloody stupidest place to be having this conversation—in a borrowed car as if she were a teenager who'd been caught stealing it.

No. She was a professional and a very good teacher. She deserved a better hearing.

"I'd rather discuss this in a different environment. Let me look into the problem and come talk to you tomorrow. I'll give you every detail."

Christina shook her head. "I'm sorry, Mairi. With all due respect to your Mr. Taylor, this school comes first. Just as the potential for scandal caused him to let you go, I need to be vigilant that no potential for scandal affects our student body here. School starts in a month."

"I'm certain I can clear this up before then. Whatever this new claim is, it will be proven false. No trouble will land on your doorstep."

"I know you're sincere, Mairi. And your references are impeccable." She held up her hand in apology. "I would like to see this resolved, but until it is and I know without a doubt it won't be resurrected again, I need to have someone else start the school year. I've already contacted a temporary teacher."

Shock paralyzed her and not only summoned rare tears but nearly spilled them. "I'm looking forward to this job, and to sending my daughter to your school. I don't want to jeopardize either of those things," she managed.

Christina nodded, sympathetic once again. "Naturally this doesn't affect Ella's attendance here. We'll welcome her and keep her safe. As for your position, I'm sure with vigilance we can get everything sorted."

"Oh, we definitely will get it sorted." She fought to keep her voice steady. "Thank you for your candor, Christine."

The head teacher stepped away, ending hope for further conversation, and Mairi had no choice but to pull slowly out of the parking lot. She was a liar, she thought miserably as she drove away. She wasn't thankful at all.

On the fifteen-minute drive to Glencoe Village, Mairi's emotions swelled from numbness to full-fledged anger. How dare Aiden? Her family had spent years of time and pounds of savings trying to help her brother, but Aiden Murray was a lost cause. And *James*? That made no sense. If he had shown up out of the blue, it was beyond concerning.

By the time she pulled up to the pretty whitewashed house on the outskirts of Glencoe, exhaustion from rehashing the past and despairing over the future had settled into every muscle. She had no idea what to do next, but there was no more time to think. Ainsley's ancient Nissan truck, filled with the tools of a busy local veterinarian's trade, was already parked in the short driveway. Mairi steeled herself and opened her door, then caught the flash of a hot pink jumper as her elfin daughter dashed around a corner from the back of the house.

"Mama!" Ella called. "You should see the garden. You should *see*!"

"I'm coming." Mairi's spirits lifting in spite of everything. "Is it brilliant?"

"Pure dead brilliant!" she cried, and threw herself into Mairi's arms.

Ainslie appeared, grinning at the grand mother-daughter hug.

"I don't think you'll have a problem convincing her to move in," she said.

Mairi hid her worry as the consequences of her exchange with Christina Sullivan struck home. For the moment, she no longer had employment, and that meant her meager savings couldn't handle rent along with her other expenses. But Ella was so happy Mairi couldn't bear to rip that away before at least acknowledging the excitement.

"How'd you manage that?" Mairi whispered over her daughter's head. "Is there a loch with a kelpie in back? Or a house brownie?"

Ainslie laughed. "No loch, sorry to say. I don't know about the brownie; they don't show themselves to humans as we well know. Will you be leaving some cream and buttered bread out after you move in, Miss Ella? To see if one lives here"

"'Course I will!" Ella's bright auburn hair swung in thick, glossy ribbons as she twirled in excitement. "Lots of cream. And honey."

Mairi smiled at her daughter, more for the twirling and joy than the plan to entice a helpful house brownie. She'd always encouraged Ella's voracious love of books, even those that brought her Scottish mythology to life. She'd never been one, however, to champion her child's unrelenting belief in the legends. She waged a constant battle between encouraging Ella's all-important free-spirit and keeping her grounded in knowledge and reality. A base in reality *had* to be strong. Anything else led to heartache. Her ex-husband and her brother proved that.

"Come on, then," Ainslie said. "Let's go inside."

It still boggled Mairi's mind that less than two months ago, she'd been in her Glasgow house, newly unemployed and wondering how she was going to find a temporary job. During a catch-up call, she'd confided in her old college friend Ainslie and, out of the blue, Ainslie had told her about the opening for a primary school teacher she'd recently seen advertised.

Ainslie Campbell. Newly engaged. Gifted veterinarian. Friends with most of the west Highland area. Miracle worker extraordinaire. She'd invited Mairi and Ella to her beautiful old home and then come up with this place to rent. And how was Mairi about repay all that generosity? By telling her everything was now mucked up.

While Ella explored every little corner of the place as if she'd been promised a pony of her own if she looked hard enough, Mairi managed to tell the news without breaking down. The way her head pounded from tension and the area behind her eyes burned with frustrated anger, her control over weeping deserved an award.

"I'm so sorry, Ainslie, I seriously don't know what to do. This was not supposed to happen, but I don't see how I can sign a lease when I don't know if I'll have a job."

Ainslie gathered her into a hug. "I'm sorry, too, Mairi. Truly. But I'll tell you exactly what we're going to do. We're heading back to Craigwarren where Catrione is going to teach us how to bake her shortbread. And when it's hot and buttery, we're going to eat ourselves silly."

"And be madder than wet cats afterwards for downing all those calories." Mairi tried to smile.

"No. We'll be fortified and able to brainstorm how to solve this *minor* setback. No bawbag of an ex-husband is going to ruin this plan. And that useless nugget of a brother of yours is at the end of his desperate rope. Once he gets nothin' from you, he'll go away as he always does."

"I don't know. He's after revenge," Mairi said. "I was the one who told the police where to find drugs in his house. Now that he's out of rehab, he wants me to lose something, too."

"We've always known he's no good. Sorry, I know he's your brother—"

"Don't apologize. He's less than no good. The only thing I can say is that he's not violent, as far as I know. He's a cheat and a liar and threatens hellfire when he's angry, but I don't think he's got the stomach to hurt or kill."

"Your mother knows the truth. Why doesn't she talk to these head teachers for you?"

Mairi gave a sigh as heavy as the weight in her heart. "Aiden is her lost boy come back to her. He was gone without a word for those six years before our da' died. Now she wants to believe him when he tells her it was all a lie. I might be her daughter. She leans on me when she needs something. But because I won't stand up for Aiden there's a gulf between us."

Mairi tried to smile away the heartache of it all until she had time to think. Instead, the first tears finally fell.

Ainslie hugged her tighter. "No. No. I can't remember ever seeing you cry. It hurts my heart even though I understand."

"I *don't* cry. There was no crying in our household. The Murrays were hardened Scots folk, and Aiden and I both got the strap if we acted like wee whingeing bairns."

"If that's the case, I take it back. You have a good, healing cry, and *then* we'll go back to Catrione."

Mairi didn't allow her weeping to give off any sound — no sobs, no hiccups. Still, when she lifted her head she left a damp spot on Ainslie's shoulder.

Ella chose that moment to re-enter the room. "Mama, what's wrong?"

Mairi wiped her eyes quickly with an embarrassed swipe of her fingertips.

"I could say 'nothing,' my love, but that's not true, so I'll be honest like I always tell you to be. I found out a bit of bad news about this house."

"Bad?"

"We can't stay here for now," Mairi said. "Things changed a bit with my job, and we have to wait to move away from Ainslie's house."

Ella contemplated the words for several seconds, and then jumped to Mairi so suddenly, there was barely time to wrap her in another giant hug.

"You mean we get to stay with Ainslie and Ewan longer? I get to tell Diarmid I'm not going away?"

Diarmid. Mairi sighed, out of energy to care the child was dead serious about talking to the brownie sprite who supposedly lived in the barn. As for staying with Ainslie and Ewan, something that clearly delighted her daughter... Her heart sank even further. She'd imposed too much on her friends already.

Ainslie squatted in front of Ella. "Yes, of course you're stayin'. For as long as you need it, Craigwarren is where you'll live. But wait..." Ainslie's brows drew together. "Tell Diarmid, you said? Brownies don't talk to people."

"He doesn't like anyone to see him," Ella replied matter-of-factly. "And he would be dead angry if I tried to spy. But sometimes, when it's getting on to night, he'll creep up and whisper what he wants to do while we sleep and tell me what he likes to eat. He said he's never had a human who would listen but not try to capture him or tell the grown-ups where he is. He said he would miss me when I moved."

"Och, Ella." Mairi shook her head. "I don't know what to make of you most days."

"Diarmid says I'm Wee Not-Quite-Red Girl."

Ainslie laughed. "Well, Not-Quite-Red, you can talk to Diarmid any time y'like, and if he's happy you're stayin', well so am I."

"I can't believe all you've done for us," Mairi said. "Especially since Ewan is trying to get so much done on the house so quickly. Then your wedding so soon."

For the first time, Ainslie turned serious. "Four months, don't remind me. And aye, well, Ewan's got new problems every day. The roof, the stonework, finding help. Can't see how we'll be ready on time, daft eejits that we are, agreeing to host this honeymoon couple and planning our wedding this soon. Ewan has one last hope, but it's a long shot."

"Oh?"

"He's asking his brother to come help him."

"Sounds like a perfect solution."

"It would be, aye, but we're talking about Noah, a man who won't get on a bus to cross the city, much less an airplane to cross the Atlantic. He's a gifted woodworker and builder but a wee bit of a hermit."

"Nobody is a hermit in this day and age."

"I said the same, didn't I? Ewan tells me I don't know Noah. And the fly in that ale is Noah is up for a new job that could start soon. There might not be enough time to bring him here and get much of anythin' major done. Ewan will try, though. Even a jumpstart would be good."

"Oh, Ains. If he does come, you'll have the house full. I'll find a way to clear up this crisis with Aiden and be gone by the time you need the space."

"Don't even think that. You know we have plenty of room. We're not a bed and breakfast yet."

"I disagree, the way you treat us. I should be paying you."

"Absolutely not. Come on. We'll stop and do a little shopping on the way home."

"Can I get some honey for Diarmid?" Ella asked.

"Aye," Ainslie said. "But Aunt Catrione should have some honey at home."

"I can't use hers all up. I need a whole jar that's for Diarmid."

"My goodness," Ainslie said. "Won't that make him a great fat barn brownie?"

"Maybe he's already fat and likes it," Ella said. "Maybe he's losing weight and doesn't want to."

Mairi stared at her daughter. The observation, so childlike on the surface, was delivered with all the seriousness of a Tibetan monk.

"I don't know about your child. It's possible she isn't well," Ainslie said.

Mairi ruffled Ella's glossy auburn, not-quite-red tresses. "Believe me, I worry."

They left the house, and Mairi had to work hard to keep from looking back with longing. Maybe this setback would only last a few days. She'd find out what her brother's angle was and how on earth James had found out. Their divorce had been civil in a "we should have known better" kind of way. She'd handled his disappearance and raised their child. She wanted only for him to disappear back into his carefree life while she figured out how to stop Aiden's harassment. Maybe it was time to brave her dysfunctional family face-to-face—if she could keep them away from Ella while she did.

CHAPTER THREE

Noah never turned his brother down. Ever. And yet, he'd done it this time.

He'd had no choice, but still guilt had eaten at him like acid for two days. Ewan rarely asked for help, but this timing was impossible. The fact that Ewan wasn't even upset only made the guilt worse.

"I knew it was a long shot," he'd said. "And I wouldn't for a minute want you to pass up a big break. I have another option anyway. Our cousin over here has a few connections."

Noah didn't understand any of their long-lost family's dynamics. He'd only heard the stories Ewan told about discovering two great-aunts and a cousin when he'd traveled to Scotland earlier that spring. Inheriting the family home had also meant inheriting the last of their mother's relatives. Callum, the cousin in question, was supposedly a royal pain the ass.

"The infamous Callum McTavish?"

"He's got access to investors with money and connections. We'll work something out."

"You said he wants to take charge and control the property. Isn't there another way?"

"Callum has ambitious ideas, but we have ways to keep him in check. Don't worry."

Noah did worry, about his brother's dilemma along with a host of other things, and he sighed as he entered the workshop that doubled as his home, thanks to the three small rooms he'd built along the back wall of the six-car garage. At least, it was home for another five or six weeks unless a dirt-cheap miracle property came his way. Today's search hadn't solved that problem.

Ewan's issue was equally time sensitive. From what Noah understood, he and Ainslie had agreed to offer a cottage on their property as the honeymoon destination for some couple that was very well-to-do. The renovation of that cottage, along with a building inspection and a certification review for running a bed and breakfast, had to be finished by mid-September.

The whole mess sounded insane. Ewan had always been practical to a fault, until he'd met this Ainslie person. Suddenly he was in a tizzy, making plans before he could realistically pull them off, acting more like Bridget than himself. Noah wanted to like the woman Ewan had fallen in love with, but he resented her for rattling his unflappable brother.

He tossed his keys in a bowl by the door and scanned the micro-apartment-slash-workshop. His living quarters consisted of a kitchenette with running water, a small bedroom, and a bathroom with a sink and composting toilet that functioned perfectly for him. A little ascetic, maybe, but the knotty pine walls were attractive enough, and the wiring and minimal plumbing were up to code. He'd only had to guarantee to the housing inspector he wouldn't be keeping cars in his living space.

The garage's owner hadn't objected to the upgrade, and Noah was perfectly comfortable while he saved money for a house. Then, out of the blue, had come the announcement that the owner was starting a business and turning the place back into a garage. Since Noah's sporadic work with the construction company wouldn't nearly cover expensive rent on a new place big enough for his needs, he was at a loss. Leo Frederickson offered the only potential lifeboat and Noah couldn't risk his chance of missing that boat by going to Scotland, even to help Ewan.

He entered his miniscule kitchen and opened the half-fridge. He kept it well stocked for its size, and he didn't think he ate like a clueless bachelor. Eggs and cheese, yogurt and milk. Meat and carrots and celery. Beer, of course. He kept pasta fixings in the large pantry along with basic canned stuff, peanut butter, bread and cereal. And a bag of Reese's Peanut Butter Cups.

He cooked more than he ate out. There was something to be said for that. But he wasn't in the mood for eating yet and simply grabbed a beer. He had emails to check. Maybe there'd be a small job requested that would take his mind off of Scotland.

He took a swig of beer and admitted the truth. The real deep-dark cause of his guilt was relief. He had the perfect excuse to avoid buying a plane ticket—and he was glad. It was not the flying that bothered him. He'd never been on a plane, but he figured that could be fun. The thought of living in a foreign house, however, with the kind of close, huggy family Ewan had been describing for the past three months sounded like a lot of work. He didn't go places. So what? A lot of people didn't. He kept close to home and that was enough for him.

Purposefully he shrugged off the unsuccessful day and the pointless guilt and walked to a microwave-sized cardboard box filled with blocks of wood. He chose a smooth, unfinished, four-by-four block of basswood. As always, the wood warmed in his hands while his fingers traced and studied the smooth, tight grain. His idea was simple. He'd create a miniature Jupiter and maybe, if Frederickson could see his vision for the ballroom statues, it would give Noah an edge. He picked up a pencil, settled into his favorite chair, and made a few initial strokes on the wood, roughing in eyes, a wide forehead, and the start of the god's traditional swept-back mane of hair. The beard curling to the top of his chest would go…there. He marked the spot. Rather than giving him a traditional lightning bolt, Noah sketched an eagle and imagined it with its head on Jupiter's shoulder. He'd done his symbol research.

He held up the block and squinted, turning the flat drawing into a three-dimensional figure in his mind. An easy smile played on his lips. He liked designing, yet in spite of all the planning he knew the final figure would surprise him. After twenty minutes, he set his creation down, itching to grab his knife and start rough-cutting, but he wanted to ponder his ideas for the lower body a little more. He'd eat and take a break to watch the Twins game. Baseball was the only thing he considered his real vice.

His phone, with its plain old-fashioned ring, startled him and he snatched it from the table, figuring it to be Bridget or his mother. He hadn't checked in during the past week. Bad stepson. His heartrate doubled at the ID on the screen.

L. Frederickson.

Damn. It was too early for a decision. Had to be a question—a clarification. Didn't it?

Answer it, idiot.

"Noah Portman."

"Noah." The deep baritone voice echoed over the phone exactly as it had in person. "Have I got you at a convenient time?"

"Yes, of course," Noah's gut slowly began tying itself into a knot.

"I want to start by telling you how impressed I was with your detailed proposal and fair bid."

"I appreciate that." The knot stopped twisting slightly.

"We've gotten both bids already and they've been presented to my board of investors. We had a tough decision, but we wanted to make it quickly."

The knot cinched again. "You said you wanted to move fast."

"Noah, I chose you all the way, but I'm afraid the board went the other direction."

The knot jerked like a hangman's noose. Disbelief and ravaging disappointment turned Frederickson's next words into tinny echoes.

"The other proposal had a timeline swifter by a third with a lower bid. And his designs were fine. I shouldn't be telling you particulars, but I'm so damn sorry. I wanted to explain."

Noah fought to respond professionally. Stupidly, he hadn't prepared for this outcome.

"I'm damn sorry, too. Is there something I can change in the bid? I'm more than happy to be flexible."

"I asked that too, but the decision is final. I'm sure your sister will be disappointed as well."

"Almost certainly true."

The only remotely humorous thing about this was an image of Bridget, pitchfork and torch in hand, green eyes full of lightning, storming into Frederickson's office to tell him what a huge mistake he'd made.

"This wasn't an easy phone call for me to make," Frederickson continued. "I was very impressed with your expertise. I hope if anything comes up in the future you'll be open to speaking again."

The pain of the initial blow was dulling, and Noah straightened. "Buck up," his father would say. To the elder Portman, that was the one thing expected of any Portman in every situation.

"I'm always open to a creative prospect," Noah said.

"Good. Excellent. Now if there's anything I can do for you in the meantime, don't hesitate to call."

Tell me what would make you change your mind.

"I'm sorry to have missed this opportunity."

"I am, too. Good night, Noah."

He stood in the middle of the room, lost as to what to do next. All at once, he was four again, abandoned by a mother. He was twelve, left behind by a best friend. He was twenty-five, not chosen by a woman. All the people he'd allowed close to his emotions.

He glimpsed the block of basswood lying on his carving table and gave a choked laugh. That had certainly become a pointless exercise.

It took several long minutes for his head to clear and his disappointment to dull. He chastised himself for infantile behavior. He was no worse off than he'd been a week ago. He had minor savings. He had skills. He'd lived like an artisan most of his life, and he would go on. He lifted his phone and opened his text threads. There weren't that many, but Bridget's was at the top, and she deserved to know.

Decision was made. Frederickson went with Zimmerman.

He shut off the phone. He wasn't going to answer any reply she'd make. That could wait for tomorrow. Tonight there was a ballgame. Vices were useful things.

The Twins were actually leading in the fourth when the pounding started on his door. He swigged the last of his Surly Furious and blew his breath through pursed lips.

"Go away, Bridget," he called.

"I won't." Her muffled voice came through the door. "And it doesn't matter whether you open up or not. You gave me a key a long time ago."

Sure enough, seconds later the door swung open.

"Twins are actually winning. Come sit down," he said without looking back.

"I'm sorry you're pining. I'm sorry about Frederickson."

"I'm not pining; I'm watching the game."

"Yeah, well, turn it off, you have a phone call."

A phone appeared over his shoulder, and Noah scowled. "What the hell, Bridge?"

"I'm the hell. Talk to me." Ewan's voice came through the speaker.

Noah sat up and stared at his watch. "What in the world? It's two in the morning there."

"Believe me, I know."

Noah finally turned on his sister. "This is stupid, Bridget. What are you doing here?"

"We're taking advantage of your weak moment," Ewan answered for her. "I'm not above playing dirty, and we know Bridget loves this kind of thing."

"What kind of thing?" Noah narrowed his eyes. Bridget only grinned.

"You lost out on a commission. Our brother has a new offer." She beamed as if it was the be all and end all of ideas.

Noah closed his eyes and groaned. "This could have waited for morning."

"Nope," she replied. "You'll be less vulnerable then. More able to make excuses."

"But I'm more annoyed now and very unlikely to agree to anything."

"Look, we honestly didn't plan this," Ewan said. "In all seriousness, Bridget called because she was worried. You weren't answering your phone. Dad and Mother are traveling so she woke *me* up. That's all."

"Bridget woke you for nothing."

"But she made a good case for talking to you now. I meant it—I will take this advantage even if it's unfair. I need you, and now you need me."

This was cruelty. Noah was angry about losing the commission—a little depressed, if he was honest. It had been a blow to his ego, although he knew it was simply business. Still, they were right; he didn't have the will to fight being ganged up on.

"What happened to our cousin helping out?"

"I put a brave face on it. Callum wants to turn us into a flipping Ritz-Carlton, and if we give him an inch, he'll take the whole bloody place—loch and craig. You come, and I can tell him we don't need his connections or his contractors. You'll be the contractor."

Ewan said nothing. He desperately wished he had the excuse of not having a passport, but as soon as Ewan had announced his engagement to Ainslie, Bridget had literally forced him and their parents to get passports in order. But this was too sudden. He needed to think.

Going to Scotland would solve his immediate problems. He had enough money to rent a storage unit here. He could move out of this place and not worry about a new one until he got back. Only stubbornness, and his fear, mild though it was, of overly affectionate Scottish aunts and uncles stood in his way.

"Don't think about this too much," Ewan said, in his creepy, mind-reading way. "Aside from saving me, I promise seeing this place will do you good. It has a way of putting things in perspective."

"I don't need perspective. Perspective changed *you*."

"Yeah, for the better. But you aren't me. I only mean you'll come and then go back home having found something you didn't even known was lost."

"You sound like a crazier version of our sister."

He laughed again. "I suppose I do to you."

Noah tried to sigh, but there was a boulder lodged in his lungs that wouldn't let air through. "I need to think about this."

"Not for too long. There's a flight next Monday. That'll give you four days to settle things, which is actually too much time. I'm tempted to book the ticket even without your official approval. You can decide tomorrow, but in the interest of full disclosure we do have one other guest at the moment."

"Guest?" The boulder in his chest got heavier.

"One of Ainslie's university friends. She and her daughter are visiting for a few weeks. They won't be in your way, but I know you don't like surprises."

"Really? Like this entire ambush wasn't a surprise?"

"Touché. Nevertheless, she's very nice. Mairi MacDonald."

"You're kidding. Does everyone over there have a cliché name?"

"No. The most common name over here is Smith."

"Whatever. Fine, I'll factor *Mah-ree* MacDonald into my decision."

"Long black hair. Pretty blue eyes." Ewan's voice rose temptingly.

"Stop it. Not applicable. She has a daughter, you said?"

"Ella. Seven years old and talks to fairies."

"Sounds frickin' adorable." Noah half wished this was a video call so he could have given Ewan the finger.

"Well, she is that. Entertaining, too. And Mairi is easy to have around. Like I said, she won't be in your way."

"I'm probably not coming. That won't be a concern."

"I won't give up hope until the last bagpipe wails."

"That's another thing. Bagpipes. The day you take that up is the day we part ways."

"No worry. It's an impossible instrument."

"Yes, of torture."

"I'm going back to bed. Talk to you in twelve hours."

After he hung up Bridget's phone and handed it to her, Noah ran a frustrated hand through his hair and tried to get a full, deep breath. He failed again.

"I know this is scary for you," Bridget said.

"Then why are you forcing it?"

"Because you need it. You'd sit here for the next six weeks, sanding your carvings, finding a hole-in-the-wall apartment at the last minute, and retreating further into your head. You're not as antisocial as you claim, but you can't see it. You need to go discover yourself."

"I like myself fine."

"Not the same issue."

He still didn't have the energy to fight her. In a brief flash of hope for a little solidarity, he took her by the upper arms and stared pleadingly.

"Come along then—even for a few days. Be the buffer."

"Between you and this Mairi?" Bridget's eyes sparked with fun.

"I don't give a rip about any Mairi or her strange child. It's the aunties, the uncle, the cousin. Ewan had to have invited you, too."

"He did, but I can't leave. I've got that field study coming up next week and hours of prep for my master's presentation. Don't think for a second I'm not totally bummed. But! Here's the other thing I brought. Double chocolate, Moose Tracks ice cream because I knew you wouldn't have any."

"Don't need ice cream."

"You can't plan a trip without it. And we need to make a shopping list to get you some decent clothes."

"We absolutely are not making a clothing shopping list."

She shushed him. "Stop fighting it, big brother. Helping you plan will lessen my envy, and believe me, I am so incredibly jealous. You're going to Scotland."

CHAPTER FOUR

"Fluff that pillow up nice and plump, Ella, like Aunt Catrione showed you. Make it look extra cozy for Ewan's brother."

Mairi watched her daughter, small of stature but dexterous as a sculptor, lift the down pillow and squeeze it to her chest. Then she shook it and dropped it on the bed, giving it three solid punches before squaring it up.

"When's he comin'?" Ella asked.

"Should be any time. We got behind helping Catrione with the lamb stew and the shortbread. That's why we're hurrying."

"I like being a maid," Ella said. "Can I put the candy in the dish now?"

"You can." She handed her auburn-haired girl a bag of chocolates and the blue pottery bowl to fill. "Then pay yourself with two pieces. You've been a huge help today."

Ella beamed. Blessedly, it was not one of her impish I-have-a-marvelous-idea-Mum smiles but one of genuine pleasure at the offer of the treat. Mairi looked around the room Noah Portman would occupy and nodded. It was neutral enough—pretty but not frilly, with pale blue walls and tan-and-blue tartan accents. Ella set the bowl of chocolates on the side table, then hugged the bag of treats and twirled with it.

"I love this kind," she said. "I should marry them."

Ella twirled often. And she loved often. Mairi seriously wondered where her daughter had come by such a free spirit, since she was nothing like either of her parents. Mairi herself was far more serious, addicted to crusading for the underdog. James was a restless adventurer but a non-dreamer. Ella, it always seemed, had to have been gifted to the world by the fairies she claimed she could talk with.

While Ella was finishing her chocolate, two gray tabby cats found their way into the room. Mairi nabbed one before it jumped onto the freshly made bed.

"Rigby, out," she admonished. "Ella, grab Eleanor please. The dog didn't come in, did he? Last thing we need is to lock an animal in here to make a mess."

"I don't think so. David Tennant doesn't like to do the stairs if he doesn't have to."

David Tennant. A handsome actor to be sure, but a rather silly name for a border collie/corgi mix. Ainslie's dog and cats—a third named Jenny was around somewhere—were adorable, but always under foot.

They finished in the room and moved into the bathroom down the hall. It had been scrubbed that morning, but Mairi made certain all the fresh soaps were in place and the main set of towels were still unused. Her thoughts buzzed through the list of chores she'd taken on that morning so Ainslie could accompany Ewan to pick up his brother in Glasgow. She was more than happy to fill her mind with anything other than her work and family situation.

It had been almost a week since she'd lost the Glencoe teaching job, and she'd made no headway solving anything. She'd been unable to reach Paul Taylor, out of town at an educator's conference, to ask why he'd called Christina last week. She'd tried the last number she had for James with no luck and still had no clue how or why Scotland's most accomplished absentee father was suddenly meddling. Against her better judgement, she'd even tried calling her brother, but his mobile numbers had never stayed the same for long, and her mother didn't have a current one either.

"You should talk to him in person," she said.

That was not happening at this point.

The lack of an immediate path forward was painful to Mairi's inner warrior—but next week, she vowed, she'd find a way to get at Aiden without giving away her location. The whole debacle was what made cleaning rooms in Craigwarren house a distraction and pleasure.

When they were done, she followed Ella downstairs and through the cozy, eclectic living room filled with its tartan throws and comfortable furniture all facing the massive fieldstone fireplace at its heart. It was no perfectly appointed, posh showplace, but its burnished and uneven dark plank flooring, bright red-and-blue carpets, and rustic decorating that included family heirlooms—like a two-hundred-year-old sword and a seventy-five-year-old set of bagpipes—made the space more inviting than any room featured in *Homes & Interiors Scotland*.

"Hullo, Catrione!" She gave a chipper call to Ewan's great-aunt, a woman as warm and comfortable as her home, who stood in the kitchen, her hands busy with a round of bread dough on a floured counter. "I think the rooms are fit as we can get them for Noah."

"I can't thank you enough, sweet Mairi. They'll be perfect. You have the same sense of the beautiful that our Ainslie does. And I don't know why I'm this nervous about Noah's arrival. I swear to ye, I wasn't as done in when I knew

Ewan was coming, and I'd never met any of the family. Noah is a special case."

"Ewan is nervous as well," Mairi said. "Ainslie told me they had to gang up on him to get him here."

"He's not a big people person, according to Ewan."

"Aye. Ella and I will take a walk and not be here when they arrive. I don't want to overwhelm him."

"You don't have to do that, darlin' girl. You feel like part of the family now."

Catrione was the other reason, in addition to the coziness of her place, that Craigwarren was special. At eighty she was a gentle force—and the sun around which everything else revolved. She could still walk five miles across the Highlands when she wanted to, chase an escaped chicken even if she *didn't* want to, and cook up a meal that would fill a Highland regiment. And her shortbread…Ainslie hadn't lied about the mouthwatering treat that came from her ovens. It was positively medicinal.

Catrione was also the happiest person on Earth now that she had her family around her. In fact, in her only sign of slight barminess, she believed with all her heart that Ewan, Noah, and their sister, Bridget, were the spell-breakers of a generations-old curse, and their presence had restored Craigwarren's family line after it had been severed the generation before. Mairi sometimes thought of Catrione Kerr as the person Ella would grow to be if her imagination wasn't reined in at some point.

"It's all right. We'll be back in a couple of hours. I'd like you to meet your great-grandnephew without having to introduce us. I told Ella we'd go looking for late-summer flowers by the loch."

"Can we go now, Mama?" Ella popped in from the living room. "Auntie Cat, can I take a bit of cream to the barn first?"

"Of course you can, my wee sweetheart. Diarmid is out of treats again, is he? Saints love the gluttonous scoundrel."

"His food is gone every morning!"

Mairi shared an amused wink with Catrione over her child's head. The barn brownie was as real as the three of them standing in this room to her. Nobody had suggested there were also three cats in the barn every night.

Catrione took a small brown pottery mug from her cupboard and handed it to Ella who held it carefully in cupped hands while Catrione poured a thick, rich stream of sweet cream to the halfway mark. Ella nodded. She would take it reverently to the barn and empty it into Diarmid the brownie's tin cup. The crockery mug would be returned, washed, and put away until the next visit.

"Have you got your wellies?" Mairi asked. "It rained last night."

"They're by the front door."

"All right. Let's go out the front then."

"Bye, Auntie Cat!"

"Bye-bye. Have a lovely walk. Bring me a little blossom if you find one."

"I will."

They were out the front door, a beauty made of heavy oak planks with hinges and a handle of hammered wrought iron, with Ella seated on the brick stoop struggling and grunting over her wellies—a pink pair she was rapidly outgrowing—when the familiar sound of Ainslie's car reached their ears.

In surprise, Mairi turned toward the long, uneven drive leading from the main road a quarter mile away. The trio hadn't been expected for another thirty to forty minutes, but sure enough, the white Vauxhall bounced into view. For a crazy second Mairi wanted to run. It was a stupid reaction, but dressed in old, saggy jeans and a favorite sweater meant for leisure not for meeting new people, a wave of acute embarrassment swept over her.

She pulled herself together as the car, Ainslie at the wheel, made it to the parking space right of the house.

"Ewan!" Ella cried, as the passenger door opened and Ella's newest best playmate exited. She'd bonded with Ainslie's fiancé and loved to tease him about the funny American way he pronounced his words. Mairi couldn't fault her daughter. Ainslie had found herself a stunner. And a really lovely person.

Ainslie exited the driver's door and waved. "I'm so glad you're here," she called. "We have someone for you to meet!"

"I wasn't going to intrude—"

Mairi stopped short as a figure emerged from the back seat, blinking in the overcast light like an owl forced to awaken in the daytime. Tall and slender but well-muscled, he had a shock of the thickest sable hair curling to his collar, like it should have been seen to by a barber weeks ago but had refused because it knew being long was definitely the right decision.

Her throat closed as if she'd suddenly developed laryngitis. Utterly ridiculous, but if Ewan was the Portman family's movie star, then his brother was its hot rock-and-roll royalty.

Ainsley scooted to Mairi's side. "Noah, this is my good friend Mairi MacDonald. Mairi, Noah Portman."

"It's lovely to meet you, Noah." Mairi shook off her physical reaction and held out a hand.

He studied it a moment, his owl-eyes blinking against her gaze as if he had to process the moment. Then his head gave a small shake as if he were finally fully awake.

"Mairi," he replied, and his fingers closed on hers.

He slipped out of the handshake in seconds, as if their palms were oiled and couldn't maintain a grip. Unlike their hands, however, their gazes held for long seconds. His eyes, as brown and rich as his hair color, showed nothing but mild interest, yet he didn't turn away until Ella started jumping.

"And here's our Ella. Her only job is to keep us on our toes," Ewan said.

"Hi, Noah." Ella bounced to within a foot of the hapless visitor. "Did ye have a good plane ride? Auntie Cat said it's terrible and long. I helped make your bed up for you. When you're all tucked into your room, I'll show you the barn, too. It's far better even than the house, and the house is bonnie braw. You'll see where Diarmid lives. And Fenella and Ailish and Juliet. Do you want to come in and have some shortbread?"

Noah stared at the child as if he'd never seen such a creature before. Mairi tugged Ella back and put a hand lightly over her mouth.

"Ella, Ella, give poor Noah a bit of a moment to arrive." She offered an apologetic smile and turned to him with weak humor. "I'm sorry. She doesn't get out enough."

"Not a problem," he replied, but gave no answering smile.

She was saved from further awkwardness by the big front door, opening like it was spring loaded. Catrione, flanked by her husband of four months, Innis, full white beard, sparkling eyes and all, bustled from the house.

"Noah," Cat called. "If you aren't the bonniest sight for these old eyes."

"Aunt Catrione," Ewan whispered to his brother.

Mairi pulled Ella back, touched by the tears in Catrione's eyes as she drew near. When she reached Noah, she took his hands, but didn't close in for one of the hugs that made her famous.

"I'm your ancient old Auntie Catrione. *Mo cridhe*—my heart—welcome to Craigwarren."

"Hello, Catrione. You're the great-aunt of a lot of legend." He still didn't exactly smile, but Mairi caught the smallest uptick at the corner of his mouth.

"I know this was a long and unplanned journey for you," she said. "And I know it's Ewan you've come to help. But it is my wish you're fulfilling. My heart is full now that I have you here."

At the gushy words, Noah's face went fully somber again and his eyes filled with shadows of doubt.

"I doubt I'm much of a wish fulfiller," he said. "But I am glad to meet you at last."

"You'll see, my sweet boy. You'll see. Would you grant me a welcome hug before I introduce you to my new old better half?"

He bent to allow the tiny old woman to wrap him in one of her safe bear hugs. Once again, the body language spoke far louder than his words. As his stiff form relaxed beneath his great-aunt's ministrations, Mairi had to wonder, again, if there was some kind of magic in the lady. The proper and uncomfortable Noah Portman looked like a different person than he'd been at first.

When Catrione released him and held his upper arms with firm, loving hands, she could barely speak. "Your grandfather, Iain, would be so pleased to know you've come home." She tilted her head. "Your adopted home—we hope.

He was a hard man, but a very good one deep inside. I wish he'd given your father a bit more credit."

Mairi laughed to herself. This was the family legend Noah would have to hear repeatedly during his stay. That his father had come, stolen his mother away to America, left the family in Scotland barren and Craigwarren on the verge of being lost to the family. Noah's mother, and by default her children, had been cut off from their Scottish roots by her father. And the whole story had been predicted three hundred years earlier. It was one of the legends she herself found adorable but could easily attribute to the whims of passing time. Catrione, however, was another story.

"This is Innis MacFarlane," Catrione was saying. "Took us seventy years but we finally caught each other this past April."

Noah shook his uncle-in-law's hand, looking rather more brave than excited. Mairi tugged on Ella's hand and stepped farther away. Clearly this was overwhelming for Noah, and it was time to implement her original plan. She touched Ainslie's shoulder.

"We'll be back in an hour or so. You get him settled. The room is ready."

Ainslie hugged her. "Thank you so much. I'm glad I got to help fetch him. One-on-one he's great. I won't even ask if you've noticed what a looker he is." Ainslie grinned. "Don't you dare tell Ewan I said that."

He was a "looker" all right, but Mairi wasn't going to admit it, even to Ainslie. That would be all she needed—her crazy friend thinking everyone needed to be hooked up with an American.

"He looks a little shell-shocked, truth be told."

"Aye, it's a lot this family, even without jetlag. But I think his solitary nature will help get the job done for us.

He'll concentrate on work more than people. He got fairly animated when he talked about the renovation."

"Well, I'll leave you to get him settled. Ella and I will help with dinner when we get back."

Ainslie waved at Ella. "Have fun. Are you going to the loch?"

"To the barn first. With cream."

"Of course. The most important task."

"All right, girl, off we go," Mairi said. "Diarmid's a'starving."

"Mama, he won't drink it until nighttime."

"When will I ever learn?"

She took one final look at Noah, who seemed to be his tall, straight self again now that he'd met the whole lot. She was about to turn away when he swiveled his head and caught her eyes again. Shock ricocheted through her system. She managed a quick smile and a wave, then took Ella's hand and went to deliver Diarmid's cream.

***

Noah had never understood the phrase "mind blown." To him, life was a series of steps that turned into a series of decisions, that turned into finished projects. There might setbacks and sorrows and aggravations, but his mind was never blown.

After the past twelve hours, he could no longer say that.

Since being ramrodded into this trip, there'd been no simple series of steps; there'd been mighty leaps in a landscape with no gravity, and no clear indication each time he leaped how far from the original point he might land. Ewan had warned Scotland would affect him. If that hadn't been a colossal understatement, there were no such things as understatements.

From the moment he'd stepped into the cool, misty air outside Glasgow International Airport, the only thing he noticed was change. The cars drove on the wrong side of the road, something he'd known, of course, but the experience confused his jet-lagged brain. Glasgow had been a mix of beautiful old European-style buildings, unique and modern bridges, and office buildings that looked like pictures of apartments in eastern Europe from World War II—so foreign to a stubbornly untraveled Midwesterner.

Then, the instant they'd left the city, there'd been green. Endless green in every shade covering valley and mountains. Anything not green was water—bright, shining, running down mountainsides and glistening in shadowed sunlight. Bridget had shown him pictures to give him some idea, but they hadn't come close to readying him for the overwhelming sensations as they'd driven along Loch Lomond.

He'd calmed as they'd driven north. Being with Ewan had made up for the long, bumpy flight, and he could no longer resent the stunningly nice Ainslie. Her tour guide's monologue, offered in a brogue he never tired of hearing, had been like a soothing song, stopping the jangling of his stretched-by-travel nerves. By the time they crested the rutted road above Craigwarren and stopped to let him take it in, he'd expected beauty. He'd heard about the famous Loch Warren, and known there'd be a small—but nonetheless way too huge—welcoming committee once they reached the house.

None of it mattered. He hadn't been prepared.

Not for Catrione's hug, which made him feel emotions he'd long ago forgotten—memories of a much younger woman whose hugs had held the same kind of warmth.

He definitely hadn't been prepared for the ebullience in Innis MacFarlane's—God help him, those names again—handshake, or the fact that each person's welcome was more enthusiastic than the previous one. Under normal circumstances such displays would have been suspiciously overzealous, but Noah couldn't sense a drop of insincerity in anyone. Catrione had even cried with joy. He didn't like being the cause of tears—no matter how happy they might be.

And then there was this Mairi person. He had imagined her based on Ewan's description as an unobtrusive uber-mama, handsome and plaid-wearing, with a pleasant expression. She was not supposed to be a woman with the smoothest sculpted features, the biggest lake-blue eyes holding wounded secrets, and hair like a stormy black cloud. She definitely wasn't supposed to have struck him dumb as a coat rack.

And the child. She was no chubby placid schoolgirl kid. She was a Disney-esque imp with wild curly hair the color of a red-brown acorn, a nose full of light freckles, and a mouth like an outboard motor running on high. She hadn't even been annoying; she'd been overwhelming. Maybe annoyingly cute. And that observation unnerved him, since he didn't know enough kids to really understand cute.

In the country less than two hours and he was exhausted. He'd been given a cozy room to rest in until dinner when he was expected to eat with the whole darn bunch of them. What he craved was his dusty home, his big-screen television, his baseball games, and his Reese's Peanut Butter Cups. Though even that home no longer existed, since he and Bridget had packed everything into storage before he'd left.

A soft knock on the bedroom door gave his churning brain a welcome break. He rose from the soft, thick mattress and opened the door to Ewan.

"Hey," his brother said.

"Hi."

"Came to see if you're okay. You looked pretty shell-shocked when I left you."

"Bah, I'm fine. It was a long flight."

"It is long. Claim jetlag. It's a real thing. If you can stay awake until eight or nine and then sleep, you'll do okay."

"I'll do okay no matter what."

"It's really good to see you, man."

"You too. It's different at home now that you aren't there," Noah admitted. "I'm not very good at being the only big brother."

"Ach, how is our Bridget?"

Noah stared at him. The tiniest hint of an accent tinged his words. "Say what? *Acchh?* You got something in your throat? 'Our Bridget'? Even I know Americans don't use that word combination. Tell me it ain't so…you're assimilating."

Ewan laughed. "I swear to you, I had no idea. This accent is impossible. If you asked me to mimic it, I couldn't. And I wouldn't. I've been teased for trying."

"You'd get worse at home."

"Yeah, well, rag on; I can take it." He gave a self-conscious smile. "I also came to bring you on a little tour before supper. I can show you the old groundskeeper's cottage you're here to fix."

"Sure. I came to work. Let's start."

Innis met them as they left the house through a back door off the kitchen. Noah had to admit, the scents emanating from Catrione's stove eased his weariness and reminded him how meager the airplane breakfast had been.

The kitchen smelled of roasted meat and rich spices with an overlying aroma that was both yeasty and sweet.

"I didn't want to leave that room," he said when they were in the fresh air of the garden, where the smells turned from wonderful food to water-rich soil and windblown grasses. Even in the north woods of Minnesota, Noah hadn't ever smelled anything this purely fresh.

"Nobody wants to leave Catrione's kitchen," Innis agreed. "You'd think she spent every moment of her day slaving over her stove, but ye'd be wrong. That girl packs more into her day than our seven-year-old Ella does."

Noah had to smile. "Girl," Innis called her. It was good, he supposed, to see true love knew no age limit, and newlyweds could be any age.

"The building we're working on is over there in that little grove of trees." Ewan pointed across the yard to where the walls of a small gray stone house showed through a stand of silver birch and the ash trees they called rowan. He swung to the right and pointed at a larger building set into a hillside with a wide set of double doors in front and two stories behind. "There's the barn. It'll give you a good look at how things were built a hundred and fifty years ago."

"It's still sturdy as the day it was built by stone masons who were right magicians," Innis said. "Same type who knew how to build the drystone walls that cross all of Britain. 'Tisn't for the simple bricklayers. There aren't many left who want to learn the art."

"And the cottage?" Noah asked.

"It's suffered more over the decades. The roof leaked years back and was haphazardly repaired. Inner walls were damaged. You'll see."

Despite Innis's warning, the little cottage's charm couldn't be denied. The front flagstone façade was built of variously sized gray and rose-colored stones like puzzle pieces, perfectly stacked as if they'd been quarried to fit with one another. The cottage was a simple rectangular box with an attached square room off the back. On the front, the flagstone façade extended to the right, forming an attractive stone archway. Through the arch lay the little house's garden.

"It's a bonnie wee place, is it not?" Innis asked.

"I admit, I've never seen anything like it before. Did people used to live in it?"

"On and off, I understand," Ewan said. "Catrione's grandfather—our great-great grandfather—had servants. I guess this was the gardener's house. It's not big, maybe thirty by sixty. There are four rooms inside. We have some plans but want to see what you think."

"And who is it coming to stay that makes fixing it up so important?"

Ewan shrugged. "A couple who'll be on their honeymoon and want a place no one has ever heard of."

"But so soon? Why did you say yes when the work wasn't done yet?"

Ewan hesitated as if he were hiding something, but that was ridiculous.

"The couple is well-to-do," Ewan said finally. "It would be a windfall and great advertising to have them come. We know it's crazy, but now that we have your help, we think it's doable."

They passed under the stone archway and Noah could see where some of the stone had crumbled away. Cursory inspection told him the cottage's foundation was probably solid, but right off the bat he worried he didn't have the expertise Innis had talked about for repairing such stonework. Most of the wood window framing along with the door and its jambs needed replacing. He couldn't tell much about the slate roof yet.

As Noah rounded a corner to the back of the cottage, an unexpected burst of high-pitched laughter stopped him in his tracks. He had only a second's glimpse of a reddish-topped mini-tornado bearing down on him before it barreled straight into his legs. Ella bounced backward like she'd hit a very hard trampoline and landed smack on her rear end in a tuft of grass. She let out a squawk like a wounded baby duck.

"Hey, what's this?" Ewan called. "Ella?"

Noah was as stunned as the girl, and before he could bend to see if she was all right, her mother was at her side. Where she'd come from, Noah had no idea; he hadn't seen her come round the house.

"Ella, love, are you hurt?"

Mairi tried to gather her daughter into a hug, but the girl brushed her aside and scrambled to her feet, an enormous smile on her face. "I'm okay!"

Noah held back a laugh. The kid was as cute as a wild rabbit, her curls straying from the band that had once held it all back in a ponytail. He had no idea what to say to a child he'd just knocked over. Then again, she'd been the one racing while looking backward. Could you put blame on a seven-year-old?

"Noah!" Ella cried when she finally looked up into his face. "You were like a constable standing right in my way to stop me."

"I'm sorry?" he said.

"It's okay. I like constables. Mama says they're our good friends and we can always ask them for help if we need it. I've never needed help before but I've talked to constables."

He stared at her with no idea how to respond. She was like a miniature elderly person whose thoughts weren't quite coming out coherently.

"I'm not a constable, I'm afraid," he said finally.

"What are you doing here?" she asked.

"Ella, don't be rude." Mairi's quiet voice held no censure, yet she clearly meant what she said.

Ella shrugged. "I only wondered."

Noah lifted his eyes from Ella's open, trusting face and met Mairi MacDonald's gaze for the second time that day. The impact of her eyes and face on his shallow male brain hadn't lessened. If anything, his throat closed even more tightly.

"I'm sorry," she said. "She was playing tag in her own little world and wouldn't stop for me. I was supposed to catch her before she rounded the corner. I... Sorry. I'm babblin' like a nutter."

"Tag," Noah said. "I know the game."

Wow. There was a brilliant response.

"Want to play?" Ella asked, her eyes bright with the idea. "You're probably really really quick."

"Ella, Mr. Noah is here to do some work for Ewan and Aunt Catrione. He's not here to play tag. We'll go on our way again and let them get to their business."

"But what business?"

"Wee Not-Quite-Red." Innis took Ella's hand and sent Mairi a wink. "We're goin' into this house to see how it can be fixed up. Have you ever been inside this old place?"

She shook her head.

"Ask your mum, then, if you can have a wee peek."

"Mama, can I? I want to see what's inside."

Noah's heart sank a little. He hadn't expected an entourage while he looked at the project for the first time. He liked to study a space quietly and get the configurations and possibilities straight in his mind. It had been one thing to have Bridget with him at the hotel. She, at least, had a sense of history and knew proper things to point out. There was nothing proper or knowledgeable about this group.

"If it's really all right with the gentlemen, Ella. And if you behave."

"I will."

She let go of Innis's hand and skipped off, disappearing around the next corner of the little house.

"She's quite the live wire," Ewan laughed. "Someone needs to find a way to run down those batteries."

"Too right." Mairi sighed. "I haven't figured out how in seven years, though, and I am sorry. We meant to be out of your way by now, but it took far too long in the barn. We had to greet every animal, you see." She looked Noah in the eyes again. "And we had to chase Juliet through the lower barn when she bullied her way out the gate. Fortunately, we'd closed the front door and she couldn't fully escape."

"Juliet?" Noah asked.

"The goat."

"Ah," he said. "She's been mentioned. A Houdini, is she?"

"That she is. And Ella is her biggest fan, sorry to say. She roots for the goat."

She stopped again and bit her lip to hide a self-deprecating smile.

"Sounds like Ella might be as much a handful as Juliet." Was that an insult? Noah had no idea, but Mairi only offered a resigned sigh.

"In many ways, yes. I'm sorry...again. This is way more than you need or want to know I'm quite sure."

"Ella and the animals keep us entertained. In a good way." Ewan sent Mairi a grin.

Noah couldn't for the life of him figure out how an entertaining child-animal circus was going to help him in the task he'd been brought here to do. He would have preferred ignoring the whole show and carrying on alone, but something about Mairi wouldn't let him go. Whether it was the accent—a little broader and sharper than Ainslie's—or the eyes, or the guileless way she spoke what came into her mind, he didn't know, but fascination had gripped him whether he liked it or not.

He managed to get ahead of her as she walked with Ewan along the back of the building. Innis went back to pointing out the places where stonework needed repair and showed Noah a spot where a window had been removed and stoned over. When they made it back to the front of the little house, Noah was creating mental lists of experts he might need to assist with the stonework. And he already knew he wanted to open up the bricked off window to lighten the façade.

They also found Ella standing in front of the door, squinting as if examining a portal to another world. Her fingers splayed on her hips, her head tilted upward, and her little mouth considered whatever she'd found with a pursed-lips O.

"Whatcha see, Ella?" Ewan asked.

"I think there's a unicorn carved into one of the stones above the door. And a thistle. And a fairy. The fairy is in the middle of the top. Do you see it? Is this a fairy house?"

Mairi groaned behind him. "Honestly, Ella. Not everything has to do with fairies."

"Not everything," the girl agreed. "But a lot of things."

Noah couldn't stop the amusement that welled up inside.

"She is magical-creature obsessed," Mairi said when she caught Noah looking at her. "I promise I don't know where she gets it."

"I guess most kids are obsessed with something," he replied, although he didn't know if that was actually true.

"I guess she could be bringing home real stray animals," Mairi said. "At least her strays are invisible and don't require house training."

He laughed in spite of himself.

"Look, Noah," Ella called to him. "See the fairy and the unicorn and the thistle?"

He had no choice but to join her in front of the worn wooden door. It definitely needed to be replaced, since large splinters were missing from the planks.

"Where?" he asked.

"There. On the stones that go around the curvy top."

He stared at three wedge-shaped lintel stones lining the rounded top of the door. The front surfaces bore the shine from decades of exposure to the weather, but with a little squinting he saw the carved lines Ella had found. To the left of the center stone was a flower with a bushy bloom and pointed leaves, to the right a horse—no, a unicorn—head. In the middle, a tiny human-like form hovered over the door with wings larger than its body.

"You know, I think she's right. They're pretty worn, but the carvings are there."

Innis joined them and stared upward. "I'll be. I have to admit, I've never noticed these. Wonder if Cat knows. Well done, Ella, my wee expert. You've discovered a very special piece of this little house."

"I wonder if it has its own brownie."

"Ella. It does not have a brownie," Mairi said with certainty.

"I think you're right," Ella said again. She was actually a pretty agreeable child, Noah thought. "There's nobody to do helpful chores for, so why would anyone live here?"

"Exactly," Innis said. "After all, Craigwarren House itself has no brownie."

"Diarmid used to live there, but he likes animals. He liked to help in the barn more than in the house."

"All right, you, lassie. Let's go inside and see if Noah can tell us whether our ideas will work."

"Who's going to live here?" Ella asked as Innis worked the handle latch and pushed open the door.

"I hope many people will get the chance to stay here," Ewan answered. "We want to make a nice place for people who come to visit Scotland and need a place to sleep for a night or two. Especially people who hike on the path through the hills."

"Brilliant," Ella said.

Noah let the others' conversations fade into the background as he stepped through the doorway into a tiny stone entry foyer barely five feet square. The right wall held a large built-in shelf, and the left an unfinished board holding four coat hooks.

He entered the main living area and took his first look. One big window left of the door and a smaller one on a side wall let in a good amount of light, and the floor was a burnished pine of some kind, mostly a dark coffee brown but mottled from rain and slightly warped from time. Still, it looked warm and offset the cold stone entryway. The room was empty save for a small wooden table and four spindly ladder-back chairs. A stone fireplace graced the end wall, the hearth filled with debris and even some recent trash like cups and paper plates.

"I think this was last used as a secret place to play cards and drink Scotch," Ewan said. "Catrione said she used to let our cousin Callum stay from time to time when he was little."

"*The* Callum?" Noah asked.

"The very same. You'll meet him as soon as he hears you've arrived."

"He's a wee piece of work is our Callum," Innis finished. "Not an evil sort, but he would as soon take over this whole place and turn it into a Highland resort destination."

"So I've heard," Noah said.

"That's why we're grateful you're here," Ewan said. "With you running the show, we aren't beholden to Callum. If he has any decent ideas, we can pick and choose."

"He doesn't honor the heritage of the family the way your auntie wants," Innis said.

"And we do?" Noah asked.

"We do," Ewan said without hesitation. "I know that sounds arrogant and doesn't make sense to you, but it will. I promise. This place really belongs to you, too."

Noah held in a sigh, not sure his brother was right. It might be partly his on paper, but he felt no ownership—this was merely another job, and he'd do it to the best of his ability. He scouted the room, inspecting places where the walls were disintegrating and the framing was rotting. It was worse than the exterior but, still, most of the bones were okay. The worst problems were in the vaulted roof and the ceiling in the small addition at the back of the cottage.

"I see straightforward fixes for most things," he said. "But I don't think there's any saving the ceilings. The roof obviously needs repairs, judging by the water stains on the floor."

Ewan nodded. "The slate cracked in one spot long ago was patched with asphalt shingles. I'd give a lot to replace the full slate roof, but I'm not sure we can afford that yet. I'm hoping a repair job will be enough."

"I'll put it on the list of things I can't do alone," Noah said. "I'll need help locating experts to break everything down and estimate costs."

"The first thing we'll look into."

They walked through the living area, peering into every corner, then they reached the small kitchen to the right of the front door."

"Everything needs to be replaced in here, from appliances to cabinetry."

"This room has amazing potential." Mairi's voice from behind them gave Noah a start.

"I think so, too," Ewan said.

"This whole place is incredibly charming. What a treasure it would be to get it all restored. Ideas basically throw themselves at you when you look around, don't they?"

A slight wave of resentment rolled slowly through Noah. This was precisely why he preferred walking through a project alone—he wasn't ready for other ideas yet. He needed a simple lay of the land so when visions were discussed, he had no preconceived ideas.

"We're a long way from decorating," he said.

"I'm not only talking about decorating," she replied. "For example, you could push this wall out a wee bit and make room for a lovely eating nook. The back addition would be perfect for a main bedroom, and there's even room for a second behind the kitchen. And can you see building a wee loft beneath the rafter beams? More guest sleeping or a reading and relaxing space? With a ladder leading up to it."

He stared at her. Her flowing ideas made his head spin. Wasn't she supposed to be on a walk with her daughter?

"I think Ewan and Ainslie have ideas for the space," he said. "I'd like to hear those first."

"Of course." Mairi's mouth thinned into a wounded line. "Just blethering. Pay no mind."

She turned away, and Noah held back an irritated snort. He wasn't trying to offend her. He'd have said the same to anyone interrupting his initial thought process.

"If you really want to make this a *good* house you need to have a brownie." Ella appeared from wherever she'd been exploring and stood in front of Noah, looking up with huge eyes. They were the most unusual shade of blue, he thought. Like pieces of pale turquoise. "There isn't a brownie here now, but if you put out some honey and bread, maybe Diarmid would tell one of his friends to come help."

As if her daughter's limitless connection to the fairy world finally flipped a switch in her head, Mairi took Ella by the hand.

"Okay, darlin'. I think we need to get on that walk of ours. These gentlemen have plans to make."

"Okay. But..." She looked back up at Noah. "A brownie will help get the work done faster, you know. They'll do stuff overnight that you don't have time to do yourself." She gave a little shrug, too wise by far for a seven-year-old. "Do you have brownies in America?"

"Uhhh..."

Behind him, Ewan started to laugh. "I have to admit, bro, I've never contemplated that question. Do we?"

"Don't encourage this," Noah muttered.

"Oh, I dunno," Innis said. "I can't say I've never wondered if it wasn't a sprite of some kind did me a good turn over a night once or twice."

Noah turned his stare on the old man. Were these people all insane?

"Ella," Ewan said. "I know you're fondest of cream for Diarmid, but did I ever tell you that once, after I decided to stay here in Scotland with Ainslie, I brought some Oreo cookies from America for him as a peace offering? I didn't know at the time that there were certain things a brownie prefers. But you say he's still here? He must not have taken offense."

"Oreo cookies?"

"Chocolate wafers with thick white frosting in the middle."

"Is the frosting like cream?" she asked.

Ewan caught Noah's eye and made a face. "I don't think you can call it real cream. Oreo white stuff is like whipped up sugar."

Ella took a turn to make a face. "Sounds weird."

How old was this kid? "It *is* weird," Noah said. "Weird to eat. Even weirder to bring to a made-up fantasy man."

He was shocked by a collective groan of warning from all three adults.

"I'd be careful what you say, brother," Ewan grinned. "Brownies are very, very sensitive to slights."

"Okay." Noah took a step back and took them all in, trying very hard not to glare. "I know I've only been here a couple of hours, and I'm an interloper who doesn't know the ways of this country. But seriously? I'm here to see what can be done in a short time for this house you desperately need renovated, and our conversation has devolved into a discussion of whether or not to feed Oreos to a mythical man."

"Oh, it has," Mairi said. "And were I you, Noah Portman, I'd embrace it. It's not worth fighting." She actually winked, her earlier huffiness gone for the moment. "Come on, Ella. We'll be going. See you at dinner, everyone."

Ella skipped to her mother's side, then seemed to think of something and skipped right back to Noah.

"Don't worry. Mama didn't believe in Diarmid at first either. I think maybe she's changing her mind a little now. You'll see!"

Mother and daughter left the cottage without another look back. Their presence had been so big they almost left a hole where they'd been standing. Noah turned to Innis only to find the man grinning as if he'd witnessed the funniest scene in his favorite movie.

"What?" Noah asked.

"She's a handful, I think," he said.

"She's like that kid in the Disney movie. That little Scottish thing. Don't anyone dare give her a bow and arrow."

"Aye, that's true enough," Innis laughed. "But I wasn't talking about the little girl."

CHAPTER FIVE

"Catrione, the butter on this potato bread is like cake icing!" Mairi groaned and sucked lightly on her lower lip to savor every drop of the warm, nutty butter sweetness that had melted against her mouth.

Murmurs of agreement from the seven people around the dinner table told her she was not the only one stuffing herself on the rich pork stew, savory vegetables and homemade bread.

"I'm glad you're enjoying it." Catrione beamed.

"I need to stop enjoying it quite so much." Mairi laughed, pulled off a square of the soft bread with its crusty brown edge, and set it on Ella's plate. "Try this, darlin'."

"I did." Ella snatched up the bread, ate it along with a forkful of stew, and then garbled out the next words through her full mouth. "The potatoes and *gravy* are best."

"Not with your mouth full, please." Mairi gave the obligatory parental admonishment.

"Hard not to, isn't it?" Noah said, and Mairi, her eyebrows rising in surprise at his words, almost missed the little wink he shot across the table at her daughter. "Talk with your mouth full, I mean."

It was hard to believe Ewan's taciturn brother had spoken, much less entered into a conspiracy with the child who'd seemed to do nothing but annoy and confuse him all afternoon. It must have happened, however, because Ella jumped on the invitation to camaraderie.

"If I didn't talk with my mouth full, I'd never get to say anything."

Chuckles erupted around the table.

"Out the mouth of babes," Innis said. "She makes a fair point."

"Well, I didn't mean we should do it," Noah said. "I only meant this is all very good. Thank you, Aunt Catrione."

"Dear boy, this is very little enough to say thank *you*. You're the one who's traveled untold miles to help us all."

"True," he said, leveling a stare at Ewan and getting an insouciant smile in return.

Mairi dipped her head to hide a grin. She hadn't been able to get a handle on Noah Portman from the moment he'd arrived. This exchange didn't exactly explain him, but it did show her a different side to the slightly irritable man who'd shut down all and sundry ideas out in the gardener's cottage earlier. At least he wasn't prickly one hundred percent of the time.

"The best news is that our new expert here says the project is doable," Innis said. "I believe he even said we could make it within our timeline."

"You really think so, Noah?" Catrione asked.

The serious demeanor he'd worn all afternoon returned and he frowned, more in thoughtfulness than anything.

"We can. There's a lot to be done, and a lot depends on whether there's a stone expert willing to help within the time, because I don't have the expertise to fix the walls. Meeting the deadline for your inspection depends on a lot of things falling into place without problems. I'll spend tomorrow putting together a detailed plan with Ewan and Ainslie. We'll make a list of supplies and maybe start laying out a work timeline."

"We'll finish clean-up and some prep over the weekend, then we'll need to take a trip Glasgow," Ewan added.

"That's moving fast," Catrione said. "I can barely believe it's going to happen. Noah, *mo cridhe*, you're a miracle worker."

"Hardly. It's just best to jump in and start swimming."

His words bore the lightness of confidence and enthusiasm for the job, but his dark eyes didn't hold the same cheerfulness. Whatever his inner feelings really were, Mairi's ridiculous analysis was silly and pointless. His real emotions were covered with a layer of protective caution. Noah reminded her of a stray pup suddenly being lavished with love and praise but having no idea how to handle the attention.

Turning away, she tried to focus on anyone else—Cat, Ella, Ainslie, all the chattering social squirrels at the table, who could carry the conversation past her obsession with Noah Portman. She knew nothing about the man except the one thing she'd been told in forewarning: he was a solitary creature—his brother's words—a reserved introvert who preferred to work alone. She'd seen hints of those things but, in truth, the reality of him was nothing like she'd expected. He was quiet but not shy. He kept himself guarded yet answered questions willingly enough.

It was his protective shell that intrigued her.

Or maybe his rock star looks turned her into a shallow person. Based on Ewan's descriptions, she'd expected a pale, mousy stick figure of a man. Instead, Noah Portman could easily relegate a combo of Cavill, Clooney, Jackman and two Hemsworths to the category of ordinary dudes.

"You don't need a swimming pool in the Highlands, you wait for the rain and then jump in the puddles." Ainslie's voice pulled Mairi from inner thoughts that were quickly careening off the rails.

With a shake of her head, she realized the line was in reply to Ella's question, "How can you jump in and swim if you don't have a swimming pool?"

Her daughter's giggle cleared away the last of Mairi's musing. "Noah, you can swim in the loch. You don't have to use puddles. Eachann won't bother with you."

Noah stared at Ella, fascinated the way a visitor to the zoo would be fascinated by a kangaroo or an exotic bird, and Mairi chuckled. She couldn't blame him. Ella was a whirlwind with no idea where her energy stopped and her mouth full of words began.

"I'm afraid to ask what would happen if *Eachann* did bother with me," Noah grimaced at Ella, who laughed again at the face.

"He's the kelpie," Ewan explained, exactly the way he'd have said "he's the neighbor."

"Sure," Noah replied.

"But he's a good kelpie. Normally they steal away little girls, but he's my friend, so he won't steal me." Ella nodded with certainty. "And you're not a little girl, so he'll not be fashed."

Not a soul around the table except Noah stopped eating or made any indication this wasn't perfectly normal conversation. They all nodded and acknowledged the information with quiet "aye rights" and "true, you don't have to worry."

Mairi bit her lip and tried not to laugh at the defeat on Noah's face. "It's a water horse," she said at last, unable to keep up the ruse as long as the others could.

Noah's eyes caught hers, his those of a drowning man pleading for a life ring.

"You know," Ewan said. "Like that old story Bridget tells now and then about the flesh-eating horse that's lost in the water, and the fairies try to help him but fail and he's stuck there forever, going after young maidens?"

"The one she says our mother used to tell her? That's a kelpie?" Noah asked. "It's a terrible story."

"Scottish fairy tales." Ewan shrugged. "They aren't for wimps."

"Delightful," Noah murmured. "I always thought our sister was traumatized as a child—this confirms it."

"Your mother would have heard such stories as a wee girl," Catrione said. "I would be surprised if she had'nae told them to you."

"I don't remember anything like that from childhood," Noah insisted. "My sister pulls out the tale like a party trick at family gatherings."

"You probably thought they were only stories," Ella said. "But Eachann is real. Like Diarmid."

Without warning, Ella picked up her paper napkin, slipped from her chair and rounded behind Innis, making for Noah's side of the table.

"Ella, come back and sit down," Mairi called. "You've not been excused."

"I need to show Noah." She reached him and searched his bemused face. "May I use the pen from your pocket?"

Bemusement turned to amusement as Noah lifted a hand and shifted to reach into his pocket.

"You don't have to indulge this," Mairi said.

"It's okay. Now I have to see the end of the joke."

"Not a joke." Ella's voice turned seven-year-old stern. "This is what to look for when ye go to the loch."

As she took the pen Noah offered, Catrione and Innis's landline phone rang from the kitchen.

"Could be Isla," Ainslie said. "She and the baby are away in Inverness."

"Baby?" Noah's head jerked up.

"My sister had a bairn four months ago," Ainslie explained. "Isla's to be part of a friend's wedding in a month, and she took her wee Skye on a two-day shopping excursion to Inverness with the rest of the party. I told her she'd better call in every night."

Innis stood and smiled. "I'll go take the report."

"Isla lets me hold Skye," Ella said proudly, even though she was engrossed in drawing on the napkin. "She never cries when *I* hold her."

"She lives here, too?" Noah's eyes widened almost imperceptibly.

"You remember," Ewan said. "Ainslie's niece who was born in the snowstorm last April."

"Oh. The one you were there for? I can't keep track of all the family members."

Mairi could see uncertainty creeping into Noah's eyes over the circle of people around him that kept growing, but Ella distracted him—maybe in a good way this time.

"See, then he has this long fish tale."

She set her drawing directly in front of him, and Mairi could make out, upside down, the child-like outline of a horse with two front hooves and a mermaid-like tail.

"So it's a mer-horse." The lines of tension in Noah's face eased.

"No! There's no such thing. He's a kelpie. A pretty kelpie. Some drawings of them are pure ugly and scary. But those are by people who've never seen one."

"And you have."

"Two times."

Noah actually smiled.

Innis returned, his features thoughtful. "Mairi, love," he called and crooked his finger. "It's for you, as it turns out."

Her heart gave a stutter. Nobody should know to call her on Craigwarren's landline.

"It's all right." Innis placed a hand on her arm, reading her worry. "It's your head teacher—the one from Glasgow."

Of course. She stood though her knees went weak with relief. Paul was the one person she'd given this number to, in case of emergency.

"Thank you, Innis."

He nodded as he handed her the phone. "Everything will be fine, lass."

She took the handset into the kitchen and leaned on a counter. "Hello?"

"Mairi! I'm sorry to call you at this number, but I wasn't reaching you on your mobile. I got back into town a couple of hours ago and saw messages from you. Is everything all right?"

She wanted to rail at him that no, nothing was all right since he'd cost her the new job. But Paul had always been a good friend as well as a mentor. She owed him a civil conversation.

"Things aren't great, Paul. I was let go from the new job today. Before I even started."

"Mairi, no. I'm terribly sorry. What happened?"

"Honestly?" She clung to her calm. "Your call to Christina Sullivan last week spooked her about Aiden."

Several seconds of silence told her he was processing the implications.

"If I caused this, I am sorry," he said.

"I wish you'd told *me* first that James had called. I haven't heard from him in over a year; a heads-up would have been helpful."

"A year?" Another heartbeat of silence followed. "Oh! No, Mairi, I didn't hear from Ella's father. It was James Senior who rang looking for you."

She closed her eyes and groaned in understanding. James *Robert* MacDonald. Her ex-father-in-law only used "James" in the most formal of circumstances. Everywhere else he was Robbie. She closed her eyes.

"That explains a lot. Robbie MacDonald is a solicitor, and Aiden knows he keeps tabs on everything he possibly can. It wouldn't surprise me at all if my brother made sure Robbie knows I left my job in Glasgow." She sighed. "I don't know how, but Aiden seems to have a way of getting to anyone he wants—first you and the parent council, then the head teacher at the school in Glencoe, now Ella's grandparents. How long until he finds me?"

"Your father-in-law, ex, did ask where you were. I only told him you'd taken a sabbatical, but the next day the police called and asked about your job and your relationship with your brother. I called Christina Sullivan because I assumed she knew what was going on and I wanted her to keep the secret."

"I'd told her I'd left the city to sort out some family issues. She simply thought I was looking to start fresh." Mairi pinched the bridge of her nose. "But she knows the story now. I can't blame her for making her first priority the school. It's what you had to do."

"I'll call her back—"

"No, Paul, don't. I appreciate it, but that won't help. Until Aiden is out of the picture, I'm a liability anywhere. I need to figure how to deal with him."

"If there's anything I can do…"

"The thing I need most is for you to keep believing me until this is over."

"That's a promise I can make without hesitation."

"Then thank you. We'll talk again, Paul. Bye for now."

"Goodnight, Mairi."

It took her several minutes to quiet her chaotic emotions, but finally her resolve hardened. When she faced the inevitable inquisition back in the dining room, she'd do it with calm and without whingeing like an adolescent. She took another deep breath and returned to the others.

Ella sat on Ewan's lap. Someone had produced drawing paper and a handful of markers, and she was chattering away while covering the paper with her favorite art subjects: fairies, rainbows, and dinosaurs with wings, which were, in Ella-world, different than dragons.

She was clearly still filling Noah in on all things magical. The poor man's eyes were glazing over.

"Are you still blethering?" Mairi drew up beside her daughter and caught her chin lightly in her cupped hand. "I believe it's time for chores. Feed the chicks and donkeys and make sure the goat gets locked up tight."

"But there's bread pudding. We're waiting for you," Ella said.

"Ah. I suppose we have to see to that first, don't we? But perhaps it's time to give Ewan and Noah a wee bit of space and rest your stories for a bit."

"Your stories are awesome," Ewan said. "But Auntie's bread pudding is worth changing the subject for, right?"

"Right!" Ella slid off his lap.

"Did Paul have any news?" Ainslie asked.

"Some," Mairi said lightly and glanced at Ella. "It wasn't the, uh, ex who called. It was his father."

Ainslie's brows curved into a high arch. "Seriously?"

Mairi nodded. "But it's all I know until I dig a bit more. A task for tomorrow." She took her seat, turned a bright smile on Ella and patted her daughter's chair. "Bread pudding and then evening chores."

"Noah! Come with us to do chores," Ella cried. "Then you can see Diarmid's house."

"Ella, I'm sure Mr. Noah is very tired from his trip. Give him a rest."

"But he wants to see it. He said so."

She lifted her eyes to Noah's. He looked like a movie star who'd been on a bender, with drooping eyes and a two-day growth of stubble.

"How long do your chores take?" Noah asked.

"Two minutes!"

"Little devil!" Mairi said. "More like twenty. Noah, really, pay the child no mind."

"I said I'd go."

"See?" Ella crowed.

Mairi didn't know how she felt about him coming along. Her mind spun with too many problems; she didn't want to make conversation with a stranger.

"It's only a goat and chickens. Honestly, don't feel obligated."

"I wouldn't mind seeing the barn again," he replied. "See how it's put together."

Well, fine then. If he wanted to brave more of Ella that was on him, but she couldn't help believing that if he were smart, he'd leave the goat and the child—and her—on their own and go straight to bed.

CHAPTER SIX

Ella charged ahead down the path to the barn, her wild curls fully freed from their restraining band, her purple bike shorts and matching purple tennis shoes catching the still-bright evening sunlight. The little black-and-white corgi-collie galloped beside her, fluffy ears flying. Mairi sighed and shook her head.

"How can she run?" she asked. "I can barely waddle after that meal."

Noah grunted in agreement. The food had been incredible, but he pictured himself having grown a roll of fat after the giant slab of rich, cinnamon-and-cream-laced bread pudding. Watching Ella run made him wince.

"Children are a mystery."

He meant it rhetorically but, in many ways, literally as well. He'd never been a kid person. Not the way Bridget and Ewan were. This child had said more words in an hour during dinner than he usually said in a month. In his opinion, Ella could win the kind of talking contest where you got the prize if you didn't stop talking in x-amount of time—and do it on any subject on the face of the planet. Physics or plumbing or, hell, kangaroo breeding.

Although he was exhausted from jetlag, the guileless Ella MacDonald, with her endless chatter, was fueling him with weird energy. All he could do was accept it as a gift that would allow him to stay awake another two hours.

"Even after seven years, she's a mystery to me," Mairi said. "I wish I could get her to tone down the fantasy stuff a little. She could use a little grounding in reality."

"I don't know, she seems happy enough," he said.

"She's definitely happy."

"I wouldn't sweat it. She's seven. Fantasies die out soon enough."

"So profound," she said.

"Realistic. Do *you* believe we're about to visit the home of a brownie?"

She laughed. "I believe we're about to make four barn cats very happy with more cream and honey." She held up the covered jar she'd agreed to carry.

"I rest my case. Your kid believes one hundred percent that a small magic person will be making sure everything in the barn is safe. Who's filled with excitement over chores, and who's doing this because it has to be done?"

She didn't reply immediately. A breeze rippled up the path and tossed at their hair, bringing the scent of damp soil, redolent grass and a hint of animal in its wake.

"So, you don't believe in brownies then? You're too grown up?" she asked.

"I believe in the U.S. kind that are fudgy chocolate squares of cake. The barn-type brownies I'll leave to your daughter."

She chuckled and it dawned on Noah he'd used more words on this walk than all during dinner. He bit back a question about how Mairi and her daughter had come to be there, uncomfortable with the thought of getting more personal. He knew she had moved from Glasgow because of family issues, but nobody at Craigwarren had divulged her story, and it wasn't his place to dig. He let silence fall and although it wasn't uncomfortable, he missed their initial ease. They concentrated on Ella as she scampered ahead.

The front of the barn was at ground level, its stonework in much better shape than that of the little cottage. Two massive green doors, their tops meeting in a cathedral point, had been recently painted, and Ella was working to throw a large lever latch when Noah and Mairi arrived. David Tennant ran in ecstatic circles around her, barking in anticipation.

"He wants to chase the cats," Ella said. "He can't catch them because he doesnae know how to sneak up."

She got the latch open, and Mairi helped swing one door wide. Noah had walked briefly around the barn's exterior that afternoon but not gone inside. To his shock, Ella grabbed his hand.

"Come and see!"

They entered a spacious hayloft, and Ella tugged him across the hay-strewn floor as if he were a stuck car she was determined to get free. They finally stopped in front of a six-foot-long, battered wooden table. In the hazy light filtering through a dozen narrow slits in the stone walls, he could see the table had been set with a pewter plate, a couple of mugs and a bowl. Beneath them was a short, dusty piece of cloth, and to one side were two pictures of gnome-like beings. To the right were two pewter candlesticks bearing fake candles.

"This is Diarmid's table. Every night he comes out and drinks his cream and eats bread and honey if we leave it. You aren't actually supposed to let the brownie know you know he's here. But Auntie Cat said Diarmid broke that rule ages ago."

"I see."

Ella still held his hand, and before he could figure out a way to extricate his fingers, she tugged again. "Now come and meet the animals."

"Don't we have to, like, pay homage here or make an offering or something?" He looked over the girl's head to Mairi.

"It's not a religion, it's just a barn brownie." Her eyes glistened with merriment in the shafts of light. "We'll pour the milk when we leave—that's the only ritual. Right, Ella?"

"Too right!"

She pulled him to a narrow stairwell in the middle of the floor, protected on three sides by walls that kept it from being an open hole. A caricature of a fairy sprite herself, with her flyaway hair and her happy flitting, Ella was down the first step practically before Noah could balance behind her.

"I think you better let Noah navigate the stairs on his own," Mairi said. "You'll pull him down in a heap if you keep draggin' on the poor man."

Noah sent her a grateful smile. Ella released his hand.

"And you wouldn't want old Diarmid to laugh at me before he knows me," he said.

"He wouldn't laugh. He'd maybe cry if you got hurt."

"Or if I squashed you."

The little girl's eyes went wide. She clearly hadn't considered that possibility. "Okay, you can climb down on your own."

He couldn't help the laugh that tickled up from his stomach. The child was either brilliant or had a brain made of sugar plums and fairies.

The actual barn made up the lower level, a space divided by hand-hewn posts and boards that formed four pens and a couple of full-size stalls. They'd barely reached the floor when a cacophony rose that sounded like a petting zoo was being strangled. Angry clucking, a series of plaintive bleats, and a loud bray that would have been bone-chilling in the dark, sent Ella running for the open back door.

"Eejit dog," Mairi grumbled and followed. "He must have run round the side to the yard. If he can't get the cats, he'll try to play with the chickens, and that cheeses off the goat."

"Am I about to witness a chicken murder?"

Mairi giggled. "No. D.T. truly only wants to herd them, but the birds are so barmy they don't know he won't touch them. Even a trained border collie would quit its job trying to sort that lot, and this dog, bein' far from trained, hasnae hope."

For the first time, Noah was fully struck by the music in Mairi's accent. It was normally a little guttural and, sometimes, when she spoke quickly, she was harder to understand than Ainslie. Now, with laughter in her voice, the shortened vowels and chopped consonants brought back vague memories of a laugh he hadn't heard since he'd been four.

"David Tennant, come now, ye wee rocket," she called. "Give off chasin' that poor chick or she'll die of a heart attack. Come, boy."

The dog immediately stopped and stared at the three humans in the barn door. He contemplated them for several seconds until Ella called as well. At that, the little dog loped toward them and Ella grabbed his collar, hugging him tightly as she pulled him close.

"Funny wee doggy," she said. "Ye think the chickens should do as ye say."

David Tennant wriggled in happiness and slobbered kisses on Ella's face. Her giggles were infectious.

"All right, all right, come on. Time to get the goat in before she decides it's night escape time." Mairi reached for a rope hanging at the side of the door, and Ella released the dog.

"Night escape time?" Noah asked.

"From what Ainslie tells me, Juliet here," she pointed out the door at a large brown-and-white goat with an impressively curved pair of horns, "has learned how to open the yard gate during the past few months. They've tried all manner of locks and ties, but she's brilliant."

As if she'd heard herself being discussed, Juliet lifted her head and stared at Noah. A strange sense of foreboding came over him as the goat's eyes met his. Again, it was ridiculous. Goats didn't take your measure and then —

Juliet let out a long, low bleat and ran straight for the humans in the doorway. More specifically, straight for Noah. He backed swiftly away and pressed against the wall next to the door.

"What's she doing?" he asked.

All he got in reply was Mairi's hearty laugh. "I think she's looking for you. Have a wee peek."

Noah liked animals as well as the next guy, but something in that goat's eyes... Cautiously he bent around the doorjamb to see Juliet standing still, her head cocked. Then she gave another call, this one sounding straight-up happy, put her head down and trotted through the barn door, past Ella, past Mairi, stopped and spun to face Noah. She had to be the biggest damn goat he'd ever seen.

"Hello, uh, Juliet," he said, more nervously than he'd intended. Mairi sputtered again, covering her mouth when he glared at her.

Juliet wasted no more time. She speed-walked directly toward him, lifted her head until her nose was even with his collarbone and snuffled his neck before starting to nibble on the ribbed collar of his T-shirt.

"Ack, what the hell...heck? She's eating me."

Mairi was nearly bent double, gasping for breath. Ella giggled as if being tickled.

"No. She's fallen in love at first sight," Mairi wheezed.

Convinced the goat wasn't really attacking, Noah pushed her nose away. "That's the stupidest thing I've ever heard. Get away now, goat. Go'wan."

Juliet merely lowered her horns and pressed her forehead against the side of Noah's leg. With a happy "naaaaa, naaaaa," she rubbed on the rough denim of his jeans.

"Scratch her!" Ella laughed. "She likes you. Oh, hiya, Fen."

Noah looked up from the goat and gave a yelp of shock, escaping Juliet momentarily by jump backward. A giant donkey head appeared through the barn door with ears as big as the flipping goat.

"Mary, Joseph, and Frank! Is this place haunted?"

Mairi literally could no longer speak. With one hand on her chest, she slapped at her thigh with the other, trying to catch her breath.

"Your mother has lost it," Noah said to Ella, who wasn't laughing *quite* as hard.

"It's not haunted," she said. "That's Fenella."

Juliet resumed her head rubbing. Noah pushed her away again. His equilibrium and his memory were returning. A goat and *two* donkeys. Four chickens. There should be no more surprises. He didn't even startle when the second long-eared head poked through the door.

"And this?"

"Ailish. She's Fen's daughter."

"And that's all of them. All the animals."

"Except the cats. But they won't come out as long as D.T. is here."

"I-I'm s-sorry." Mairi managed a squeaky apology between snorts.

"I don't think you are."

She slapped her thigh again. "Make it stop. I can't breathe!"

Juliet nibbled at Noah's pocket and he growled at her. She rubbed her forehead on his shirt hem. "Ella, where does this animal live at night?"

Ella took the lead rope from her mother and looped it over Juliet's neck. She tugged but Juliet was clearly happy where she was.

"C'mon, Juliet! C'mon! I'll pour your food."

Juliet braced all four legs, and Mairi, still holding back chuckles, wiped her eyes and took hold of Noah's left biceps.

"C'mon, goat whisperer." She pulled him gently forward. "She'll follow you. Second pen there on the right."

As predicted, Juliet followed Noah more than willingly, and a few minutes later was safely confined and munching her food pellets, even as she kept raising her head to keep watch on Noah's whereabouts.

"That goat is not normal," he said.

"Sometimes animals take a liking to someone." Mairi shrugged and leaned against the pen, keeping her eye on Ella, who filled two flat pans with chicken feed.

Noah had no response. He didn't dislike animals. He wasn't afraid of animals. He'd had a dog growing up—a great dog. But dogs didn't live long enough, and he'd never craved having a pet in adulthood. He had no desire to start attracting animals with crushes.

"She'll stay in for the night now?"

"So far, the chain around the gate and post along with being in at night seems to hold her."

"You and Ella are pretty expert even though Ewan said you've only been here a while."

"Three weeks and a few days, but Ella took to the barn on day one, and nighttime feeding became her chore. Ainslie trained her well."

"You've known Ainslie a long time?" He sounded like an interrogator, but it would be good to know more about the woman his brother had proposed to after only three months.

She eyed him with slight suspicion, then nodded. "Aye. Since secondary school. S-2, I think. We were maybe thirteen or fourteen."

"She seems nice—based on four hours of knowing her."

Her features relaxed, and she smiled. "Aye right, I understand. Is she good enough for your brother?"

He leaned against the stone wall opposite her and laughed in mild self-deprecation. "I guess that was obvious."

"She's the best, Noah. I promise. Generous. Works like a demon, she does. And I've never known her to be as happy about anything or anyone as she is about Ewan. He's a lucky man."

"She's lucky, too. And I can say the same. Ewan's different than I've ever seen him."

She studied him again, like a teacher singling him out in front of the class.

"You don't like this, your brother and Ainslie?"

"No, no. I'm happy for him. I don't know her, that's all, but I'm sure I will."

"Aye, you will." She straightened. "Right then. Ella, let's get chores done—do you need help rounding up those chicks?"

He was glad when her attention turned from him. She'd read him a little too easily, and that went well past his comfort zone. He stood back, watching mother and daughter round up the chickens and send them squawking into their night enclosure, then feed the donkeys who, he learned, stayed outdoors in nice weather. When it came time to throw their hay into an outdoor feeder, Ella finally required Noah to leave the barn and officially meet the mother-daughter donks. He dutifully scratched each between its foot-long ears, and Ella beamed.

"Mammoth-eared donkeys," she informed him. "Aren't they adorable?"

"I can't think of a better word," Noah replied dryly.

With that, Ella went back to chattering nonstop, and Mairi was back to apologizing by the time they returned to the weirdly set table in the loft and were pouring cream into a bowl for Diarmid.

"Thanks for your help, Diarmid!" Ella called to the emptiness. "Have a good night. Oh, and this is Noah. Don't be mad if he doesn't believe in you yet. He will."

"Really?" he asked.

"You're the one who advised me not to sweat it, if you remember," Mairi whispered.

"Maybe I was wrong."

She chuckled and started to speak when a soft chiming from her pocket halted her. She pulled out a cell phone.

"I rarely have service, especially out here." A frown tugged the corners of her mouth down. "What the devil? It's James's mother."

James…Ella's absentee father.

"Aren't you going to answer it?" he asked.

"I'd rather not," she said, but then huffed out a breath. "Oh, fine, the old hen." She jabbed at the screen. "Hullo? Sorcha?"

Dark clouds of annoyance quickly replaced the sunniness in Mairi's features.

"We're fine. Ella's fine. That's right, we're away and keeping it quiet for a time. Yes, my brother... He what? Excuse me, but why would Robbie think calling the police is something he should do?"

She searched for Noah's eyes then, and though anger had begun to spark in hers, she managed a pleading look and covered the phone with her hand.

"Would you take Ella back to the house? I'm sorry, I'll be right there."

"Are you all right?"

"Aye, 'course."

"Come on, Ella," he called. "Your mom's going to finish her call. We might as well get back before they send out the search party."

She laughed. "They won't."

Mairi offered a tight smile of gratitude and turned away. Her tone when she spoke into the phone was menacing as a wolf starting to growl. "Sorry, Sorcha, but you need to trust *me* on this."

Noah suddenly didn't want to leave her alone with such mounting anger, but he guessed she didn't want Ella to hear more.

"Bye, Diarmid," he called. "I'm happy to pretend you're here."

Ella gave him a surprising strong punch in the arm. "Don't tease him! If brownies get angry, they'll leave."

"Sorry, Diarmid," he called, giving Ella an exaggerated wink.

She put her hands on her hips and shook her head. "Don't listen to him," she called. "He's a silly grown-up."

Mairi was suddenly beside her, hand over the phone again. "If I see you punching a grown-up again, no matter how silly, you'll miss a night of chores, wee missy."

"I'm sorry," she said.

"That's a threat?" Noah asked. "Usually, you give a kid *more* work."

Mairi rolled her eyes and turned away again.

"Sorry, Noah," Ella said again.

He shrugged and held out his hand for her to shake. "It's okay. Really. I'll be nicer to Diarmid."

She pursed her lips in satisfaction and gave one swift nod. In her mind, she'd won the round. He and Ella were a quarter of the way back to the house when he heard Mairi's voice behind them rise in fury. He made out only a few words, but they left him inexplicably concerned.

"She absolutely is *not* staying with you…"

"Mum's mad at Gran," Ella said matter-of-factly.

"I'm sorry. I wouldn't worry."

"Gran is nice but bossy. Especially with Mama."

How disturbing was it that a seven-year-old could one minute be defending an invisible barn sprite and the next minute be coolly rational about a shouting match between two people who should be closest to her? Adults could be real donkey-holes. They reached the house, where he turned Ella over to Cat and Innis.

"How'd it go?" Ewan came down the stairs from the upper floor and grinned. "We sort of threw you to the chickens, didn't we?"

"To the goat," he said. "That animal is a menace."

"Uh oh, did she try to headbutt you?"

"More like try to drag me into some warped animal love match."

Ewan stared. "I don't even want to know."

"Smart."

"I'm sorry we abandoned you. I admit it's been a treat to have Ella take on the night feedings. It's only half an hour of free time, but Ainslie has started using it to plan her appointments for the next day. Still, you don't even know Mairi and Ella. We should have gone with you."

Noah waved him off, his mind still on Mairi and her phone call.

"All's well?" Ainslie joined Ewan on the steps.

"I assume," Noah said. "Mairi got a call as we were leaving. I think she said it was her ex-mother-in-law? I didn't hear much, but she was pretty angry. She asked me to bring Ella back."

"Ack, Sorcha MacDonald. She's a special one."

Noah had to chuckle. "Ella said she was bossy."

Ainslie's smile was stiff. "Ella loves her gran, but, aye. Bossy is a kind way to put it."

Once again, a phone interrupted them. Noah hadn't heard this much phone ringing in months. Ainslie grabbed the nearest landline handset and smiled.

"Isla," she said. "At last."

"She's as much a fretting mama as a big sister," Ewan said. "That baby of Isla's has an overabundance of maternal caretakers."

"And no doting uncles or great-uncles?" Noah cocked a brow.

"Well, I can't say that." He grinned.

They moved to the living room and within minutes Ella appeared, nibbling a small square of shortbread. Noah stared at her.

"Seriously, where are you putting that?"

Ella shrugged. "I don't know. Ewan, will you play that card game with me again?"

"Klondike? Sure. Bet Noah would watch a game, too. Unless he's ready to crash—it's been a busy day coming all the way from the U.S."

"You two go ahead and start. I'll be back in a few minutes."

Ewan nodded. "Long as you're hanging in there."

"I'm fine."

Admittedly, his eyes were heavy and his brain was starting to process like a turtle in sludge, but he wanted another hour or so to try and fool his body into thinking it was simply a late night. But more than wanting to battle jetlag, he couldn't get his mind off Mairi, fighting her phone battle alone by the barn. She had to be done by now, but ten minutes had passed, and she wasn't back yet.

It was exactly none of his business. He didn't barge into the lives of people he knew well, much less strangers he'd known for five hours. She wouldn't want him asking about her personal problems, and he didn't want to know. But something about the quality of the anger in her voice, not righteous but worried—as if she were bracing for a fight, had triggered a rare empathetic reaction.

He was nobody's white knight.

Besides, Mairi MacDonald had been a single mother for years; she didn't need a knight of any color. Even he, dull as he was about human nature, knew that. He repeated all these things to himself as he pushed open the back door and stepped onto the deep back deck, scanning the path to the barn but seeing no sign of Mairi. Still chastising himself, he stepped into the yard.

Two minutes later, halfway to the barn, he found her. The happy, laughing woman no longer existed. Instead, she was an angry wasp buzzing in a ten-foot circle, periodically sending an innocent dirt clod flying with the toe of her shoe.

The obvious fury in her movements released the knot of concern in his stomach. He'd chauvinistically half expected to find her sitting in a corner, weeping or frightened. He was more than glad to know he'd been right in the first place; she didn't need him.

Still, she was pissed off, and nobody liked to be pissed off alone.

She lifted her head and stopped pacing when she heard him approach. "Oh, go away," she called. "I told you I'd be back when I was ready."

Apparently, she *did* want to be alone.

"You're wearing a path in the walkway."

"Might be, but seriously, Noah, I'm fine, and if you're wise, you'll go back."

He stopped and almost did as she asked. Then he saw the smear of dust across one cheek.

"You're upset."

"Nae." She shook her head. "I am not upset. I'm feckin' homicidal."

"That doesn't sound good for me."

She stared at him as if he'd grown an extra head and asked her to dance. And then she covered her face with her hands.

CHAPTER SEVEN

For a moment, Mairi feared he was going to wrap his arms around her. She heard him move forward and then stop, and she pressed her fingers hard against her eyes to ease the burning. If she let her angry tears fall he'd go all sympathetic on her, and even a touch from him would be unacceptable. She didn't know him. What she needed was for him to leave. He shouldn't have come back.

Paradoxically, she was stupidly glad he was there. A decent human being to remind her that, in reality, her world wasn't completely filled with arseholes.

He didn't touch her.

At last, with a sigh of relief and no small measure of embarrassment, she dropped her hands and faced him. Even though it was his own fault that he stood there, her heart went out to him. Handsome but wary, eyes nervous with uncertainty, he was the very picture of a fish out of water.

"Should I run?" he asked, humor belying his discomfiture. "Or, maybe you'd let me just walk away slowly."

He wasn't supposed to be funny. He was supposed to be an anti-social recluse. What was he doing being charming?

"I really am fine." The calm in her voice surprised her, considering the anger still boiling inside. "I got angry after that phone call and I didn't think it a good idea to bring it back up to the house."

That was more than she wanted to tell him, and she clenched her teeth to prevent more words from finding their way out. He wasn't a flamin' barkeep, although she had to admit a wee dram—or not so wee—would have been welcome.

"It sounded like a tough conversation. I'm sorry."

"Aye. But it's nothin' for you to be sorry about. Just people I'd happily leave in the past but for the fact I have a child. I would'nae lose her for the world. But I'd lose her grandparents without a second thought and no bloody mistake."

She blew out a breath. Clenching her jaw obviously hadn't worked. But even if she was set on talking, she shouldn't be swearing at the poor man.

"I don't know what you're dealing with; it's none of my business. But if I can do anything to help…" He trailed off.

"Aye right. Thank you, but nobody can help."

She meant it. Nobody *could* help. Her ex-in-laws had always been sanctimonious and unpleasant people, but tonight they'd gone a step too far. And the more she replayed the conversation she'd just had with Sorcha MacDonald, the hotter her anger burned.

"Okay. But there's always help if you're willing to ask for it. Or so my mother used to say."

Talk about sanctimonious! She nearly called him on it, tired of people acting as if she were a child who needed life lessons, but as her anger began to boil over, she registered the look on his face and stopped. Bewilderment was the only word that came to mind. Noah looked as if he had no idea why he'd said the words or where they'd come from. He was such a strange man — kind yet confused all at once. Her anger vanished in one resigned breath. She didn't have the time or desire to figure him out.

"The only help will come from myself. From me gettin' off my arse here and going home to take care of a brother who's nothing but a blight on the earth. He's done causing grief. I don't care what he does to me, but now he's muckin' with Ella."

She swung away and took three steps toward him and the house.

"Okay, hold on." For the very first time, Noah *did* touch her, very gently catching her upper arm as she made to pass him. "I told you I don't know what's going on, and I don't care. But it sounds like you need a calmer plan."

She jerked from him and fear momentarily overpowered her anger. Sorcha had been dead serious, and the threat hit with full force. *She's not safe with you or your family, Mairi. She needs to be with us, where we will make certain she's protected.*

"They want to take her away!" she blurted before she could halt the words. "So don't you tell me I need a calmer plan. I need a heavy, blunt object to swing at a few heads."

"First, you need a deep breath."

"How dare you?"

"You said it yourself. You shouldn't bring your full anger to the house."

"I can say that. *You* can't. How is it you think you can give me advice as if I'm the seven-year-old?"

"I have zero advice. Are you leaving here tonight to bludgeon these people, because if you are doesn't that make me an accomplice?"

She stared. The man was daft. "Of course not, and I can't very well drive to Glasgow at this hour."

"See, that's at least a part of a plan. Are you going in the morning, and are you taking Ella?"

"For the love of St. Mungo, who are you?"

For the first time, he smiled. "Just a stranger trying to talk you off a ledge."

His cheerful, rational reply only stoked her irritation. "Well, stop. If I want to jump, I'll jump. And the operative word there was 'stranger.' It should stay that way. I'm going in now whether you think I'm ready or not. Stay here as long as you like—should be a lovely sunset across that field in about fifteen minutes."

She left him looking even more bemused than before. It wasn't fair or even adult, but she'd gotten herself too tangled up in illogical anger to try and redeem herself. He'd only been trying to help, but she didn't want his advice, and she'd never admit he'd been right—about needing to be calm when she got to Ella. Or about needing a plan that sounded rational when she presented it to Ainslie and Ewan— because she was definitely going to Glasgow, but she most certainly could not take Ella.

She managed the smallest of glances over her shoulder. Noah remained in his spot, but he wasn't staring after her. Giving her space? Wounded by her attitude? Taking her advice on the sunset? She didn't know, but contemplating the unknowable allowed her to slow her indignant march and, reluctantly, do as he'd instructed and take a breath.

Over a lifetime of being, as her father had always said, "passionate," she'd certainly had enough practice learning how to cool down when she was angry, and she promised herself she'd never have stormed into Craigwarren house and ranted about Sorcha in front of everyone.

Evidently, nowadays she only ranted in front of infuriating strangers whose opinions didn't matter.

Aye right, Mairi MacDonald. Good thing he's not worth thinkin' twice about, because now he *thinks you're as nutters as the goat in the barn.*

It didn't matter. *He* didn't matter. She knew she'd bitten his head off for trying to show basic human kindness. But he wasn't supposed to be basically kind — that wasn't what had been advertised. He shouldn't have returned to the barn.

This shouldn't be making her angry.

She wasn't really angry at him. Was she?

Yes. He'd told her to calm down — nobody should tell an angry person to calm down, especially a person he didn't know. That was a societal rule everyone should know to follow.

Her mind circled through her fury — at Noah, at Sorcha, at her brother. At herself.

She'd been hiding out at Craigwarren in the name of protecting Ella, but that had been a mistake. It was time to solve the problems not hide from them.

She glanced back one more time. To her surprise, Noah had squatted and was stroking one of the two barn cats that must have been off hunting earlier. The first pangs of regret filtered through her confusion. She'd made him her scapegoat — considering Juliet's obsession earlier, the word was pretty funny — but she'd been genuinely annoyed with his smug advice-giving. She wanted to stay annoyed.

Why then was she suddenly, miserably, envious of that cat?

***

Ewan had promised Noah several things on the drive from Glasgow International to Craigwarren. First, that there would be haggis. Second, that there would be a lot of renovation plans to coordinate, but he'd be in charge of them. Third, that there would be rain. As he sat alone in front of the slowly decaying stone fireplace in the cottage, Noah contemplated the haggis and the planning. He hadn't expected the two to go together but, then, he hadn't expected to be sitting with a notebook on a raggedy wooden chair in a leaky Scottish cottage, either.

The haggis had been fine. He hadn't dreaded it the way he understood many visitors did. His diet at home might consist of simple ingredients and peanut butter cups, but he still liked all kinds of food. Despite its internal organ ingredients, haggis tasted like hash, and eating it as part of Catrione's full Scottish breakfast, while simultaneously studying a spreadsheet and two rough idea sketches for the renovations, had felt like a total Scottish immersion.

Afterward, in order to digest both the breakfast—eggs, bacon, toast, oatmeal-no-it's-not-it's-porridge, grilled tomatoes, baked beans, haggis, and black-pudding-don't-ask-okay-it's-blood-sausage—and the spreadsheet filled with cost estimates, Noah had requested an hour alone in the cottage to make his own assessment and deal with promise number three.

The rain washed gray, green, and blue colors into the landscape, and wasn't unpleasant, just insistently monochrome. Though the rain didn't pour down it did penetrate—as if it possessed microscopic eyes that guided it between fibers even in his rain jacket. He hadn't gotten soaked in the two-hundred-yard walk from the main house, but neither had he stayed dry.

He looked at the notebook in his lap and read over the five things he'd written.

1. Clean (fireplace, old furnishings, sweep, walls)
2. Add loft—feasible?
3. Add window—feasible?

4. Requires help: stonework, sheetrock, framing potential loft.

5. What can't be done in five weeks: build new cabinetry as well as renovate.

It was a broadly unspecific and semi-depressing list. Truth to tell, he wasn't sure most of it could be finished in five weeks. Even after Ewan's repeated, and stubbornly vague, explanations, Noah didn't understand why his brother had undertaken this project. He'd been here a whopping four months. To start something of this magnitude on such a short timeline only seemed to prove his usually careful sibling was not himself.

He stood and shoved his pencil into a back pocket, spinning slowly to study the room exactly as he'd done not ten days before at the Broadburn Hotel. What he'd seen of this country and its people so far indicated the whole place was permanently under the influence of some kind of pervasive and dangerous magic mushroom. The mists, the rain, the obsessive adherence to endless generations of family ties, had addicted the locals to fairies and brownies and, it seemed after hearing stories of his new-old Scottish relatives, continuing battles over ancient clan rights.

But that wasn't all. Animals—goats in particular—were affected, children were indoctrinated, and their mothers...were indecipherable. Proven last night when he had been temporarily under the influence himself. Returning to the barn to "check" on Mairi MacDonald? He never did such things. Live and let live was his credo. Her reaction to his misguided chivalry had shown him clearly, he shouldn't listen when some unfamiliar spirit moved him.

He was here solely to organize his brother's crazy project, execute it as best he could, and get back home. If it didn't finish, he didn't want anyone to say it was because he hadn't given his best clear-headed shot. He would chalk up the Mairi MacDonald mistake to jetlag fog.

At least she and Ella had been long gone this morning. Running errands, he'd been told. He shook his head to banish the thoughts. He didn't need her in his mind any more than he needed her in front of him.

"Hello? Anyone home?"

His heart sank at the bright brogue until the voice registered: Catrione not Mairi. He turned to the doorway and his great-aunt entered. Except, everything about her was wrong. What he knew of Aunt Cat after a single evening and morning was not a lot, but one thing had struck him from the start. She was warm, homey, and anything but fancy with her neat, sturdy clothing and her pretty, shoulder-length gray hair worn held back with a simple ribbon.

The Catrione who now stood in the cottage had been thoroughly made over.

"Why, hello, Noah," she said, leaning a folded umbrella against a wall. "I'm very glad to find you here."

It wasn't Aunt Cat. Her eyes were too sharply focused, her haircut too professionally perfect, her soft blue sweater not nearly tweedy enough. And then he remembered—in time to greet her.

"You must be Great-Aunt Cairstine."

Her eyes softened, and her smile blossomed. "Sure that certainly warms an old heart. I'm pleased you know of me."

She stepped farther into the room and held out her hands. Noah took them, as was clearly expected and wondered if this was what it was like to meet royalty.

"Of course, I do. I'm learning a lot about family, and I've tried to memorize the important members."

"Ah, and I can hear you have the Cameron silver tongue."

"Only if that means we tell the truth."

She shook her head with a smile. "My point is made. Forgive me for arriving unannounced. We knocked at the house but nobody answered. I'd heard rumors you were not wasting any time getting to work, so we took a chance you'd be here."

"I'm happy you did. But 'we'?" he asked.

As if hearing his cue, a second person appeared in the doorway, folding his own dripping umbrella and shaking water off the sleeve of his jacket.

"There are two of us," he said. "Good to meet you. I'm your cousin, Callum MacTavish."

The man had an overwhelming presence, his ebullient personality eclipsing his mother's polished one in a single short sentence. A head of red hair and a neat beard made him a poster boy for Scotland even sans a kilt. Instead, he wore jeans and a pale green polo shirt beneath his black jacket.

"Callum. Another famous family member."

He laughed heartily and held out his hand. "I'm sure the stories are much more infamous and as far-fetched as yours are to me."

His handshake reminded Noah of Ewan's: firm, confident, a little forward. A salesman's handshake.

"You know, I doubt anything you've heard about me is far-fetched," he said mildly.

"So, what do you think of our little project?"

Our project? Noah studied him without answering right away. This was how he was going to play it? Try to influence the newbie—the one he'd surely been told was a quiet and unsophisticated artisan. He smiled.

"I'm getting a handle on it. Nice place. I think it'll make a decent holiday cottage."

"I've always thought it could be lovely." Cairstine gazed up at the ceiling, actively dripping in four spots. "Do you think you can handle the many repairs it needs?"

"I do," he replied without hesitating. "With a little expert help in a few areas. I have the skills; we'll see if I have the time."

"Well, you know," Callum said. "Ewan and I have talked at some length about his plans. If you need help, I think I could be of service. All you have to do is ask."

In his own conversations with Ewan, Noah had heard much about Callum's ideas and grand plans, but he wasn't ready to reveal anything about what he did or didn't know. Let the man think he was the clueless Yank. Clueless people could learn a lot.

"Much appreciated," he said. "Nothing to ask for yet, but I'll keep you in mind as a resource."

Callum's eyes narrowed slightly at the brush-off, but he nodded. "Good, then."

"What are your first thoughts?" Cairstine asked.

"There's a lot of work," he said. "The roof and the deteriorating walls will be the biggest projects. After that, it's reworking the rooms and cosmetics in here."

"So much potential," she said. "It's a blank canvas."

Noah stood back, not sure whether to be amused or annoyed as the mother and son pair began a slow walk around the space.

"Not much has been done to it over the past thirty years," Cairstine said. "I remember my brother, Iain, your grandfather, sleeping out here on occasion. He wasn't always the most loveable person, and I'm sure your grandmother enjoyed those nights. I know your sweet mother thought it a marvelous playhouse."

The mention of his mother brought more unexpected memories from the previous night. What had he said to Mairi? "There's always help if you're willing to ask for it." He remembered his mother as the perfect playmate. A smiling presence always there to laugh and comfort—until she'd gone away. The memories had been reduced to good feelings over his lifetime. Any real memory pictures had always been shrouded in misty vagueness, never talked about by his father. Now, quite suddenly, the mist was lifting and he could hear his mother's voice as clear as the rain pattering on the slate above him. She had said exactly those words whenever he'd been frustrated about something.

"Noah?"

He blinked at his great-aunt. "Sorry, I was thinking about what it might have looked like then. You knew my mother?"

"Of course, dear boy. A brighter bonnier girl there never was. Showered with love and spoiled like a wee princess, since she was the only child. 'Twas a sad day when she left for America."

That sounded almost like an accusation, and Noah bristled slightly until Cairstine patted his arm.

"Your grandfather, the stubborn old man, made a bad choice cutting her out of our lives, but I think Elise made *her* life a good one in the short time she had. I like to believe she's very happy her bairns are coming home to visit."

Cairstine's speech pattern was much different than Catrione's. She had closer to what Noah thought of as an English accent and used fewer words he didn't understand. But even though her diction was less homespun and her mannerisms more proper than her sister's, the words about his mother felt sincere. She lacked Aunt Cat's warmth, but he liked this great aunt, too.

"I don't know much about her life," he said. "We all have such vague memories of her."

"A tragedy," she replied. "But you are here, and that's an honor to her memory, however vague. Now, tell us what you envision for this space. I've always thought it would be wonderful to make this all one large, blended room. What do they call that nowadays, an open concept?"

Noah frowned. Based on the few sketches he'd discussed with Ewan, Ainslie, and Catrione, "open" wasn't a concept they'd even considered. To him it sounded like a modern but terrible idea.

"Interesting. Very contemporary."

"Exactly." Callum, who'd been prowling the perimeter of the room, stopped beside the door of the one bedroom. "Remove this wall and the kitchen's as well. Add some counter space instead—an island, say. Delineate the sleeping area with floor coverings or shelving. That way, the fireplace heats the whole space and it doesn't feel like a drafty stone building."

Either the man was an interior designer, or his mother had coached him on what to say.

"Also interesting. It does limit the number of people the space would sleep and cuts back on the amount they can charge guests. On the other hand, if you leave the bedroom, add another, put in a sleeper...heck you could potentially sleep six. Build a small loft there—you've got room for eight."

He smiled, knowing Mairi would rag on him mercilessly for pilfering her idea, but he'd decided he liked the suggestion. He'd thank her later.

"Sounds like you have your mind and plans made up." Callum's gaze held the slightest challenge.

Noah adopted what he hoped was an unsophisticated artisan's smile.

"No. It's not my space to design. The only thing I'm sure of is that I can keep the look of the old stone building but still make it warm, not drafty."

"Confidence is good." Callum chuckled. "If you do go the direction you've described, however, you probably *will* run out of time. My contacts can help. Let me know if you need a crew."

"I've heard you have people," Noah said.

"That I do, and they're yours for the asking." Callum rubbed his hands together. "Okay, then, Mum. Shall we get on to the errands?"

"Aye. Yes. Noah, it was—"

A hard, insistent knocking on the door interrupted Cairstine's good-bye. Like a drum roll, it continued until the door banged open and Mairi rushed through, out of breath.

"Noah, I'm sorry to interrupt, but is Ella here?" She looked two steps short of panicked, but when she caught sight of the other two in the room, she stopped. "Callum MacTavish?"

He stared right back and his brogue thickened in surprise. "Oy, nae way! Mairi Murray? Haven't seen you since you and Ainslie were at Uni. What're you doing here?"

"Visiting. And looking for my daughter. Shocked as I am to run into you, I've nae time for a reunion. I need to find her. Have ye seen her, Noah?" Her brogue came thicker and faster. Noah shook his head.

"I'm sorry, I haven't. Is she in the barn?"

"That's the first place I looked. I left her in her room for no more than fifteen minutes. When I went to fetch her, she was gone. I admit it isn't the first time; she wanders without thinking. I swear I'm lockin' her up like Rapunzel when I find her."

"So, it's been what, about twenty minutes she's been gone?"

"Or so. The thing I worry about is her goin' to the loch. She's smart, but she fancies she knows where the kelpie's cave is. It's bloody rainin', there are plenty of places to slip, and she's nae a strong swimmer. I'm off to check there. If she comes to you, can I trouble you to bring her to the house?"

"I'm coming with you," Noah said hastily. "Where's Aunt Cat?"

"Due back any moment. She and Innis ran to Glencoe."

"Aunt Cairstine? Any chance you can stay here until we find her?"

"Of course."

"I'll stay with her," Callum said. "I'll be useless walking to the loch without my wellies. Didn't think I'd need them."

Noah glanced at his cousin's leather shoes. Wouldn't want to ruin them looking for a lost kid. He shrugged. "Sure. Maybe look around outside here? Check the barn again?"

To his credit, Callum's frown lasted only a second. "I'll do that."

Noah grabbed his coat and put his hand on Mairi's back to guide her out the door.

"How old is the child?" Callum called.

"Seven, going on twenty," Noah replied. "If you hear someone talking to fairies, it's Ella."

CHAPTER EIGHT

The actual rain fell more gently than the drumming against the cottage roof suggested. Noah left his jacket hood down, letting the drizzle dampen his hair and the fresh breeze carry away the mustiness of the cottage. Mairi, on the other hand, drew the zipper of her thigh-length mac higher, shrugging into its protective shell. What did you say to a mother worried about her child? His success rate for comforting her was a fat zero percent.

"I'll look wherever you send me. Has Ella gone off like this before?"

"I wish I could say no, but what I said is true. She wanders."

"Too bad we don't have a bloodhound instead of a sawed-off border collie."

"Aye, but the dog's gone too. Daft thing loves to run as much as the girl does. I'm hoping they're together."

"Then we'll find them."

"I'm sure. Although part of me thinks it would be better for her if we didn't." Silence fell and lingered for several seconds before she added, "I don't mean that."

"I know you don't."

They headed toward the house, silence poised between them. He vowed not to offer any advice. She knew potential runaway-girl destinations far better than he, who'd seen exactly two hundred square yards of a four-hundred-acre property. The last time he'd tried to help, she'd stalked off like a beautiful but furious cat. This time he'd follow her lead.

"Thank you for coming. I...want to apologize for last night."

He'd been so focused on not aggravating her that the words didn't register at first.

"Apologize for...?"

"I know better than to stalk away from a fight. It's been a rough week, and my ex-mother-in-law was the last straw."

"Or I was." He offered a shallow smile. "It wasn't a fight. You don't have to apologize."

"I've a reputation for getting angry first and thinking later. You'll figure that out soon enough, so I might as well admit it straight away. I know better, but it still gets me in trouble."

"It's not all on you. You were right that it was none of my business. I'm sorry, too."

"That's kind of you." She hesitated. "You're not how they described you, Noah Portman."

"Oh, I probably am. This helpfulness isn't actually like me."

"I don't know. You've jumped in to play the chivalrous role twice now. A person doesn't do that if it isn't in his nature."

He half chuckled. "Chivalrous. I've been accused of many things, but never that."

They stopped in front of the main house, and Noah took in the long driveway and the expanse of hills stretching into the gray rain.

"Where to?"

"The loch." Mairi pointed. "That's the place I most fear she went."

"Why would she come out in the rain?"

"Oh, why does Ella do anything? She'd live outdoors if I let her. She knows better than to do this, but her head is awa' wi' the fairies more often than I like. I'm sure she only planned to be gone two minutes looking at something she imagined she saw, but in Ella time, that's two hours."

"All right. Let's go find her," Noah said.

The path they followed was a narrow trail of packed grass, and the wet weeds and greenery along the sides soaked their pant legs in minutes. They called for both Ella and David Tennant to no avail, and the rain slowly ramped up again, forcing Noah to raise his hood.

"Would she really come down here in this?" he asked.

"Honestly? I can't imagine. And the dog is usually good at coming when called." For the first time, Mairi looked legitimately worried and clearly torn. "I don't want to waste my time here if it doesn't make sense, but, if she went near that water…"

"Tell you what. You keep going to the loch. I'll go back and check along the road. She hasn't been gone that long. I don't think she's far."

"Aye, that's a good plan." She hesitated and put a hand on his forearm. "But am I pathetic for wanting to stay with you? You keep me from panicking."

"I promise there's no need to panic." He had no idea why he'd said that, yet, strangely, he utterly believed the words. "But as I said, I'll come wherever you want me."

She sighed. "This is silly. Go. I'll meet you back by the house with or without my daughter."

Noah gave one nod and turned, then turned back. "You're not pathetic."

She bit her lower lip. "Aye, right. Thanks."

Noah trudged back along the narrow path, and when he'd gone far enough that his voice didn't overlap with Mairi's, he called out for Ella and then the dog. After a second round of calls, he heard a cheerful little yip and his heart beat double time with hope. Sure enough, David Tennant bounded toward him, soggy black-and-white coat plastered to his body, doggy muzzle smiling in delight at finding a human.

"Dog!" Noah cried. "Where's Ella? Huh boy? You were with her, yeah?"

The dog cocked his head at the word "Ella," and Noah repeated it. "Ella, boy. Where is she?"

If he expected the little collie-corgi to turn into barking, eager Lassie and lead him to the lost girl, he was disappointed. David Tennant simply met him with wiggling rapture and planted his stubby front legs on Noah's thighs to beg for a scratch.

"Come on, where's your dog pride?" Noah asked, obliging the animal though its hair was disgustingly wet and tangled. "Ella. Where's Ella?"

Again the dog cocked its head. Then he jumped down and waited as if looking for a command.

"You're not helping."

He thought for several seconds and made a decision. Turning on the saturated path, he backtracked until he reached the spot where he thought he'd left Mairi, and called for her. David Tennant ran past him, came back, dove into the weeds, and came back again. Finally, Mairi appeared, breathless.

"Did you find her?"

"Not quite, but the dog found me. He's no bloodhound, but maybe he can take us to her."

"I bet he can. If she was at the loch, D.T. would be there, too. I'll come with you."

They retraced their steps with David Tennant, who circled them in playful excitement, not looking able to track a squirrel much less a missing girl. Mairi jogged to the house to see if Ella had returned, but came back shaking her head.

"Innis is now out looking, too." Her face had gone slightly paler. "He thought of a little thicket out in the woods, beyond the cottage, that she might have found."

"She's hunkered down somewhere waiting out the rain," Noah promised.

"I'll murder the wee bugger."

He grinned at her rolled r's. *Merder the wee begger*.

"Oh, hug her first. Maybe consider chaining her to her bed. A little less messy."

She sputtered and covered her face with her hands, avoiding a laugh by dragging her fingers down her cheeks with a growl of frustration. "That girl would follow Will O' the Wisps to a mud house if she thought she'd find a friendly spirit. Her latest is wanting to meet Ghillie Dhu."

"I have no idea what any of that means."

"Will O' the Wisps are mischievous little creatures made of light that lead you astray into the woods or marshes. Ghillie Dhu is a male fairy who's very shy, but cares for children. We do have one or two kindly sorts in our legends, if not many."

"How do children in this country ever sleep at night? All your fairy tale heroes are Freddy Kruger."

"Raise 'em tough in a tough land we say. But I admit, I do wish Ella wasn't quite this immersed in the tales. A little more reality wouldn't do her ill."

"Well, like I said. Lock her in the house. Easiest solution."

"Aye, I'll build Ella her own house in the woods—" Mairi stopped short and let out a short, aggravated breath. "Gah, clueless woman, I am! Of course. Come on."

She grabbed his wrist, pulled him onto the long driveway, and started sprinting away from the house. Up a short rise, on the green expanse to the left of the road, was the row of three tiny stone outbuildings Noah had seen when arriving at Craigwarren. He'd paid them little mind then, since he'd been focused on the stunning sight of the big house and the loch beyond it.

"What are these?"

"I never think about them. From what I understand, they aren't used for anything these days, but if I remember, one or two are unlocked. Would there be a more perfect playhouse? How could I forget?"

At last David Tennant galloped off ahead, barking as if he'd finally scented—or remembered—what he'd forgotten.

"Better late than never?" Noah asked.

"Eejit dog. Good thing he's pretty."

They passed next to more drystone walls and came to the first gray fieldstone house. It looked about fifteen feet square and seemed to be structurally sound and sturdy. Centered in front was a solid wooden door flanked by two cobweb-strewn windows.

"What were these buildings?" Noah wondered and reached the door handle—a long, slender wrought-iron handle that swung some kind of latch inside.

"No idea."

He swung the door handle and though it stuck slightly before giving way, once it did, the door pushed open easily.

"Noah! Mama!"

Ella's happy voice greeted them like a bubbling stream. The child looked up from a seat on some kind of large can and grinned. "I'm having tea with Rupert while I waited for you."

"Ella Anne MacDonald!" Mairi rushed past Noah and grabbed her daughter off her makeshift stool in a hug so tight, the little girl squirmed.

"Stop! I can't breathe."

"Oooh, you're lucky you can. You scared the livin' bejesus out of me! What were you thinkin' leaving the house without telling anybody?"

She let the girl loose and, to the child's credit, she hung her head in contrition.

"I know. I'm sorry. I only went out to see if the rain tasted like anything. I even put on my mac and wellies. But then David Tennant ran off. I called and called but he didn't come back, so I went to catch him. It started raining harder and I came in here. I was going to come straight back, but the handle broke and I couldn't get the door open again."

The tone of the room immediately changed, and Mairi pulled Ella close again. But not before she shot Noah a raised-brow look. "What'd I tell you? She only went out for a wee moment."

Noah chuckled. "Maybe a soft velvet rope or chain."

"What?" Ella asked.

"Never you mind. I'm sorry you got trapped. I'm sure you were frightened," Mairi said.

"I wasn't scared." Ella stuck out her bottom lip in disdain. "I knew you'd find me. D.T. knew I was in here. I told him to get you."

"Did ye, aye? Well, he was short of useless," Mairi said. "But you weren't scared at all? What if you'd had to sleep here all night?"

Ella shrugged. "Maybe I could have broken a window. I just thought of that."

Noah couldn't keep the laughter to himself any longer.

"Not sure you have to worry about this one," he said.

'It's why after only seven years, I have gray hairs." Mairi turned back to Ella. "I can't tell you how relieved I am you're all right, but you put everyone in a spin by leaving the house. Even Innis is out looking for you because everyone was worried."

 "I'm sorry, Mama."

Noah turned away when Mairi hugged the girl for a third time. An unsettled trembling danced in his stomach at the combination of frustration, relief, and unconditional love he witnessed between them. Not that he hadn't been hugged and loved by his stepmother—really the only mother he'd known—but he hadn't been a brilliant entrepreneur like his brother or a gregarious friend to all like his sister. He'd been the quiet, watchful kid—the suspicious one, according to his mother.

He'd never thought of himself as suspicious; he'd simply never been one for displaying his feelings to the world. Which was why he'd been right when he'd told Mairi all this chivalry wasn't him.

He strolled the perimeter of the small room while Mairi finished with her daughter. The space was mostly empty. An old wooden stepladder stood mid-room, draped in a large white sheet. Half a dozen old paint cans were spread around, one under the tented ladder and one next to it where Ella had been sitting.

When he spotted a small, neatly piled stack of lumber in a back corner, his heart started its own little dance. He'd never been able to resist a stash of wood, and upon inspection this was a mini treasure trove. Four pine boards, one-by-eight and maybe six feet long, lay smooth and straight at the bottom of the pile. On top were a dozen more boards of various sizes and lengths. But the best find was a half-dozen four-by-four post pieces of a much harder wood. He picked up a ten-inch length that had been sawed off a longer post at an angle. His eyes widened in delight.

"Cherry," he murmured. "In perfect shape."

"You found a cherry?"

Ella stood behind him and leaned over his shoulder. Literally. Against him. His first instinct was to move away, but he took a breath instead and held out the block.

"No. A piece of cherrywood. From a cherry tree."

"Can I see it?"

He handed her the block, picked up another slightly longer piece, and ran his fingers along the pinkish-brown grain. For the first time since arriving in Scotland, he felt as if he knew what to do next.

"What do you do with it?"

"I could make almost anything I wanted out of this piece of wood," he said.

"A bed?"

Noah laughed. "A little one. Maybe a boat. Or a dog."

"David Tennant?"

"Maybe."

"Eachann?"

He struggled to remember what Eachann was. Right, the thing in the loch. "Like what you drew last night?"

"Aye."

"I probably could carve something like that."

"All right now, miss. That'll be for another time. We have to get you back to the house and call in the search and rescue teams. Then, I think it'll be the rest of the day indoors for you. Maybe a few chores."

The first whine he'd heard from the girl filled the small space. "Mama, I'll be good."

"You're always good, my darlin', at coming up with things I never expect." Mairi kissed the top of her head. "Come now. It'll only be simple chores. Makin' supper for all of us and cleaning the loo. Maybe scrubbin' the kitchen floor."

"Ma-*ma*!"

Mairi laughed.

"Before we go, I have one question." Noah held out his hand for the wood Ella held and she passed it to him. "You said you were having tea with Rupert. Who's Rupert?"

Ella looked around as if searching the room and then shrugged. "He's gone. He was the bogle who comes here once in a while to play. When I got stuck, he was stuck, too, so I made this tent and we had tea." She pointed to the ladder.

"You made the tent?"

"I got the sheet, climbed up the ladder and put it over. Easy."

The ladder was not enormous, but it was probably six feet. Mairi groaned.

"Merciful Lord, you'll be the death of me before I'm forty. Get on wi' ye, mad girl."

"A bogle?" Noah asked.

"A goblin. Mostly harmless but likes to cause mischief." She waved her hand. "I'll just get you a book; it's the only way you'll keep up."

Ella skipped all the way back to the house and was greeted like returning royalty. Catrione plied her with shortbread and fresh milk once she heard the story of being locked in the little building, even though Mairi tried to insist the child shouldn't be rewarded.

Noah had brought two pieces of the cherrywood with him and asked Cat if she knew what they were for.

"Not a clue, *mo cridhe*. Innis might know, or they may have been there for decades. If you need them, I'm sure you can have them."

"I should go back to the cottage and release Callum and Aunt Cairstine from their duties."

"Callum and my sister?" Cat looked stunned.

"They showed up to look around about forty-five minutes ago. They said nobody was at the house."

"Och, we went to the grocers in town. They must have driven straight down. Cairstine wouldn't walk a muddy track in the rain. Did Callum behave himself?"

"He gave me renovation ideas, but that's all."

"I'm sure he did. You send them up here."

"I'll tell them. I'll find Innis, too."

"Thank you, sweet boy. And you come back in an hour yourself. It'll be time for lunch."

"Aunt Catrione." He tried to look stern. "I've gained four pounds in two meals. How can I possibly eat already?"

"You'll need to store up energy for all the hard work ye'll be doing. I promise it's nae more than a bit of bread and fruit."

He sighed and shook his head at her but then kissed her on the cheek. Another thing he never did. What was wrong with him? This place *was* bewitched.

He never used that word either.

He was out the door, off the porch, and had pulled his hood back up against the steady rain when the back door opened and Mairi rushed out onto the back deck.

"Noah?"

He turned. She had no mac on this time, just a slightly baggy, loose-knit white sweater over a pair of fitted jeans. He hadn't paid her looks any mind beyond the obvious superficial, chauvinistic notice of how pretty she was, but as the rain quickly dampened the sweater, splattered her jeans, and landed like diamonds in her black hair, something jolted in his belly and hitched his breath. Instead of being model-slender, she was curvy and natural, and a little wild-looking. She fit against the rainy landscape as if she'd been born in a storm.

Before he could respond, she was down the two shallow porch steps and stood in front of him.

"Thank you," she said. "You didn't have to take time to come with me but I admit it, I was worried. Silly now, but I was very glad to have you along."

She grasped his upper arms, the jacket slick with rain, raised up on her toes and kissed him on the cheek. Light as a hummingbird barely touching a flower.

Stunned at the gesture, worried by the zip that raced through his body, he could only stare. Then he shook his head. "It was no big deal. I'm glad Ella is fine."

She smiled. "Until I tie her to the bed."

"We really need to stop saying that now," he replied.

"I suppose. Well, off you go. You're gettin' soaked. Thank you. Again."

She turned and flitted back to the house, and Noah gaped after her until she disappeared. He turned toward the cottage, the two pieces of wood tucked safely under his armpit beneath the jacket, his thoughts as far from safe as they could be.

"*I'm* getting soaked?" he muttered.

He really needed to stop trying to help people.

CHAPTER NINE

She needed a plan. The day had been so full of weird happenings, she almost believed Ella's magical creatures were at work. First the child had pulled her disappearing act, then Callum MacTavish—a person she'd never liked, even when Ainslie had dated him at Uni—had stayed for lunch. Though her friend was no longer bothered by Callum, besotted as she was with Ewan, Mairi didn't think the man had changed a bit. He was still silky smooth, still talked like a knock-off watches salesman, still had a plan for turning any project into money.

At least the family had mastered the art of nodding and smiling at the man until they could change whatever subject he was on about. Mairi would have been fine had they shown him the door, but she was a guest herself and had no such say-so.

Then there was Noah. She could have blamed the inability to solve her own problems on any of the day's misadventures, but in truth, Noah was the culprit. He'd been around for a day and a third, but he already felt like a fixture. Even when she'd been furious with him, he'd made her stop worrying about Sorcha and Robbie and the fact they were pushing for Ella to come and stay with them. This morning when she'd panicked, imagining the worst as she always did, Noah had been there again, reassuring her with his quiet, calm voice, his practical assessments, his humor. For a short while, he'd even gotten her to stop fretting about her brother and her ex-mother-in-law.

The reprieve was over. With no more adrenaline-pumping excitement, her biggest concern was how to keep Aiden and Sorcha from finding out exactly where she and Ella were staying. Aiden would continue harassing them. Sorcha would, honestly, try to take Ella away.

"If you feel the need to run and hide away, Ella can't possibly be safe. Robbie and I can protect her." Sorcha had argued

Holding in a sigh of frustration, Mairi stood from the chair in the living room where she was pretending to read and walked to the kitchen table. Ella had insisted on drawing in the company of Noah and Ewan who were studying floorplans and discussing the supplies they needed.

"Here's the best picture of Eachann." Her daughter handed a drawing to Noah as Mairi approached.

Noah held up the paper. "Amazing. More detailed than the one last night. Exactly what I needed."

"Is she bothering you?" Mairi asked. "Don't let her interrupt your work."

"Not at all," Ewan said. "She's showing us what Eachann really looks like, but she's been very quiet."

Mairi tousled Ella's hair. "As she should be when everyone is working. Best behavior is a requirement, right, Ella?"

She nodded dutifully. "See, Mama?"

She really was a good little artist when she took her time. This detailed kelpie looked exactly like a horse's front half combined with a mermaid's back half—if the horse was a bit

My Little Pony bonded with a tail covered in neon green and purple scales. It was adorable, actually. Noah caught her gaze, gave a nod, then went back to his own papers.

Mairi frowned. After their warm interactions that morning, his standoffish reaction seemed odd.

"How goes the planning?" she asked. "Sounded earlier like Callum had a lot of suggestions."

"He always does," Ewan said. "In this case, I doubt we'll use many of his."

She moved around the table and stood behind the brothers, peering between them to check out the two sets of plans. They were filled with surprisingly practical ideas and, she noticed with a moment of satisfaction, both included a loft overlooking the main living area.

"I like this one." She pointed to the drawing in front of Noah. "Two bedrooms and the loft rather than one bedroom, a loft, and two sitting areas. Sleeps more people, and you could put a reading-slash-sitting area in the bigger bedroom."

Noah slanted her a look that held no irritation, unlike at their first meeting, but he clearly didn't relish unsolicited input. It was his least attractive trait, but this time it made her laugh.

"Sorry," she said.

"No, you aren't," he retorted.

"Aye, in fact. I'm not." She leaned forward, resting her hand on the table between him and Ewan and pressing forward until their upper arms touched. There was no give to his—only lean muscle. A man who worked with his whole body. "I see one more thing. You've got a laundry and clothes-drying space between the kitchen and the new bedroom. What if you moved the kitchen up and put the drying space down here, next to the front door? That way, guests wouldn't have to drag through the space in wet clothes after hiking and could hang things right up."

"Huh," said Ewan.

"Go away," said Noah. But a tic at the corner of his mouth belied a bit of mirth.

"Fine…" She adopted her best affronted tone.

Noah looked up. "I should have thought of that."

It felt ridiculously like a compliment from the laird of the manor.

"Thank you. I know it depends on where the plumbing is right now. Not easy to move that, so changin' the kitchen might not work. It was only an observation."

"Ainslie will like it," Ewan said, and Noah nodded again.

"We'll look at it."

"Here, Noah, it's all done." Ella slid her drawing across the table, and Noah picked it up again.

"This is exactly what he looks like?"

"Uh-huh." Ella's curls bounced with her decisive nod.

"Okay."

"Why the portrait of Eachann?" Mairi asked.

"He wants to learn to carve kelpies." Ella clapped in pure excitement. "He can make lots and sell them."

Mairi drew back in surprise. "You can do that?"

"Carve them or sell them?" Noah gave an amused smile.

"Oh! Carve. A kelpie."

"He can make anything out of wood," Ewan said. "Been carving things since he first found a paring knife and a piece of soap."

Ella's eyes went wide. "You can't *carve soap*. It's like water only slippery."

"Don't people buy bars of soap anymore?" Noah snorted.

"Nae, modern people like their pump bottles." Mairi laughed. "Do you really carve soap?"

"Not anymore. But it's how I learned. A big thing in Cub Scout troops."

"I want to be a Cub Scout," Ella said. "They're more fun than Brownies—even though Brownies are named after brownies. They had Cub Scouts at my school in Glasgow, but then we moved here."

"We'll be going back, love," Mairi said quickly, a pang of guilt assailing her.

Ella shrugged. "It's okay. I'd rather be here than in Cub Scouts."

"That's gratifying." Ewan grinned.

"Ewan, are you still planning to go to Glasgow?" Mairi asked.

"Yes, in a couple of days after we get the spaces in the cottage measured off. Probably Friday to Saturday. The bigger home improvement stores are there."

"Here's why I'm asking." She hesitated. "I need to make a trip there, too, but I don't want to overlap yours. I'd like to leave Ella here, and though it should only take me a day, that's a lot to ask."

"Don't be silly. I won't speak for Ainslie, but she isn't planning to come, so I'd venture a guess that if we ask, she, Catrione, and Isla will happily watch Ella. But, look, why don't you come down with us? It's silly to waste the gas on two trips."

"Oh no. I couldn't. I have several places to go and you do, too. It's Tuesday. I could go tomorrow or Thursday."

From the prickling at the nape of her neck, she knew Noah's gaze had turned to her, but she assiduously avoided looking at him. He'd had enough to say about rash plans last night. She'd made one that was only slightly less rash and she didn't want to work it out in front of him. She only needed to know she could leave Ella without causing undo work for everyone who was being so kind already.

"Whatever you need to do," Ewan said. "All's done with your car now?"

"They tell me so, aye. New hoses and a couple of belts along with a radiator patch, poor old thing. I'm afraid when it comes to cars, I'm a stereotype. If it works, great. If it doesn't, I splash down the cash."

Noah slapped his brother on the back. "That's you, too, isn't it, bro?"

"Not to mention you," Ewan protested. "You know who the mechanic is in our family."

"Bridget," they said together.

"We can change oil and tires," Noah said.

"And windscreen wipers and washer fluid," Ewan added.

"Wind*screen*?" Noah wrinkled his nose. "It's only been four months. Stop talking that way."

Ewan only grinned. "You'll see. It rubs off quickly."

"Catrione and Ainslie are taking a long time to feed the animals," Mairi said. "Hope everything's all right."

"It's because you wouldn't let me help," Ella said. "You said I'm supposed to do chores."

"But you *like* that chore." Mairi patted her head.

At that moment, the back door opened and let in the sound of pounding rain along with Ainslie, Catrione, and Innis.

"Well, that was our turn to get a shower out o' doors, wasn't it?" Catrione shook her arms letting water pool on the floor. "Been a right ugly day."

"Forecastin' more the morrow," Innis said. "Then maybe a bit o' clearin'. August and her schizophrenic weather."

"It didn't help that Juliet got out again," Ainslie said, pulling back her hood and fluffing her wet hair. "Eejit goat worked the latch before we got it chained. Ran clear to the cottage and made us come at her from three sides."

"Sell her, I'm telling you," Innis said. "We'll get a well-behaved goat."

"Pish, she's lonely. I still think she needs a friend," Catrione said.

"I'm never chasin' two of those bedeviled creatures." Innis grumbled. "You get another. You milk 'em alone."

"You say that now, auld love." Catrione patted his cheek. "You'd be there in a trice."

Innis shucked his coat off and hung it on the wide peg board beside the door. "Women, human or goat, are all of a mind, boys. Remember that. They get ye comin' and goin'."

"But Juliet is safely tucked into the barn now?" Ewan asked.

"She was there when we left," Ainslie said. "That's all I know. She's getting smarter by the day."

"Smart goat," Ella said, absently doodling on another piece of paper.

"All right. Now that everyone is in and safe, it's bedtime for you, wee troublemaker." Mairi kissed Ella's crown and looked at the picture of the goat she was drawing. "Finish that and I have a question for Ainslie, then off we go."

Ella looked up. "Can I stay with you and Auntie Catrione while Mama goes to Glasgow?"

"Oh, for the love, Ella!"

Ainslie laughed. "I'm sure I don't know what the whole story is, but of course. You can stay with me any time."

A full ninety minutes later, after Ella had bathed, told everyone in great detail about getting locked in the little house, run around to give everyone goodnight hugs—even Noah, who looked more surprised than happy—it was quarter of ten and the child was finally asleep. As were Catrione and Innis. She'd also heard Noah go to his room. Isla and the baby were still away until morning, and Ainslie and Ewan were closeted away talking plans for their December wedding.

The house, for the moment, was hers. And she crept quietly down the stairs to the living room, supremely grateful for the time to think.

Nobody had questioned her plan to go back to Glasgow, and nobody had asked her what she was going to do once there. She wanted to go to her school and talk to Paul Taylor once more. Find out exactly what Aiden had said to him. As for Aiden himself, maybe their mother was right. Face-to-face, reading his body language in person, might be the best way to confront him. She was tougher in person anyway—it was time he saw that.

"Hey." The voice from the armchair closest to the fireplace made her jump and, with no small amount of embarrassment, give a screech. "Sorry. I didn't mean to scare you."

She closed her eyes and willed her heart to stop thundering. To her chagrin, it ignored her completely. Noah had changed from the plain gray T-shirt he'd worn all day to a lightweight heather-brown sweater. His beard had filled in slightly, though it was still a sexy scruff, and his thick brown hair had dried into a cute tangle of waves.

She could have stared at that picture for an hour, but her gaze fell to his hands where he held one of the blocks of cherrywood and a short knife-like tool. At his feet was an open sheaf of newspaper covered with shavings of curled wood, and as she watched, his knuckles flexed and the veins on his hands bulged into relief as the tool bit deeply into the wood creating more curls.

"I don't want to interrupt you," she said. "I thought everyone was upstairs."

"I was. I came down to get the newspaper and never made it back up."

"You really do carve."

He nodded. "It's partly my job, but mostly my escape. You're not interrupting. You're probably looking for an escape, too. I'm in *your* way."

She shook her stare loose and sat on the arm of the oversized sofa across from him. "I admit, it's hard to find a quiet place around here, much less an empty one. Ainslie says it wasn't this way only a few months ago."

"When my brother arrived." Noah's sigh carried across the room.

"Ewan has changed things. For the better they say."

"We're still adjusting to it ourselves. He left a lot behind back home."

"You sound a wee bit resentful."

He looked up, his features carefully neutral. "I was at first. He's my best friend. But why would I wish him anything but happiness? I can see his love for this place is genuine."

"And Ainslie?"

A smile toyed at the corner of his mouth. "I can't think of a single negative thing to say. They're perfectly matched and permanently attached to each other."

"Such a romantic endorsement." She gave a little laugh and shifted off the couch arm to settle into a cushion.

"Seriously, I like her. Never seen Ewan this relaxed and happy."

"I feel the same about Ainslie. It took someone special to make her re-order her life and find real happiness."

"You went to school together, you said."

"Aye. Known her a long time." She leaned forward. "Can I ask what you're carving?"

He gave a small shrug without looking at her and reached behind himself to pull out Ella's drawing. A frisson of excitement slipped down her spine.

"You actually are carving a kelpie?"

"Why not try? It's appropriate to where I am. Something I've never made before. If it works, it's for Ella."

"Really? She'd be thrilled."

"Don't tell her yet. If for some reason it doesn't turn out, I don't want to disappoint her. I'll eventually get one right."

"Disappoint that child? I don't believe that's possible, but I'll nae say a word. Does it bother you to have someone watch?"

He shrugged again. "No. Long as they don't hang over my shoulder."

"I'll stay over here, then."

He looked up and their smiles met. A ripple of awareness meandered slowly from a crop of goose bumps on the back of her neck to her stomach where it spread into rivulets of pleasure. It had been a long time since genuine attraction had made her this giddy.

"Way over there," he agreed.

She watched him a few minutes without speaking, enamored by the movements of his hands, the sure way he turned the block, and the easy concentration in his face. She let her worries slip again to the back of her mind and simply enjoyed being in his calm presence.

"You're heading into Glasgow tomorrow?"

His question broke the spell and brought all the worry flooding back. It also raised a wall of defensiveness.

"I have several people to talk to there."

"Are you sure you want to go alone?"

That wasn't remotely the question she'd expected. She'd been sure he'd have a caustic reason she shouldn't go at all.

"I've lived in Glasgow all my life; it's not like I'm going to the far reaches of Tibet without a guide."

He chuckled. "I never thought you couldn't do it. Whatever you're dealing with, I thought maybe moral support might make it easier."

"I—"

He held up his hand. "I swear I'm not gonna give you advice. It's an observation, nothing more. I have no idea who you're going to see, and you don't have any reason to tell me."

Her wall crumbled a little. She could see, and feel, he was sincere. It was the most caring thing anyone had offered her in a long time.

"My brother. Maybe."

He stopped carving and looked at her again. "Maybe?"

"If I can find him. I also want to talk to Paul, my old boss, and maybe Sorcha—to reassure her that Ella is fine."

"There you go, you've made a plan."

She sighed. "Only very loosely thought out."

"Tell you what." He set the block at his feet and stood. "I'm going to get us a couple of those ales I was offered earlier. And you're going to run this loose plan by me so you can finalize it."

"I don't need—"

"Do you drink beer?"

"Aye, 'course."

"I'm thinking you at least need that."

She could find no argument to make. He left and returned with two opened bottles of Belhaven Scottish Ale.

"Okay?" he asked, handing one to her.

"Thanks."

He held his bottle up for her to toast with a clink and returned to his chair. They each took a first taste and sat back.

"It's good," he said. "I'd always heard Scotland wasn't known for its beer."

"Clearly our reputation rests on whisky," she agreed. "But craft brewing is up-and-coming."

"I do intend to go home with several good Scotches— whatever is most highly recommended."

"Good luck finding consensus on that." Mairi grinned. "You're not planning to stay, then?"

He snorted. "Hardly. How cliché would that be? Two brothers up and moving across the world at the same time."

"Unlikely." She nodded.

"Okay," he began. "Lay out this plan for me. Where are you going first tomorrow?"

That, she thought, was an excellent question.

CHAPTER TEN

The A-82 wasn't busy on a Wednesday mid-morning. Commuter traffic into Glasgow had thinned, and now cars carried primarily tourists and day-trippers, judging by the number of vehicles stopped at scenic pull-offs. Ninety minutes into her two-hour drive, Mairi's stomach quivered with anxiety, despite Noah's helped in creating a blueprint for the trip. Rather than a willy nilly circuit amongst all the people who, in her mind, needed sorting out, she had a plan that had seemed supremely logical the night before. She'd start with Paul, ask him exactly what the police had called him about, and what he knew about Aiden's threats. That would help form the proper questions to ask her ex-father-in-law and, if she could find him, Aiden.

One step at a time.

The closer she got, however, the more her plan lost focus. What she wanted, what her gut wanted, was to skip all the preliminaries, ignore the roadmap she and Noah had drawn, and surprise her brother with the blazing anger he deserved. He needed his turn to be cowed.

She took a deep breath. This was her nature—fighting against all the world's problems, but Noah was right. Running off anywhere half-cocked was never a plan.

Besides, Aiden had never been easily cowed, and ranting at him would simply give him the upper hand. That would be far worse than what she was living through now. To change things, she needed to show her brother she was the smart one. That had been Noah's biggest piece of advice—after she'd spilled her whole family story, as if the Bellhaven last night had been truth serum instead of ale.

Airing her family history was something she avoided— almost at all costs—but rather than distress her, as delving into the personal usually did, telling Noah had happened as easily as taking off a coat and handing it to him. His genuine empathy, combined with a calm, uncanny ability to turn her resentment of the past from anger into a plan, had made her feel in control rather than victimized, and validated for the first time in months.

She'd told him how Aiden had first turned to drugs in secondary school and later, at age twenty, disappeared for half a dozen years—during which time, the face of their family had changed.

Aiden had missed Mairi's marriage and the birth of his niece. He'd missed the diagnosis of their father's severe heart disease. He'd been nowhere to be found when Mairi divorced and moved in with their parents to become caregiver to their father as his health declined, and ineffective counselor to their mother as the loss of her son and imminent loss of her husband tortured and drained her.

Then, miraculously, Aiden had returned a few months before their father died. Like the prodigal son, he'd been feted and celebrated, and he'd promised his wounded family that he was clean and would stay that way. Mairi honestly hadn't resented his return, glad he seemed to have found his way, and grateful because their mother had rallied, allowing some of her spark to return. Three-year-old Ella had found a brand new, super fun playmate in Uncle Aiden, and the last months of their father's life had been happy.

Aiden, however, had kept his promise less than a year before sliding back into his old ways. Mairi had known he was using again even before she'd found a substantial stash of cocaine he'd hidden in, of all places, the family room. He'd tried to claim some friend had put it there to set him up, but Mairi, now a fierce mama bear and a school teacher, hadn't put up with his lies. She'd gotten the truth—with no help from her mother who insisted they should be loyal to Aiden—that he was *holding* the drugs for a friend who was the dealer. Mairi had gone straight to the police, then as now choosing the safety of her daughter over family loyalty.

Aiden had been sentenced to three-and-a-half years in prison and six months in rehab. As of six weeks ago he was out and seeking revenge. Mairi had ruined his life. Given him a permanent blot on his record. She owed him, and that meant helping him "get back on his feet."

"He wants money from you, but *would* it even get rid of him?" Noah had asked. "Or will he keep repeating the cycle? You need to go after him like an investigator and not an angry sister."

Easy to say, she'd told him. Prison had made Aiden slippery as a greased codfish. Nothing stuck to him or held him. Even his threats were veiled and delivered in roundabout ways. Following a plan to be smart first and emotional later made her shake her head in wonder at herself. She'd been dealing with her family's shite antics in her own private way for donkey's years, and suddenly an American visitor she'd known for two days had breached the closet door and seen all the skeletons. Two nights ago, she'd bitten Noah's head off for offering advice. Now she'd promised to follow it.

As she entered the outskirts of Glasgow, her home turf brought out the fear and second-guessing again. What if she failed at this mission? Where would that leave all this cool, calm planning? She forced away her doubts and tamped down her anger. She wouldn't fail, that was all. She could be overly passionate, she knew it, but she was also not a one-trick horse. She'd been standing up for herself and her daughter her whole life, and she'd do it now. She'd take the steps, rearranging or skipping them in any way it took to stop Aiden's campaign against her.

Step one: get off her arse, talk to Paul, and start problem-solving.

***

Now that he had a plan, Noah finally, gratefully, got to spend a morning doing something besides stare at stone walls and make notes. He'd found both a step and an extension ladder, set the first up inside the cottage and the second against the front façade so he could inspect the roof. But even though he was eager to study the unfamiliar slate roofing and see how it was put together and where it leaked, he'd promised not to climb onto the slippery, wet roof until Ewan could finish a business call and come spot him. After climbing halfway up the ladder for a quick survey, he agreed it would be foolish to crawl around the slick tiles alone.

He waited inside the cottage, noting exact measurements of the walls and the ceiling heights and scribbling the final dimensions in his notebook. After an hour and a half, he felt as if he had a handle on the project. He, Ewan, and Innis could easily handle framing and sheet rocking two new interior walls for the bedroom and closet, and they could build the loft as well. They needed experts to repair the stone and slate, and Ewan had found a contractor to meet with in Glasgow. Hamish Fletcher Stone Craft was supposedly a premier company for new and vintage stonework repair, but his small crews were always busy. All Fletcher had promised was that he'd look at plans and see what he could do. Whether the cottage could be finished in a month depended almost entirely on being able to get workers in time. If they could, and if everything went smoothly, Noah believed this project could happen, but there was little room for error.

As if the thought caused its own jinx, a horrendous metallic crash from outside made Noah jump six inches straight off the floor. The heart-stopping screech that followed could only have come from a very young person — like age seven — and Noah's heart leapt into his throat, choking him with fear. Only one thing could have fallen with that kind of disastrous clang — and a thirty-two-foot ladder could kill a child.

"Ella? Ella?" he called desperately. The girl had a recent history with ladders, after all.

"Juliet! No! What are you doing here?" The indignant little voice sent blood rushing to his head, and he nearly stumbled, dizzy with relief.

He burst through the front door, unconcerned about the force with which it slammed open.

"Ella?"

Sure enough, the ladder lay on the ground. Ella stood beside it, hands on hips, staring at Juliet munching grass beside the cottage wall. The girl was clearly in a precocious state of pique, and the goat's jaw worked in a frenzied circular motion, as if fearing the hammer would fall any moment, depriving her of the smorgasbord. When Juliet caught sight of Noah, however, she lifted her head abruptly, let out an enthusiastic bleat, and made a beeline for him at a fast trot.

"Oh, for crying out loud! Stop, stupid goat." He held out a hand to protect himself but looked to Ella. "Are you okay? What happened?"

"Juliet went under the ladder and knocked it over. It was loud! It scared me."

"Believe me, I was scared, too. Did it fall close to you?"

"No. I just saw it."

Noah's shoulders relaxed a notch further. If anything had happened to her... "What's she doing here?" He pointed to Juliet.

Ella's little shoulders lifted to her ears. "I don't know. She must have got out again."

Noah rubbed his eyes. He'd had such high hopes for the morning. "I suppose she has to go back to the barn then."

"I can help."

He studied her small figure. "And what brought *you* here, Ella?"

She was surprisingly subdued compared to her normal energized self. She looked at the ground before lifting her eyes to his.

"Mama said I'm to say thank you for finding me yesterday by helping you for one hour. I should pick up all the papers and trash layin' 'bout the cottage and then do any other work you say. But it's only if you want me to, and I'm not to talk to you too much, and go back to Catrione whenever you say."

She'd obviously memorized the instructions, and Noah's resentment at being interrupted softened. Poor kid— she had to be looking at this as a punishment.

"I see. And do you think you can handle clean-up duties?"

She nodded.

"Okay, here's the deal. I'll let you help if we can start with putting Juliet back."

At that, her eyes brightened. "That's easy."

"Is it?" He finally grinned at her. "Somehow, I don't think getting Juliet to do anything she doesn't want to do is easy. Like staying in her paddock."

Ella giggled. "She doesn't like it there."

"Apparently. Let's try anyway."

They coaxed the reluctant goat back to the barnyard and Noah found the place where she'd pushed an old board aside to escape. He and Ella trucked up to the garden shed where Catrione kept some basic tools and found a hammer and a couple of long fencing nails. He gave the hammer to Ella and they headed back down. Following her instructions, she said nothing, and Noah began to feel like some kind of feared Dickensian children's workhouse master.

"It's weird when you're quiet," he teased. "I won't tell your mom if you talk."

She smiled at the ground. "She says grown-ups don't always understand my stories and a few at a time are as good as Christmas."

He had to laugh. Clever Mairi.

"I suppose that's true. But you don't always have to tell stories. You could tell me when you start school. What grade will you be in?"

"I go in three weeks, but I don't know if I want to because it's a new school and Mama won't be teaching there, so now I won't be in her class."

"I didn't know you were going to be in her class."

"In Glasgow, we had three fourth-year classes, and I wouldn't be in hers. Here there is only one teacher for each class."

"Ah. And you were okay having your own mom as a teacher?"

"Aye. She would have to pretend like she wasn't my mum in school. She said something happened to the job and they couldn't give it to her. But here's a secret—I heard her talking to Aunt Catrione, and it's because of my uncle. Everyone knows he's sick because he takes bad things that make him act mean."

"Bad things?" How much did Ella really know and understand, Noah wondered.

She shrugged. "I think they mean drugs. He tells people Mama is a bad person and then they don't want her to work for the schools anymore. But he's a bawbag."

Noah coughed. "Are you supposed to say that word?"

Ella's eyes glittered with impishness. "It's rude. I didn't think you'd know. Mama says it's cute how you don't understand all the Scottish words."

She was only seven, but Noah's face heated in embarrassment. *Cute?* Well, fantastic.

"I understand that one well enough now," he said, and her hand flew to her mouth to cover a giggle. "I won't let on that we discussed it."

She sputtered again, clearly pleased she'd gotten away with something grand.

They reached the paddock and Noah leaned against the gate.

"I'm sorry about your uncle. I'm sure your mom will work it out. I think she'd like to get her job back."

Ella nodded. "Uncle Aiden needs to go to jail."

He had no idea how to respond. The conversation was veering into subjects no seven-year-old should have to discuss. He certainly wasn't comfortable going there with her.

"We'll let your mom get help with that, okay? How about you help pound in these nails and we try to keep Juliet in for a while. We have work to do."

"Pure brilliant!"

The goat made her unhappiness clearly and loudly known once the fence was fixed, and Noah shook his head at her in warning.

"I wish I could say I'm sorry, but this needs to stop. Your job is to keep watch over the barn, not wander around outside it. Now stay put."

"Aye, stay put!" Ella echoed.

They headed back to the cottage, Ella still carrying the hammer as proudly as if she'd repaired the fence herself. Though her efforts had gotten her no more than four or five actual strikes of the nails, she'd tried hard.

When they stood together in the middle of the cottage's living room, Noah surveyed the space, trying to figure out something for the kid to do. He finally settled on having her clean out the fireplace, filled with empty cans and bottles. After that, if need be to use up an hour, he'd have her gather the newspapers that littered every room. If he hadn't known for certain Mairi would check to see that her daughter had actually done what had been asked, he'd have sent her back to the main house already. He didn't want to take advantage of the child and, if he was honest, he didn't relish the distraction she was sure to bring.

Twenty minutes later, however, he had to give Ella credit. She'd studiously filled the two bins he'd brought down from Catrione's garden shed for the very purpose of collecting trash. One held recyclables and the other garbage to be thrown away. She'd happily gathered newspapers as well, piling them neatly, and finally, all on her own, she'd pointed out a small closet filled with miscellaneous papers and books she offered to sort through. She certainly was a bundle of industriousness, and bright as a little professor. She also said very little—another surprising sign of obedience. This Ella was a different child from the one he'd known the past two days.

He took the time to start demolition on the kitchen wall he'd be moving, getting rid of shelves from a storage area between the kitchen and existing bedroom, and removing doors from the ancient cabinets they were replacing. He'd made decent progress when the silence in the cottage finally registered. If he remembered anything he'd been taught about children—and it wasn't much—it was that if they were silent, things weren't good. With the second flash of panic that morning, he abandoned his task and went searching.

Ella sat on the bedroom floor surrounded by several piles of old books and papers. Noah stopped in the doorway. Some of the books were tattered, others simply dusty, but the cause of Ella's silence was a thick leather-bound book in her lap. With her head bent nearly to the pages, her almost-red hair hung like a curtain between Noah and what she studied.

"Hi there," he called.

She popped up her head, looking slightly guilty. "Sorry. I found these pictures. I started looking at them. Sorry."

"Nothing to be sorry for, you're fine. Pictures?" He hesitated for a moment, then approached and lowered to sit on the floor beside her.

"There are lots of Craigwarren and maybe some of this cottage. And I think some of them are of Aunt Cat and Cairstine because there are ladies who aren't old, but they look alike. See?"

She pushed the large book—a hefty photo album—halfway onto Noah's leg. He stared at the pictures, some black and white and a couple in faded color. Slowly he picked out details, starting with the two women, identical as Ella had described, standing before the same wooden door that still graced the front entry of Craigwarren's main house. Though the women had to be at least forty years younger than they were now, he recognized their eyes and mouths.

"You're right," he said. "This has to be Aunt Catrione."

"And Cairstine! This one is Aunt Cat." She pointed to the twin on the left.

"How do you know?"

"She has on a jumper and blue jeans. Cairstine has on a fancy dress. Aunt Cat says she was like me. She didn't like to wear dresses a lot."

Noah raised his brows, impressed. "Logical thinking. Well done."

He turned the page. All the pictures seemed to be from a single event, a family gathering centering around a baby. Groupings of men and women posed in front of the house and in various combinations on the lawns. In each, someone held a babe that looked to be six or seven months old. One or the other of the twin sisters appeared in many pictures, but they were the only people Noah could identify.

Ella turned another leaf, and Noah did a double take at the five-by-seven photo centered on the page. The twins stood on each side of a man, perhaps in his mid-forties, who looked eerily like Ewan, if he'd been aged slightly and his features sharpened. Noah tapped the image.

"He looks familiar."

In a lightning flash he knew why. These were the three siblings: Catrione, Cairstine and their brother... Noah's grandfather, Iain Cameron.

A strange, hollow burn started below his breastbone as if he were looking at something he missed terribly and couldn't get back. The sensation made no sense. He knew nothing of the people in the photo. Still, his eyes were drawn to the picture as if it contained a mystery he had to solve.

"Let's look at the first pictures again," he said.

He found Iain twice more in group pictures, a handsome man with a pleasant expression but stern, watchful eyes—the one feature that Ewan, with his lively gaze, hadn't inherited. Noah also noticed for the first time a couple of children playing in the background of several pictures. They were maybe ten, but he had no way of knowing who they were.

"Kind of cool," he said, and then it dawned on him that he wouldn't have given two flying figs for old pictures of people he didn't know when he'd been seven. Ella wouldn't find any of this cool. "Sorry, we don't have to keep looking at the same ones over and over."

"I'm looking for fairies. Sometimes they show up like little circles in the pictures." At that, the little girl grinned. "They like to photo bomb."

Noah snort-laughed at her imagination, surprised at how glad he was to have it surface. Leave it to Ella to turn a boring activity like looking at ancient photos into a treasure hunt. He turned the page, and then one more. His hand froze. Centered on the right-hand page was another enlarged picture, and his fingers hovered over the face of a girl maybe eleven or twelve years old who looked very much like his sister, Bridget. In her lap, she held the baby from the previous pictures.

He had seen no more than half a dozen pictures of this person in his life, and those had been of a young adult woman, but there was no doubt in his mind who it was. His throat tightened.

"What?" Ella asked and put out a small forefinger to touch the picture. Noah fought a ridiculous urge to do the same. "Who is that?"

"Her name was Elise," he managed.

"Elise? That's pretty. How do you know?"

"She was my mother."

CHAPTER ELEVEN

A head teacher's office was supposed to impart a feeling of seriousness and consequence to students called to their fate within its walls, but Paul Taylor's office had always been the opposite. As Mairi settled comfortably onto a sturdy, padded chair in front of Paul's paper-strewn desk, she took in the eclectic mix of fantasy posters—dragons and winged horses—and colorful book posters from *Kidnapped*, to *The Water Horse*, to *Katie Morag*, and felt a ripple of homesickness for the school and the man. Paul had always been Mairi's inspiration as a teacher and leader, and they'd been fast friends since he'd hired her seven years previously. No matter what she got out of this visit, it was good to be back.

"I'm glad you came, Mairi," he said. "Now I can see for myself you're doing all right, but equally importantly, I can tell you, again, how sorry I am I confused your ex-father-in-law for your ex-husband. I should have known."

"I've thought about it, and I'm sure Robbie knew exactly what he was doing. He didn't try to avoid confusion," she said. "He and Sorcha have strong ideas about raising children, and they've never thought Ella has had enough 'structure.' Now that they're worried about my brother being around again, they're lobbying to have Ella move in with them until this is settled."

"They can't possibly think the rumors about you being involved with Aiden's problems are true after knowing you. Why would they believe a convicted drug dealer?"

Mairi fixed him with a sardonic look. "Not a clue, Paul. Who would ever believe someone like that of me? Other than a council of school parents perhaps? Parents who'd force a teacher go on leave rather than stand up for her?"

He had the grace to drop his gaze. "I'm sorry, Mairi. I had—"

She held up her hand. "It's different. *Slightly*." She gave him a last pointed look and then sighed. "Sorcha and Robert don't believe I've anything to do with the drugs, I'm sure of that. They simply don't think I can keep Ella safe from her uncle—never mind I have done exactly that for seven years, and their *son* is the one gallivanting 'round the globe God knows where. They're annoying, but haven't they always been? What I want to know is exactly what the police called you about after you talked to Robbie. I was never suspected of anything. What or who made them start asking questions now?"

"I honestly don't know. The detective I spoke to said he'd been asked to look into your relationship with Aiden Murray. He asked specifically if I knew where you lived, and I confirmed your Glasgow address. That seemed to satisfy him. He asked why you were not in the school's employ and I said you hadn't been permanently let go, only granted a leave of absence. Then he wanted me to confirm that Aiden Murray is your brother and asked if he lived with you. I told him that you absolutely did not live with him and you aren't close."

A shiver of unease slipped through Mairi when Paul shifted uncomfortably in his chair as if wishing he didn't have more to say.

"What?" she demanded. "What else?"

His features held genuine unhappiness. "The inspector finally asked me point blank if I'd heard or had any reason to suspect you were involved with your brother's drug history—if that was why you were on leave. I told him the question was insulting, and when I asked why he even had such suspicions, he wouldn't elaborate."

"I can't imagine my ex-father-in-law having any kind of information about my brother or me," Mairi said. "And Aiden? Whatever it is he wants from me, involving the police only calls attention to himself." She bit her lip. "I don't like this."

"Nor I. But this is why you're on leave for now. It's too big a mess."

"A load of pish," she fumed. "The way things are twisted around, it's a wonder they don't have the net out for me."

"Oh, they do want to talk with you, but I was able to hedge because not once did they come out and ask specifically if I knew where you were. I thought that odd—or fortuitous—but I got by telling the police exactly what I told Robbie MacDonald, that your leave was for personal reasons, that you would never be involved in anything to do with drugs, and that I trust you implicitly." He caught her eyes with a steady gaze. "I do trust you. I told you that when we spoke a few days ago and it hasn't changed. I want this worked out as much as you do."

Mairi sighed sadly, but for the first time since entering his office she relaxed. He was serious, and she trusted him in return. Paul was caught between their friendship and his absolute dedication to the well-being of his school and students. She was on leave because it was best for the school and for her, and she couldn't expect him to cover for her forever.

"I'm sorry," she said. "I appreciate you more than I can ever say. I'm sorry I've asked you for so much, and if anyone else calls, please be as honest as you need to be. It's not your job to solve this."

"I wish I had answers, Mairi. I do."

"Somebody has them," she said, worrying her lip again. "But where to go next? I don't know. Won't do me any good to confront Aiden until I know exactly what he's planning."

"For what it's worth, I have advice."

"All right."

"Go to the police. I believe they might lead you to the next step. They can, perhaps, even help you take it. You've got nothing to hide."

The thought gave Mairi chills. She wanted to walk into a police station even less than she wanted to confront her brother. Still, the advice was sound.

"I'm afraid you're right. It is the logical place to start."

"This will get sorted, Mairi. I know it. I'll have you back as soon as it is."

"Dear Paul. I'll move back the minute you say the word."

They both stood, and he strode around his desk to take her hands. With a firm squeeze, he lifted them both and dropped a kiss on her knuckles.

"Keep in touch, please?"

"'Course I will."

Keep in touch.

In tired frustration, Mairi set her forehead against the steering wheel of her newly-repaired Kia. The only people she wanted to keep in touch with were all in the Highlands—her daughter and the saintly friends watching her. Sweet Catrione, though not a day over sixty in her energy level and demeanor, was nonetheless eighty years old and shouldn't have to watch a seven-year-old who was a constant flight risk. Ainslie, incredibly busy with her house plans, her vet practice, and her upcoming wedding, shouldn't have to run extra laps checking on a friend's daughter. Ewan had to work. And Noah...

The thought of him gave her an unexpected jolt in the pit of her stomach, and her skin flushed hot. All he wanted was to avoid people drama and get going on the cottage, but he was better with people than anyone—himself included—gave him credit for. If Ella had done as she'd been instructed and gone to offer help, had Noah been annoyed? To that end, should she have trusted her daughter alone with a man they barely knew?

Trusting Noah made no common sense. A flash of guilt replaced the fluttering in her belly. This whole feckin' mess was warping her thinking. Just because he was nice, practical, good with her daughter, and was carving her a kelpie didn't mean he couldn't be a closet psychopath.

No. He wasn't.

Still. *She* was a mother. And he was a stranger—for all intents and purposes. She took out her phone and called Craigwarren House. When the very man in her confused thoughts answered, she literally couldn't speak. Why would the new stranger and not Catrione or Innis answer if nothing was wrong?

For the love, Mairi MacDonald. Why do you let your mind go immediately to the darkest place?

"Hello?" he said again.

"Noah? Is that you?"

"Let me ask. Ella, is this me?" She heard muffled, twittery, little-girl laughing and every dark worry vanished. "Yes, I'm told it's me. What can we do for you?"

She laughed, too, at his ridiculous response. "I called to make sure all was well. I'm suddenly fearing it's not. You sound properly bewitched up there."

"No, we're just the inmates in charge at the moment. Ainslie is in Inverness taking a class. Ewan's in town talking to a potential client, and Catrione and Innis went to pick up Isla. I think that accounts for everyone. If you want to speak to one of the aforementioned, I'm afraid you're out of luck for the next fifteen minutes."

"I really called to talk to Ella."

"Oh! Why didn't you say so? She still happens to be here."

A moment later her daughter's cheery voice came on the line. "Hi, Mama!"

"Hi, Ella. How's everything?"

"Brilliant!"

"Did you help Noah like we talked about?"

"Yes. But he said I'm not allowed to help anymore because I find too many interesting things."

"She's a very distracting child," Noah called from the background, and both of them started laughing.

"Ella, I told you not to bother him."

"I didn't mean to. But he liked the pictures of his mum, so we stopped working."

Mairi stared out her car window, utterly confused. "I have no idea what you're talking about."

"I found a picture album. It has pictures of the way the old cottage used to look. *And* there were pictures of Noah's mum and that Callum-man when he was a baby. Did you know Noah's mum was sixteen when Callum came, and her name was Elise? And Noah has only ever seen about five pictures of her until now."

Mairi rubbed slowly at a deep line between her brows. Poor Noah. "I did not know all that. It sounds like you've had a good history lesson. And everyone's all right? You and Noah are okay until Catrione gets home?"

"Aye. Noah made us sandwiches and we took cookies from the jar without asking."

"Dear me, wee burglars are you?"

"Aye." Her laughter rolled again, delighted that Mairi was almost envious of the fun they were having.

"Can I talk to Noah, then? Long as you're all right."

"Aye. He has to go back to work soon. Bye, Mama."

"See you soon. Be properly good?"

"Aye."

When Noah returned with a quiet, "hi, again," the warmth of his flat, nasal accent filled her with reassurance. He was taking care of her girl. She now trusted that for sure.

"I was joking you know," he said. "She's been fine. She helped a lot."

"Until...?"

"She found a stash of old books. One of them was a photo album from about forty years ago. There are some pictures that kind of took me by surprise. It's my fault we stopped working, not hers."

"Then I'm glad. Pictures of your mother, she said?"

"Yeah, almost a little spooky—like seeing a ghost. I wanted to find out what they were about so we brought the book up to Aunt Cat. She found some other albums, too. We pretty much blew an hour looking at old pictures."

He was positively verbose. Being with Ella had clearly infected him.

"Sounds like it was a good hour."

"It was interesting. And you? How is your trip going? Everything all right?"

"Paul has convinced me to go to the police and find out what Aiden's saying that's making everyone suspicious of me."

"Hmmm. That isn't something you planned, was it? Are you okay going alone? Do you want Ainslie or one of the others with you?"

He'd spoken her exact fears, but she pushed the doubt aside. Paul had said it: she hadn't done anything wrong. The police weren't her enemy.

"I'm fine. I just want to know what they think. Then I'll decide where to go next."

"That sounds good. Would you check in after you talk to the police? It would be nice to know how things went and it's good to know...good for Ella to know...that you're okay."

His request warmed her further. He cared—however casually. It had been a long time since anyone had cared whether she checked in or not.

"I will. Thanks for keeping an eye on Ella."

"No problem."

"Talk with you soon."

"If we don't answer, we're wrangling the goat back into her pen again."

"I don't even want to know."

"Best not," he agreed.

Detective Inspector Mark Donnelly led Mairi into a space that looked like a cross between an office and a crime drama interrogation room. In addition to a desk along one wall and a small table in the center, the room boasted a flat-screen television, a case filled with reference books, and a counter with a small coffee maker and a rack of six mugs. It gave off a vibe that was equal parts innocuous and terrifying.

The DI wasn't exactly intimidating, but neither did his unflappable, dry demeanor lend itself to a friendly chat. He set a mug of coffee in front Mairi, moved around the table to take a seat across from her, then picked up a pen and scribbled her name and the date on the pad of paper before him.

"Good of you to come in, Mrs. MacDonald," he said. "We've been hoping to ask you some questions."

"I've been visiting friends."

"So you're still not back in Glasgow?"

"For the moment I'm not."

"May I ask where you are staying?"

"I'd rather not say exactly until I know my brother can't find me and my daughter to harass or harm us."

"Your brother is Aiden Murray?"

"More's the pity." She set her lips angrily but then forced herself to take a calming breath and relax. Sarcasm would not be wise when speaking to police. "Yes."

"Why are you concerned he might harm you or your daughter?"

"He's made threats and false accusations to and about me that cost me my job. He's a drug addict desperate for money, so I'm concerned about everything he might do. To be honest, I'm here hoping you can shed some light on what, exactly, I'm up against."

DI Donnelly scratched his thinning brown hair as if it helped him think. "Normally I prefer to ask the questions, but I'll go along since you've come in voluntarily. Am I to understand that you haven't had contact with your brother recently?"

"Not in person for over a month. Maybe six months ago, he claimed I had partnered with him a number of times to help sell drugs. I was interviewed by police but the accusation was deemed to be false. Still, I had to take a leave from my teaching job because it worried our parent council. More recently, in a direct way, he's cost me a temporary job in a different school. I'd like to know how he managed it."

"And where is this temporary job?"

"There isn't one. I don't have it."

DI Donnelly sighed again and sat back. "I'm afraid I can't help you if I don't know where you've been and for how long. Establishing an alibi is critical for you."

"An alibi? Why is that?"

He flipped several pages on his pad and read silently a moment. When he lifted his eyes, they were apologetic but still hard.

"We spoke to an anonymous source who claims to have knowledge of drugs currently hidden in your home, and that you know about it. They assert you are also allowing people other than Aiden Murray to use your property. We've been working on getting a search warrant, but now that you've come forward, perhaps we can simply get your permission to enter your home and look for ourselves."

Mairi's pulse pounded in her ears, dampening the inspector's voice and filling her head with the pressure of disbelief. *Anonymous source?* There was nothing anonymous about it, as far as she was concerned, and the list of incriminating things Aiden could have planted in her house didn't bear imagining.

"Who is this anonymous source?"

"I'm not at liberty to say more. We're looking into this person as well. But it isn't your brother."

"Oh, I think if you actually do dig, you'll find it absolutely is."

"Would you care to explain why you think so? Or *know* so?" His brows drew together in a more serious question.

Her heart pounded so hard it nearly choked her. If she didn't give permission to search her house, she'd look like she was hiding something. The sickness rising in her stomach, however, told her if she did allow the search, they'd find whatever Aiden wanted them to find. Suddenly she could picture *herself* in prison this time, and Aiden laughing hysterically as he skipped town.

A surge of indignation bubbled up from deep within her and, mixed with concern for Ella, blew away her choking fear. She pushed back her chair and stood, glaring at DI Donnelly. Let him see exactly how a mother bear would fight.

"Do you want to know why I left the city? Because I didn't want my seven-year-old daughter to be anywhere near Aiden Murray when he planted things in the place she lives!"

"Are you telling me you knew this might happen?"

"Not this exact thing, but something. He's desperate to get me in trouble."

"Are you telling me that if we search your house, we *will* find drugs?"

"I don't know for certain, but I'd bet a fair amount you will."

"And if we do? That will put me in an interesting spot, won't it? I'm more inclined to believe you than your brother. But this *tip*, if you will, didn't come from him. Maybe it came from a concerned outside party. If I do find drugs on your property, how will I know that you denying knowledge isn't an elaborate way to confuse the authorities?"

"For the love of saints and sinners! Maybe by looking at my record of zero involvement in drugs ever."

"You turned your brother into authorities three years ago."

"For the same reason I moved away now. To protect my daughter."

"I appreciate that, but you understand this is a lead we have to follow."

Mairi set her jaw and said nothing.

"Give us permission and I'll send my constables to your place now to start clearing this up."

Mairi took a long, silent moment to calm her boiling anger. Donnelly's reasonable coolness infuriated her as much as Aiden's unmitigated gall.

"Fine, Detective Inspector, you can search. If there's nothing there, I'm on my way without another word. If you do find something, and I expect you will, you'll have to prove I wasn't where I say I've been."

"And where is that?"

She shook her head. "I'll tell you when I have to."

CHAPTER TWELVE

"She's *where*?" Noah stared at his brother in disbelief.

"Being held at the police station in Glasgow—until someone can get there and confirm she's been here at Craigwarren since the end of July." Ewan paced the kitchen, his hands at his back, his brain clearly racing. "They found drugs in her house, and she needs an alibi to prove she wasn't in the city during the time they were placed there."

"Drugs?" Noah's mouth went dry. What on earth had she stumbled into? "Then somebody definitely has to go help her."

"Of course I'm going—but I wish Ainslie was here. She's Mairi's best friend, and always has the right words. Most importantly, she has the distinct advantage of not being a Yank."

"And she won't be back until late tonight." Noah let out a long breath. "We were going to Glasgow day after tomorrow anyway, right? I'll go with you today and after we help Mairi, we can do our business."

"And I'll be comin' as well." Innis stood from his seat at the table where he had a large seed catalogue spread in front of him. "Not to give offense, but yer right, lad. An auld Scotsman might help, even if he is a Teuchter."

"A...*chookter*?" Noah frowned.

Innis chuckled. "What the Glaswegians affectionately — or maybe not so affectionately — call any of us who don't hail from their city. At any rate, I might lend a bit o' weight, aye?"

"I would appreciate you more than I can say, Innis, if Aunt Cat can spare you. I can call Fletcher Stone Craft and see if we could meet earlier. Aunt Cat," he called to their great-aunt listening from the kitchen, "would it be all right if we steal your husband and leave Ella with you? I know that means you'll have all the kids with little help."

She laughed. "Aye, take the auld geezer. He hasn't had a good boys' outin' in four long months of ball and chain, has he? Isla is good with Ella and holdin' wee Skye is never a burden for me. You three go. Poor Mairi, that girl can't buy a thimbleful of luck with a hundred pounds and Jack's magic beans these days."

Noah exchanged a look with Ewan, who raised a brow and shrugged. "What can I say? She's got a million of 'em."

"Oh, *wheesht* now, a million whats?" Catrione entered the room, sidled up to him and reached to tug gently on his ear.

"A million sayings I'll never ever remember but wish I could."

He put an arm around her and gave their elderly aunt a squeeze. An unfamiliar twinge of envy tugged in Noah's belly at the closeness the two already shared. It left behind a more recognizable sense of loss — the kind he'd felt so often in his life. Ewan had changed over the past four months, but Noah had convinced himself it was all a passing fad, that his brother would tire of the novelty in Scotland, miss home, and come back.

Now Noah glimpsed the truth. He might never have seen Ewan this way before — happy, relaxed, able to roll with the punches—but hard as it was to admit, this Ewan was more genuine than he'd ever been in his corporate office. He *wasn't* going back.

"You have the devil's own silver tongue," Catrione said, then turned to Noah. "And you, I think, have the angels'."

"He always was the angel," Ewan laughed. "Quiet and well-behaved."

"That's enough of that." He'd never been good at accepting compliments, even teasing ones, and brushed this one away. "We've got our mission."

"All right then," Ewan said. "I don't expect to stay overnight, but grab extra clothes in case this isn't as simple as it should be."

"Surely they can't keep Mairi in jail?" Noah asked.

"Depends on what they believe she's involved in. They can keep her twelve hours before they have to charge her, but I honestly doubt it'll come to that. We'll get her out, men."

"Aye right, blether on, the three of you," Catrione scolded. "You aren't bloody white knights goin' to rescue a damsel. She's perfectly able to do that on her own. She needs you to say she's been here for a month and that's the quit of it. Go and do your duty and no peacocking about."

Noah had to laugh. How Cat managed to reprimand with such sweet sternness he wasn't sure. The urge to bend and give her a kiss on the cheek was unfamiliar, but he obeyed it anyway.

"Yes, ma'am," he said.

She beamed. "Aye, the angel's tongue."

The "cell" where Mairi waited was more like a small office room than a jail. Despite Catrione's admonition, Noah admitted he'd expected to find Mairi in a cold, gray room, cowed and desperate for release. Instead, he could see her through the glass in the door, sitting on a thickly padded chair with a magazine in her hands, the furious circling of the foot she had crossed over one knee her only sign of agitation.

When the constable accompanying him and Ewan opened the door, she leaped from the chair, her mouth forming a surprised O of relief, but her eyes filled with an anger that had clearly been festering for three hours. He entered first while Ewan stopped to ask the constable if Mairi was free to leave.

"Sorry we took so long," Noah ventured. He didn't blame her for being pissed off.

She stunned him by running three steps and throwing her arms around his neck. "Thank you for coming along! Now you've found two MacDonald girls locked in little rooms with no key to get out."

He held her stiffly at first, his surprise growing when she didn't let him go immediately.

"It's going to be okay," he said. "Innis is with Columbo out there. He'll sweet-talk him."

"Thank heaven for Innis. Someone needs to be nice, because I'm definitely no longer sweet of the month around here. They all know I'm ragin' mad. This is so much ridiculous shite."

She continued to hold onto him and, at last, his arms softened across her back and he gave into a sense of protectiveness. Her head reached to the tip of his nose, and she smelled of citrus and spice along with coffee and the slight mustiness that filtered through the whole station. Her thick black hair draped across his arms like velvet, and he could have held her all day. She made him feel exactly like the knight Catrione had warned wasn't required.

Sorry, Auntie, he thought. A guy had his fantasies.

"I'm sorry," he said aloud. "This wasn't part of your plan. I should have stayed out of things and maybe you'd have avoided jail time."

She pulled back, her scowl far cuter than it should have been. "You weren't responsible for this. I changed the plan myself, coming here to the station rather than going to find Mother or Aiden or Robbie. I didn't expect the whole drugs-in-my-house thing, but believe me, your voice in my head from our talk last night probably saved me. You warned me to stay calm no matter what. Had you not, I'd have been far ruder than I was."

"You weren't rude." He grinned.

"I called our favorite DI out there Inspector Clouseau."

"You did not!" He couldn't help himself. He pulled her close again and let her hair muffle his laughter. A flurry of shivers danced through him as her giggles sent puffs of warm air ricocheting against the skin of his neck.

"I did."

"All right, miss," the constable said. "Come with me."

Noah released her reluctantly and shook his head. "You'll have to apologize if you want to actually be sprung from this joint, you know."

"I'll apologize when he does."

"A bad attitude is like a flat tire. You can't go anywhere until you change it."

She stared at him as if he'd turned into Donald Duck and quacked the words. He laughed. "What? I must have heard that from my stepmother a hundred times when I was a kid."

"I'm sure your mother is a lovely person, but I hope the rest of her material was better than that."

"It's true, though. Right?"

"I say, sometimes a bad attitude gives you inspiration." She wrinkled her nose like a stubborn five-year-old, and Noah laughed again.

"Come on before you have any more inspiration. Did they feed you? Maybe you're hangry."

She started to protest, but then scrubbed her fingers across her forehead in resignation. "I suppose you could be a wee bit right."

Moments later, they all stood before Detective Inspector Donnelly's desk, hardly a crew of super heroes, Noah thought wryly. Mairi like a miniature Amazon warrior ready to strike given the right—or wrong—provocation; Innis, amiable as Santa with his unruly white beard; Ewan, reasonable and in control; and Noah himself, with no idea how he'd come to be standing in a Scottish police precinct when all he'd reluctantly agreed to do was fix up a small house and then go home.

His brother had warned him Scottish magic would snare him. The only thing he could attribute to magic at this point was the Craigwarren goat's ability to get through impassable fences.

"All right, Mrs. MacDonald," DI Donnelly said. "We've got separate statements from these good people that indicate you've been in the Glencoe area for the past four weeks. There's no evidence you had drugs in your house or in your possession before that time, since the accusation was made only a week ago. You're free to go."

"Thank you," Mairi said, her words clipped but civil.

"I'd like you to remain available if we have more questions. We did send a constable to…I believe it's your mother's house, to try and speak with your brother. She was told he's out of the country until next week. We'll be on the watch for his return. I'll let you know when he's been located."

"I would appreciate that," she replied.

"May I suggest you go back to Glencoe for the time being, rather than continue to hunt for information yourself? If keeping your daughter safe is your priority, you are better off there."

She bristled slightly but held herself together. "Mr. Donnelly, this needs to end now, so one of us has to find my brother. When he learns this mad scheme didn't take, he'll try another."

"We'll locate him."

"I…" Her shoulders sagged for the first time. "I apologize for the Inspector Clouseau remark earlier. It was uncalled for."

Noah nodded, giving her an encouraging smile even though, in his mind, it had been clever as snubs went.

"No worries, Mrs. MacDonald. I quite liked Inspector Clouseau."

They trooped to the parking area together, the men jubilant, Mairi more subdued. Noah hardly blamed her. It was three in the afternoon and she'd spent half the day in a holding cell.

"Here's mine." Mairi stopped at her car, parked a half dozen spaces from Ewan's forest-green Range Rover.

"You know the city better than we do," Ewan said. "Where should we go for an early dinner?"

"The Hen and Gander is good for pub fare," she said, "but honestly, I don't know if I can eat a thing until I go talk to my mum and see if she's covering for Aiden, since she protects him like he's three rather than thirty. I know she feels she almost lost him all those years he was away, so she refuses to believe he's back into anything to do with drugs. Mum does everything in her power to keep Aiden with her. I need to find out if he really is gone."

"Are you sure, lass?" Innis studied her. "He wasn't wrong, was Donnelly. Might be best to let the police shake the trees for your brother. You don't want him to focus on you and Ella more than he already does."

His suggestion got a thoughtful amount of contemplation, but then she shook her head. "The person most important to my mother after Aiden is Ella. If I tell her Aiden's actions have caused Sorcha and Robbie to want Ella taken from me and, by association most certainly her, she might be more honest."

"Okay, but *I* have a suggestion." Noah said. "I think you should eat first. Remember how being hangry was responsible for Inspector Clouseau? You don't want a worse nickname for your mom."

"Like Mommy Dearest?"

"Ouch," Noah said.

"Fine, she's not that bad. But she is pathologically blind when it comes to Aiden."

"What if you skipped your mother this trip and waited for Ainslie to see her with you?" Ewan asked. "Maybe she can be a calming influence."

"Mother always liked Ainslie," Mairi agreed. "But I'm tired of waiting for this to get solved. I want to protect Ella, but what kind of an example am I, hiding away?"

"An example of a smart, patient woman who knows when to go for the jugular?" Noah shrugged.

Her mouth twisted. "I really hate your insightful brain, you know. Your calm one, too. Also, stop with the backhanded compliments."

"I never said it was *you* who was smart and patient."

She grinned at him and he wiggled his brows, enjoying the teasing.

"No, but you implied I *could* be. From you, that's high praise."

"Ouch again. I must not be a very nice person."

"Terrible person."

"Knock it off, you two. I vote we go eat," Ewan said.

He shot Noah a raised-brow question that clearly asked what he was playing at, flirting with Mairi. He wished he knew. Every time he was around the woman, his vows to keep silent and his normal lay-low personality went out the window.

Innis put a grandfatherly arm around Mairi's shoulders. "Aye right, here's what we'll do. Come eat, Mairi-love. If you want to go to your mother, we'll send the two young lairds here off to check with their stone man, and I'll come wi' ye to face her. She'll be polite around a crazy auld man.

Or a younger one with an intimidating foreign accent might be equally effective. Noah's unbidden thought made him freeze. Damn. This country was infecting him with some kind of Scottish brain-eating curse. He'd known Mairi a mere three days, and yet he wanted to watch over her like a clan chief from the crazy family history his siblings were always going on about. He didn't do protective. He did careful. He did cool. But after their time together the night before he wanted to see this trip through with her—a desire based in zero logic and pure chauvinism. Catrione had said it: Mairi didn't need him or anyone to fight her battles. And it made far more sense for Innis to accompany her—the king of the group rather than a knight or a squire.

"Noah?"

Mairi's voice dragged him out of his reverie, and his face heated as if she could read his thoughts. Kings? Knights? Squires? What the actual hell?

"Sorry," he said. "Sounds like a plan."

"I asked what sounded good to eat." Her brows knotted quizzically.

He blinked, feeling more foolish than ever. "Sorry, I was thinking about stone fences," he lied. "I'll bow to the group's wishes since I've never been to a restaurant in Scotland."

Even to his own ears he sounded more distant than he meant to, but he had to stop falling into the teasing and bantering. His job was to finish the cottage, and that was all.

Mairi studied him for a moment, but then she smiled and nodded. "Hen and Gander it is."

Twenty minutes later, Noah sat in front of the biggest piece of fried cod he'd ever seen. The menu pick had been easy—a person could rarely go wrong with fish and chips. At home, however, fish and chips meant three pieces of fish, four or five inches long, and a potato's-worth of French fries. What lay before him was twelve inches of golden cod, enough thick brown chips to save a starving country, and a bowl of bright green mashed peas topped with a pat of sunny yellow butter.

"This could feed a small nation's population of children," he said aloud.

"And it isn't one of those dishes that looks better than it tastes," Ewan said, taking a forkful of his meat pie. "They know fish and chips around here—better than in England, they'll tell you."

"Too right we do." Innis sliced off a piece of his fish with the edge of a fork.

Noah felt Mairi's eyes on him as his fork bit into the crunchy coating of his piece and floated through the white, flaky cod. Watching her watch him, he widened his eyes in amusement and popped a generous hunk in his mouth. It melted better than butter and chocolate on his tongue, the fish mild and tender, the coating perfectly crisped and spiced.

"Oh my gosh," he said, not caring that his mouth was full.

Mairi grinned, obviously pleased. "Right? Try the peas."

The mashed version of his childhood favorite vegetable spread across his tongue like candy. He savored the flavor, thick and rich and buttery and improbably familiar. He dug his fork into the peas again and stopped, staring at the bowl as another memory rose like a ghost.

"More mush peas, Mommy."

"Of course, sweet Noah, my wee pea eater. You'd eat the entire bowlful if I allowed it, wouldn't you? Now, if you could teach your baby sister to like them as much as you do, all would be perfect."

He lifted his gaze to Ewan's, his heart racing. "Mushy peas. I called them mush peas. Our mother made these."

Ewan's eyes shone. "You remember?"

"Why have I never thought of these things before? I could hear her in my mind."

"It happens frequently, bro," he said. "Dad kept her from us and we never talked about things we remembered. We were little kids, but I swear being here slowly unlocks what things we *do* have hidden in our brains."

"It's unnerving."

"It can be, but I advise that you embrace it. Bridget doesn't have it all wrong. The family story is rich, and it's part of who we are."

Noah wasn't sure he wanted to embrace anything. Remembering his mother was disconcerting and powerful. He wanted to push away the recollections as much as he wanted to sink into their warmth.

"Weird," was all he could say.

He had a hard time pacing his eating after that. The peas disappeared followed in quick order by the fish. Everyone tucked into dinner like starving lions around a successful hunt. Conversation lightened as Innis steered it temporarily away from the seriousness of Mairi's family issues. It was only after everyone had turned down the opportunity for dessert that the subject of what to do next arose.

Ewan's phone rang.

"Ahh, it's Fletcher," he said. "Maybe we can meet with him yet today."

As soon as he answered, his call was followed by Mairi's bright mobile ringtone, and she pulled the phone from her purse to check the ID. It took less than a second for her face to blanch and her hand to start shaking.

"Mairi?" Noah asked, concern blossoming.

"I swear she's half witch. She knows I'm talking about her."

CHAPTER THIRTEEN

"Hello, Mother." Mairi answered her phone with feigned cheeriness.

"Mairi Marie?" The talent her mother had for sounding sad and shrill at the same time had amazed and annoyed her since childhood. As did the way she used Mairi's ridiculous, redundant full name. "Do you know the police were here lookin' for your brother? They can't leave him alone. You need to do something."

Her mother's "you must come help" cry was nothing new, but Mairi's clenched jaw sent a tic up through her temple. Today she was out of patience.

"We aren't having this conversation on the phone."

"Well, where will we have it, may I ask, since you've vanished into thin air?"

"Lucky for you, Mother, I'm in Glasgow today. If you want to see me, I'll come now and we can talk."

"Oh, nae, dinnae fash." Her voice faded into long-suffering wistfulness. "Aiden isn't here. He's the one you need to talk to."

Mairi rolled her eyes and caught sight of Noah, watching her like a careful guardian. Why he wasn't annoying the hell out of her, she didn't know. For some reason, since that first night when she'd thought him nothing but a busybody, he now made her feel like maybe there'd be a soft place to land if she fell. She hoped her weak smile looked grateful and not like the grimace she tried to hide.

"Believe me, I want to see Aiden, but absolutely not to have tea and blether about his poor life. He just got me three hours in a holding cell, and I have a few words to say to the great coward, and to you about seeing him for what he is."

"A holding cell? What did you do?"

"What did *I* do? Your son literally had drugs planted in my bedroom to get me in trouble with the police. That's why they want to talk to him. Tell me the truth. Is he honestly gone?"

"He needed a break and went to meet friends in Leith. Said he had some business in Edinburgh as well."

"I can guess what kind of business," she muttered and looked to Noah again. His calm features gave away no emotion, although his eyes were keen. She relaxed slightly. Her insides might roil when dealing with her mother, but there were calm people around her and she could—would—draw on their strength. "Why did you tell the constable he was out of the country?"

"I didn't want them to follow him to Edinburgh," she said plaintively. "He can decide what to do when he gets back."

"You're sure he's coming back?"

What a relief it would be if he actually did leave the country. Then again, maybe he'd simply turn into a shadowy presence dogging her forever.

"Oh, aye. He's helping me fix up the back rooms so he can have his own space. D'ya see, Mairi? Our Aiden's a good lad, makin' up for lost time."

Mairi's decision changed her entire outlook toward the rest of the day.

"Good lad, Mother?" She snorted in derision. "Look 'ere. When he returns you let me know, right?"

"Mairi, you wouldn't turn him in for no reason, would you, love?"

The "love" didn't move her, couched as it was in her "poor me" tone. "Never for no reason, Mother."

"You asked if I wanted you to come now. Do you have my Ella with you?"

"Of course I don't. I won't bring her anywhere near Aiden."

"Oh, Mairi. That's not right. He's a loving uncle to her."

Like any addict, Aiden could be sweet as honey when he needed to be, and he'd always been fine with his niece. But Mairi would never allow Ella to be a reward or a pawn.

"When I know Aiden is no longer a threat to me or to your granddaughter, you can have a fine meet-up with her. She'll love that."

"Och, pish, Mairi. He's not a threat to her."

"That right? He's making accusations about me that have Sorcha and Robbie threatening to take Ella away. Until you're willing see what Aiden's doing, Mother, Ella stays where she's safe."

"Take her away?"

"They don't think Ella is safe either, and they want her to live with them. Think about that, right?"

"Mairi, girl, I know he's still angry wi' you, but he's not doing what you're accusing him of."

"I know you think so."

"I'll talk to Aiden." It was more of a promise than she'd ever gotten from her mother, but Mairi would believe it when she heard such a "talk" with her own ears. "I hope you'll tell Ella I love her."

"I can promise that much." Mairi straightened in her chair. "Right then, if you need anything, you can call me." It was a relatively safe offer, one her mother was unlikely to take. For all her weaknesses, she did know how to survive day-to-day, if somewhat gracelessly.

"Come visit soon, Mairi."

"When Aiden is back, aye? Bye, Mother. Take care."

She rang off and sat still as a rock, feeling like she'd gone six rounds in a boxing ring. Slowly she shook off the call's aftermath and looked at the three men who watched and listened. Ewan was done with his call, Innis smiled at her, and Noah reached across the table to cover her hand. Shock at the touch zipped up her arm.

"You're good with your mother," he said. "Your hand is still shaking, though. I'm sorry."

She wanted to crawl over the table and let him hold her entire shaking body.

"Oh, nae. I'm not good with her at all. I lose it more often than not."

"Don't be so hard on yourself. We couldn't hear everything, but what did come across is that your mom is passive-aggressive, and you didn't fall for it. You were firm and honest, and though you could have used Ella as a weapon or a bargaining chip, you didn't."

She wanted to weep with relief. It's all she ever wanted to hear, that she wasn't making mistake after mistake. She missed the security of his touch when he let her hand go.

"That's nice of you," she managed. "Thanks."

"Noah's right," Innis said. "And now it's up to her. We'll be needing another trip or two back here to the city, and we'll help you keep track of your eejit brother. Meanwhile, Ewan's talked to Hamish Fletcher, and he's agreed to come and see the cottage in person on the morrow. All that's left today is to pick up what supplies we can and head for home."

"That would be fantastic," Mairi said.

"You talked about going to see your ex-in-laws. Do you still need to do that?" Noah asked.

"You know what? I've thought about it. They don't need to know I can get into Glasgow easily. Let Sorcha think I'm far away. She'll call again, I've no doubt."

Noah grinned. "What did I say? Wait to go for the jugular."

She laughed, relief beginning to ease her tension. Not a thing had been solved, and she still had no way to get her job back, but she'd taken a few steps and knew more of what she was up against. The idea of leaving the suffocating city for a cool Highland breeze gave her a flicker of optimism for the first time in weeks.

"If you'd rather leave right away, I'd be happy to ride back with you and let the lads run their errands." Innis's offer warmed her.

"Oh, Innis, you're wonderful. Thank you. I'll be very happy to get back to Craigwarren and Ella," she said. "But would it be presumptuous to ask if I could come along to the building materials warehouse? I'd fancy something completely different than what's happened so far today, and I've never spent much time looking at building goods."

Ewan grinned and rubbed his hands together. "I almost asked you, but I thought you'd rather get back home quickly—back to Craigwarren, I mean."

"I'd like to come."

"You could tell Ainslie what you find and compare thoughts."

"That would be great fun. Ainslie has bags of ideas; I know, because we've talked about them." Mairi set her worries fully aside. "I'll take pictures."

"Hey, you aren't going to take over my project, are you?" Noah cocked his head, managing to narrow his eyes and smile at the same time. "You'll stick to colors and decorating?"

She batted her lashes. "I was waiting for some kind of chauvinistic remark. I didn't think it would come from the man who not a minute ago was my champion."

He shrugged and winked. "No chauvinism intended. Just protecting my turf."

"I can respect that, but if I interpreted the most recent floorplan sketches correctly, you did take one of my ideas already. I can't be that bad."

"Didn't say you were bad. I'm saying I'm territorial."

"At least he's honest," Ewan laughed. "Temperamental artist."

"Nae. You told me last night you don't mind people watching you work. That doesn't seem too temperamental to me," Mairi said soothingly.

"The key word is *watch*. The hermit reputation is justified."

"Bah," she said, and pushed her chair back from the table. "I haven't believed that from day one."

Considering how badly her day had begun, Mairi had trouble believing it when things improved, but tramping through aisles of fixtures and tile and flooring, wainscoting and garden paving stones, was more than an improvement—it was good as a seaside vacation. She listened, rapt, while Noah explained to his brother and Innis about studwork timber, cladding, and support beams. She snapped pictures for Ainslie, bantered with Noah about flooring choices, and searched through a small selection of roofing materials, including slate, the prices of which took everyone's breath away.

By the time Noah had supervised the purchase of enough wood to frame in the cottage's loft, the new drying room and the bedroom and kitchen walls, Mairi was as excited as if they were renovating her own home. Noah's knowledge and detailed measurements, written precisely in a plain black notebook he carried in a back pocket, impressed everyone. They ordered drywall to be delivered—at a pretty cost but still cheaper than getting it from a smaller supplier in Inverness or Glencoe—and Noah had his eye on a traditional set of hardwood cabinets for the kitchen, calling Mairi's choice of a small but substantial island impractical.

Mairi thought his choices boring, but she said nothing and simply took photos of what she liked, vowing to win Ainslie to her side. The men wouldn't get to make all their monkishly ascetic choices without a fight, but it wasn't as if she had a right to a voice in this project. It was simply fun to fantasize and even more fun to spar with Noah over colors and styles.

She didn't analyze her fascination with him or their up-and-down relationship. He met her where she was at and empathized or criticized as the situation demanded. The bottom line was, she could talk to, or argue with, Noah and never worry that he was anything but an honest man.

Once Ewan's used Range Rover, of which he was inordinately proud mostly because he'd mastered the right-hand drive, had been loaded to its roofline with all the lumber, it was clear there were only two spots for passengers.

"Good thing Mairi drove her own car," Innis said. "I'll have a ride back, now that you've filled my seat."

"Let Noah go with her." Ewan slid a sly wink to his brother, and Mairi turned away, heat rushing to her cheeks.

"Brilliant," Innis said. "Perspective from yet another native tour guide."

"Not sure how *brilliant* a guide I'll be bein' a city girl. Now if he wants to see more of Glasgow or Edinburgh…" She hoped nobody could hear how crazily her heart pounded at the thought of two hours in the car with Noah Portman.

"Put me where you want me. I'm easy," he replied.

The words didn't ring with boundless excitement, but when he climbed into her car and offered a bright-eyed smile that said he didn't detest the arrangement, she relaxed.

"That trip was more successful than I'd hoped," he said as they wound through the Glasgow neighborhoods toward the River Clyde. "With all the framing wood, I'll be able to get a lot done by the end of this weekend."

"It is exciting. You can do this all yourself? I mean, it's a heap of work."

"It would be ideal to have a couple extra sets of hands, but we'll manage the interior. The stonework and roof…there's no question that has to be hired out."

"You know," she offered hesitantly. "I'm happy to be another worker if it ever helps."

He turned his head and his smile turned mischievous. "You don't think we'd murder each other before we were done? Miss Let's Put Pink in the Bathroom."

"It wasn't *pink*," she huffed. "It was coral. And it was an accent tile. It goes with the pale reddish tinge in the outside stone."

"Because you can see the outside from inside the bathroom." Noah laughed and held up a hand. "I'm kidding, I'm kidding. But see what I mean?"

"I do. Still, I think I'm necessary to your success." She chuckled. "Bring out your feminine side."

"Seriously? That's really a thing?"

"Too right. Most guys need a little help."

"Does it work the other way?"

She pursed her lips, thinking. "Nope. Girls already have an innate, tough masculine side."

"Admittedly, I've never met a wimpy girl. Or a wimpy woman."

"Based on how many girls? Or women?"

He drew back. "A little personal, isn't it?"

"I guess. I didn't mean it like it sounded. We don't know each other well enough to compare dating histories. I was thinking of how Ewan talks about your sister and your mother. They sound strong."

"Bridget is optimism wrapped in a hurricane. On the surface she doesn't seem tough, but her depth is pretty formidable. My mother is…hard to quantify. Tough and focused, but caring. We love each other, but she's always related better to my extroverted siblings. She spent a lot of time trying to bring me out of my shell."

"Now there's some fodder for a psychologist." She grinned to show she was teasing but he didn't respond.

She glanced at him, startled by the half-glazed look in his eyes—as if he'd gone somewhere and left his body in her passenger seat.

"Y'okay, then?" she asked.

He shrugged as if warding off a chill. "Yeah, sure. I…this place is weird. I keep having the strangest memory flashes of my real mother. My birth mother I guess I should say since Amanda is of course a real mother. My mom—my Scottish mom—I remember mostly as my first playmate. But something she said just came to me. It's the second or third time I've heard her voice in my head."

"What did she say?"

He rubbed self-consciously at the corner of his mouth with a thumb. "Stuff you'd say to a kid, I guess. Nothing."

"Come on," she urged. "Bring her to life. I'd love to know about her."

He was never short on advice, but he didn't talk much about himself, and he hesitated before he finally spoke. "She told me I was different from my brother and 'wee' sister, that's all. That I would…be all right, be fine, if I opened up even if it was frightening."

The story moved her in a way she didn't expect. "Aww, Noah, that's a lovely thing for a mother to say. You must have been a wee bit shy."

He scoffed. "I was three or four. Aren't all kids shy then? It's mostly an odd thing to remember."

His eyes held a slight haze of uncertainty, as if he didn't quite believe what he'd said.

"*My* daughter was never shy. If I hadn't gone through twelve hours of labor with her, I'd think she was an alien being."

"Hah, you aren't the least bit shy. Ella's no alien."

Mairi wrinkled her nose in a scowl and shook her head. "When I was young, I was the 'big girl' to my younger brother. I was the responsible one, the one who could handle anything. I cooked, I cleaned, I helped. Aiden was the beautiful boy, the one who needed patience and careful teaching. Trust me, I got sick of that really fast, and when I was thirteen, I got a real job, delivering papers and helping at a local vet surgery—one reason I bonded with Ainslie in later years. I arranged things as much as possible so I wasn't around to help at home, and from that point on I became the ungrateful one until I moved back home before Dad died. Now my help is expected."

"And you still offer it."

"My da' was a decent fellow. He worked hard, though, and wasn't the strong presence we needed. That Aiden needed. He softened my mother's rough edges—she was always a little narcissistic, but she got even needier after he was gone. It's aggravating, but she's my family, and she loves Ella. I do what I can."

"Tells me a lot."

"Well, I know you didn't really want to come to Scotland, yet look at you. That tells me a lot, too."

"Aren't the two of us simply amazing and perfect?"

She laughed. "That we are. Come on, let's cross the famous River Clyde."

"It's famous?"

"It's not the longest in Scotland but Glaswegians think it's the most important. After we cross, I'll drive past the Museum of Modern art and show you the Duke of Wellington wearing his traffic cone hat. A bit of Glaswegian city humor. You'll love it."

They talked all the way back to Craigwarren, although Noah was always succinct and careful in his questions and answers. But she liked that. He didn't push her and he didn't push her away. For someone who supposedly lived mostly alone, he was a man comfortable in his own skin who appreciated his gifts. They laughed easily. He told her about the big hotel renovation commission he'd lost to another artist and about the apartment he'd had to pack up in a whirlwind four days before coming to Scotland. He even admitted to being concerned about needing to hunt for a new place immediately upon getting home in five weeks.

Those five weeks didn't seem very long when she thought about it. And the way he talked about the tight schedule he and Ewan had laid out for the cottage renovation, she knew the time would fly. By the time they arrived at Craigwarren, it was nearly nine o'clock and fully dusk.

"Thanks for the ride home," Noah said.

"Thanks for the company."

"Ewan talked about unloading the lumber tonight in case it rains. I should probably help them."

"I can—"

"You see to Ella. If she's still awake."

"Och, she's a night creature. If I get her to sleep by ten, even on a school night, it's miraculous. But, aye, thanks. I'll see how she is."

"We didn't talk much about your day," he said. "I'm sorry you sat in jail all that time."

It seemed a million hours ago, but she nodded and shrugged. "It wasn't as hard as what I hope my brother will face when this is all behind us."

"That's my girl," he winked. "Planning the win already."

His casual "my girl" should have blown by unnoticed. Or annoyed her. But suddenly, there didn't seem to be anything he did that bothered her or escaped her notice, but that wasn't a good thing. She had too much baggage and he had too little time for them to even consider attraction. Then again, she amended, it was too late to stop the attraction. All she could do was avoid acting on it.

"Oh, I'll win," she vowed. "He's controlled my life in one way or another for far too long."

"There you are!" Catrione bustled from the house before they even reached the door, followed by Ainslie who got to Mairi first.

"Are you all right? I'm so sorry I wasn't here to help you. I hate that you went through this."

"I'm fine, I really am," Mairi said. "It's no more than a grand story now."

"Can't fool me; it was not that grand. But I'm afraid you'll have to fill me in later."

"That I will, but what's going on?"

Ainslie looked from Mairi to Noah and pressed her lips together in a tiny grimace. "What would you like first? The two crises or the good news?"

CHAPTER FOURTEEN

"Is Ella okay?"

Why that was the first question out of Noah's mouth, he wasn't sure, but Mairi looked at him with such gratitude, he was glad it had been.

"Ella is perfect," Catrione said. "Everyone is fine. Everyone except the goat and the donkeys."

"Oh no," Mairi said.

An evil person inside of Noah wondered if maybe the goat was dead. Okay, he wasn't that despicable, maybe Juliet was simply gone—as in run away. In that case he wouldn't mourn. Juliet needed a goat psychiatrist. He had no feud with the donkeys—he'd only met them once, and they'd been curious but not, thank God, interested in a love relationship.

"All right, good news. Let's have it," he said.

"I might have found you a crew. Of two," Ainslie replied. "I have a client who's fallen on hard times with a husband injured and out of work. She has a son and a nephew, both twenty years old who are looking for jobs. They aren't professional construction workers, but they grew up on farms and are happy to follow directions. They'd be more helpers than a real crew, but if you feel they'd be useful we can hire them. Up to you."

"Help would be good," he said. "I don't know if there'll be much to do for another few days or a week, but after that... Sure, let's give 'em a try."

"But the crises?" Mairi asked. "Not sure I want to know."

"Well, to start, the feckin' goat got out and beelined directly to the cottage." Ainslie looked Noah in the eye and obviously had to work hard to keep a straight face. "You have definitely become her person, Noah. When you didn't come out to play with her, she worked the latch on the door—"

"Worked the latch?" He couldn't believe it.

"Okay, she broke the latch."

"Why are you smiling?"

"It's that or weep. Juliet made herself quite at home inside. We found her chewing on some books in a corner of the bedroom. Let's just say she left her gate open, and Ailish decided to follow her. We found the donks in the kitchen."

"Are you kidding me?" Noah let out a breath hard as a Highland gale.

"We've only had time to get them back to the barn, but not to, uh, clean up. They didn't exactly use the loo."

He closed his eyes and scrubbed at his forehead, not wanting to contemplate the implications of her report. Goat and donkey crap in his work space? Before he could ask the extent of the mess, an appalling sound burst beside him, far more upsetting and grating than the foot of poop he was picturing in the cottage: the high-pitched squeal of three women laughing hysterically.

He glared at them. "Aunt Cat, you too? Thanks a lot."

"Oh, *mo cridhe*, it's your face. You do look as if it's an epic crisis. I'm sorry, but this is a nothing problem. Annoying. Perhaps closer to infuriating until we find a way to contain Juliet. But we will."

He wasn't assuaged, but the women were clearly no longer serious about crises. They chortled their laughter like gleeful hyenas. Finally, he reached for Catrione's hand and made her look at him.

"Is that really it? Animals in the cottage?"

"Oh no," she said, and took a breath, wiping her eyes. "The real crisis is that the inspectors have moved up the inspection date. We now have a little under four weeks."

Anyone who knew him, knew Noah was not prone to anger. Even now he didn't exactly lose his temper, but for several long moments he bit his lip trying to figure out why this didn't feel like just another problem to solve. This felt like...like piling onto the new guy. He didn't even know why he was being asked to do this crazy thing. Why it *had* to be done by September what now, sixth? And it was August ninth.

He did carvings for a living. He did framing and drywall part time. He was an idea guy, not a real contractor.

"This is insanity," he said as calmly as he could. "It was crazy before, and the train just jumped the tracks. Where's my brother? He needs to start explaining why this is so da—"

Ella appeared at the door, and Noah bit back his curse. She looked like that crazy Disney cartoon again, all frizzed red curls and a long nightgown covered in little woodland animals.

Animals. He'd never understood why people kept animals. Like goats.

"Why it's this important," he finished.

At his words, Ewan appeared behind Ella, his mouth twisted in a wry smile. "We aren't off to a very auspicious start, are we?"

"That depends," Noah replied. "When do I get to know exactly what's going on and why?"

"Let's go down to the cottage and I'll tell you."

Ella finally launched herself out the door and wrapped her arms around Noah's legs, shocking him into speechlessness.

"Hi, Noah! Guess what? We found some more pictures of the cottage. Back then it was cool, but didn't have donkey poo." She belly laughed, and Noah rolled his eyes. She let go of him and hopped to her mother. "Hi, Mama. I'm gonna go to see what books Juliet ate in the cottage. Did you have a good trip?"

"I had an adventurous trip, and we're going to talk about that while we put you to bed. You can see Juliet's book the morrow."

"But I want to see what they did!"

"You've been in a barn, Ella. No need to see it recreated in a house." She gave a little snort and sought Noah's eyes. "Noah can take pictures."

"I don't think so," he said.

"Please!" Ella cried. "Please, Noah."

"Aww, how can you resist that adorable face?" Ainslie said and caught Ella's cheeks between her palms before bending to plant a kiss on her nose.

"Because she bothers me." Noah stared at the little girl, who laughed at him.

"I'm the biggest bother he knows," she said. She returned to Noah and lifted her arms to him. With only the barest hesitation, he hoisted her up and let her wrap her slender arms around his neck. "Good night. That's really what Isla said I could come and say."

"Well, good night then. Sleep tight. Don't let the donkeys poop in your dreams."

Her continued little peals of laughter and the pixie cuteness aimed at him swept away the last of his irritation.

"Pee-yew. Okay, I willnae."

He let her down, and Mairi shook her head. "I don't think you're any more grown up than she is."

"Don't blame me. I didn't start the whole excrement conversation."

The cottage reeked of that conversation when he, Ewan, and Ainslie stepped through the front door, but the physical damage wasn't as bad as Noah had imagined. The tiny, pellet-shaped goat droppings were the worst, scattered across the floor of two rooms like rounds of carelessly fired BBs. Ailish had left only one steamy pile that was easily picked up with a manure fork. Ewan filled a bucket with water and scrubbed the spot with piney floor cleaner while Ainslie and Noah chased the goat pellets around with mostly ineffectual brooms.

Eventually, however, the disaster was cleaned up, the room smelled woodsy, and Noah pulled three ladder-back chairs out from the small table, pointed Ewan to one of them and Ainslie to another before he joined them, leaned forward and folded his hands on the scarred tabletop.

"This is it. Tell me right now why we're planning to bust our butts for an unreasonable deadline. What possessed the two of you to try and do this in such a short time?"

The pair exchanged a resigned look, but one that also held excitement.

"You're right. I should have told you from the beginning, but we were sworn to silence."

"Really." Noah cocked a disbelieving brow.

"Sounds like made-up theater, but it's true," Ainslie said. "The guests we're expecting are indeed honeymooners, but the bride is a member of the extended British royal family. Normally, she's far enough down the line that nobody would pay any attention, but the groom is a Dutch sailor who was involved in breaking some world records before there was an accident a couple of years ago, and one of his team members was killed. Bottom line is, the marriage is controversial, the British tabloids are speculating like crazy, the parents on both sides want to avoid bad press at all costs, and all the kids want is to be happy and a place to honeymoon that nobody has ever heard of so they can have a week of peace."

Noah almost laughed. The crazy story had to be made up.

"Where did you find these people?" he asked.

"A few months ago—" Ainslie began.

"The night I arrived at Craigwarren," Ewan added.

"That's right!" They shared a smile Noah found a little too sweet, but he waited them out. "I took him to see Loch Warren, and we came upon a woman and her son who'd been hiking and gotten lost. She was Dutch, her wife was American, and they'd been separated on the trail. We brought them here, fed them, and got the family back together. Turns out, Anke, the Dutch mom, is this sailor's cousin. When all this broke, she thought of us."

"And you randomly said yes." Noah scowled.

"We said no," Ewan replied. "And then it got surreal."

"Are you trying to say it wasn't already?"

Before Ewan could answer there was a tap on the door. It pushed open and Mairi appeared. She grinned sheepishly, and Noah's stomach did a flip of happiness. He tamped it firmly down.

"Hiya," she said. "Wee bratty girl is asleep and I thought maybe I wouldn't be too late to help. It smells like I am a bit, but…?"

"The mess is cleaned up, but you're not too late," Ainslie said. "Come and sit. You might as well hear this, too. But you have to take the oath of silence. The story goes no further than the pair o' you, on pain of death."

She laughed. "Intrigue and secrets? This sounds like a braw club to join. Why do you look like you've been offered a bowl of glass to eat?" She rocked into Noah's upper arm.

"Because it's a meeting of the crazy club."

"Brilliant. Where do I sign up?"

They told her as much of the story as they'd shared with Noah, and Mairi gulped it all in like it was the best candy she'd ever tasted.

"I can't tell you how much I need something like this," she said. "So, what's the weird part?"

"The queen has given her blessing to the marriage and specifically requested we be the official honeymoon destination. The couple will even get minimal protection."

"The Queen." Noah stared. "As in *of England*, not like Narnia or Disneyland."

"As in Elizabeth Two, mother of Charlie, stepmother to Camilla, grandmum to William and Harry."

"You're telling me Queen Elizabeth has contacted you."

"No, of course not. Not directly," Ainslie said. "A letter from her undersecretary's secretary or something. But she does know of us, and that we're, and I quote, 'a warm, secluded, beautiful spot filled with exceptionally nice people.' I mean, there really wasn't much choice given a royal endorsement like that, was there?"

"Holy mother of mutton and gravy!" Mairi drummed her hands on the tabletop in glee. "This is unreal, Ainslie."

"We've literally sworn to keep this a secret until after the couple is gone," Ewan said. "But afterward, if they enjoy it, they'll make an endorsement, and we can't buy that kind of publicity. Not that we want to handle thousands of bookings, but an infusion of cash around here is needed, and this would be a big startup boost. Did I mention they're paying a premium rate for their week's stay? Enough to recoup a great deal of what we spend to fix this little place."

Noah's head spun with the implications. He still couldn't believe he wasn't asleep and dreaming the whole story, but on the off chance he wasn't, his brother had laid out a scenario that meant no backing out of this deal. And no skimping on the quality or the freaking Queen of England would hear about it.

He shook his head, trying to make the others around the table disappear back into the peace of sleep. When they didn't, he turned to Mairi.

"Holy mother of what did you say?"

They all broke into laughter.

"Yeah, well, when something can't be done, you downplay breaking the news." He stared them all down defensively. "And this can't be done."

For a moment, the shock on Mairi's face was almost worth the moment of cruelty. Even Ainslie's eyes held disappointed doubt. He relented with a sigh.

"Easily. It can't be done *easily*. This fairytale couple, Sugar Bunny and Prince Gorgeous—"

"Amy and Finn, actually." Ainslie giggled, her eyes liquid with relief.

"Them too. They may have to sleep in a finished room next to one that's unfinished. Or maybe they'll have to cook on a camp stove. Maybe we'll get everything mostly done. I'm just saying, it isn't a fairy tale on this end. Royal or not, we have zero wiggle room. I'll not only need the two boys you found, Ainslie, we need all hands on deck. And I know everyone has other obligations."

"I have one meeting this week," Ewan said. "The first international client for Portman and White."

P and W was the advertising agency their father had started with his late partner, now run by the original White's daughter, Julia. Ewan, once in line to take over for their father, now desperately wanted to make a go of bringing the agency international.

"How is that going over with Dad and Julia?"

"They're cautiously excited. But I can still make the cottage a priority."

"I've been working on getting some backup help a couple of days a week," Ainslie said. "Busy season will taper off this month, but I know I'm the weak link. I'm sorry."

"Don't apologize," Noah said. "It's a team effort and we all have jobs."

"I don't." Mairi shrugged. "Have a job that is. Like I said, I'm a city girl so I have few qualifications, but I can follow orders."

"I know you can give them," Noah teased.

"About colors and designs—absolutely. Ainslie, you and I need to talk."

"We do indeed."

"We're screwed." Noah dodged out of the way when Mairi waved a hand as if to smack his upper arm. "Let's get this show on the road first thing in the morning. Who's around to help me finish tearing down the kitchen wall?"

CHAPTER FIFTEEN

A shrill wailing woke Noah in the pitch dark, and he squeezed his eyes shut against a nightmare starring mewling brown-and-white goats galloping through his garage back in Minnesota. He shuddered in his bed, glad for the interrupted dream, until the wail came again. What the...? Was the stupid goat outside the house now? What was wrong with that mentally disturbed animal?

The sound came again, more sustained this time.

No, not a goat. A baby.

For a long moment, his sleep-deprived brain could make no sense of such a thing. Then everything came back in a rush of clarity. Ainslie's sister Isla had returned home yesterday, but he'd barely caught a glimpse of the seventeen-year-old before rushing off to Glasgow. He'd not seen her baby at all. What was its name? Earth? Fire? Skye? Skye.

He rubbed his eyes and opened them. The only illumination in the room came from an old-fashioned clock radio on the bedside table. Two forty-seven a.m.

The crying didn't stop. In fact, it grew in volume momentarily and then he heard footsteps in the hallway followed by the creak of stairs as the wailing baby was carried down to the living room. He pulled the edges of his pillow up around his ears, but the interruption to his sleep had him aggravatingly wide awake. After only two full days, he could still chalk it up to jetlag, but he was so tired he should have been able to sleep through zombies.

But evidently not babies.

He'd spent so little time around infants he had no idea if this would be a regular occurrence now that Isla was home. Honestly, the last baby he'd held had been his own sister.

She's a wee bit of a thing, isn't she, Noah-love? Hold your arm under her head like so…

"Stop it," he growled into the dark.

This mother's voice thing was getting ridiculous. Ewan had told him about the strange memory games this place had played on him—comforting bits of the past, he'd said. To Noah they were more disturbing than comforting. Nobody could remember this many things from young childhood. Certainly not holding a baby when he was two-and-a-half.

And yet, four or five times now he'd heard words clear as if they were being spoken in his ear. Some, like the ones he'd heard the day before, he hadn't wanted to share even though Mairi had pressed for details. They'd been too personal. Embarrassing, truth be told. He could still hear them.

You are different, Noah. You aren't like your brother or your sister. When you learn to open up and let people in, even a wee bit, you'll find you will be able to understand them and their souls better than most.

His face went warm in the dark. It *wasn't* real. And yet, he could hear her sweet brogue as if she spoke in his ears. His mother had known him inside and out the way only a mother could. The way his stepmother never had. He hadn't always been wary of closeness, although he'd always been quiet, content to watch and capture moments he could draw or carve rather than aspire to work in his father's ad agency or get a Ph.D.

Only after his mother—his best friend, his best playmate—had left him; after his best friend had moved away in middle school; and after the girl he'd believed was The One found the man she thought was The One and it wasn't Noah, had he decided it was easier to keep all but his closest family at friendly arm's length.

He'd never considered himself damaged or bitter, but he knew himself. His mother—or whatever dreams were putting those voices in his head—was wrong. He had no insight into people's souls. He liked people, but he sure as hell didn't understand them.

He listened again. Skye was still crying and, for the first time, concern blossomed. He had no idea how to tell if babies and mothers were okay. He lay still for several more minutes, working to slow his racing thoughts. A goat bleating. A beautiful, dark-haired woman in a small holding cell. Rain. A right-hand-drive car skimming along the highway beside a world-famous loch. A baby crying. His mother, with flowing auburn hair, rocking the baby on a big porch swing. *Sometimes she just needs to be outside, to smell the fresh air, to know she's not stuck in her crib...*

"Aaach!"

He threw off his covers and sat up in the dark. Enough. Fumbling for the lamp, he turned it on, filling the room with pale yellow light. He stood, stretched, and went for his jeans on the chair across the small room. He dragged them on, grabbed a fresh T-shirt from his not-yet-unpacked suitcase, and pulled the gray cotton over his head. It was an old favorite from a long-ago trip to the Rocky Mountains, soft and faded, an old friend he took everywhere.

The living room lights brightened the upstairs hallway enough that he could find the steps. Quiet cooing voices mixed with the baby's plaintive crying, and he followed the sounds to the main level. In the living room, he found Isla, tucked into the rose-colored armchair that seemed to be everyone's favorite comfort spot. She looked young and exhausted, her thick blonde braid frayed, her eyes bleary but wide and attentive. Noah followed her gaze and saw Mairi, arms full of crying baby, walking and bouncing, and crooning so softly he couldn't make out the tune.

His heart gave an unexpected flip. She looked up and smiled softly. "Oh hullo."

"Having a party without me?" he asked.

Isla's head swung around, and her wide eyes filled with consternation. "Noah! Oh, I'm sorry we woke you. Truly. We can't seem to comfort her."

"It's all right," he said. "I'm sorry she's unhappy."

He said the damnedest things these days.

"She's normally a very good baby," Isla said. "She'd been sleeping through the night the past couple of weeks. I hope she isn't sick."

"Now then, she doesn't have a fever," Mairi said. "She ate fine. She isn't scrunching up her wee legs or screaming outright. She's been away a few days, and her routine is all off, so she's annoyed with the world for the moment."

Noah rounded the sofa and sat, giving Isla an empathetic smile. "You look tired."

"Aye. Tired for four months. But it's all right, isn't it? I've a lot of help. Usually Ainslie gets up with me, but she's actually out on an emergency call."

"At three in the morning?" Noah glanced at the door as if that would bring her back.

"Bein' the only vet in forty square miles is as bad as being a new mother. She gets called out a fair few times like this. But look, Mairi is a saint, too."

He did look. Mairi bent over Skye with a calm demeanor that countered Isla's worried features. So young. Isla looked like a babe as well, willowy and wan. He'd never known how women did it—bore so much emotion.

"I have an idea," he said, shocking himself with the words and wishing he could take them back.

"Oh?" Mairi asked.

He swallowed, feeling foolish. "Take her out on the back porch. Sit in that big chair for a minute or three. Let her see the stars."

The women exchanged surprised looks, probably wondering if he'd gone to bed drunk. Then Mairi gave her shoulder a quick why-not lift, and Isla nodded.

"Grab that blanket beside you, it's chilly this time of the morning," Mairi said, and approached Noah with the fussing Skye.

When she held the baby out to him, he held up his hands. "Oh no, I don't do babies."

"Clearly you must; it was your idea. Give it a go. We haven't had any luck."

He was the master of crazy voices in his head, not of calming infants. He tried again to refuse, but suddenly Skye was in his arms, her little face red from crying, fists clenched like tiny walnuts, wails rising at the change of cradling arms beneath her.

"Here." Isla draped a second blanket over her daughter, and Noah stared helplessly.

They gave him no choice but to make his way slowly to the back door, the bundle he carried feeling as unstable as nitroglycerin, as priceless as a whatever-dynasty vase. Mairi opened the door, and he shot her a disgruntled glare. If she was going to follow him, she could as well do this. He felt like a grizzly carrying a hummingbird.

Then the crisp air enveloped him, and he couldn't help but lift his face toward the spot where the Highland peaks surrounded the vast Craigwarren property. A three-quarter moon gave the sky a silver cast, and he could make out a faint handful of stars. His first clear night since arriving. Slowly, he dared to adjust the baby's position in his arms and, awkward though it felt, he tilted her so she faced out and toward the moon. The breeze swirled, not cold but cooled by the night.

Skye gave a sharp cry and then gulped before redoubling her efforts.

"I don't blame you," he said. "Some nights suck. But...you aren't stuck in your crib at least. You can be outside in all this fresh air..."

The words from his imagination embarrassed him, but he didn't look at either Mairi or Isla to see if they'd heard. He tried bouncing his arms the way he'd seen baby-savvy people do, and Skye gave another gulping hiccup. Clumsily, he changed to a sway. In truth, she didn't weigh much more than a block of carving wood. And wasn't that kind of what she was? A new little human block, waiting for the world and the people around her to shape her?

She cried another minute but the intensity waned slowly and surely until, finally, Skye's wails turned to kitten-like sobs and then hiccups and then silence.

"I don't believe it," Isla whispered. "He's a miracle worker."

"I am not," he replied quietly. "I threatened to take her to the moon and back if she didn't stop crying."

"Did ye, aye?" Mairi laughed. "Pish, Noah. You're a natural."

"Got it from my mother." He meant it as a joke, but his chest tightened as the bizarre truth of it hit home.

They stayed on the deck, listening to the breeze in the trees, marveling at the stars, and watching Skye fall asleep. When the baby hadn't opened her eyes in long minutes and her little hands had relaxed into the folds of her blanket, Noah handed her back to Isla.

"Maybe she'll stay asleep now," he said.

"Go, grab what's left of the night," Mairi told her.

For the first time, Isla had tears in her eyes. "I can't thank you both enough. I usually handle her waking up fairly well, but I was lost tonight. I'm sorry I woke you."

"Isla, believe me. This is motherhood. Ups and downs, success and failure, thrills and depression. Sometimes all of those things in five minutes. You were perfect. It does take a village, you know. Truly it does."

"I have the best village." She smiled shyly at Noah. "Guess my girl has two uncles now. Thanks again."

"Nothing to thank me for. Guess Skye and I both like the night air."

"You coming, too?" Isla asked.

"Go ahead," Noah said to Mairi. "I'm going to fight the jetlag down here for a few minutes."

"I thought I'd make some tea to help put me back to sleep," she said. "I'm happy to make two cups."

Tea at three-thirty in the morning was a step too far into his sensitive side for this evening. He was freaked enough by all the night whisperings and emotional baby bonding.

"I'm good," he said. "But I'll keep you company while you drink it. Maybe I'll advance the progress of Ella's kelpie for a few minutes."

They sent Isla and Skye to bed, and while Mairi brewed her chamomile, Noah retrieved his cherrywood and carving knives. When he sat on the sofa ready to work, Mairi sat beside him, cupping her steaming mug. Her nearness warmed him as much as any hot drink would have, and he relaxed into his task, loving the familiar feel of the wood, reveling in knowing the bite of his blade was true and exactly where he wanted it. This task—this art—he *could* control.

"You were amazing," she said.

"I wasn't. I went with the flow. I don't plan to take up baby care anytime soon."

"Such a curmudgeon."

"Now you're getting it." He smiled.

"I learn more about you every time we're together, and I'm more convinced than ever your marketing department needs to revamp its promos of you. You're okay, Mr. Portman."

"Huh," he grunted, and chiseled away a large section at the kelpie's throat. "I'll have a word with them. Wouldn't expect much, though. I get by fine on this reputation. And for the record, I think you're okay, too, Mrs. MacDonald."

She yawned and took a two-handed sip of her tea, then settled back with a contented-cat smile and curled her legs beneath her. He waited for her next topic of conversation, but she stared almost dreamily across the room without a word. After several more sips, she stretched to set her mug on an end table and leaned her head back on the cushions.

"We should go to bed," she sighed.

"I suppose." He studied his carving, pleased with the way the head was emerging. It looked as he'd wanted, like a refined version of Ella's drawing. "Go ahead. Just a little more and I'll go, too."

"Mmmm. I'll wait."

He roughed out the shape of Eachann's front legs, and as he shaved thick curls from along the line of what would be the fish tail, he felt the weight of Mairi's head slip onto his left shoulder.

A thread of awareness wove through him and he gazed at her sleeping form. Adjusting the wood in his left hand so he could carve on without disturbing her, he finished shaping the curl and thickness of the tail and then, finally, put the carving on the table next to him, wrapped the sharp knife into its leather pouch, and started to wake Mairi.

He stopped instead, reluctant to move.

Carefully, he shifted until Mairi lay on her side, her head in his lap. He snugged himself into the sofa corner and drew Catrione's thick tartan wool throw off the cushion backs, draped it over Mairi, and leaned back, resting his arm across her shoulders. He closed his eyes...and the next thing he knew, someone was shaking him gently awake.

"Noah?" the voice whispered, and he squinted one eye open. The shadowy figure morphed into Ainslie. "It's nearly five in the morning. What are you two doing here?"

He'd sunk deep into the cushions and his neck was stiff. Mairi hadn't moved.

"Hey there." He yawned. "Long story. Crying babies and jetlag. Wait, are you just getting home?"

"Aye. It was a shite night. But a little girl's pony is likely going to be okay, so I'll take it. Did you have a tough night with Skye?"

"Nothing a little stargazing couldn't fix."

"I'm too tired to ask. And I'm too tired to ask how all this came about." She waved at Mairi still snoring delicately on his lap. "Move upstairs or not. I'm off to get two hours of sleep and meet you in the cottage."

"Don't you dare. No demolition for you until you have at least three hours."

She grinned. "Well, you aren't going to suck at bein' a boss, are you?"

"Hah. Just don't let this happen again."

"Goodnight, Noah. Goodnight, Mairi."

At that, his sleeping beauty stirred for the first time. "Hmmm? What?" she murmured.

"Time to get up and head down to the cottage," he whispered.

"Oh, you are evil." Ainslie waved. "You're on your own."

"Get up?" Mairi scrambled to sit and blinked furiously. "It's dark. What happened?"

"Aww, Mairi. We slept together for the first time. I'm nothing special, but it hurts you don't remember."

She swiveled her head back and forth, focusing on the room, gaining her bearings. "We fell asleep here?"

"Like Skye looking at the stars. Ainslie woke us."

"I'm so sorry."

"Stop it. Why are you sorry? I was tired, too. Now we can drag ourselves upstairs and get a couple more hours."

"We don't have to go to the cottage yet?"

He laughed. "No. Come on."

"I was pretty comfortable right here."

"Okay, but I was a little cramped, so if we stay here, I'm on top."

"Chauvinist. What if I want to be on top?"

The whole joke made him happy—and also more than a little uncomfortable, in more ways than one. He stood, afraid if he did stay, he'd kiss her like he was suddenly imagining doing. Nothing but the result of strange dreams, interrupted sleep, and exhaustion, he promised himself, then clasped her hand and pulled her up.

"Next time," he said. "For now, it's separate beds. There are children in this house."

"Oh boy, do I remember. Well, thanks for the nap. Next time I'll tone down the excitement."

"No, it was good. Best time I've had in ages."

If only she knew how close to the truth that was.

Noah got the desperate idea to build Juliet a temporary pen right in the cottage's back garden, the moment he found her grazing fitfully in the yard later that morning as if awaiting his arrival. When she saw him, her call of genuine joy was unmistakable, and her charge was fast but no longer intimidating. Noah spent a full minute petting her and telling her in the nicest possible voice what a horrible goat she was, and how he didn't have time to keep fixing her dumb pen. After the attention, she went back to grazing but followed him or the sound of his voice wherever he went.

Innis arrived to help first, and snapped his fingers in inspiration as soon as Noah told him his idea for containing Juliet. From the back of a gardening shed near the main house, he unearthed a roll of chicken wire fencing, a dozen slender, metal electric wire fence posts, and a spool of narrow-gauge wire.

"Years ago, Cat kept chickens," he said. "We saved this much. It should do."

In half an hour, they'd erected a ten-foot circular pen next to the rear door, complete with a makeshift gate, all but invisible unless a person knew where to look for the wire twists keeping it closed. Juliet followed Noah willingly into her new play yard, found the mound of hay dropped for her and sniffed at the heavy rubber horse ball stolen from the donkeys' paddock. Noah took another minute to stroke and praise her before letting himself out the gate.

"All right, Dumb Juliet," he said. "I don't know why I'm indulging you, but this is a crazy place and you're living proof. Now I'm right inside, I'll visit when I can, and I'll leave the door open if it doesn't rain. Welcome to goat daycare."

She didn't look up when he left her. An auspicious start.

By ten o'clock, everyone was in the cottage, swinging sledgehammers, pulling nails, toting old boards outside, and unhooking the ancient appliances. The weather held, the back door stayed open, the goat made no attempt to escape, and Noah marveled at the difference a day made. Yesterday he'd been staring at a project he'd half feared would never get started. By early afternoon, two walls had been demolished and removed, the old stove and under-counter refrigerator had been lugged outside, and Innis had contacted a refuse company who said they could have a dumpster in place after the upcoming weekend.

The good luck even extended to their meeting with Hamish Fletcher, the stone expert, who appeared as promised and poked and prodded the exterior walls, the fireplace, and the spot where Noah wanted to add a window, with the scrutiny of a surgeon pinpointing where the incisions needed to be made.

"Aye, she's a beaut of an auld huis isn't she?" Fletcher said when he'd taken all his notes. The man was easily sixties, with a mustache that flowed into old-fashioned muttonchops from beneath a straight, aquiline nose. His sharp brown eyes missed no detail, and he actually wore a brown canvas utilitarian kilt. It had no plaid pattern but bore a full complement of pleats and leather strap buckles at the hip. With it, he wore a plain brown T-shirt and bulky socks, slouched over thick-soled work boots.

"I have one like that," Ewan whispered.

"The skirt?"

"Yup—but don't say that out loud, you'll get a lecture on kilts. It took me a while, but I've worn it hiking several times. Worn the tartan one twice. They're amazingly comfortable."

"So I've heard." Noah curled his lip. "Just don't bend over when I'm around."

His brother shrugged. "Commando isn't required."

"Good to know."

"You'll get yours for the wedding."

"Oh, gosh." Noah batted his eyes. "Something wonderful to look forward to. And the girls are wearing tuxedos, right?"

Ewan slugged him lightly in the arm. "I'd hit you harder, but I said the same things when I was new."

"You're still new."

After nearly half an hour of inspection, Hamish Fletcher met them in the cottage at the little table. His paper tablet was filled with notes, and he tapped the top page with the end of his pen.

"So," he began. "Lots of work, as ye know, but not beyond repair. There's a fair amount of mortar deterioration, but we can repoint it without replacing those stones. I've found a few stairstep cracks—happens when the foundation settles—but there's no bowing or foundation failure yet, though we may need to reinforce the back sou'west corner. I don't think there's a need for any tear-down or major rebuilding, unless we run into something underground I can't see.

"There are about a dozen stones along the back that have spalled...the face has flaked off," he explained, when Noah knotted his brow in confusion. "Could be a bit of cracking let water in. If it's not serious, we can patch or replace the stones. A bit of moss growing in the same places. All repairable.

"Far as fireplace in here goes, the chimney needs a bit o' fixin' and I'd consider replacin' the stone flue with a modern insert—safer. But, all-in-all, for a cottage over a hundred, this auld girl's in bonny condition. Built by a master in her day."

"It's as good a report as we could hope for," Noah said. "First question. Can you start work and get it finished in a little over three weeks?"

He pursed his lips and thought. "We could. Just. Assuming it doesnae rain every day."

Ewan laughed. "Well, that's a gamble we all have to take, isn't it? How about a rough cost estimate? I understand it would be a pure guess, but we'd have a vague idea."

"Repointing is approximately eight or nine pounds per square foot. Replacing stones a bit more. With the fireplace, the outside walls, the spots inside and the new windae. I'm guessing we'll be in the neighborhood of twenty-five hundred pounds. Maybe less."

Noah let out a long breath, but Ewan didn't blink. "Close to what my research showed. You said you don't do slate roofing?"

"Nae, don't touch it any longer. Too heavy for the dodgy back. Best slate tile man I know is actually in Edinburgh these days. I can give you his number if it's of interest."

"Please," Ewan said. "I've one other name. I'll check with them both. It may be cost prohibitive."

Hamish Fletcher nodded. "Cost a wee fortune those roofs. But they'll last you a hundred years if you care for 'em."

He promised to have an official quote on the stonework by the next day. If it was satisfactory, he could start work the following week. His positive assessment was only made better by Catrione's arrival with a lunch feast of cold meats, fresh bread, a brick of sharp cheddar, and a big serving bowl filled with fresh fruit.

"And if you're good, I've a pretty little sponge cake for a treat," she said. "Still baking but done soon."

Noah knew the day was charmed when the cake arrived, along with Great Aunt Cairstine. At first he tensed when he saw her strolling down the drive with Cat; he dreaded dealing with his cousin even when things were going well. Cairstine, however, hugged him warmly and apologized for her son not being with her.

"Callum is in Aberdeen for the week," she said. "He knows how much work this is going to be, and he'll be willing to help when he's back."

"Thank you, Aunt Cairstine. I'll definitely let him know when we need him," Noah said, with no intention of letting him know anything. "We've two other workers coming next week as well."

"You're off the hook with your cousin." Mairi sidled beside him as Cairstine bent over the cake with Cat. Her whisper in his ear sent a rain of gooseflesh down his spine.

"For an entire week," he agreed. "It's a gift."

"Never liked old Callum much," she said. "Utter twonk, so self-confident every minute. You've gotten plenty done without him."

"*We've* gotten it done. And by the time he's back, we'll have the wall studs in place and he'll have no say in the configuration of the rooms. After that, Ewan can deal with his input."

"Once more, I'm impressed. You do know what you're doing. It's been fun being on your crew."

The compliment warmed him. He liked recognition as well as the next guy, but from Mairi it felt like a knighthood.

Damn. Knights again.

"That's nice of you. Let's see if that holds up when we get closer to the deadline. I might be a twonk, too."

"You could never. Today is a good omen. I think you're not only going to pull this off but it's going to go smooth as silk."

His stomach gave a nervous twist and he placed a finger against her lips and tried not to notice the softness against his skin.

"Shhh," he said. "Don't jinx it."

CHAPTER SIXTEEN

Through the weekend and into Monday, Mairi did worry Noah was right and her breezy prediction would jinx the project, but it didn't seem to be so. In a first indication they were off to a successful start, Juliet remained in her round pen. Then, to Mairi's delight, Ella adopted the job of official water girl, ferrying drinks and snacks from house to cottage in an ancient wheelbarrow Innis repainted for her in a fresh, cheery orange. The task kept her from wandering off—a relief that left Mairi free to work inside the cottage.

By the Monday afternoon, Hamish Fletcher had dispatched a crew to start the stonework, Noah had booked two men to bid on repairing the roof and—best of all—Bing and Bob joined the crew.

They were actually Gerry and Danny, the Smith cousins. Only twenty, they were best friends but yin and yang. Hilarious Gerry, with a physique like a Christmas snowman and antics that made it hard to tell whether he was simply a goof or really two bubbles short of level, was such fun, nobody cared that his strength was definitely stepping and fetching, not leading.

Danny, on the other hand, the straight man to his cousin but equally gregarious, had a head for problem-solving and a voice for singing. From his first day, he'd serenaded them with everything from "Loch Lomond" to The Proclaimers' "I'm Gonna Be." But his favorite song catalogue was The Beatles, and his favorite song turned out to be "Ob-La-Di, Ob-La-Da," which took no time to become a permanent earworm.

"We're in one of those old Hope and Crosby 'Road to' movies. *The Road to Kilt Land*," Noah had complained after their first hour of one singing. "Right there we have Bob." He'd pointed to Gerry and then Danny. "You're Bing."

The boys had no idea what the reference meant, but they good-naturedly accepted the teasing nicknames, and by the end of the day, nobody remembered their real ones.

By Tuesday dinnertime, the new bedroom was framed in, the kitchen wall had been moved, the floor was swept and every inch of the little cottage was cleared, and the support beam for the new loft was ready to be hung next morning. No jinx. No setbacks.

Mairi sat at the dinner table with the rest of her temporarily adopted family, exhausted but exhilarated as they all were. She'd found solace the past five days in lifting and holding and carrying until her limbs and back ached. The labor filled her thoughts with things other than her mother, brother, and lack of a paying job. Best of all, she got to work with Noah. She didn't tell him how uplifting his calm words were, or how much peace she got from his quiet smiles, but she took those gifts gratefully and drew strength from them the few times she did panic about her brother or the fact that her mother hadn't called.

"You all must be ready to take a vacation. The inside of our wee cottage looks quite amazing." Catrione passed a platter laden with pork chops to Noah, who started right off with two thick pieces.

"No vacations." He laughed. "I can't afford to stop being a tyrant overseer now. We're on a roll. But it looks good, doesn't it?"

"I knew you were the one to call," Ewan said, two chops filling his own plate.

"Don't thank me yet. There's a long way to go."

"Still, I can see it," Mairi said. "Simple but functional. Wait until we get some coral-colored tile in that kitchen and bathroom and it will all pop."

"There it is," Noah rolled his eyes. "The takeover starts and there's not even wallboard installed yet."

"Wasn't born yesterday, was I? If I say things often enough, by the time you're ready for finishing touches, you'll be so sick of me you'll give in to make me stop."

Ainslie lifted her glass of wine. "This is why we've always been friends. You're carrying our mutual vision forward since I can't always be there when I'd like."

"We're outnumbered, man," Ewan said. "Give in gracefully and things will go a lot smoother."

Mairi loved the way Noah played his role as pessimistic curmudgeon. He harrumphed like a put-upon husband, but he never lost the twinkle in his eye. She wasn't sure he knew it was there, but this week it had flared more often—within a smile of satisfaction when a floor joist fit perfectly, or when they deemed the wooden plank flooring was sturdy and level enough that refinishing it was not only cost effective but desirable.

"I knew better than to let girls into this club, but I did it anyway," he said. "Guess it's on me."

"You'll be happy in the end," Mairi promised, patting his arm. "Promise."

They all tucked into dinner, bantering happily, and were beginning to groan about over-full bellies when the front door bell rang. Innis took his napkin from his lap and frowned.

"The only one who always comes at dinnertime is Callum. If he's back in town…"

Ewan stood to answer the door, and they all heard the agitated voice that greeted him.

"Is the other Mr. Portman here? He needs to come. Quick as you please."

"He's here. What's wrong?"

Noah jumped from his seat as if spring-loaded and rushed from the dining room. Mairi, Ainslie, and Catrione all went silent with immediate concern. Ella, astute enough to know when the atmosphere had changed from upbeat to worried, stared with wide eyes when Innis followed Noah.

"Is everything okay, Mama?"

"I'm sure it is," she replied, her heart thundering.

"Bing?" She heard Noah's calm question.

"It's a roof truss," he said. "I went back into the cottage to get my water bottle and hat, and the truss is near broke in splinters. I…I don't know what happened but you need to come look."

"Has anything collapsed?" Noah asked, still calm.

"Not that I saw," the boy replied. "But it doesnae look good."

"Where's Bob?"

"He's in the doorway watchin' it. Said he wanted to be able to describe it if anything happened."

"Of course he is," Noah said. "Okay, let me get a jacket, the wind's come up. Run down ahead of us. Make sure your cousin is nowhere near the problem. If something has weakened, I don't want him underneath it."

"He's not Einstein, but he does love livin'," Bing said. "I'm guessin' he's well awa'."

Mairi's stomach knotted with fierce worry. She caught Ainslie's eyes and though neither said anything, they both nodded.

"We have to go along and see what's happening," Ainslie said. "We've invested in this, too."

"I want to see," Ella said.

"Absolutely not this time," Mairi said. "Not because you don't deserve to, you worked hard all this week, but because it really could be dangerous. Later, if it's safe, I'll take you down and help with your barn chores."

For once, her daughter didn't argue her case, but her eyes lost none of their growing fear. Mairi beckoned for her, held her to her in a fierce hug and kissed her head.

"You don't have to worry, my sweet. Everyone will be very careful. We might have to get someone out to fix the roof quickly, right?"

Ella clung to her, but her slender little body relaxed. "I hope it's just the roof."

"Or a saggy old board. It's a good thing Bing and Bob noticed it. They're good helpers."

Ella pulled away then, smiling at last. "I like Bing and Bob. They're funny. They sing funny songs."

"That they do."

It wasn't a full-on disaster, but it was well on its way to becoming one. Exactly as Bing had described, one of the old timber roof trusses had split. It bowed downward like a splintered twig beneath the slate tiles in the back of the cottage. It still held its section of roof but it wasn't clear what would happen if it broke. Perhaps nothing, or perhaps there'd be a domino effect and the entire roof would crash into the new framing.

"The luck couldn't hold forever," Noah said.

"I don't know why not. We deserved good luck," Ewan groused. "I was hoping we'd get by replacing only a third of the slate. I don't see how that's possible now."

"Yeah." Noah rubbed the back of his neck as he stared up.

"Why all of a sudden now?" Mairi asked. "This has been standing for better than a hundred years."

Noah shook his head. "We've done a lot of pounding and shifting of things in this space. It's the same principle as vibrations in a mountain snow wall. The wrong frequency causes an avalanche. I truly worry this is a potential avalanche."

"That's so not good," Ainslie said, her voice thick with emotion.

"It's a given we don't work in here until the roofing experts look at this." Noah's mouth tightened painfully as if the import finally hit him fully. He growled out curse. "This is exactly what we don't have time for."

Mairi wanted to hug him the way she'd hugged Ella and chase away his worry as easily as she had her little girl's. But adult worries weren't kid worries, and she knew a hug couldn't fix his time crunch fears. Still, she wished.

Ewan clapped a hand to his brother's shoulder. "Hey, we knew we had to take time to talk to the roof guy anyway. We'll spend the morning with him and then we've got plenty to do. It's not too early to get fixtures and appliances ordered. We won't waste any time."

"I know."

"There's nothing more we can do tonight. Let's brace the broken truss with a beam and that's good enough."

Mairi stepped beside Noah and surreptitiously took his hand. It took a few seconds, but his fingers responded, slowly squeezing around hers. A quicksilver shiver dove for her toes.

"Come and help Ella and me with chores," she said. "Juliet's been a very good girl this week. She'd not be turning down a bit of a scratch from her true love."

He looked down at her, dark amusement replacing the unhappiness in his eyes. "You have a distressingly wicked streak."

She smiled innocently. "Aye, but Juliet will thank me."

Juliet seemed more than grateful as she followed Noah and Ella around the barn as if they had clover and sweet treats dripping from their pockets. Mairi had no reasonable explanation as to why the ridiculous goat had taken such a shine to Noah, but if it was annoying to him, it was endearing to watch. His grousing about the animal had diminished as her penchant for charging him waned. She seemed content now to be his shadow, and he mostly ignored her except for the absent strokes he bestowed when they stopped at a pen or a feed pan.

Ella was no less in heaven than Juliet, surrounded by animals and two adults who were a captive audience. She skipped through her tasks, chattering and baby-talking to each animal as she closed it in its pen for the night. The whole exercise left Mairi the closest she'd been to content since leaving Glasgow. Pretending this was all normal life—revamping a cottage, trekking nightly to the barn, watching Ella blossom and show off for a father-type figure who actually treated her like the special kid she was—gave her a much-needed moment of fantasy. For Ella, it was kelpies, fairies, and brownies. For Mairi, it was an illusion of caring family. It wasn't real. But it was nice to imagine.

Darkness hadn't yet fallen when they locked up the barn, but gray clouds filled the sky and the brisk breeze smelled like rain.

"When I go to school after next week, it won't stay light very long anymore," Ella said. "I won't be able to go visit Eachann except on weekends."

"School starts already?" Noah asked.

"In a week." For the first time in several days, Mairi wasn't able to push back the sadness that scooped out a hollow, empty hole in her stomach over the loss of her own classroom full of students on the first day of school. Were her life not a comedy of errors, she'd be in her room already, giving it last-minute touches and reading her students' names over and over to familiarize herself with them even before they met.

She'd meant to keep in touch with Christine Sullivan at Westmuir, but she hadn't had the heart to face rejection yet again.

Feckin' Aiden. Where was he?

"Hey, you okay?" Noah's quiet voice brought her back.

"Aye, fine." She offered a small smile and then shook her head. "I was thinking how much I'll miss teaching."

"It's unfair," he said.

"'Tis that. But it's life."

"Mama would have been my teacher!" Ella said.

"Right. You told me that before, didn't you?" Noah replied. "I'm sorry."

"Can we please go to the loch because it's still light? I want to leave Eachann a treat." Ella switched subject direction like one of the leaves flying from the surrounding trees. She reached into the front pocket of her jeans and, twisting her wrist in a scooping motion, pulled out a generous handful of Fenella and Ailish's grain.

"Ella!" Mairi tried to sound stern, but sputters gave her away. The girl knew all the angles.

"I want to tell him that I have to go to school and I won't see him much. He'll be lonely."

"Ella, y'wee dreamer. That beastie, if he's all you say, is nae a normal kelpie. He shouldn't miss visits from a sweet girl—he should be stalkin' you. You should be deathly afraid of him."

She winked at Noah, who scrunched his eyes closed in disbelief. "These stories," he said.

"I'm not afraid. All the fae at Craigwarren are friendly. Most of them don't act like they do in the wild because they like it here. Eachann has a relative, though. An *each uisge* who lives in a much bigger loch. He's very mean. I wouldn't ride him. He would drown me properly."

Mairi rolled her eyes at Noah. "Sorry," she said. "I really will get you a book one of these days."

He laughed. "I guess an...'*aach ooshka*,'" he tried mimicking the words with minimal success, "must be something worse than a kelpie?"

"It's another type of water horse. Can turn into a handsome man and entice girls to a watery grave. Or, if you ride one, your hands will stick to its mane and, same fate. Kelpies have lots of legends associated with them."

"Unbelievable."

She waved a hand. "Not to worry. Evidently our kelpie has amended his ways."

"Well that's a relief."

The rain started halfway back to the house. It drizzled at first, but just before they reached the back porch the heavens broke open. Squealing and laughing, Ella made it in the door first, and Noah gallantly held the door for Mairi. They were nearly drenched when they stood in the kitchen.

"Oh, darlin' girl," Mairi said. "I think Eachann is going to have to wait for his treat. We'll plan on it tomorrow."

Ella scrunched her elfin features in thought and finally nodded.

"Hullo, my three." Catrione met them with towels and distributed them. "It's turned into a good night not to work. I think you should all take baths and showers and get warmed up."

"Sounds perfect," Mairi said. "Ella and I will do that. Then I'm coming down for a dram and good company."

"Or," Catrione beamed. "I can give Ella her bath. We just gave wee Skye hers. You two can get dry and go out on the town to warm up. Have your wee dram at the Black Thistle. It'll do you both good to get away from here. Fill the well for the morrow. Noah's had nae time at all to see any of the town."

Mairi shrugged and looked to Noah.

"Random idea," he said.

"Not really," Catrione said. "Ainslie is out on a call. Ewan actually went with her—he does that now and again so she doesn't have to drive the back roads alone in the dark. Brilliant boy. They may stop by town for a fortifying pint themselves."

"Oh, let's go." Mairi grinned. "Ella, you'd be okay with Aunt Cat and Isla?"

"Can I hold Skye?"

"If she's still awake, aye, of course."

"Remember, Mama, we have to go visit Eachann before we go shopping in Edinburgh."

Mairi's skin blanched. *Edinburgh. Well shite.* She'd forgotten all about the promised special trip for new school shoes and a school bag and a grown-up lunch in New Town. She drew in a breath to hide her forgetfulness. She'd figure it out, even though, at the moment, thinking of Edinburgh forced her to think of Aiden.

"That's right," she said. "We'll make plans tomorrow."

"Come along, my pretty girl," Cat said, and smiled at Mairi. "You two do what you wish. We'll be fine."

Noah withstood Mairi's pleading eyes for a long minute before giving in. She knew he wasn't a lover of crowds, but Catrione was right. He should see a little local color. It was a Tuesday; the place wouldn't be horribly crowded.

"The fact that there will be no lovesick goats and no *Eachann-ooshkas* are the clinchers," he said. "They both kind of scare me."

She patted his arm. "No shame in that. An immersive course in Scottish mythology with Ella MacDonald is a lot for a beginner."

***

The Black Thistle was a good-sized pub, uncrowded on a weeknight. Noah had expected a stereotyped dark and moody British pub house, but this one was far from a cliché, with walls done in honey-colored oak wainscoting and sky blue walls, and a hefty horseshoe-shaped bar, its wood surface well-worn, sporting at least two dozen gleaming gold tap handles lined along the front edge. At the open end of the horseshoe, fifty Scotch bottles were arranged like regimental soldiers on four glass shelves. Glasses hung from wooden racks. Bottles of liquor and mixers lived in an open cabinet beneath the whiskies.

Noah liked the atmosphere immediately and liked it even better when Mairi pointed to a table in a far corner with a view of the entire pub.

"This is nice," he said once they'd seated themselves. "Newer than I expected. Although I don't know why I expected anything in particular."

"Been around quite a while but got a re-do ten years ago or so, I understand. I've only been here once. Ainslie says it's a local favorite, not a tourist destination."

He had to admit it was nice to get away. Since his arrival, it seemed every move he'd made had been in response to a crisis or a deadline. Though neither had disappeared, here he had no choice but to set them aside. Slowly his shoulders lowered, his spine relaxed against the back of his chair, and his racing brain—until now halted only by Ella's talk of things fantastical—slowed on its own.

"What'll you have?" she asked. "First round's on me. A thanks for bein' that patient with Ella."

"Patient?" Noah thought about the word, surprised. He'd never considered patience something he needed with Ella. He didn't understand her, but she did intrigue him. "She makes me laugh. It's no big deal."

"That's sweet of you, but as I've admitted before, the obsession with all things mythological is wearin' even on me. I often ask myself why she couldn't be interested in computers or dragons or Disney princesses."

"Would it matter? I think she'd talk our ears off about whatever she liked. And are kelpies that much different than dragons?"

"As usual, words of wisdom from the master builder. You're right. I just don't want her to annoy you. She'll be in school next week and we'll get a break."

"She doesn't annoy me. And don't lie, you'll miss her."

"Of course I will. Still, even Eachann will be glad of a rest."

He had to laugh at the image of a half horse, half fish resting on the bottom of a lake with a relieved smile on its face. "It'll definitely be quieter. What did she mean about going to Edinburgh?"

Mairi let a groan slip free and dropped her head to her forearms folded on the table. "I promised to take her shopping before school. We don't really need clothes because of school uniforms, but she needs good school shoes and trainers, socks and underthings." She lifted her head. "Before all the shite rained down, I thought it would be a nice outing for us, maybe even for a couple of days. Now, I don't know when I'll fit it in. Plus there's the whole..."

She hesitated and Noah covered her hands with his. "Your brother is there."

"I don't know that for sure, and Edinburgh is huge. I'd never accidentally run into him. Still, I'd be watchin' over my shoulder the whole time."

"Whatever you decide, don't skip this because of work on the cottage. You can take time for your daughter—that's most important."

"Thank you."

"Besides, you have no personal reason to be invested in the renovation. You're a guest here."

"But one they're not letting pay her way. I buy food. I help with housework. That's all I've been able to do. And they've been so wonderful."

"I'm starting to see how Ewan got hooked. These people treat me as if they've known me my entire life."

"In many ways, they have. You should have seen your great-aunt getting ready for your arrival. You were far more important than this crazy semi-royal couple coming for their honeymoon."

Noah's heart warmed even as he laughed at the whole ludicrous situation.

"Can you believe that story? The princess and the sailor? Like I stumbled into a cartoon."

"It's kind of far-fetched. Still, I looked the sailor up, and it's all true. Past scandal, six years ago. The Dutch people adore him, but the family of the sailor who died still blame him. This marriage is actually making headlines."

"Okay, time for that drink." Noah laughed.

"I say Scotch to start. Do you know what you like?"

"Anything."

"Peaty? Mild?"

"Surprise me."

"Got just the thing."

He watched her walk to the bar, tall, swaying in a perfect, graceful combination of confidence and femininity. A wave of rare contentment washed over him. He liked her. He liked even more being with her, and that hadn't happened with another person in a very long time. It had been unnerving him the entire past week as he'd tried to keep from getting too close, but she wasn't overly flirty or clingy or…frightening. She'd become a friend. And if she was a particularly attractive friend, well, he'd take that benefit. Tonight, he let himself be unafraid of Mairi MacDonald.

"Laphroaig," she said proudly as she set his glass before him. "Have you had it?"

"Don't think so." He ran the glass under his nose. It smelled like a campfire, and he laughed. "A little smoky?"

She wiggled her brows and he sipped. The smoke exploded against his tastebuds and he choked while his eyes started to water. Then the rich, oaky amber spread across his tongue, ending with salty vanilla. He'd never tasted anything that complex.

"Wow," he said. "Is this one you like?" He pointed to her glass.

"Nae, not a fan of the smoky Islay whiskies. I like a light, smooth Speyside or Highland Scotch. But?"

"You know, I do like it," he said.

"You must be a true Scotsman."

He started to deny it, but caught himself. He supposed he was. Half Scottish anyway.

By the third sip, he was ready to claim his heritage, and by the time he'd finished three-quarters of the glass, the Scotch had freed his tongue and allowed words to flow as easily between him and Mairi as rain down the hillsides outside Craigwarren house. Music, books, movies, the amount of capital Ewan had to be laying out for the cottage...one subject morphed effortlessly into the next. They avoided the serious topics that had been their mainstays and let people-watching serve as entertainment.

Noah got round two: dark, nutty, imported porters this time, and they drank more slowly, letting the alcohol lead them on engrossing, drifting conversations. They forgot to people watch. Noah found he was perfectly happy watching nothing but Mairi's face.

In his growing haze of relaxation and happiness, he studied her waves of thick black hair and wondered what it would feel like to the touch, if it would be as weighty in his fingers as it looked. Fascinated, he studied the way her full lips rounded around her sweetly accented words, and her eyes, as rare a blue as a rainless Scottish sky, mesmerized him.

He didn't realize how completely he'd lost himself until a deep, hearty voice interrupted their intimacy from ten feet away.

"Well, if it isn't the newest of my newfound cousins. And with an old friend of mine, no less. Noah. Mairi. I'm surprised to see you both here on a work night."

The unwelcome voice dragged him from peaceful contentment to disorienting reality. As Callum approached and Mairi's happy laugh disappeared along with the warmth in her eyes, Noah's resentment blossomed. It was unreasonable. Callum had done nothing to warrant anger, and yet the swagger he brought with him to the table fueled Noah's irritation.

"So. Callum. You're back."

"I am." He pulled out an empty chair and sat without invitation. Noah didn't miss Mairi's glower. "I hear good progress has been made on the gardener's cottage. A braw start, Mum says. But I also heard you've been burning the midnight oil since you haven't much time. Having a deserved night out?"

Somehow, he made the question sound anything but complimentary.

"Well deserved." Noah held his gaze to emphasize the words. "We've a good crew."

He refused to give Callum any details. He didn't trust the man's attitude. Beneath the table, Mairi set a hand on his thigh in a touch of solidarity and welcome reassurance that Callum hadn't broken the connection they'd started to make.

"Ah, the crew. I heard you took on those two Smith boys. I'd keep a right close eye on those two weapons if I were you. They have a reputation for taking very little in their lives seriously. If you want quality work, I can find you better."

Genuine anger flared in Mairi's eyes. "They're lovely boys, Callum," she said. "I'll not have you sayin' another word."

"Just offering my expertise." He shrugged as if her admonishment meant nothing. "It's your project."

"Too right it is," she snapped.

Noah was almost proud of the anger that he'd learned firsthand could ignite like flash powder when Mairi was riled, but he calmed her with a touch to the middle of her back, where he rubbed a small, gentle circle over her spine.

"What else can we do for you, Callum? Buy you a drink?"

Mairi scowled, but he simply waited—and was surprised by the next voice he heard.

"Yes! Let us buy you a drink, Callum. I hadn't heard there was to be a family reunion."

Noah had never been so happy to see his brother. Mairi relaxed beneath his touch and lost her frown when Ainslie rounded the table to give her a hug.

"Glad to see you're back from bonnie Aberdeen, cousin," Ewan said.

"I'm glad you all missed me," Callum retorted.

"Och, nobody ever misses you." Ainslie slapped a hand on Callum's shoulder. "Life is much bigger and louder when you return."

Callum ignored her. "A drink then," he agreed. "I can hear from the main man's own mouth how things are going at the family project and offer my help. I'll be there on the morrow. Help keep an eye on your two farmhands. One of 'em at least has trouble tellin' two ends of a heifer apart."

Mairi's chair nearly fell backward from the force of her pushing it back and charging to her feet. "Didn't I tell you there wasn't to be another word about those lads?"

"Ho well! Here's a lass hasn't lost her spunk over the years." Callum arched his brows suggestively. "Gotta love a woman who's grown into her passion."

Mairi pierced him with unadulterated fury, and Noah stiffened at the man's rude cockiness.

"That's enough, Callum," he said. "Let a good beer keep your mouth quiet now." Mairi sat, and he took her hand. "Ignore him."

"And a valiant defender. I never realized how dull it was around here without family." Callum sat back again. "Rather than you buy me a drink, the next round is mine. Then I'll be on my way. I was just passin' through after a meeting. Been a long week, but I've time on my hands now. Tell me when to show up."

"Kind of you," Ewan said. "But not tomorrow. There's a broken truss, and roofers are coming. We won't be in the cottage."

"Oh no. Roof problems are serious. And expensive." He quirked a brow and gave the tiniest confident lift of his chin. "Remember, I've got access to money and more expertise than you currently have."

"We won't be needing your money," Ewan said. "Now behave yourself and order that round you promised."

CHAPTER SEVENTEEN

Mairi tossed beneath her bed covers all night, jarred by the evening's events and emotions, and unsoothed by the rain driving against the roof. Rain normally relaxed her better than any lullaby, but tonight it only agitated the company of butterflies in her stomach and the jumping nerves everywhere else.

She didn't know what to make of the evening at the pub. She'd been completely at ease and comfortable with Noah before Callum, the feckin' rocket, had blown in. Then her emotions had mutinied. She didn't know whether to admire the Portman brothers for their calm handling of their cousin or to smack them for it. Callum wasn't going to change—why should Ewan keep appeasing him? Why was Noah completely passive with him?

Not that she'd done herself proud, yelling at him like he was the PE class bully. She never lost her cool with students though, truth to tell, seven-year-olds weren't as annoying as Callum MacTavish.

She smacked her pillow with a fist berating herself for her own hypocrisy. She hadn't done any better with her mother or brother and made just as many allowances for her family.

She sat up, raised her knees, and wrapped them with her arms. The rain drummed like a military tattoo on the roof, the walls, the ground outside. Her smart watch read 4:00 a.m. Remembering Noah's composure, she buried her face in her blanketed knees.

Why wouldn't the man simply leave her head? She'd known him barely two weeks and he was the opposite of everything she'd ever imagined wanting in a partner: homebound, quiet, conflict averse, prone to telling her to be calm… But was that *really* what she didn't want? With James, she'd had the adventure-loving, passionate mate. That had gotten her nothing but heartbreak. Noah was steady, talented, brilliant. He complimented her. He laughed with her. He was wonderful with her daughter.

He sent shivers through her entire body simply by holding her hand. By—she nearly melted back into her bed with the memory—rubbing her back like she was something precious. And even by telling Callum to let a beer close his mouth when the man had insulted her. By making her wonder desperately, like a schoolgirl with a crush on someone well out of her league, what it would be like to kiss him.

Damn it, she wanted to kiss him—at least to try it. It had been ages since she'd had such a desire. But he was completely out of reach. He made it clear he wanted no entanglements, that relationships didn't interest him. That aside from the whole he-lived-in-the-U.S. thing.

She forced her brain to stop spinning by throwing aside covers to creep out and use the bathroom. She never made it to the door. Her phone rang, sending her heart into cartwheels of fear and her lungs into asthma-like panic. Gasping, she lunged for the mobile and recoiled at the name on the screen.

Aiden.

If the ringer hadn't been loud enough that she feared waking others, her panic might have made her ignore him despite all her bold threats, but she swiped the answer icon.

"Hullo, sis," he said before she could speak. "Sorry to wake you, but I didn't want to give you a chance to ignore me. Clever, right? Gives me the advantage."

"Makes you a feckin' coward." Her whispered words were knife sharp. "Calling in the middle of the night? Why are you afraid to face me in person?"

The chill that frosted her nerves from his dark laugh drove away the last of her sweet thoughts of Noah.

"Meeting you in person has never done me any good, Mairi. Showin' you exactly how selfish you are has gotten me much further. Hear you lost another job. Guess parents are a wee bit leery of a teacher with drug connections."

"Think again, brother. The police know I have nothing to do with you or your pathetic attempts to frame me as something I'm not. You haven't won anything."

"Haven't I? It doesn't really matter what the police believe, does it? They also have nothing on *me*. They can't prove I did anything either. But guess who does have doubts? Your dear mother-in-law. I'll bet you've heard from our Sorcha by now, haven't you?"

"She's no threat." Mairi's hands shook uncontrollably. She was reacting to his taunts, not controlling him. The problem was, he was right. This whole situation was about what people thought and feared.

"She could be. I know where you are."

"You don't."

The slight hesitation told her that, in this case, she was still right. But he countered anyway.

"You're close enough to Glasgow to drive in and talk to Mum. It's only a matter of time before I find the right friend."

"You come near us, and you'll see the ways I can stop you."

"Nae," he laughed again. "Were that true, you'd have me already. What you *do* have is the means to help your family out of some serious difficulties."

"Oh, difficulties have you now?" She laughed cruelly. "Is that what you call drug addiction? You have the utter bollocks to accuse me of owing you *anything* when you've sniffed, snorted, and shot up every pound of your inheritance, then borrowed from Mum and left her in debt?"

"You don't know anything about what's going on with me or Mum because you're selfish and think only of yourself. And I can keep on telling people who you really are for as long as you want to play this game. You can stop it, Mairi. With one simple act. I need five thousand pounds. You have it; don't try to tell me you don't. That will get our mother current on her house and me out of your life."

"Are you bloody serious? You're going to all this trouble for that amount of money? Get a feckin' job."

"Thanks to you, again, I'm unemployable. One look at the record *you* gave me and it's a 'no thank you all the same.' And now you're getting a taste of that treatment. Doesn't feel too good, does it?"

She ignored the rant. "Still taking no responsibility, 'eh, Aiden? Can you even pretend to imagine what your life might have been like if you'd, oh, I don't know, *not* started taking drugs? If you spent one quarter the time cleaning up your sad self that you spend threatening me, you'd have no problems."

"Don't you lecture me. That's so sanctimonious and typical. You haven't helped us since Da' died, so you're going to help now with the money, sister. It's simple."

"You know full well I haven't got it. It's tied up in a trust I can't touch. I knew you'd piss away anything you could get, and you've proved me right ten times over. Well, what Da' left me is now your niece's. Done and dusted. I'm not your ticket out of trouble."

"I'm back in Glasgow, but you're my ticket out. You'll get the money, Mairi."

"Or what?" She took a deep breath and softened, trying to channel Noah but knowing full well it would do no good. "You threaten? I'll go farther away. You can't really hurt me unless you've turned into a murderer as well. But meet me. In person. In Glasgow. Work this all out with me instead of acting like a cartoon criminal, and I'll help you get whatever you need."

"We've been down that road. Rehab is a crock of shite. Now it's my way…or you might find you and your little girl aren't as safe as you think."

"That sounds like a threat I can take to the police," she said, her stomach rolling wildly. "You've overstepped."

"We'll see."

"No!" She'd had it. "Now it's the police who'll find you, Aiden, and they'll do the talking. Hide where you like, Glasgow, Edinburgh, England, Wales. It's my turn to direct this show. No money, Aiden. You wait and see."

She hung up and turned the ringer of the phone down. As suspected, he called back, but she didn't answer. When the phone went dark, she waited. He called again.

He quit after that…and that's when she finally wept. She'd made big statements but, in reality, she had no way of keeping the vows she'd made.

She didn't cry long. When she was done raging inside, she lay back and tried to find at least some sleep, but she really did need the bathroom now, the fear roiling in her stomach adding to her distress. She made it down the hall and sat for five long minutes while her insides calmed and her hands stopped shaking.

She'd report the phone call to her favorite DI Donnelly. She'd call her mother and make sure Aiden was back at home. She'd make a trip to Westmuir Primary and update Christine Sullivan. It wouldn't get her job back, but she'd look proactive. Noah was right. It helped to have a step-by-step plan.

On the way back to her room she heard the first of several movements from downstairs. Curious, she stood at the top of the staircase and listened. Someone moved through the kitchen, first quietly and then, clearly having donned shoes, more distinctly. She heard the deadbolt on the back door slide and the door squeaked open and then closed. Who would brave going outside in this horrible rain?

She hurried back to her room. Her window looked onto the back garden, and a faint brightening told her she'd managed to stay up until dawn. Not that it would be anything bright or pretty in this dreich weather. She stared into the dim, rain-soaked yard and saw nothing at first. Then she caught sight of him. Noah. Hunched against the rain under a heavy poncho, with a drawstring hood that made the back of his head look like a ruched laundry bag, and squelching through the grass in new wellies. Even from behind, she recognized his long-legged stride heading for the cottage. Within a few seconds, he was out of sight.

She was too crazy from Aiden's call and too foggy from drinking to analyze her actions or care whether Noah wanted her with him or not. He wouldn't be heading to the cottage in the dark and the rain if there wasn't something wrong, and she wasn't about to let him face it alone.

She found him in the middle of the living area floor, squatting with a flashlight that played over a scene of devastation. The rain crashed on the roof like they were in a metal barrel being beaten with hammers, and the din seemed to shriek, "your lucky week is over." Her heart plummeted.

"Noah?"

"Welcome to disaster." His voice rasped from his throat and got lost in the rain splashing onto the floor in a curved waterfall. "What are you doing out here?"

"Following you. I heard you leave the house."

"There's nothing you can do. Nothing either of us can do until it's light. There's no electricity out here at the moment. You should go back."

"Look, it's been a shitty night ever since Callum showed up at the pub. I haven't slept, my brother is an arsehole, and now the roof is literally caving in. You are *not* adding to the cluster by pushing me away."

She hadn't meant for her voice to go shrill, but they'd become friends and, by heaven, she wasn't going to let him turn sourpuss loner on her now. He looked over his shoulder, his shadowed features shocked. He stood.

"Push you away? I'm trying to give you a chance to avoid pneumonia and depression for no good reason."

"Pneumonia? I grew up here. This is a balmy summer rain. You're the one should be tucked in bed. Are you going back in until its daylight?"

"In a bit." That calm, reasonable voice both soothed and infuriated her.

"Then that's when I'm going in, too. How can we get lights back on?"

"Change a fuse in the box outside, I'm guessing. But I'm not doing that in the dark and driving rain. Stupid design."

"Agreed. What exactly happened?"

"That cracked truss gave way. We know some of the asphalt patches were leaking and the collapse is right under the biggest patch. My theory is the truss was damaged back when the repair was made and shifting things down here followed by heavy rain was the last straw."

He aimed the flashlight to the ceiling. An eight-to-ten-inch hole gaped between exposed rafters, and raggedy edges of asphalt shingles draped around the edges like overhanging lichen. Rain fell through the hole in a light shower, but most of the water rolled in from the sides.

"Damn it," Mairi said. "I'm so sorry."

He moved the beam downward again and swept it across the floor. The old boards had soaked up the water and were stained for a solid six feet beneath the roof hole.

"Nice, huh?" he asked.

"I know this cottage has nothing to do with me," she replied. "I don't live here. I have very little reason to invest in it. But I feel like a part of me was just mugged and beaten."

He nodded. "The saying is true. Shit happens. What're you going to do?"

She glared at him. How could he be so bloody calm? "Good question. What *are* you going to do?"

He frowned. "I'm going to bring Ella's wheelbarrow in here to catch what water can be caught. When the rain stops, I'll put a tarp over the hole. We'll tell the roof guys this is has become an emergency, and we'll assess and fix it if we can. What else is there?"

He was infuriatingly logical, as unemotional as if he'd been programmed to keep emotion inside. Between her brother, who threatened with a cruel single-mindedness, and this man who held his emotions in check like he was afraid of them, for one crazy-feeling second, she'd had enough.

"For God's sake, Noah," she cried. "There's raging against the unfairness of things. This will cost you time you don't have, and you're acting like it's a skinned knee. Damn it, yell at something. Tell me you're sick of getting walked on by cousins, by goats, by rain. Be a feckin' normal person instead of a perfect saint."

"Stop." He spun to face her and seized her upper arms. Exactly as she'd wished, his eyes filled with more emotion than she could read. "You think I'm not angry? Not mad at the whole damn world right now? I have no idea if this can be repaired in time. No idea what the roofers are going to say. I have no idea what to do, Mairi, but tell me what possible good it does to fall apart."

"It clears the brain." Her anger drained in the face of his utter frustration, and she lowered her eyes. "For me, it gets the anger out of my head and then I can think."

"Fine. Your way is to solve things by yelling, by getting a reaction. I don't know how to face a problem that way, but if you don't think I'm pissed as hell and swearing at God for his *acts* right now, you're wrong. So, swear you will never call me a saint again."

Now she saw it perfectly in his eyes—the hurt and sorrow she'd accused him unfairly of not having. With her reactionary fury, she'd robbed him of the dignity that made him who he was, even though she'd gotten a little of the honesty she'd craved.

"Noah, I'm sorry, I—"

He crushed off her words with his mouth against hers, shocking her, and sending bolts of lightning through her belly and down her legs, rendering them steady as matchsticks. He wrapped her with his arms and pressed deeper into the stunning kiss like he was a dying man and she was a cure. His hungry mouth searched hers unapologetic.

When her surprise dissipated, pent-up desire took its place. She pressed back, inviting his tongue into her mouth, responding with her own, tasting the sweet hint of rain from his lips. He suckled her tongue, released it, and softly scraped his teeth against her bottom lip, feeding the greedy butterflies in her stomach with pure pleasure.

He stopped, with a groan, as suddenly as he'd started. "Sorry, sorry," he whispered.

The words touched her lips with warm puffs of breath, and before he could pull away, she interlocked her fingers behind his nape and held his head close.

"Absolutely no apologies. I wanted that. I still do."

"But I...we..."

"Have been thrown together for reasons I don't understand. Maybe neither of us belongs here, so let's not belong here together."

"You're right. We *don't* belong together."

He smiled with a touch of sadness but kissed her again, softly this time. She angled her head and returned it, calmer but no less filled with desire as relentless as the rain. When they parted, she placed her fingers on the warm skin beside the corner of his mouth.

"I don't know why this is happening, so let's do it your slow way. One step at a time,"

"I don't know," he replied. "Your way might be better. Rage and yell, because this isn't smart."

She was the one to finally pull from their embrace, but she trailed her fingers down his arms and caught his hands. "I think kissing you *stopped* my rage. Maybe smart is relative."

"Even if we want this, I don't see any scenario where smart can be used to describe it."

The words were tender. Resigned. She smiled.

"Heaven help me, I think I've wanted to kiss you for a while, Noah Portman, and I've no regrets. I'm only sorry I go so crazy and keep asking you to be who you aren't. It's a shite time, but I can tell you, it's better because I've met you."

He brushed a drop of rain off her cheek. "I've no regrets either, but it'll be a long time until I believe I'm the best thing for you."

"You don't have to be the best, but for the moment you're pretty close."

CHAPTER EIGHTEEN

"Maybe we simply have to face reality and let the couple know the place won't be ready." Ainslie voiced the words everybody else held inside and all gazes dropped morosely to the tabletop in Catrione's warm, dry kitchen. "There's such a thing as killing yourself and still failing to meet the goal."

"I don't have the expertise to know what the possibilities are," Ewan said, giving Noah a sad shake of his head. "I have to make the decision, but I need your best guess. I'm sorry I brought you into this craziness."

Noah honestly felt awful for him. His brother rarely guessed wrong on a business gamble. "You don't have to be sorry. I came kicking and screaming of my own volition." A few smiles returned at half strength. "Obviously we need to talk to the slate guy and see what he can do and what it will cost."

"Yeah, of course," Ewan said.

The only good thing about the rain was the fact that the crews at Roofing Solutions wouldn't be working in it, so the owner, Tristan Hewitt, could come that morning.

"The floor is another matter—I doubt we can save the old wood now. The wet boards will have to come up because they're soaked through and you don't want mold, but they'll take days, maybe a couple of weeks to dry through, and even if there's no warping or other damage, we need to be much further than installing flooring ten or fourteen days from now. Bottom line, I can eventually figure out if the work can get *done.* You'll have to decide if you can afford it."

"We had a budget—our assets combined were about twelve thousand pounds. I guessed relatively accurately on stonework, and I came close on framing and sheet rocking. We figured in appliances and some furnishings. But I was pretty far off on the roof. I figured forty or fifty replacement tiles. I knew if I had to replace the whole thing it would be prohibitive. This would push us over the limit for sure."

A melancholy silence fell until Catrione entered with a piping-hot pan of sweet rolls.

"Sugar to drown your sorrows," she said.

Murmurs of genuine appreciation rose, and Noah looked to Mairi, knowing she loved her sweets. She sat with her eyes downcast as if she hadn't noticed the enticing caramel scent or the yeasty invitation to dig in and forget any associated guilt. He frowned in concern. She was reliably the life of the table, but her clear worry set her apart this time in a completely different way. It was a little strange that she was taking this setback so hard.

And then he remembered something. A passing reference when she'd been berating him before the kiss. The stunning kiss he had no one to blame for but himself and that still both thrilled and scared him. A kiss he had no time to fret over or relive until they got through the rest of this morning.

"My brother is an arsehole," she'd said. He'd barely thought about it because it wasn't new information. But why had she brought it up randomly then, when she hadn't mentioned him in days? "I haven't slept. My brother is an arsehole."

Suddenly he knew. She'd spoken to him. It was the only thing that could have turned her anger to depression. He sought her hand beneath the table, and when he squeezed she finally forced her face to brighten.

"Need to talk?" he whispered.

Her smile widened at that, and she leaned toward his ear. "That offer is like porn for a woman, you know," she whispered back.

"Trust me, it was accidental. I'm serious, though. Is it Aiden?"

Her eyes rounded slightly but she nodded. "I can tell you later."

"Or we can go check on the fuse box."

She dipped her head. "We could."

They were interrupted by pounding on the back door. Innis hefted himself out of his chair and went to open it. Bing and Bob entered like an entire squad of rowdy soccer fans.

"It smells like a wee bit o' heaven in here!" Bob called. "How can I get myself invited to breakfast?"

"You say 'please,'" Bing told him.

"Please!" Bob grinned and stood beside his cousin behind Ewan's chair.

"Help yourselves," Ewan said. "You got my message."

"Oh aye," Bob said. "Sounded right wicked so we detoured down to the cottage first. Had a look 'round. It *were* bad. Noah, it soaked through under our bedroom wall. I'd say about thirty percent o' the floor is lost."

"Yeah, thanks," Noah replied, scowling at the news that was hardly news anymore.

Bing gave his cousin a cuff on the shoulder. "He knows that, y'rocket. We didn't come to tell him his floor's wet."

"No, but it's good to know we're all on the same page."

Needed laughter rang around the table. The line hadn't been that funny, but it was ridiculous and fit right into the morning.

"We checked it out for another reason, as well," Bing continued. "When you said in your message the floor had been soaked and probably ruined, I remembered some'at. Another of our uncles built a huis in Edinburgh. He got sent the wrong flooring for his lower level and the company didnae want it back. They shipped the new, and the extra's been sittin' in Uncle's garage for round eight or nine month. Says he's been too busy to get rid o' it."

"He'll gi' ye the lot, you know." Bob licked caramel off his finger, already done with one fat roll. "But you'd have to fetch it yer sel'. It might not be enough for the whole cottage, but for a couple of rooms I think there'd be plenty."

"Are you joking?" Ewan asked. "Tell me you're not joking."

Bob looked at Bing and shrugged, confused. "Nae. Not a joke. Are *you* joking?"

Bing patted him on the shoulder. "I would never joke, y' know that." He looked at the group, then singled out Noah for an eye roll. "Y'gotta love him. He's like a loyal dog."

"Well, the pair of you are saving our bacon," Noah said. "Brilliant genius or loyal dog—we love you."

"Bacon is good," Bob said and then held up his hand before Bing could touch him. "I know what he means. I'm not *that* much of a dog."

"What color is the floor?" Mairi asked. "It's not purple or anything?"

"It's not *coral*, is it?" Noah added, and shot her a horrified look that made her laugh for the first time.

"It's a dark brown is all Uncle said," Bing replied. "Was supposed to be a light oak. Other than that, I havenae seen it."

"At the moment, I don't care if *it* is purple," Ewan said. "It's free. Can I get your uncle's number and talk to him? I want to make sure this is all legitimate."

"Yeah, 'course."

"You guys get the details," Noah said. "I'm going down to see if I can get the lights back on now that the rain is tapering off. And if the flooring deal is real, I have an idea, but I need to talk to Mairi. Wasn't there something you said about a shopping trip to Edinburgh?"

He felt guilty taking her hand as they headed down the driveway to the cottage. The kiss earlier could be chalked up to attraction and hormones and a reaction to disaster. Holding hands like this somehow intimated more, something proprietary, as if there was a connection between them beyond simple chemistry. He didn't want that; he *couldn't* want that.

At the same time, he wanted it the way he wanted air. The way he craved something he could trust. And that was insane, because in the long run, Mairi was the least stable thing in his life.

Too many roller coaster feelings.

As he had a hundred times already during this trip, he reminded himself he didn't do these kinds of emotions. No holes in slate roofs, no insane deadlines, no crazy brothers, garrulous little girls, or arrogant cousins. Certainly no dark-haired women who kissed like Scottish angels but would disappear from his life in less than a month.

He did easy commissions, Reese's Peanut Butter Cups, televise baseball games, and one day at a time. He did uncomplicated.

And still he held her hand.

"It could work, couldn't it?" she asked. "A day trip to Edinburgh? Pick up the flooring. Visit a couple of stores."

"It would solve two problems, anyway."

"I did think of one negative. It's August."

He laughed. "Has been for a couple of weeks."

"No. I mean, every August, Edinburgh hosts a huge arts festival. That draws big enough crowds, but the problem is that along with it is the Edinburgh Festival Fringe—and that's an enormous proper zoo."

"Zoo?"

"You've heard of the Royal Mile, the main thoroughfare downtown between the castle and the Palace of Holyroodhouse?"

"Ah, sure."

"During the Fringe, it and every street around it, is jammed. Something like six or seven hundred performers and artisans put on shows, free street art performances, and sell things. There are crazy people, super-talented people, shows for kids, raunchy things, funny things. It's fun but mad. Parking, eating, staying anywhere will be difficult. We can manage if it comes to that. Just a warning."

"Sounds fantastic," he muttered.

"Call it a little cultural immersion," she teased.

"Completely out of my comfort zone," he admitted. He didn't even like going to fairs and carnivals when he went to sell his own work.

"It's good for you. Expand your horizons."

"Whatever you say." He put the thought of crowds out of his mind and paused, reluctant to bring up the subject they really needed to talk about, hating the thought of ruining their light-hearted mood. It was surface lightness only, however, and he gave her hand another squeeze, hoping it would at least show support. "We can worry about Fringes and crowds later. Tell me about Aiden. What happened?"

The mood shifted but, to his relief, this time she seemed more resolute than depressed.

"He called. At blessed half past four this morning. Scared the devil out of me, to be sure, but then he made me so angry I could have crawled through the airwaves, or the cell waves, whatever the technology is, and done him in on the spot." She looked up. "And now I hope he doesn't actually die somehow, because I said that."

"I'm your rock-solid alibi, I promise."

"I knew I could count on you."

She told him the details—Aiden's demand for cash, his threat that he could find her, the accusations that she was an ungrateful sister and daughter...and Noah's heart broke for her. For the first time he, the professed nonconfrontationalist, believed he'd found a person he could punch, given the opportunity.

"What can I do to help?" he asked. "Find him? Stalk him? Push him down on the playground?" They stopped in front of the cottage door. "Sorry. I'm not trying to treat this lightly. You can push him down as well as I can."

"Yeah. Well, I like a good smart-arse, thanks."

She raised her eyes to the door's three arch stones carved with the thistle, fairy, and unicorn Ella had noticed on Noah's first day. She leaned into him and stared wistfully.

"Such a lovely thing—somebody carved these symbols as a sign that this place is watched over by the good things in Scotland—the national flower, the national animal, the kinder spirits. All I've ever wanted is this—a place that's safe and permanent. I came as close as I ever have with the job in Glasgow, but Aiden, my mother, James...they've been determined to keep things hellish. I will win, Noah, I will. But sometimes I'm tired of waiting for the right time, you know?" She turned to face him. "You can't do anything about that, but you listen and you believe me, and that's more than I've had in a long time."

It was the perfect moment, the perfect opportunity to kiss her again. She raised her head, he lowered his, and the inches between them begged to be closed. Noah hadn't allowed himself to think about the power of their kiss that morning. It had been the confusion of the moment. This moment was no less fraught, but his stomach quivered and the primal part of his male brain finally dragged his imagination to the inevitable. This couldn't be passed off as heat-of-the-moment. This was pure and simple wanting her.

It was also wanting to give her all the things she'd admitted wishing for—the things *he* wished for: safety, permanency, trust. For those things, they were each other's worst solution. Reluctantly, his neanderthal brain protesting, he drew back and cupped her cheek in one hand.

"No kiss to make it better?" she said, her voice carefully neutral.

"Believe me, I'm thinking of even more effective things than a kiss. But I'm not sure they actually *would* make it better. It was good...better than good...this morning. I don't know what that meant, really. Let's take it slow."

Her careful expression relaxed into understanding. She stepped forward and closed the gap between them by wrapping her arms around his torso.

"If ever I thought you might take advantage of a girl in an emotional state, that worry is gone."

"Mairi, I didn't mean—"

"It's good, Noah. It's gallant, even. I'm not used to that. This time, your way is the right way."

Her gentle acquiescence made him want her more. Made his body spring to life with a rush of desire masked as tenderness. He impulsively dropped a kiss on the top of her head and then pushed her away.

"I'm writing that down to blackmail you with later."

"I'll live with it." Her eyes reflected a little of the smoky desire he was fighting.

"Let's go turn the electricity on."

As if there wasn't enough electricity already.

The free floor offer was legitimate, and Bing and Bob's uncle would be thrilled, he told Ewan, to be rid of the fifteen cartons of laminate that had been taking up space in his garage. News from the roofing inspection, however, was not nearly as good. In fact, it was about as bad as it could be. Too many slate tiles were cracked and damaged to be salvaged. Six more roof trusses were found to have rot issues. The meager insulation contained mold in some places. The only reasonable option was to replace the roof along with the insulation and the trusses.

The only positive was the relatively small size of the cottage and the single roof gable along with standard size trusses, so the projected cost was "only" eight thousand pounds. Give or take.

"Holy—" Noah stopped himself, even though Ella was out of earshot, drawing at the dining room table. He sat with the rest of the family in the living room, looking over the worksheet Hewitt the roofer had filled out. "It's what, ten thousand dollars?"

"It's the whole budget." Ewan covered his mouth with his palm.

"Free flooring doesn't quite make up for it, does it?" Noah said. "What are our options?"

"Two." Ewan laughed humorlessly. "Find the money. Cancel the booking. The first is preferable but not likely. The second..."

"There's one other solution." Ainslie's voice came slowly, reluctantly.

"Nope." Ewan shook his head. "Not Callum."

Innis gave a laugh. "There's a switch. Ewan is usually the one willing to give his cousin the benefit."

"I don't like it either," Ainslie said. "But one thing Ewan's taught me is that if we keep tight enough reins on Callum, we can make deals. If we draw up a good enough contract..."

"He'll want something besides money in return. He'll want some kind of control over what's done with the property."

"We won't let him," Ainslie insisted.

"Let's back up," Noah said. "Setting aside the money issue—not a small thing, I know—can the work even get done? We have seventeen days to the inspection. For that, the wiring, plumbing, roof, insulation, and structural work have to be done. Then there would be tiling, fixtures, painting, cabinets, and appliances to finish in another ten days. We have those of us here plus Bob and Bing, plus Callum if he's serious about swinging a hammer. We can do the inside work barring any more floods. Can the roofers fit us in?"

"Hewitt said they could. It would take them the week."

"Another question," Mairi asked. "Say you decide to postpone opening the cottage—cancel the royal booking. Do you still plan to finish it eventually? You wouldn't abandon the project?"

"No, of course not," Ewan said.

"Then the roof has to get fixed or patched no matter what to avoid more damage than has already been done."

"True."

"I have money. Some. It's in a trust. There's a penalty for cracking into it, but it's doable. I'd like to help—for all you've done for me and Ella."

Once again, Ewan shook his head. "That's amazing of you, Mairi, but no. It's in a trust for a reason, we know that."

"I wouldn't use it all—just enough to help."

"Mairi, you can't exchange your future for a small cottage roof," Noah said. "You're generous, always thinking of ways to help others. But we know there's another way."

"I wouldn't regret it," she said softly. "I'm invested in this, too. Know it's there if all else fails."

Noah ignored the amused looks from the others and placed an arm around Mairi's shoulders to give her a squeeze. He popped a kiss on her forehead. "Thank you."

Ewan straightened in his armchair and gave a nod.

"Okay, here's the plan for the next two days. Noah, Mairi and Ella, take your trip to Edinburgh. Pick up the flooring. Gather your energy. I'll book the roofers." He paused and then took Ainslie's hand. "I'll talk to Callum. I won't ask him for anything yet. I'll see what his reaction to the problem is. I'm not completely out of ideas—even when it comes to him."

"If anyone can handle him, you can," Ainslie said. "I trust you."

Trust, thought Noah. That word again. Trust was hard to come by and inconstant, but Ainslie definitely seemed to have found it with Ewan. Maybe he'd never find it for himself…but at least he was starting to believe it existed in the world.

CHAPTER NINETEEN

It was hard to stay pessimistic in Edinburgh. Mairi loved Glasgow, loved her city, its quirky humor and singular accent. But for sheer bombastic, elegant, outsized fun, Edinburgh was only ever out to impress. For day trippers and tourists, the tough underbelly of the capital, as it did in all large cities, stayed hidden. The Old Town, crowned by Castle Hill and flanked by Holyrood Park and the green bluffs of Arthur's Seat was venerable and beautiful. The New Town, hardly actually new, was filled with gardens and green spaces and bustled as much as any cosmopolitan city.

They started Friday mid-morning on Princes Street where Mairi felt like she got her sea legs back in mothering, not just with Ella but with Noah, too. She had to laugh at the way the two bonded over their distaste of shopping for clothing. Ella wanted to spend all her time at the small electronics gaming store, where Noah showed her a few of the latest computer games and gadgets—things fairy-mad Ella was just discovering she liked, thanks to school.

Mairi forced them to look at shoes and managed to get her daughter into two pairs she didn't actually hate. She engaged Noah to help pick out school socks, and Ella was much more amenable to her new anti-shopping soul mate's antics and taste in colorful hosiery—one of the few places she could be creative with school clothes.

Ella whined at picking out new underpants and shirts, but complained less over white blouses that would accommodate her purple and gray striped uniform ties. When Mairi had squeezed and cajoled all she could out of her daughter in terms of school clothes, they made their way to a children's boutique where Ella got the pick of the store for a new play outfit.

"Anything you need to shop for while we're here?" she teased Noah, as they watched Ella skip through displays of pre-ripped-knee jeans, sparkly unicorn tops, and fluffy sleeveless vests.

"You know, I could use a set of model paints. Is there a hobby store in a place like this?"

"I'm sure."

"If not, it's fine because all I really need is lunch," he said. "This uses as many calories as running a marathon."

"Ach, poor man. No worries, lunch is on the agenda. We can wander back to The Mile and find a street vendor or one of the good pubs there. What sounds good?"

"Fish and chips. I've been craving them since we were in Glasgow."

"Pub it is," she said. "Ella will eat a burger or a meat pie."

"You're such a great mom," he said, surprising her.

"I...thank you. What brought that up?"

"The way you direct her when she doesn't want to be told what to do. The way you distract her—and me, for that matter. You make un-fun things fun."

Her cheeks heated and she shrugged, pleased with the unexpected compliment. "Come on, you're calling shopping 'un-fun'? You did a great job picking out *How to Train Your*

Dragon socks. All in the right colors, too. You're a natural shopper."

"Because." He looked around to see if Ella was occupied and slipped a quick kiss onto her nose. A tiny arrow of electricity zipped to her shoulders. "You made it fun."

"I see. And I get a kiss for that. Brilliant."

"Friends." He shrugged. "A friendly kiss only. Between friends."

"You're two bags shy of a whole shopping trip, aren't ye, lad?" She liked the return to silliness between them and loved being away from the stress of Craigwarren's cottage woes, if even for a day.

"Oh, I hope not. I don't have two more bags of shopping left in me."

"These, Mama!" Ella came toward them, a pair of purple leggings in one hand, and a wide silky shirt busy with bright, rainbow-striped sleeves and, on the front, purple and pink blocks of color behind the image of a flower garden being prowled by a fanciful cat.

"That is the definition of bright," Noah said. "I like the cat."

"It's definitely you, love," Mairi said to Ella as she checked the size. "Let's get it."

Twenty minutes later, they'd found Noah's hobby store where he bought the paints he wanted. They stowed their shopping bags in the car in a tiny, out-of-the-way car park where they'd found one space, then took the bus back to Old Town. Mairi clung fast to Ella's hand in the crush of people making their way down The Mile toward St. Giles' Cathedral. Ella was in heaven, gaping at the street performers, laughing at funny signs bearing bad jokes.

"Why don't you play poker at the zoo?" Noah read.

Ella doubled over. "Too many cheetahs!"

They saw Darth Vader and a cadre of Stormtroopers. They saw dragon costumes and fairy costumes, and Ella declared she wanted to grow up, come to Edinburgh and be a fairy.

Noah seemed mesmerized, but Mairi couldn't tell if he was fascinated or shell-shocked. He stopped at one point, staring in bewilderment at a group of eight men and women dressed like peasants. Their sign identified them as the Society of Slow Walkers and they progressed up the street at the speed of one step per two seconds. He watched for long minutes and the group never changed its excruciating pace. Finally, he literally burst out laughing.

"I don't get it," he said.

"Nothing to get. It's Fringe," she said. "It's all about being out there."

Mairi found the crowds fun. People were either gawking at performers and hawkers, or doing the performing and hawking.

"Are those people dead?" Ella asked, when they came upon a group of six people lying in various states of motionlessness in the middle of the street."

"Do you think they are?" Noah asked. "They look dead to me."

"Me, too." Ella nodded in certainty. "What will happen to them?"

"Maybe the street sweepers will come and sweep them up. Everything should be cleared off by tomorrow before they start to smell bad."

"Oh my Lord!" Mairi said. "Noah, really."

Ella burst out laughing, holding her belly. "That's so funny!"

"Hey, you said fringe. Trying to get in the spirit." He raised his brows and shrugged.

Secretly, she was proud of him for dealing with the crowds, but she wouldn't tell him yet. She made a face. "But dead people jokes…"

"Let's go to that show!" Ella pointed to a pillar covered in placards and a sign that advertised "The Naked Magicians. Sleeves up, pants down."

This time Noah snorted in laughter. "Is that better than dead people, Mom?"

"It is not!" She laughed, too. "You can go when you're older, darlin'. Not today."

"Hey, here's another one," Noah pointed to a sign. "What's orange and sounds like a parrot?"

Ella read the answer. "A carrot!" Giggles erupted yet again. "I get it. Carrot. Parrot."

"Yup." Noah nodded. "In the U.S., we call them dad jokes. Dad jokes are the stupidest jokes on the planet."

"Oh, we call them that, too," Mairi said. "I'll pit ours against yours any day."

"Did I just hear a gauntlet drop?"

"What did the Scottish man say when the barkeep took his pint away? Where'd my Glasgow?"

He shook his head. "That was stupid but not good enough. This one: I asked my dog what was two minus two. He said nothing."

She covered her mouth with her hand to hide the sputter. "Are we really going to do this?"

"I hope not. How about we find those fish and chips?"

"I'll tell you a less nice one later."

"Naughty dad jokes? My, my, the Scottish are earthy, are they?"

"Sheep jokes and all."

He grimaced. "I forgot about sheep jokes. Even we know about those."

"That's too bad."

They stuffed themselves at a small fish and chips restaurant a block off The Royal Mile. After two bites, Noah was laughing and happy, teasing Ella and coming up with more ridiculously stupid jokes. All Mairi wanted to do was sit back and watch him, listen to his flat, pretty accent, and soak in the fun her daughter was having. This side of Noah Portman didn't come out very often, she guessed, and she wished she could find a way to change that.

"I think fish and chips are your kryptonite," she said when none of them could eat another bite. "You lose your super powers of seriousness."

"I'm thoroughly embarrassed," he said. "I didn't expect to like this place at all. It sounded like my worst nightmare."

"Told you it would be good for you."

"Bah. It's you again. And her." He jabbed his thumb at Ella. "She knows too many jokes. I'm actually not sure I'd like this place without all the weirdos and dead people."

"Who says it's any different once the Fringe is gone?" Mairi winked. "Auld Reekie is weird all the time. Elegant. But weird."

"Seriously bad nickname," Noah said.

"Auld Reekie!" Ella giggled. "Because it used to stink."

"It did, but Auld Reekie actually meant Old Smoky," Mairi said. "Where those lovely Princes Street Gardens are I pointed out this morning—used to be a loch where they *actually* dumped the dead bodies. And the sewage. And burned all the refuse."

Noah and Ella exchanged triumphant looks. "See!" Noah said. "I told you they'd know what to do with those dead guys."

"You two are terrible."

"Aye, we are pure brilliant terrible!" Ella held up her hand and Noah high-fived her.

Mairi's heart soared at the growing relationship. She refused to think about what would happen when Noah went back home. His brother lived here now; Noah would visit. Ella would understand—you had to learn to understand as you got older.

"Are we done here?" she asked. "It's nearly three. Our appointment with Bing and Bob's uncle Mac isn't until six. What do you want to do for the last two hours, love?"

Mairi winked at Noah, fully expecting the answer she got.

"The Everything Bake Shop and wee Greyfriars Bobby."

"I would have been disappointed had you forgotten those." Mairi kissed Ella's head.

"Bake Shop?" Noah groaned.

"Don't worry. A walk to wear off lunch first. We need all the luck we can get back at Craigwarren, wouldn't you say? A trip to David Hume's toe and then Greyfriars Bobby and we should be set for fortune. Then we can eat dessert."

"I'm just gonna follow," Noah said. "Learn as I go."

She led them back through the throng to St. Giles' Cathedral, where the statue of philosopher David Hume stood at the end of line of people.

"He was one of our most enlightened scholars, they say," Mairi explained. "Here's the fun part. One of his big deals was trying to overturn superstition and darkness, but people line up to give his big toe a rub for good luck."

"I am not even surprised by this," Noah said. "In a land of creatures who drown children, why wouldn't adults rub a statue toe to ward off bad luck?"

She laughed. "Come on, take your turn."

Noah groused good-naturedly the entire two-minute wait and then rubbed the statue's toe, worn to gold by the millions of hands that had preceded his. He held Ella up to follow suit, and when Mairi had added her touch, she nodded.

"That'll help."

"I'm sure it will."

They headed toward the castle esplanade on the three-block walk to Candlemaker Row, but didn't escape The Mile before Ella begged to put money in the tip jar of a woman in a long white hoop dress, her face and hands painted a creamy white as well, her lips cherry red, her expression blank. Once Ella had deposited her pound note, however, the woman put a whistle in her mouth, gave several short blasts, pulled some marionette-like strings and hoisted the skirt to reveal white garters, knickers, and stockings.

Ella screeched with laughter.

"And you said I was inappropriate," Noah laughed.

"Yeah, well, death and garters. I'm an equal-opportunity bad parent."

The white lady lowered her skirt, blew Ella a kiss and then made a heart with her fingers and pointed at Noah. He grinned like a fifteen-year-old and saluted her.

"Can we pay her again, Mom?" he asked.

"Absolutely not. I'll corrupt a kid, but not a grown man."

They left her with a last wave and Mairi took Ella's hand. On her other side, Noah leaned around her while they walked.

"Hey, Ell? Is it okay if I hold your mom's hand, too?"

Her face brightened. "So you don't get lost?"

"Exactly."

He grasped her hand gently and squeezed. This time it felt familiar and right. She literally could not remember the last time she'd been that contented.

"Whose toe are we rubbing this time?" Noah asked.

"No toe, but a nose. A little bitty dog named Greyfriars Bobby. He belonged to a police watchman and when the man died, the dog guarded his gravesite for years.

"Aren't there movies about that dog?"

"Several, aye. Whether the story is strictly true is something curmudgeonly old scholars like to debate. But I choose to believe it. One family took care of the dog and paid for his license and collar. That's in the wee Museum of Edinburgh. It has to be true, right?"

"Can't argue with a museum."

Once on Candlemaker Row, Ella remembered the way to the statue from the same visit the year before. She tugged so hard on Mairi's hand that she slipped free and zipped down the sidewalk. The crowds were not nearly as suffocating as they'd been, but Mairi still called for her to stop. Ella looked over her shoulder.

"Come on, hurry!"

"Incorrigible," she said.

"We ought to be able to keep up with a seven-year-old." Noah jogged forward, pulling her along.

Ella stayed in sight for the last half a block to the little fountain and statue. She stopped, and Mairi didn't notice anything untoward...until she watched Ella's shoes levitate from the pavement.

She shrieked when she realized someone had grabbed her daughter, and she jerked from Noah's hold, running all out. "Ella!!"

"What the hell?" Noah shouted and passed her at a gallop.

Faintly, she heard Ella's voice—and her blood ran colder yet.

"Uncle Aiden!"

As Noah reached her, Ella twisted and slipped free of Aiden's arms, landing on the pavement in front of him.

"Don't do that, I'm not three," she said, her hands on her hips, her head tilted back.

"Who the hell are you?" Noah stopped and gave Aiden a sharp shove backward. "What would possess you to grab a child off the street?"

"Easy there, Rob Roy. The girl's my niece. Reckon I can say hullo if I've a mind to. Hiya, Mairi. Took you long enough. I was beginnin' to think you wouldnae come."

Mairi could barely catch her breath, the fear and anger all but closing off her airway.

"This?" Noah sounded equally breathless now. "Is Aiden?"

"Uncle Aiden, you're supposed to be Glasgow."

Ella sounded like a miniature head teacher scolding a disobedient student. She'd been told Aiden had some problems and that she was never to go anywhere alone with him. But she had enough of a relationship to be polite to her uncle.

"I was in Glasgow," he said. "But when I heard you and your mum were coming here to shop, I wanted to surprise you. I happen to know Bobby here is your favorite place to visit in Edinburgh. I was right, wasn't I?"

Ella nodded. "I like to rub his nose."

"Do you need me to lift you?"

Aiden put his arms out, and Mairi's growl caught in her throat when Noah stepped between him and Ella.

"I don't think that's a good idea," he said. "What *is* a good idea is that you walk away. Another place would be better for talking to Mairi."

"Hey, Mairi. I didn't know you had a new Galahad in your life." He held out his hand. "Aiden Murray."

Noah didn't reciprocate, nor did he speak again. Mairi wanted to kiss him for trying, but instead she placed a hand on his arm. He took a step back and took Ella's hand.

"I've got her."

"You two rub Bobby's nose. Aiden and I will be right over there." She pointed to a concrete flower planter ten feet away and caught Noah's eyes. They were no longer carefree. Anything but. "Thank you."

She grabbed a fistful of leather jacket sleeve at Aiden's wrist and jerked him toward the planter.

"How dare you?" she said under her breath. "How did you know we were here? What do you think you're doing?"

"That's three questions, two of them redundant," he said. "Did I surprise you?"

"You're a rotten piece of work and surprise isn't the word. How did you find me?"

"A bit of investigation after we talked, although most of it was pretty intuitive once I put some thought into it. Don't know why it took me this long."

He gave a junkie's sniff and Mairi recoiled. He would look relatively normal to anyone who passed him, but she could see how much thinner he was than when she'd seen him last. His skin was pale, as if he'd spent months indoors, and the faint circles under his eyes weren't from lack of sleep. He'd been a handsome man once, broad-shouldered and square-jawed like their father. Now, though his hair was neatly trimmed and his face clean-shaven—their mother's influence, no doubt—he looked older than his thirty-two years and his eyes were wary and leaden.

"Who told you I would be here today?"

"Nobody told *me*." His grin was humorless. "They may have told who they thought was an inspector from the Glasgow police, who wanted to confirm you were safe since they'd heard *I* was back and looking for you."

"Nobody near me would believe that."

"I think it was a miss Isla Campbell who had the fear for you put in her by our inspector. She got a wee bit flustered and let on you were not in Glasgow, and were safe from your brother. And that you wouldn't be home until late from picking up building supplies in Edinburgh."

Mairi's heart sank. Isla knew not to tell where Mairi and Ella were living, but she was young and would have been intimidated by police.

"Let me guess—you were the 'inspector'?"

"Not me. An acquaintance. I'd heard you got a new job, then thought about where you might stay, and it made sense you'd be with a friend. It took a while to remember all your geeky hens from school, but then I thought of good old Ainslie, the book nerd…the animal freak. If anyone would hide you, she would. I looked up where she lived, found the three primary schools closest to her, and called each one asking for you."

The man was mad-scientist insane.

"Unbelievable. You've got your own Uni education. You're not supposed to be stupid, yet here y'are, putting as much work into stalking me as you could be into a real job."

"Never wanted a desk job like our dear old da'."

"So you went to school to become a drug addict. Brilliant. You'll slip up one day and that'll be it."

"But not today. It was simple to convince that nice head teacher that the police wanted to talk to you about your brother. One step led to another. Here I am and now I have you."

"You have nothing. What do you expect me to do?"

"I need you to get me that six-thousand pounds."

"Five, you said."

"Price has gone up. People are waiting for payments. I have overhead. I told you about Mum. Time for you to be part of the family, hen."

"You're no family of mine anymore. Go away, Aiden. If you show up anywhere I am, or Ella is, I'll have the police waiting. If you go near my house in Glasgow, you'll be caught. They're watching for you."

He laughed. A genuine, mirth-filled chortle of condescension. "I'm simply a brother asking family for a loan. You've made far more threats than I have."

"I swear I'll get a restraining order."

"There are many ways around those."

It was like arguing with a mobius strip. She always ended up in the same place.

"There's nothing else to talk about, Aiden; I've got nothing for you. Go someplace else to escape whatever drug dealer wants your skin, because that's what this is about. You owe someone, and you can't pay them. No sympathy from me, brother."

"That's me gone then, but now you know your little haven in the Highlands isn't safe anymore."

With cold fury, she grabbed for the neck of his white T-shirt beneath the unzipped leather jacket. Crumpling it in her fist, she stepped close and glared two inches from his smirking face. "I am not afraid of you. I'm sad to have lost my big brother, but that's *your* fault. Leave us alone."

He shook free and shrugged his shirt back into place. Raising his eyebrows, he pointed at her.

"We'll be talking, Mairi."

He turned and sauntered down the sidewalk, melting into the crowd. As soon as she could no longer see him, her legs turned to paste, and she slumped onto the edge of the planter. A second later, Noah was beside her and Ella in front of her.

"Uncle Aiden was mean to you, wasn't he?" she asked.

There was no point in lying. "He's not well, sweetheart, you know that. And, yes, he's being mean. But it's just words. He's not going to hurt us."

"Brave girl." Noah gathered her close. "You got rid of him."

"Maybe," she said. "I'll tell you later."

Her stomach roiled and her hands shook uncontrollably over the lie she'd told her brother. She was scared to death of what he could do now—this was her nightmare come to life. But she couldn't let Ella know. If Noah could make up phrases like "brave girl," then she could pretend long enough to get them all home.

"That surprise is over, thank goodness," she said brightly. "How about the bake shop and then back to the car? We still have all those boxes of flooring to pick up. Do you think Ewan measured right? Will fifteen cartons really fit in the old Sorento?"

"Shhh," Noah whispered. "You're babbling. It's okay."

She buried her head for a moment in his shoulder and took deep breaths, loving the warm scent that had become familiar and comforting. She straightened and smiled gratefully.

"I'm okay. Come on. Chocolate sponge for me."

"Fern cake! No, millionaire's shortbread!"

"I'm still full," Noah said.

"Not too full for *that*!" Ella pulled Mairi up. "Let's go!"

They set off, outwardly cheerful, but there was no denying the cloud that had settled over the day.

CHAPTER TWENTY

"Oh, bugger all, I cannot believe this. What happened to all the good luck we were supposed to have gathered from the statues?"

Mairi stood staring around the miniscule room, and Noah had no idea what to say to comfort her. He couldn't believe their situation either. The only positive was not having broken down on the A-82. Instead, Mairi's twelve-year-old Sorento that had supposedly been repaired three weeks before, had refused to start in the parking garage, leaving them stranded in the heart of civilization.

"It's less than a day's delay," he said. "I suppose it could be worse."

"Och, I hate that phrase. It's bad enough. A little box of a room. All together. How's this going to work?"

"You and Ella on the bed. Me on the couch. Look, you were brilliant finding us even this much. It's clean; the landlady seems nice. It's far better than the car ~~leaving the~~ street with those dead actors."

He peered at her, hoping to make her at leas~~t~~ smile, but he knew it wasn't the room or the car ca~~using the~~ unhappiness. She wanted to get as far from Aide~~n as she~~ could.

"They were funny." Ella climbed onto the bed, jumped twice and landed on her seat with her legs crossed. "Look, Noah! See what I can do?"

"You're a regular trampoline expert."

Ella repeated her trick three more times, and neither adult bothered to tell her to stop. At least someone hadn't a care in the world. Mairi set her shopping bags along one wall and sighed. Noah ran a hand softly down her back.

"Take a break. You've been solving problems for the past two hours."

"I'm sorry," she said. "I should be grateful there's actually a solution to all this, but I don't feel grateful for much at the moment." She hesitated and lifted her eyes apologetically. "Not true. I'm very grateful I'm not doing this alone. I'm glad you're here."

He chuckled. "That's nice. Same here."

"And you found the mechanic, and talked to the uncle, what's his name, Mac? It's a team effort."

"I could be persuaded that the toe or the nose brought us a little luck when we discovered our garage attendant has a friend who fixes cars." Noah shrugged.

"And that we found a room at all. I can give those to the statues, I suppose."

The mechanic friend had looked at the Sorento, diagnosed a dead alternator, and arranged for a tow. Noah had struck up a friendly conversation, during which he'd discovered the man had recently started woodcarving as a hobby. That, and the fact that he had a six-year-old daughter, had garnered them a promise to replace the part first thing in the morning and have the car ready before noon. Such serendipity had to be some kind of luck or magic.

Uncle Mac worked during the day, but after a little negotiating, he agreed to take his lunch break when Noah had the car back. All-in-all, even though their room had barely enough space for a double bed, a sofa, a small desk and three people to turn around, they were fine and the problems were solvable.

Mairi flopped onto the sofa and yawned. "I still can't believe I spent seven hundred pounds less than a month ago getting bells, whistles, hoses, battery, and probably the flippin' James Bond ejector seat fixed, and they missed a dying alternator."

Ella jumped off the bed and sat on Mairi's lap, facing her with legs on either side of her thighs. She placed a palm on each of her cheeks, squeezing to make her lips pop out.

"What's a James Bond ejector seat?"

Mairi laughed. "Something that shoots the bad guy's seat out of the car with the bad guy still in it."

"We *have* one of those?" Her eyes shone with the imagined excitement of all she could do with this amazing ejector seat.

"I'm sorry, no we don't. I was being silly."

"It would be good to be able to shoot people out of the car." She mashed Mairi's face together again and laughed.

Mairi shook her head to escape. "Why are you torturing me?"

"To make you look happy. Don't be sad about Uncle Aiden. Some day he will prob'ly get better."

Mairi crushed Ella tightly to her chest throat with a half laugh, half sob. "My kind, marvelous girl. I hope you're right. Uncle Aiden needs to get better."

She pressed her lips together, holding back sudden tears. Out of the mouths of babes. Babies like Ella were still pure of heart. When did all that change in a person? When did a person figure out that not everything could be fixed?

"Now," Mairi said, sniffing and gathering her composure. "It's almost eight o'clock. We picked up those supplies on the way here. You can have one of the biscuits and some milk. Then brush teeth and it's bedtime."

"And the book Noah bought me."

Mairi looked up at him, gratefully. "And the book."

"But no pajamas." Ella pursed her lips.

"You can sleep in your knicks and undershirt tonight."

"And you and Noah, too?"

Noah snorted and turned away. There were far worse fates he could think of—in fact, he couldn't think of anything nicer—than seeing Mairi stripped of her jeans and soft yellow sweater in bed. But that was the most inappropriate thing he could be contemplating in a room with her daughter present.

"Grown-ups don't have the best underthings to sleep in. I think Noah and I will use our jeans and shirts. And tomorrow, maybe you can wear your new clothes if you like."

"Aye, brilliant!" She jumped off of Mairi's lap and ran to Noah, throwing her arms around his legs. "You get to sleep in your clothes. Like camping!"

He placed his hands on her slight little back and pulled her into a standing hug, finding Mairi's eyes again.

"Yup sleepin' in the clothes. More's the pity."

He really loved how her cheeks pinkened before she dipped her head away and smiled.

A narrow sliver of light from the B&B's hallway showed beneath the room's door, allowing just enough brightness for Noah to make out the dark shapes of furniture. He illuminated the time on his watch. Just after three. The couch wasn't winning any awards for bed of the year, and he shifted position, dragging his lone blanket over his shoulders. As he tried to settle, he heard a soft "oof" from the bed, and Mairi's muttered whisper, "Ella, you sleep like a flipping starfish."

His shoulders shook in silent laughter. Then Mairi gave a full-fledge grunt, got out of bed, and started to walk around it, passing in front of his uncomfortable bed. He reached out and caught her leg, garnering a squeal. She jerked away before starting to laugh.

"Noah! For pity's sake, you about stopped my heart."

"I'm sorry. I heard you mumbling about Ella."

"She's taking up the entire bed. I've moved her a dozen times if I've done it once and the best I can do is get her into the middle half."

"Heck, if you're sleeping with a bed hog anyway, come sleep with me."

Her theatrical intake of breath made him laugh out loud. "Mr. Portman. How dare you suggest such a thing?"

He sat and swung his legs over the front of the sofa, caught her hand and pulled her to sit beside him.

"I evidently have no moral code. I'm not suggesting; I'm begging."

"Everyone has a moral code. Yours just isn't of a very high standard."

"I've been trying to keep it high where you're concerned. That seems to have quit working."

He drew her against his side and tucked the blanket around their legs. She snuggled into his embrace and rested one hand against his chest. "I think this is the most comfortable I've been since climbing into bed. She's always been a horrible child to sleep with."

"Other than Ella the horrible, are you okay?"

"Fine."

"No, I mean honestly. It was a traumatic day."

She didn't answer right away. Finally, she sighed. "Seeing Aiden *was* traumatic, and if I'm honest, I'm nervous about what he'll do. He knows where I am now, and I think he must owe someone big money. He's angry for the way his life turned out, he's in deep trouble, and I'm his chosen target for a ticket out."

"Do you think he'll turn violent?"

"Not the Aiden I've always known, but if things are very bad, who can say?"

"The police need to know about this."

"They do. And I'll call about this latest run-in as well. The trouble is, he hasn't physically done anything to me that would get him arrested."

"He's intimidated you. Threatened. Now he's stalking."

"Perhaps I could convince them of that, aye. But he is truly slippery, and I think he has someone helping him. I don't know how to stop him short of actually paying him."

"That's a terrible idea," Noah insisted. "It's a temporary fix that will only jeopardize Ella's future."

"But maybe a long enough fix that he'll find another source of money."

"Honey, it lets him win and he can come back again and again."

"I admit, thinking of him winning is one of the things that stops me."

"How about this? You're safe from him right here, right now. When we go home, you'll tell everyone what's going on and we'll put our heads together to figure it out."

"It sounds so easy."

"It should be. He's a bully and bullies can be stopped."

"I want to think I'm smarter than he is, but so far I'm not. He's not above using Ella to get to me."

"You know we'll all do anything to keep you and Ella safe."

"Thank you."

She rubbed her hand slowly up and down his chest as if for comfort. He closed his eyes and let the goose bumps from her touch have free rein throughout his body. She squirmed to get closer.

"This is awful to say, but I'm glad we got stuck here. My child's only ten feet away, which makes her a very effective chaperone, but I can still think of one or two adult activities that are pretty quiet."

She lifted her face to him, and he cupped her chin before dipping to meet her mouth with his. Swirls of pent-up anticipation exploded into a kiss that bypassed gentle and dove straight to excited exploration. Their tongues met and danced. Mairi moaned happily and scrambled onto his lap, miraculously avoiding losing their connection. Long, sweet moments later when they did break the kiss, Noah grasped her head with both hands and changed the angle of his mouth. She straddled his thighs and pushed closer, their heads bobbing together, the kiss softening at last.

"You are an amazin' kisser, Noah Portman," Mairi whispered against his lips.

She let her fingertips slide along his jawbone and up to his ears, then she buried them in his hair. Electric zaps raced down his neck and spine.

"And you make electricity," he replied, trailing shallow kisses down her chin, across its point and back up to her ear, where he nibbled until she moaned again and her head fell back, exposing her throat.

"Look who's talking."

He slid his hands along the indents of her waist and settled on her hips. Slowly drawing her tighter to him, he reveled in the shards of pleasure darting into his core. He knew the inevitable reaction could lead to nothing, but he didn't stop her from rocking gently with each thrust of her tongue, the rhythmic undulation sharpening his pleasure into desire.

His hand moved again, this time tentatively, around the curve of her seat, up to the hem of her lightweight sweater, and beneath the knit to the soft skin of her back. Higher he roamed, until he realized there was no bra to unclasp, no undergarments to impede his search. There should have been no surprise, but there was—along with another deep thrill.

"Sweet," he whispered.

"Convenient," she returned, and arched her back, allowing him to slip his fingers beneath her arm and meet the swell of her breast.

Soft, firm, generous—he wished he could look at her, tell her how stunning she was because that's how she felt to his touch. When he found the peaked nipple, her breath released in a long, slow stream that ended in a whimper. The sound sent a whiplash thrill to his groin.

"I can't even tell you how long it's been since anyone has touched me like this," she said. "And I can't remember it ever being this good."

"Talk about a woman who knows how to build up an ego." He shifted beneath her. "Not to mention a few other things."

She coughed out a laugh. "Uh-oh," she said.

"We kind of have to slow this train down," he said. "The chaperone..."

"I know. But I really don't think I want your hand to move."

He pressed his kiss back into hers and rolled her nipple beneath his fingers. She gasped into his mouth and he switched hands, giving the same attention to the other breast before finally withdrawing.

"I have to stop. The cold shower is down the hall and I don't want to go there."

"Aye. Sounds like a miserable idea."

He lifted one of her legs and twisted beneath her until he could lie on his side, braced against the couch back. When she lay facing him, he hooked her top leg over his hip. Then he grabbed the pillow he'd taken from the bed and bunched it beneath their heads.

"Don't know how long you can stand this," he said. "But we'll manage a little while. You know I didn't *want* to stop."

"I didn't either."

He kissed her slowly, and she responded with languid strokes of her tongue, soothing and easy. When they parted, he placed one hand on her head and held it, wishing he dared tell her she was safe with him, but knowing she didn't need him to protect her. Probably didn't want him to protect her. But he could comfort her, and let her do the same for him. It had been a long time for him, too, and even though this was all a terrible idea, for the moment, he truly didn't care.

They slept, cramped and curled together, until light crept in around the edges of the window and he woke to a soft kiss on his cheek.

"I should crawl in the last little while with the girl," she whispered. "Probably best she not find us atop each other quite yet."

"I suppose. We should pretend to be good role models."

"She could do worse for role models, I promise you that. It's six-thirty. Sleep a bit longer."

He closed his eyes, smiled and nodded.

The next thing he knew, Ella was standing over him, staring so quietly he actually heard her breathing and awoke with a start.

"Hi," she said.

"You are a strange child," he mumbled and rubbed his eyes.

"Time to get up. Mama says we're going out on the town after breakfast. She says we have time to shop for something for Skye before our car gets done."

"Here's what I'm thinking," he said. "I'm still sleeping and you're a nightmare I'm having."

"I'm not a nightmare!" Her laugh bubbled from her like spilled soda pop.

"You are if you're talking about shopping. Go away."

"Nae, I willnae. Get up!"

He laughed. "All right, look out. I'm up."

The morning passed much more calmly than the day before. They stayed away from The Royal Mile, concentrating instead on Victoria Street, which Ella loved because it was the street Harry Potter's Diagon Alley was based on, curving down a hill lined with tall shops and colorful buildings. They found a stuffed dragon Ella insisted Skye needed. Mairi found a bookstore and they spent half an hour browsing.

Finally, she dragged Noah, almost literally, into a kiltmaker's shop, where she attempted to educate him on clan tartans. He saw the rich red and green plaid that she said matched Ewan's dress kilt—the Cameron tartan. Her MacDonald clan was one of the oldest, she said, and showed him one of many plaids the family claimed, her favorite a dark green with navy blue, red, and black.

"You should try one on," Ella said.

"You should," Mairi agreed. "You'll need one for the wedding. You'll be back for the wedding, right?"

His brother's wedding. Nobody had even mentioned it the past two weeks. Mid-December was only four months away.

"I expect I will," he said, not really understand the confusing mix of emotions the idea brought. Leaving. Coming back. Saying good-bye. Getting home. What was he doing getting knotted up about this place, not to mention over the people?

"So...try one on," Ella said again.

He was saved by the ring of his phone, and he grinned. "Ha! Don't have time. This is our car dude."

"Car dude. Car dude!" Ella clapped.

He took the call outside the shop, and when he'd finished, Mairi appeared with a plastic bag bearing the shop's logo. She held it out.

"What?" He eyed her.

"It's not a kilt, y'eejit. But you haven't a single tartan that I've ever noticed. This'll represent for now."

He peered into the bag and pulled out a red, green, and blue tartan newsboy-style cap. He'd never considered such a thing, but it pleased him.

"Let's see," she said.

He settled it front to back on his head, and Ella clapped again. "Brilliant!"

"Handsome," Mairi said, and her eyes were serious and glistening. "It suits."

He turned and looked quickly in the glass of the shop door. The cap's low profile was subtle enough that he didn't feel conspicuous.

"It's great," he said sincerely. "Thank you, Mairi, but this is a lot."

"Nae," she replied. "A perfect impulse buy. Wear it now."

"Should I?" he asked Ella with a wink.

"Aye because it's handsome."

"How could I ignore such a compliment? I feel properly dressed now. Let's go get Mom's car."

The car ran perfectly. They found Bing and Bob's uncle's house, and the jovial Mac Smith met them precisely at noon to help load the fifteen boxes of new floor into the Kia's hatchback. Though it was filled to the top and the weight was not insubstantial, the little black Sorento and its new alternator purred them easily out of Edinburgh.

Noah felt like a weight had been lifted from him once they were out of the city. It had nothing to do with Edinburgh itself; he'd liked the town. He liked the crazy fringe festival, liked the elegant, jolly atmosphere, and he especially liked the time with Mairi that Edinburgh had gifted him last night. But the things that had precipitated the trip and the apprehension over all the tasks yet to be accomplished were heavy.

He wanted to get back to Craigwarren, where the air belonged to the grass, breezes, and sounds of late summer, rather than scents of street food and the crush of bodies. Where, he realized with surprise, he felt at home. Where Mairi and Ella would be protected and safe. Where, despite all the work that awaited, the closer they got, the more he believed they could get all their problems solved.

He watched Mairi surely and competently driving them home, down the wrong side of the road that still confused his brain, and he sighed. All his optimism was likely no more than the happy, curled-up, cramped night of interrupted sleep talking. And that intimacy was something he wasn't at all sure he could, or should, find again—even in the Highlands.

CHAPTER TWENTY-ONE

They returned Saturday evening to a chaotic mess that couldn't have made Noah happier. In his absence, Bing and Bob, with Ewan's help, had pulled up the old wooden flooring and separated it into ruined versus useable planks. Stone masons' paraphernalia—mortar-coated wheelbarrows, trowels and trails of dust—littered the area around the fireplace, and he learned the work on it would be finished Monday. A rectangle had been chalked out in the back wall for the new window and a thick, black tarpaulin had been secured to the hole in the roof, which the roofers would begin repairing after the weekend.

Supper that night was treated as a special occasion because, in Catrione's words, the family was whole and home safe again from all adventures. The only thing to dim the celebratory mood was the announcement that Callum was arriving after dinner to talk.

"Don't worry," Ewan had promised. "It's not what you think." His demeanor was a little too bright and upbeat for Noah not to worry, however, and a slow, smoldering concern grew in his gut.

It didn't help that Mairi was also subdued and serious. She'd disappeared after arriving back at Craigwarren to make some phone calls, but when she'd resurfaced, she'd put off reporting on them. "Later," was all she'd say. Noah wanted her to tell everyone what was happening, but it wasn't up to him to share her stories, so he was stuck, clueless, in the middle of every issue, and the optimism from his drive home had shrunk to faint hope.

"Come take a walk." Ewan invited him after dinner. "I'll tell you the latest."

They headed down the front driveway to the long road leading away from the house. As they passed the three houses lining the drive, Noah remembered Ella's bogart Rupert—the one who'd shared tea under the ladder—then pushed the lighthearted memory away. He needed to stop letting Scottish creatures into his thoughts.

"You've clearly decided to go ahead and try finishing the cottage," Noah said. "And Callum is coming to talk so—"

Ewan stopped him with a quiet hand on his shoulder. "Callum works with a good contractor from right here in Glencoe. I've seen his work and I think it would be smart to get him for the interior taping and finishing. You and he can do it a lot faster than the rest of us. Callum is bringing him along tonight so you can meet him."

"But that won't be cheap."

"No." Ewan hesitated. "So, I've made another decision. I don't need your approval, but I want your blessing."

Noah slowed, his wariness doubling. "What's going on?"

"I'm going to sell the cabin in Minnesota."

He might as well have sucker punched Noah. Not six months ago, Ewan had purchased a log home ninety minutes from his old office in Minneapolis. It had been planned as an escape, a respite from the city, and Noah had made all the renovations to that interior, too. Then Ewan had found Scotland, and the cabin was now a retreat Noah and Bridget used on weekends and holidays.

"That's your dream home."

Ewan's smile held more than a little wistfulness. "It was. And I feel like it's as much or even more yours than mine because you did all the work. And I would love to keep it— for you, for Bridget, for Ainslie and me when we visit. But I've done some research, and it's worth a lot more now than even half a year ago. The profit I could make would fund every bit of the reno here. We'd be free of worry and, most importantly, free of Callum's influence. It's an almost-perfect solution."

Noah's heart thrummed in disappointment. What Ewan said was true, but it also tore at the very last of his ties to home—his real home. Until that moment, Noah hadn't fully realized all the things he'd never said, never challenged about Ewan's recent decisions. He didn't want to say anything now, didn't want to confront his hero of a big brother with the sorrow and disillusionment all those decisions had caused. They weren't Ewan's problems.

On the other hand, he thought about Mairi and the problems she couldn't solve with her own brother. Maybe, if words had been spoken soon enough, Aiden's life might have been different and the rift in Mairi's family wouldn't have happened. Didn't Mairi always say sometimes you had to stand up and rage?

"I've never questioned your choices," he said reluctantly. "And if this is what you need to do, you're right, you don't need my permission. But I have to ask. Do you really know what you're doing here?"

"What's that mean?"

Noah held up a placating hand. "I know how that sounds. All I mean is, it's been four months, Ewan. *Only* four months. And you're ready to sell your old life and invest it all in something you've barely experienced. That has never been you. From where I stand, it's rash, and I worry."

He waited for the backlash, for Ewan to come back at him with defensive excuses and even anger. But his brother's brow furrowed in thoughtful concern, and all Noah saw was him working out exactly what to say. Finally, he nodded.

"You aren't wrong. This is, by all measures of my entire life, insanity. I know Dad doesn't remotely understand my defection. I know you feel like I abandoned you, Bridget, and the whole family."

"No, I—"

Ewan took his turn warding off the refute. "In some ways I did exactly that, I know. But the thing is, I can't explain, even to myself, what happened when I came here. I learned I was living Dad's life back home, not mine. I found that Bridget has always been right—we need our heritage, and since discovering it, I want to live it here. It's crazy, but it's right for me."

Noah wanted to challenge him, to let his anger out the way Mairi did and tell his brother he was hurt and mad. Except…he couldn't. He might not feel them as deeply, but he understood every word Ewan had said. He, too, felt the pull of this place. He'd heard their mother speak and believed himself crazy. He'd soaked in the watercolor scenery and the essence of the legends until they felt familiar, even though he'd spent little time immersed in the landscape and history the way Ewan had. A part of this was in him, like it or not.

"I don't believe all the crazy stories and family legends Catrione tells," Ewan continued. "But the stupid thing is, I *want* to. I think Mom, our Scottish mom, had to have believed them. The things I remember about her point to all her words and stories and advice being based in magic. Not *real* magic, but real power. This powerful place."

"Damn it." Noah groaned and looked toward the towering Warren craig named for an Englishman who'd adopted this land three hundred years before any of the relatives now living here had even been part of the universe's design. "I don't want to know this. I had a life that was nice and simple. I'll never be rich. But I didn't need to be. I didn't have enough entanglements to need much and I liked it that way. Now I have so many entanglements, I've no idea how to sort them out."

Ewan grinned. "Mairi."

Noah snorted. "Not even. She's beautiful. She's got a great kid. She's a nice enough distraction. But she's got her own troubles and much as I'd like to, I can't sort them out either."

"White Knight syndrome. I had to get over that. I had to be taught how to get over it."

"It's not that. Well, I don't know, maybe. But Mairi doesn't need a knight. She needs a hitman."

Ewan sputtered. "Uhhh, okay. I suppose that's one way."

"You know what I mean. Someone needs to catch her brother doing something that'll put him away."

"She needs a bigger family to keep him in line."

Something about that gave Noah pause. He'd been thinking of his family as her family. But they weren't. She had actual relatives of her own. He shook his head, not sure why that mattered and not able to follow his skittering thoughts to figure it out.

Ewan stopped walking and turned toward him.

"I'm happy, Noah. I've learned I can't make anyone else believe that, but if *I* believe it that's all that matters. And the practical me isn't gone. I haven't lost the work ethic. It's just that I figured out the future doesn't have to be fully planned *this minute*. In some ways, I think you've always known that. I often envied your lifestyle, doing exactly what you wanted, using your skills, making the world a kinder place."

"What the hell?" Noah squinted at the ground, half embarrassed. "Envy me? This is a little too much new-age, oversharing, Kumbaya shit, bro."

"Yeah, it sucks." Ewan laughed heartily. "Ainslie's fault. She makes me talk about…emotional shit. Look, I'm not trying to be a new-age jerk and tell you stuff to make you change your mind or your life. I'm just saying I've found my—"

"Don't you dare say 'bliss.'" Noah gave Ewan's shoulder a friendly shove.

"Say what?"

"You found your bliss. Bridget says that all the time." He lilted his voice, "'Ewan found his bliss and you should find yours.' It's annoying and girlie as hell."

"I was going to say found *myself*, but okay. And you found your bliss a long time ago, Noah. Now you need to find where you're going to follow it."

"Jerk."

Noah turned his thoughts back to the original topic. He did love the cabin in Minnesota, but it wasn't his. He'd made it attractive inside, and the work had gone as smoothly as sailing on a glass sea. This project, however… He had more emotional investment in the stupid, impossible cottage here than he'd ever had in the Minnesota log house.

"Sell the cabin," he said. "You're right, it's a perfect solution. Let's get this cottage done so I can go work on my bliss."

Because he knew how he'd do that as clearly as he knew how to plan a trip to Mars.

Noah liked the contractor Callum brought to them. John Acheson walked through the cottage with Noah and Ewan, Callum in tow, and Bing and Bob in the background "to hear the plan." Acheson showed his expertise with several good suggestions for insulation, easier placement of support beams, and praise for the basic soundness of the old building.

"I'm finishin' a frame-up this mid-week," he said. "Were you to get your floor and framing done by Thursday, I can gi' ye time over weekend next. It's a small job. Puttin' up the amount of board you're talkin' and taping the lot could be done in three or four days, including dry time and sanding."

"That would be fantastic," Ewan said.

"I couldn't do it that fast alone," Noah agreed. "I'd be grateful for the help. We could probably get some of the wallboard started. I've done a fair amount of that."

"Aye, so've we," called Bob. "We've been slappin' up walls for me da' for donkeys' years."

Callum shot them hotly annoyed daggers. "Slapping up walls is exactly why we've hired an expert. You two haven't been alive for donkeys' years."

"We're very old souls." Bob gave him a beatific grin and Noah stifled a laugh. "Nae need to be feart, Mr. McTavish. We know what we're doin' and no mistake."

Noah still never knew if Bob's happy dolt character was real or completely intentional. Either way, he discombobulated the stuffy Callum, and that was worth a lot.

"No mistakes?" Callum said. "That's the whole intention."

"You said you've swung a hammer, Cal," Ewan said. "You can come by next week and keep watch over the pair. You might be impressed."

"You know I said I'd help." Callum wrinkled his nose. "I'll be here."

"We should have a houseful Monday," Ewan said. "And it's not supposed to rain for a few days. We could be in luck."

Luck.

Noah thought of the two Edinburgh statues. Among he, Mairi, and Ella, they'd good-naturedly gathered six hands' worth of luck, but was statue luck like cat lives and get used up one good thing at a time? If so, how much Hume-and-Bobby magic had they spent?

He scoffed at his thoughts again, right up there with thinking about bogarts and kelpies. This whole country was filled with silliness. Nonetheless, looking around the shell of the cottage, he couldn't stop thinking it would be awful damn helpful if the silliness could be real.

***

"Here you are."

Mairi slipped out the back door and shut it silently behind her. Noah looked up from his carving and straightened on the bench.

"Here I am."

A fan of small creases formed at the corners of his eyes as his easy smile met her. She studied him for a long moment, taking in the line of his jaw, strong but not angular, the breadth of his forehead, the deep sable of his beard shadow, the way his thick brown hair touched the back of his collared shirt just enough to flip the ends upward.

"I'm interrupting your first quiet minute," she said.

"You are not. Come. Sit. Is Ella asleep?"

"Fell like off the top of Warren Craig."

"She's something else. Narrates her life as she goes and it's always amazing."

Mairi laughed. "I guess she does that."

"But you." He cocked his head to look at her and then removed another curl of wood with his knife. "I'm more worried about you."

"Don't be." She didn't want sympathy. She didn't really even want to talk, but she never seemed to be able to stop around him.

"You're dealing with a lot."

"Everyone is."

"You know what I mean. You talked to people today. Are you all right?"

Her sigh sounded heavy even to herself, but she relaxed as she'd known she would if she could be with him. "I'm fine, Noah. I am. I feel as if I talked to everyone. My mother isn't mad at Aiden only worried about him. Nothing new there, aye. I didn't tell her I'd seen him. I'll save that one."

Noah frowned but nodded.

Mairi sat and bent one knee, wrapping it with her hands and resting her heel on the bench. "I talked to Paul Taylor. Told him about Aiden. Told him I want my job back."

"And?"

"He wants to give it to me. He'll keep negotiating with the parent council."

"So, no change."

"Not really. Then I called Christina Sullivan from Westmuir right at home on a weekend, daring old me. Told *her* I wanted the job I'd been hired for and why it would be safe to let me teach. Figured if by a miracle I got both offers I'd be in the driver's seat for a change. She said the person she hired to replace me is only temporary and she needs more details. More proof I'm not dealing with a dangerous person."

"So, no change there either."

She shook her head and rested her chin on her knee. "But they're both thinking about me. It's not immediately helpful, but it's not unhelpful."

"Open channels are always good."

"And, the best for last. I called Sorcha back because she is a grandmother and I promised to check in. Told her once again Ella is fine. She, of course, still thinks Ella is far from fine and is quite certain she needs to go stay with her and Robbie. They can take her to her old school every day and make sure her life is not disrupted."

Noah stared a moment before he could speak. "Because taking her away from her mother would not be disruptive at all."

Her heart swelled in gratitude. The man got it. She couldn't help it; she threw her arms around his neck and buried her face against her shoulder. "Right? Why am I the one they don't trust?"

He twisted to set down his carving and take her fully into his arms.

"I don't know your brother. In the five minutes I was around him yesterday, I saw a cool, unflappable dude who double-speaks like a grifter. My take was, he has no passion only desperation that he's learned how to control. You, however, are incredibly passionate—in wonderful ways. You jump in to fix things and people hear your passion before they see your control."

"So it's because Aiden is calm and I'm a hothead? Brilliant."

He placed his lips against her ear. "You're the one teaching me that sometimes it doesn't pay to play it cool. That's all I'm saying. Aiden will get his."

"He's a bloody eel. Whenever I think I can prove something, he gets away without his fingerprints anywhere near the problem. I swear he has a double."

"Maybe you were right and he has help."

"You think?" She pulled away, even though she wanted his lips to stay on her skin for the rest of the night.

"Ewan said something this evening. That you need a bigger family to help control your brother. Your family isn't big…but you do *have* one."

"You're saying my mother is actually helping him?"

"Maybe in some ways—believing him, lying to the police, covering for him. But more importantly, she might also know who *else* is helping him—even if she doesn't know she knows."

Mairi rubbed her forehead, lost. "Lovely double talk, that."

He smiled. "It's only a theory, but think about it. Your mother knows who comes to see him. She's heard names. Maybe one of them is the one who does Aiden's dirty work."

It sounded far-fetched and overly complicated, like a television script. The whole thing was a rabbit hole she didn't even want to peer into. And yet…what wouldn't she try to get her brother out of her life?

"I think you've watched too many *Law and Order* episodes."

"Maybe," he laughed.

"This is too much to think about any more tonight," she said, her stomach sinking because, in truth, she had no idea what else to think about.

"Then don't," he said. "Take a break. What do you think about this?"

He handed her the carving, and she held it almost reverently, astonishment growing the longer she stared. The head was exquisite. He'd refined the rounded, toy-like pony head from Ella's drawing and made it more horsey, while still leaving it looking like her creation. The fish tail had the same twisting bend Ella had given it, but the forked fin at the end was delicate and filigreed. The front horse legs were sturdy and sinewed.

"I don't know what to say. It's...perfect. Stunning."

"I have to finish the tail scales, then paint it like her drawing."

"She's going to lose her mind over this."

"I'd like to give it to her after the first day of school. It's only two days away now, but I should be able to finish."

"She'll treasure it always."

"Take me to the loch," he said, surprising her with the abrupt change of subject. "Would you believe, in two full weeks, I've never been there? I've never taken one of those hikes into the hills Ewan is always raving about. I know it's getting dark, but you know the way, right?"

"Been there many times following Ella. You know? She's been very good about sticking close to home since you've come."

"Stifling her spirit."

"Hardly. Helping her mother keep her sanity! Come on, I know where there are torches. We can find the way."

"And pitchforks?" he asked.

"What?"

"Torches and pitchforks. Going after Eachann."

"No! We call—"

"A flashlight. I know. It's my inept American humor. Besides, I don't really want to go after Eachann. I kind of want to see him. Like Ella says she does."

She leaned back and stared, amused and pleased by the unexpected admission. "You're making me think you need to start wearing a kilt, man," she teased. "Believin' in kelpies and such. You're sounding the proper auld Highlander."

"Ewan said it. I don't believe in them, but I kind of want to. And I lowered myself to rubbing a bronze toe in public. I mean, what the heck? Might as well go all in."

Loch Warren was blanketed in purples and blues, the clouds limned in enough final sunlight to give them gold edges and tip the inky water with yellow highlights. The ripples spread slowly, lending a deep and mysterious air to Eachann's domain.

"I've not been here this late before," Mairi said. "It looks much different. Haunting."

"Pretty awesome," he replied.

They found a flat rock and sat. He put an arm around her shoulders, and they watched the very end of sunset in silence. When darkness finally engulfed them, he kissed her temple.

"I didn't see him, did you?"

"Nae, not tonight. It's okay. He doesn't know us."

"Didn't Ella say she knows where his actual cave is?"

"The little devil wean. It's off to the left. She found it herself the second day we were here—another time we had to look desperately for her, only to have her come meet us on the path, shoes and socks drenched, pure innocent joy on her face. The 'cave' is a deep depression in the rocks and the only way to get there is to scramble over a short boulder field. It's not hard. If you're a fair amount over three-and-a-half feet tall."

"She is an adventurer."

"She's in trouble half her life." Mairi laughed. "She supposedly knows now not to go anywhere near it without an adult."

Noah looked to the left and made a short, waving salute. "Thank you, Eachann. Hope to see you one day. Sleep well."

"You are barmy tonight, aren't you?"

"Don't have many more days left to try out Scottish craziness. Monday the work starts in earnest and there'll be some long nights." He sat quietly. "I do like this, though. It's like nothing back home."

"Could you ever see yourself staying here?" She wasn't really serious; she knew the answer.

"Like Ewan?" He laughed. "Two for two on the Portman brothers? I don't really think so. Another place to fall for and then have to leave one day."

She'd known the answer but it made her sad anyway. "Why would you say that?"

"Everything disappears after a while. Everyone moves on."

"Why are you so afraid of people leaving, Noah? You're here. I'm here. Whatever happens next week or the week after, is it really that bad?"

"It might be. The way I'm flirting with disaster right now? The way I did with you in Edinburgh when I know it all has to end? Another goodbye."

"Who said goodbye, Noah? Who hurt you enough to make you set yourself apart?"

He shook his head. "It's not that. I'm not a man ruined by his only great love."

"Promise?"

"Yes. Oops, dust speck." He brushed a thumb beneath her eye and removed the soft touch too quickly. "No tragic love affair, except maybe with my mother. Freud would have a field day. Whatever else I forgot over the years, I never forgot the day my father told us our mother was gone. To Heaven, he said, but that didn't help because people don't come back from Heaven. I knew that even at four. She was my best friend when she died. Ewan was in school and gone most of the day. Bridget was only little. The loss stayed with me.

"My mother Amanda, the one who raised me most of my life—always told me I was born to be more solitary than the others. She—everybody—tried to make me make friends. And I could do it. But it hurts when best friends leave, too. And when girlfriends leave. Even brothers when you're an adult and understand these things. I don't think I ever got mad, but every loss proved life was easier when I made my own schedule, lived according to my own timeline, picked my own levels of friendship."

"So, this friendship, ours, is not one you're picking? It's flirting with disaster?"

"Oh, I *am* picking it—but it's now at way too high a level for my comfort."

"People come in and out of our lives all the time," she said. "That doesn't have to keep us from enjoying new things or new people. Does nae mean this," she leaned toward him and kissed the corner of his mouth, "is going to be a disaster."

He turned slowly sliding into the kiss and slipping a hand up the back of her neck to bring her mouth tight to his.

"Doesn't mean it isn't," he whispered.

CHAPTER TWENTY-TWO

Monday came and passed in a haze of people learning how to choreograph movements around everything from rolling out wool insulation, to nail in subflooring, to fetching boards, wheelbarrows, nails, and tape measures.

Callum showed up and proved he could work with others as long as it was neither Bob nor Bing. He and Ewan worked on insulation and finished in less than two hours. Bing and Noah weren't far behind with plywood subflooring, Bing crooning "Maxwell's Silver Hammer" multiple times and Bob hitting the side of a wheelbarrow whenever an anvil strike was called for. At least they did until everyone forced him to choose a new song and got "Sunshine on Leith," and, later, a handful of actual Bing Crosby songs he'd proudly learned after researching his nickname including "Pennies From Heaven" and "White Christmas."

Bob turned out to be the construction site equivalent of a surgical nurse. He heard every conversation, handed people equipment without them asking, fetched supplies, and carted things away, always with a wisecrack or an over-obvious reply. Even Callum couldn't complain.

Roofers clambered over the old slate tiles and, once subflooring was in, set up scaffolds to reach the underside of the roof. Noah kept tabs on it all, and once his part in laying flooring was done he recruited Bing to help start constructing wall frames.

The time shot by, and when Innis and Catrione, Cairstine and Isla brought lunch, the ham sandwiches on thick slices of rich sourdough bread were devoured in minutes, a fruit compote disappeared, and a welcome case of Belhaven light ale washed everything down.

By the end of the afternoon, the fireplace was finished including the new flu and electric insert, and the stone mason had set up to finish outdoor work the next day. The subflooring was in, the roofers had old insulation out of the rafters and were ready to tear off slate tiles and replace half the trusses.

When the five-man crew left the cottage and flopped onto the grass out front with more beer to wash away the dust, Catrione and Cairstine appeared with trowels, shears, and clippers in hand after spending the afternoon in the cottage gardens. They wouldn't get all the new plantings from Cat and Innis's long-range plan in, but even the start was going to be beautiful.

Noah had never had such a productive day in his life. This pace couldn't continue as the work got more detailed, but his optimism finally soared. As a bonus, he hadn't had a minute to dwell on the night before, when he'd ignored every warning he'd given himself about the dangers of playing the attraction game with Mairi.

They'd returned to the house and talked until after one in the morning about every unimportant subject that came up. As it had the night at the pub, sharing flowed between them easily as Ella chattered and Bing sang, all while Noah finished Eachann's wooden scales and gently sanded the last rough spots smooth. All of that would have been fine, but then they'd slept together. Sadly—or thankfully—he'd been stubborn enough to keep it to actual sleeping, but like holding hands, sleeping with her, however sappily chaste it had been, was almost more intimate than casual sex. Sex would be hormones. Sleeping beside her was caring. Wanting her close.

He didn't do close.

Hours later, Catrione stood at the head of the table after dinner and addressed Ella with sparkling eyes. "So, little Ella, kelpie hunter, fairy keeper, and a work hand at the cottage we will desperately miss, this is your last night before school starts, aye?"

"Aye," Ella echoed. "It'll be all right, but I'd rather stay here.".

"It *will* be all right," Catrione said. "Nonetheless, we must mark the end of summer with somethin' special. What have you been asking for most days the past month?"

"Cranachan?"

Catrione inclined her head. "Is it still on your wish list?"

"Are we having it!"

"I thought it was time. Come along. You can help me serve."

Ella hopped up and Noah turned to Mairi. "What is this magical thing, Cranachan?"

"Like a little trifle."

"A parfait," Ewan explained.

"Raspberries, oats, heather honey, and Scottish whipped cream." She leaned forward to whisper, "The grown-up versions will have the oats soaked in our best Scotch."

The glasses appeared, and Ella proudly set one in front of her mother and the other before Noah. He had to admit they were pretty, layered bright red and white with thin layers of crispy brown between. In the middle of the table, Catrione set a platter of shortbread, each piece layered with a base of chocolate. Her version of millionaire's shortbread.

"Give it a go," Mairi said. "Pretty traditional, this one."

He dipped his spoon into the thick, creamy, layers and when the sweetness hit his tongue, he moaned.

"No way," he said. "This isn't real."

"Taste the whisky in the crunch?" Innis asked. "Not your usual sweet pudding, aye?"

They ate until they were ready to explode, and for once Mairi didn't even limit her daughter. When they were done, Ewan and Ainslie shooed Catrione into the living room.

"For that meal, you get the night off," Ainslie said. "Everyone go. We've got this."

"Can I show you my school uniform?" Ella asked Noah as soon as he sat. "It's nicer than my old one. That was a plain gray skirt with a green jumper. This one has purple in it."

"By all means, let's see."

She dashed up the stairs and returned five minutes later wearing a plaid pleated skirt of purple, black, and green, and one of the white shirts she'd gotten in Edinburgh. She carried a tiny gray blazer with purple edging on the lapels.

"It's kind of pretty," she said.

"That is an epic skirt," he said. "And the blazer is, in a word, awesome."

She laughed. "I like that word. You say it a lot. Awesome."

The landline phone began to ring then, and Innis looked to the handset. "Who would that be at this time? I suppose someone working with you on the cottage?"

The ringing stopped and a moment later, Ainslie stepped into the room, her expression uncertain. "Mairi," she called and brought the phone closer. "It's Sorcha. She wants to talk to Ella."

Mairi's mouth closed into a tight line while she contemplated the news and then she held out her hand for the receiver. "Hullo, Sorcha. How are you? What can I do for you?"

Noah watched, impressed with the calm Mairi showed. She was proving his observations perfectly—using her control when she needed it.

"She's here. Getting ready for bed in a few. Big day tomorrow." A pause. "I'm sure she'd like that. I can put her on speaker for you. Hold for a mo'." She covered the speaker and smiled at Ella. "It's Gran MacDonald. She wants to wish you happy first day."

"Okay!" Mairi pushed the speaker button. "Gran!" Ella said.

"Hullo my girl. How are you? Having fun staying with friends?" The woman didn't sound old, and her voice cajoled.

Mairi raised a brow and in reminder for Ella to give away no information.

"It's fun. I get to draw a lot and help cook and with chores. But tomorrow I have to start school."

"Yes, I know. How do you feel about that?"

"Good. I'll be in P4."

"Already. How is that possible?"

"I turned seven last November."

"Yes, you did. How do you feel about going to a new school? Won't you miss your old one?"

"I'll miss my friend Ava. But it's okay, this school has pretty uniforms. I'm wearing it to show Noah. It's purple and green." Mairi winced but Noah shook his head. Nobody knew who he was.

"Is Noah a new friend you're staying with?"

"No. He's staying here, too."

"So there are lots of people staying there?"

"Why don't you tell Gran about the new cat shirt you got?" Mairi said quickly, and shot a dark look at the phone. "She's fishing," she whispered, and Noah nodded.

"A new cat shirt?" Sorcha asked.

"For after school. It's purple and has rainbow colors on the sleeves."

"My, you have lots of purple. Well, it's almost time to say good night, Ella. Have you visited your new school? Do you know your teacher?"

"Aye. Mrs. Cowan. But soon as Mama gets her new job, guess what? I'll be in Mrs. MacDonald's class!"

"Is that so?"

"Right!" Mairi jumped in. "Time to say goodnight for now, Ella. Bath and earlier bed tonight."

"Okay. 'Night, Gran."

"Have a wonderful first day. One of these days soon, Grandad and I will come see your new school. We'll surprise you."

Mairi grabbed the phone and turned off the speaker. "Thanks for ringing, Sorcha. Talk soon. Bye now."

She disconnected, her features drawn and tight, her eyes bright with annoyance. Still she managed a smile for her daughter.

"Time to take the uniform off, jump in the bath, and then color or read before bed. How about we plait your hair and make it curly but not flyaway for tomorrow?"

Ella made the rounds to say good night. Noah accepted her hug and gave her an extra squeeze. "I'll see you in the morning. Don't want to miss the whole uniform when it's all on."

"I'm wearing the purple dragon socks tomorrow too."

"Can't wait. Sleep tight."

He'd offered to do Ella's barn chores that night, allowing her to spend more time preparing for school. Ainslie went with him, and by the time they returned Catrione had picked up a cross stitch she'd started. Innis had his nose in a book. Ewan was going through more cottage checklists, and Ainslie sat beside him at the table. Noah dug out the paints he'd bought in Edinburgh and set them up at the end of the table. When he brought out the kelpie carving, Ainslie took one look at it and squealed.

"My word, Noah! That is unbelievable."

"It's for Ella. Her vision of Eachann mixed with mine. I'll paint it and give it to her tomorrow to celebrate the first day in a new school."

"Told you he had a magical talent," Ewan said.

"People around here use that word far too much," Noah said. "It's a horse and a fish. I've done plenty of each. It's not magical." Despite his protest, the compliment pleased him.

"She'll love it," Ainslie said.

"That she will." Mairi entered the room and took a seat across from Noah. "Is it okay if we watch this last part?"

"I would have hidden in my room if I cared." He chose a container of deep russet brown paint and a medium bristle brush. He didn't paint a lot of his carvings, most people liked them natural or stained. But he had a vision for this piece based on Ella's original sketch. "Ella says Eachann is dark brown, right?"

"That's exactly what Eachann means," Ainslie said. "Brown horse. Borin' old name."

"I can pronounce it, so I like it," Noah said and made the first stroke.

Mairi's eyes followed his brush. He liked having her watch—and wasn't that something new? "How are you after Grandma's weird phone call?" he asked.

"Aye, that *was* odd," Ainslie agreed. "Think she got whatever information she wanted?"

Mairi sighed, her eyes clouded with worry. "I'm really not okay. She completely gave me the crawlies. The whole thing about surprising Ella with a visit."

"She doesn't know where we are, does she?" Ainslie asked.

"I know that's what she was fishing for. And now she has Ella's teacher's name. All she has to do is look up where a Mrs. Cowan teaches."

"It's a common name. That could take a while."

"Even so, Aiden knows we're here. He'll tell her, I'm sure."

"*What?*" Ainslie cried.

Mairi finally told the story of their Edinburgh meeting.

"We have to do something," Ainslie said.

"I agree, so I talked to that DI in Glasgow again today."

"That's great." Noah looked up and smiled. "And he listened?"

"I think, maybe, he finally agrees I'm not making all this up. Aiden hasn't done anything he can be arrested for yet, but they'll watch him more closely now."

"Then they'll catch him up," Ewan said. "He'll make a mistake."

"I can only hope."

"I'll be honest. I didn't like the way your ex-mother-in-law was probing, either," Noah said, finishing the main horse body color and rinsing his brush. "But I don't think you need to worry. You're taking Ella to school and picking her up."

"She also has us," Ainslie added. "We've got you."

"I honestly don't know how I'd have made it through the past month without you."

"You don't have to wonder, do you? We'll help you get Aiden sorted."

Noah finished the carving almost two hours later and was pleased with the final result. The tail glistened with touches of neon and scales tipped in gold. The horse's eyes were focused but not mean or angry. He didn't look friendly, but he looked like he could be a friend. He hoped Ella would like it.

That was silly. He knew she'd *like* it. But he also knew little girls liked fuzzy, cute things. This wasn't a cuddly toy, but over the years maybe she'd come to think it was special.

He and Mairi talked into the morning again. The new habit was close to feeling like an obsession, but at least by the time he sent her—reluctantly—to her own room this time, she insisted he'd helped assuage her worries. If this was an obsession, it was worth the risk if Mairi slept better.

Ironically, he slept like crap. Swirling dreams of kelpies, grandmothers with shaded faces, and worries that he was getting too close to Mairi MacDonald, left him feeling heavy and drugged the next morning. It didn't help that fresh-scrubbed Ella in her skirt, blouse, purple-and-green striped tie, and the blazer that made her look like a miniature Wall Street exec, made his heart nearly thump out of his chest at the idea that someone might hurt her.

"Let me come with you to pick her up this afternoon?" he asked. "It's a silly feeling that I should."

Mairi didn't question the silly feeling, she simply agreed to bring him.

After that, though the heaviness of concern didn't quite dissipate, the day was nearly as successful as the one before. Bob was reliably full of comic relief. Callum remained condescending of Bob's lack of mental acuity, but mostly avoided him. Bing worked like a demon on flooring with Ewan, and Noah and Callum built the frames for the bedroom walls, the new kitchen, and the drying closet.

The crowning moment came, however, three hours after lunch, when the five of them, along with an excited Innis, hoisted the solid wooden beam that would hold the loft's floor onto wooden posts they'd anchored to the floor joists that morning.

"We'll get Callum's contractor to double check it all," Noah said. "But I think tomorrow we can put in the joists for the loft floor. We'll definitely be ready for him. Might even get a few sheets of wallboard hung. And it's looking like the rain's gonna stay off for another couple of days." He stared at where half the roof sported new triangular trusses and the base for the new slate tiles. "They might get the roof secured by the weekend. Men, you might all pull this prank off."

Their self-congratulatory back-thumping was interrupted when Mairi stepped through the door.

"Look at what I'm seeing here!" she exclaimed. "This is pure dead brilliant, you lot. I can see the rooms!"

"It's coming," Noah said.

"And that free flooring? I love the dark, dark color. It's going to blend *so well* with the coral accents everywhere."

"You're mean, aren't you?" Noah growled.

"And proud of it. Do you still want to ride along to school?"

"I do." He turned to Ewan. "Can you four finish the last of this? I'll be back in less than an hour."

"Goin' to get Ella?" Bob asked.

"We are," Mairi said. "Make sure her first day was fun and safe."

"I've heard 'bout your brother. Sounds a right wanker that one."

Mairi's smile twisted. "He kind of is."

"Well, we've got your back, aye."

Mairi offered him a grateful hug that made him beam, and Noah gave him a pat on the back. Young Bob really wasn't as clueless as he sounded.

***

Mairi sat at the table with the rest of the family, laughing at Ella's stories from the day. She liked her teacher but not as well as she would have liked her mama. She liked science because they were talking about insects and she was going to like insects. Her new friend Amy was kind of lazy, she said, and didn't like to skip rope or play dodgeball at playtime. In PE, Amy walked when they were supposed to run. But she was funny and she liked to draw, too. Though she liked to draw cats and flowers and people. She'd never tried drawing a kelpie.

Ella's chattiness brought lighthearted happiness to the table, and even baby Skye contributed. Since it was the first day of school and Skye was now four-and-a-half months old, Isla had decided to school her, too, on a first taste of solid food. Ella begged to be the one to give Skye the first spoonful of rice cereal and Isla took pictures as Ella doubled over with laughter at the baby's shuddering, scrunched-up faces.

When everyone had laughed their fill, and the ricey disaster on Skye's cheeks had been wiped away, Noah took his turn.

"So, I have something to commemorate Ella's first day in a new school," he began.

"What's commemorate?" Ella asked.

"Celebrate," Mairi said. "A special award so you remember the day."

"For me?"

"For you." Noah nodded. "It's mostly because you're so cheerful. A lot of kids won't talk about school at home and that makes us lucky."

"What's the award? Is it like a present?"

Ella honed straight in on the present part, but Mairi's heart swelled in her chest. This man. So full of surprises. Smart and clever, talented but modest. Funny. An effective boss.

An amazing kisser.

She'd spent the last three nights—more if she counted Edinburgh—trying to figure out how she was going to get used to him leaving. She held no illusions. But she wanted to hang onto *him* as long as she could. He gave her confidence every day—and later she would tell him he'd given her another plan, too. The more she'd thought about asking her mother about Aiden's friends, the more sense it made. Now that DI Donnelly was taking her a little more seriously, maybe she could give him another name to look into...

She watched Noah hand her daughter a pink box Catrione had found for him.

"What is it?" Ella asked, taking the box with surprising reverence.

"Something we talked about a while ago," he said.

She pulled off the cover and dug through a wad of white tissue paper. She stopped momentarily, her eyes widening, and at last she lifted out the kelpie. Mairi had already seen it finished, had watched it come alive over two weeks, and still it took her breath away—like something conjured from the heart of a tree.

Ella stood as still as the carving itself and said nothing. Finally, she touched the horse's nose with her finger. Then, suddenly, her lip trembled and her eyes welled with a flood of tears that spilled like little rivers from both eyes.

"Ella! Oh, sweetie, what's wrong?" Mairi asked.

Noah looked momentarily distraught.

"It's Eachann," she said.

"It is," Noah replied. "The drawing you made for me turned into this."

As suddenly as she'd begun to weep, Ella ran to where Noah stood and reached for him. He squatted and took her in his arms.

"I love you, Noah! This is the best present I ever got!"

His face crumpled slightly, and he worried his lip. "Aw, sweetie. It's just a little carving."

"It's the most beautiful carving in the whole entire world! You made it?"

"I watched him, love," Mairi said. "He did make it. Out of that wood he found when you got locked in the little shed."

Ella clung to him a long time, and when she finally let go, her face tear-streaked but dry and back to being excited, she danced around with her kelpie, showing him off to everyone.

Noah, however, turned away, and Mairi saw his shoulders sag. Quietly she moved to stand in front of him and took his hands. "Hey. You okay?"

"Nope." He half-laughed and blew out another breath. "I…that was some reaction. I don't know if I deserved that."

"Of course you did. I told you she'd love it."

"It, yes. Not *me*."

Mairi laughed. "Well, you're worth loving. You did a special thing for her. She knows."

"I guess." He sniffed a little and smiled. "Let her play with it a while. I need to go out to the cottage and check on a couple of things for tomorrow. I'll be back in a few minutes."

She peered closely into his eyes, troubled by the shutters she started to see coming down behind their normal golden hazel spark. "All right. You need help?"

"I don't." He squeezed her hand. "I can't tell you how happy I am that she loves it. I loved making it for her."

He left then, and in his wake there was a strange hollow void Mairi found more worrisome than any call from Sorcha or Aiden.

CHAPTER TWENTY-THREE

Mairi told Ainslie the next morning she was heading for Glasgow after dropping Ella off at school. She'd not seen Noah again the night before. If he'd come in late from the cottage, he'd sneaked in when she wasn't watching, and his reaction to giving Ella the carving both worried and slightly annoyed her. She couldn't figure out what had caused the extreme emotion, but whatever it was, he hadn't even returned so Ella could say good night.

He also didn't know her plans for the day, and she hated that it bothered her.

She reached her mother's house just before noon, laden with lunch—a pair of sandwiches from her mother's favorite shop, and two pieces of lemon cake from a neighborhood bakery. She greeted her mother warmly and welcomed the hug she got in return.

"It's lovely of you to visit," her mother said. "I miss you."

"I miss you, too, Mum. And Ella does. She started school yesterday."

"She's growing fast. I'd love to see her."

"Soon," Mairi promised.

"I wish I knew where you were. I would at least know you're both safe."

That surprised her. Aiden hadn't told his mother where they were? She didn't know what that meant, but since he knew it hardly mattered if her mother did, too.

"I'm staying near Glencoe. With Ainslie Campbell."

"Ainslie! Such a beautiful, smart girl. You two were close as two peanuts in a shell. She's a veterinarian if I remember."

"She is. A very good one. She's engaged to the new owner of Craigwarren. You've heard of that property. Out near Kingshouse."

"One of the oldest family properties still around. She's there?"

"Aye. It's beautiful. Ella loves the Highlands. She's wild as a little sprite."

"And you can't come home yet?"

"Not yet. I want to help Aiden get settled first."

"Aiden? Why, he's settled right here. We're fine, Mairi."

"I know." She gritted her teeth and remained pleasant. "I talked to him a few days ago. He's asking for help. For some money."

Her mother looked crestfallen for only a moment, then nodded her head. Sheila Murray had once looked very much like Mairi. At fifty-nine, she held onto her looks in a thin and fragile way, her black hair now streaked with silver, her green eyes sharp but aged more than they should be. She was still smart about many things—the world, the community. It was only when it came to Aiden she wore blinders.

"Aiden is too generous," she said. "He's always treating us to something new. He loves to buy me small gifts though I tell him not to." She held out her hand. "Two weeks ago, he brought me this ring. It's an aquamarine, my birthstone."

"Pretty, Mum but based on what he said, he oughtn't be splashin' down such cash."

Sadness etched deeper lines into her mother's face. "I'm afraid you're right."

"I'm thinking about helping him." The lie came with difficulty. She was a terrible actor, and there were more white ones to come. Her fingers shook as she picked up her sandwich. "I want to be sure if I lend him the money, he'll use it to help you both and get back on track. The other thing he said is that he has a friend, one who's been helping him, but is also a little down on his luck? Which one is that, do you know?"

"I don't know many of his friends. He goes out. They rarely come here." She took a thoughtful bite of her sandwich.

"If he wants to help a friend, that's fine. But maybe I can find out a little more and know how to better help, too." She wanted to gag on her fake sweetness. This whole scheme suddenly seemed like a stupid idea. Even if her mother came up with no names, she'd surely tell Aiden about this conversation, and that would only make him suspicious.

"He's got a good heart, Aiden. I know you don't trust him, but he always wants to help people. I know one of his friends. He has come 'round a time or two. Magnus. Magnus Ferguson, I think. I know Aiden has given him money to help him out. He's that generous."

She couldn't believe it had been that easy. There was no way Aiden was giving money to anyone to help him out. Magnus Ferguson was shaking Aiden down! It had to be that, or he was simply a bloke Aiden had crossed and now owed. She tamped down her excitement. Magnus Ferguson could be a legitimate friend. She could still be on the road to infuriating her brother. But she had a name. It was something.

She spent another hour with her mother, looking at old pictures. Finishing the cakes. Acting the dutiful daughter. As long as she didn't have to talk about Aiden, it wasn't that hard.

"I need to head back now, Mum," she said. "I wanted to pop in for lunch, but it's over two hours back, and I need to pick up Ella at four."

"Bring her back for a visit soon."

"I will."

"And thank you for trying to help Aiden. It makes my heart glad."

"Sure, Mum."

She'd help him all right. With any luck at all, right into a prison cell. She'd have to deal with her mother's heart later. She pulled away but within two blocks, found a parking spot next to a small neighborhood park. As fast as she could, she pressed the button labeled DI Donnelly. He answered on the second ring.

"Donnelly."

"This is Mairi MacDonald, Inspector. I have some information for you."

He took down her story and Magnus Ferguson's name. Then, after asking her to hold for several minutes, he returned.

"It's interesting, Miss MacDonald. That name is on our watch list. He does have a record. If I can tie him to your brother, we might have something. I can let you know."

"Thank you. And this isn't to tell you your job, Mr. Donnelly, but I know my family. If my mother tells Aiden of our conversation, he'll warn this Ferguson. If he can be found soon, it might be helpful."

"I agree. I'll speak with you soon. Thank you for the information."

It was a huge change from the Donnelly who'd kept her in a holding room after finding drugs in her kitchen. The feeling of relief at simply being believed was enormous.

She found Noah in the cottage after supper that night, after he'd been friendly but distant during the meal and disappeared immediately afterward.

"Hiya," she said. "Am I bothering you?"

"Of course not. The inspection is in eleven days, and now the push is on. Acheson is coming to help with plasterboard tomorrow. I want to have a head start."

"Oh aye, sure. Makes sense."

"You went to see your mother. That's good. Did anything come of it?"

"It did. You were right, I got the name of a supposed friend Aiden has been paying and I gave it to Donnelly. I wanted to thank you for the idea."

"You're welcome."

He turned to lift a small piece of plasterboard into place with a cutout for a light switch, and pulled a hammer and nail off his tool belt. He didn't offer a single word...and Mairi's natural anger bubbled to the surface.

"What's wrong with you?" she asked.

"A lot of people have tried answering that, with no success."

"Stop bein' a feckin' weapon, Noah. Look at me and tell me why you're doing this. Acting this way."

His shoulders drooped. For a long moment he simply stood, but at last he straightened, and when he turned, his eyes were stern.

"You want to know why things have changed? Fine. You deserve to know. It's because I was Ella's age once. I know what it's like to lose somebody at that age. She's already got a father she can't trust and an uncle who's threatening her. I won't let her say she loves me and then turn around and leave her like they have. If you aren't going to protect her, I have to."

Mairi's full anger spilled over in a hot rush.

"How dare you? How dare you tell me I don't know how to protect my daughter or know what she needs? You listen to me. What Ella needs to learn is the exact *opposite* of what you learned. She needs to know that people are mostly wonderful. That if someone comes into your life for two days or two years or twenty years, they're a gift. And if they leave, it isn't her fault. It might be sad to have someone move away, but she can keep in touch. *That* is what I will tell her when you leave. Not that you abandoned her. I don't tell her that about her father. She thinks he has a wonderful job."

"Sounds like a nice thing to tell her. Wish someone had tried it on me."

"For God's sake, then try it now. The whole world isn't out to depress you, Noah. Everyone in the universe isn't thinkin' about you every feckin' hour. You're only on the minds of the people who care about you, but those people can't help you if you're convinced they're out to hurt you."

"Mairi, it's not that simple. You and my sister…you can't make the world look like lollipops and rainbows for everyone. People get hurt if you don't take them seriously."

She had nothing else to say. He'd made up his mind to be exactly the caricature hermit she'd first heard he was. And he had shut down right in front of her.

She opened a manilla envelope she'd carried down from the house and drew out a sheaf of two dozen papers along with several photographs. With an angry flourish, she tossed them onto a worktable.

"Here are the latest orders and some color samples. If you check them against the pictures you and Ella found, you'll see we tried to match some of the original décor of the cabin. You'll be thrilled to know there's not a coral tile in the lot. Freestanding cupboards that will do until there's time to order custom cabinets. There's even a small kitchen island. Some end tables. A couple of rugs. A living room set. It's all been vetted by Ainslie, Catrione, and Isla. They'll look pretty. The whole place will look pretty. Everything should start arriving after the inspection.

"It'll be another hard push to get all the tiling and finishing done, but you're a great leader. With your guidance, it will look great for the newlyweds. That's all the report I have for you. Congratulations, Noah. You were right—you can get this done."

Her anger turned to pain when his features didn't change.

She turned and took two steps. He stood in front of her on the third. Her breath caught and her pulse raced with hope at the sorrow in his eyes. At least it was an emotion other than indifference. He grasped her upper arms.

"Please, Mairi. Understand. I can't change who I am."

She stared. Anger, annoyance, hurt...all warred within her. Some might look at his worry for Ella as noble. To her, it reeked of cowardice. She set her jaw.

"Dinna fash, Noah, of course I understand. Better than you think. It *is* hard to change. Thing is, I wasn't askin' you to. I know who you are and that you need to go. It didn't matter. But I will miss the friendship. Unlike you, I need all the friends I can get."

***

Noah had no idea how he managed the pain of the following four days. The work on the cottage went better than he could have hoped for, but with Mairi, there was no more progress on the friendship. In fact, there was negative progress. He believed he'd been true to himself and truthful about his reasons for pulling away from the relationship with Mairi and Ella, but he also knew she thought he was the living embodiment of every Scottish term for a dickhead she knew.

She was true to her word as well. Never once did she let Ella think there was anything wrong. They didn't hang out as much. He didn't read to her as often. But Mairi explained that Noah was on a deadline. He'd talk later. She was, in a word, kind.

By the end of Sunday, the inside of the cottage had been transformed. Stark white walls created all the spaces Ewan and Ainslie had imagined. The seams were taped and sanded, the loft had a sturdy floor and railing, and a showpiece ladder to serve as a staircase.

At seven o'clock, the entire family walked from the main house to the cottage to celebrate what Ewan dubbed the end of Phase Mission Impossible. Callum had gone home, but Bing and Bob remained, still cleaning up.

"My brother *has* accomplished the impossible," he said. "He organized a group of people who know next to nothing about building and turned them into construction workers. He coordinated the actual experts and sweet-talked them into turning themselves inside out for us by breaking all speed records. Look where we are now. We have six more days to get the wiring to the new rooms, install the bathroom and kitchen fixtures, the last half of the roof tiled and the last of the foundation work finished. Compared to what already done, it's a walk in the park."

Everyone clapped and cheered. Ella, sitting on a folding chair with Skye in her lap, clapped the baby's hands together, too. Innis, never one to skimp on a celebration toast, poured out glasses of Scotch and wine and juice for Ella.

Noah held his glass of Scotch while Ewan made the toast, and instinctively searched for Mairi. When she caught his eyes and then quickly flicked her gaze away, the pain was too much. He had to fix what he'd done, and he could only think of one way to try.

Ducking into the kitchen space, he found the pad of paper and pen he kept for scribbling notes as he worked. He tore off one sheet and wrote a fast list: *Eejit, bampot, rocket, bawbag, diddy, nugget, spanner, weapon, arsehole...* He drew several blank lines beneath the words, folded the paper, and made his way to Mairi, who stood beside Ainslie and Isla.

"Can I steal you for a minute? Please?"

She bit her lip and studied him a long moment, then she relented. "To where?"

"Just across the room." When they'd gone far enough, he handed her the paper. "Read it."

She opened it...and slowly began to giggle. "What in the world?"

"All the Scot speak I've learned over the past three weeks. I know there are more. Add them. Mairi, I'm sorry. I did this all wrong."

"Oh, aye, y'did, laddie." She looked at her list. "Diddy, will do. A spineless idiot."

"That's actually pretty kind."

"I'll think about more."

"Can we talk later? I will properly apologize. I'm not changing. I can't. But I threw our friendship in your face and that was unforgiveable. It took me four days to figure it out."

"That's better than five days. And not completely unforgiveable."

"I can't stand not knowing if they've learned anything about Aiden's drug buddy. I need to know if you think Ella is still safe. What's Sorcha doing?"

"I *would* like to talk. I don't know what Sorcha's doing; I haven't called her. Don't know anything about Aiden either yet. Ella has been perfectly fine." Her words rushed out as if they'd been pent up.

"Back porch after Ella's in bed."

"Done." She started to turn but then faced him and put a hand on his forearm. Her eyes glistened. "Thank you."

He wanted to kiss her. He missed kissing her. But that was not what this apology was about. He'd been serious— he hadn't changed; he wasn't going to let the physical take over again when he was mere days from leaving. This was about respecting her, not pleasing himself.

Mairi and Isla took the little girls back to the house first. Catrione and Innis followed shortly afterward. When Ainslie took a call on her emergency phone, she waved at Ewan and told him she'd take it outside.

"So," Ewan said when the brothers were alone. "I saw you talking to Mairi. Are you going to fix things with her?"

"I'm going to try. I got too close to her and Ella, but I'm leaving and I refuse to be another person who hurts them. We've become friends. That's the relationship I want to fix."

"You sound exactly like I did. I wasn't going to stay. Ainslie knew that. We tried to plan the opposite of what you are, a hot two-week affair. It didn't remotely work. Skye came along, Cat and Innis got married, Dad got sick. Two weeks were up and we'd barely had ten minutes alone much less time for a tryst. Still, it worked out. It could for you, too."

"I'm too set in my bachelor ways," Noah joked, though it didn't feel funny.

"It has nothing to do with being a bachelor. It has to do with you letting go. You could stay, you know. What have you got going on back home? Your stuff in storage. Maybe helping me sell the cabin. I have those three little driveway houses I'd like to upgrade at some point. The big house needs repairs I can't do. You'd have jobs here forever."

"Tempting as it is, this is your life. I don't think it's mine."

Ewan grasped the back of Noah's neck and pulled him forward, giving him a pat on the cheek. "The offer is permanently open, man. Now I'm going with Ainslie."

"I want to make sure Bing and Bob got on their way. I haven't seen them since the toast."

He checked every room to make sure all was secure. Bing's car was gone, so he knew the cousins had left. He was shutting off lights when his cell phone rang. He pulled it out of his pocket—and froze. For an instant, he couldn't make himself answer, but finally he slid the icon.

"Noah Portman."

"Noah! Glad I caught you right in the middle of lunchtime. This is Leonard Frederickson. Do you have a minute?"

"I do. Mr. Frederickson, this is a huge surprise."

"I'm sure it is. I have an enormous apology and some groveling to do. I'll start by admitting up front I hired the wrong man for my hotel renovation. Not to disparage anyone, but the personalities, the timelines, the workmanship, isn't in line with what I'm seeking."

Noah's heart was making an attempt to pound through his chest wall. "Oh?"

"The groveling goes this way: how soon can I talk you into accepting this job? And what additions to your bid will make it even more attractive?"

"Mr. Frederickson, I'm more flattered than I can say, but there are a few things you need to know before I can give you an answer."

"I can deal with almost anything, Noah, as long as the answer is that you'll work on my ballroom. Now tell me, what can I do for you?"

CHAPTER TWENTY-FOUR

The silence in the living room hung for so long after Noah's announcement, Mairi was sure she could hear birds weeping outdoors. Finally, Innis cleared his throat.

"Of course, we don't like that he's leaving us earlier than planned, but what we can't forget, is that our Noah has been offered the chance of a lifetime. What a braw job he'll make of renovating a historical building. Congratulations, laddie, we're happy for your success."

Mairi *was* happy for him, but she doubted her face showed it.

"Thank you," Noah replied quietly. "It's only a week early. I'll be here for the inspection plus three extra days in case of problems. Time for lots more shortbread."

He'd gotten the new job offer two nights before. The very night he'd met her on the deck and they'd put their friendship back to rights. She couldn't lie to herself any longer—she had no idea how she'd live without his presence. Until he'd broken the news about accepting the job, a part of her had hoped he'd extend his stay to help Ewan. Surely the longer he stayed the more time she'd have to convince him their friendship could grow into more.

Hopes as fanciful as Ella's kelpies and brownies.

Nobody was surprised by his news. Everyone was, just as Innis had said, sad but happy. She alone had taken it as if he'd dropped a bomb.

He stood in front of her before she saw him coming.

"I'm sorry, Mairi," he said. "I wanted to tell you first. Ewan jumped the gun."

"I'm not angry. This is wonderful news for you."

"As my sister says, this could build a career."

"It's what you deserve."

His smile turned wistful. "I'll be back in four months for the wedding. You and Ella could come and visit the states, too. There's lots to show you. We have legends in Minnesota, as well."

"She would love that, Noah." A hint of disappointment clouded his eyes and she placed a hand on his arm. "I would, too."

Almost as if the Highlands were as pissed off over Noah leaving as Mairi was, or maybe because the entire malevolent Unseelie Court of fairies decided six days before the big inspection was a great time to cause trouble, the good fortune of the past week ended.

First to go bad was the weather. From sunny summer blue, the skies turned back to charcoal and ink, and rain fell as if trying to turn all of Craigwarren into a new loch. Roofers had to finish the last quarter of the roof shouting warnings, gripping safety harnesses on the slick tiles, and sending curses ringing through the yard.

Next came the notice that the shipment of six new windows, including the one to be installed where there was of yet no opening, had been delayed for a week. This meant there was no way the energy-efficient double glazing could be installed before the inspectors arrived. Nobody knew how much of a deal-breaker that might be.

While the rain whipped and the roofers slid and furnishings began arriving to be stored in the empty driveway houses until the rain stopped, Bing and Noah managed to get the wiring done, including installing a new breaker box indoors. The new bath, shower and toilet arrived. Surprisingly, Bob had actually installed two toilets in his young life and got that done in a snap. The tub and shower followed but when that didn't go nearly as smoothly, Ewan sprang for a plumber to come hook things up.

Mairi helped in every way she could, mostly to stay near Noah. There wasn't time for much besides crunch work and eating, which was a good thing because the closer they got to inspection day, and Noah's departure, the harder it was to keep her feelings platonic. He'd become a part of her, but no matter how much she wished for closeness and kisses, he had turned gentlemanly as a monk.

By Inspection Monday, everyone's nerves were frayed, and everyone who could pray prayed. Two hours before the inspector's appointment at 1:00 p.m., the fae played a final trick by prodding poor Juliet, who'd been a model goat citizen for almost two weeks, into madness. Mairi followed Noah and Ewan to the cottage after lunch for one final obsessive look around. They'd done all they could. The wiring, the plumbing, and the windows were the biggest worries—until they opened the front door.

Juliet greeted them with a long, mournful bleat and trotted, agitated, to Noah's side. A cursory look around showed them numerous trails of little round goat pellets and several sheets of chewed paper from Noah's notebook. One white wall corner bore a tannish smear of mud where Juliet had obviously scratched an itch.

Despairing, Mairi looked to Noah, fully expecting signs of a meltdown at last. He'd kept his cool faultlessly during the trials that week, but this kind of last-minute disaster could have pushed tranquil Tibetan monks over the edge.

To her shock, Noah bent forward, braced his palms on his thighs and started to laugh. She'd never heard him surrender so completely to any emotion, and pretty soon he'd given up standing and sank to the floor, guffawing until he could hardly breathe. He wrapped one arm around Juliet's slender neck and buried his face in her coarse coat.

"I think he's over the bend," Ewan said, barely controlling his own laughter. "I thought he'd get mad. Instead, he's *gone* mad."

"Juliet, old girl," Noah gasped from the floor, "if this isn't the most fitting christening I could have imagined. We've come full circle, haven't we?"

"Noah, are you all right?" Mairi asked.

"Sure." She could almost hear the air getting dragged into his lungs. "I don't know why she got out of the pen or how she got in here, but I almost don't care if the inspector finds goat shit in here. Maybe he'll think it's funny, too."

"Oh no, no way." Ewan stood next to his brother, placed a toe under his butt and pried upward. "Get your ass up and take your goat outside. She can graze in the rain until we sweep this up, and then I'm chaining her to her fence until this is over. Animals in a human dwelling will get us banned from certification for life."

Noah's eyes sparked with fun. He didn't look crazy when he stood and ran his hands over Juliet's coat with loving care. "I'm even going to miss the damn goat."

Mairi's eyes stung with tears while she laughed.

The inspection took less than half an hour and couldn't have been more anticlimactic if it hadn't happened at all. After the pressure cooker they'd lived in for almost three weeks, following the woman with her check-off sheet and answering her few impersonal questions, felt ordinary as ordering burgers from a drive-through.

Will the goat pen be permanent?

No.

The windows will be installed when?

They arrive in one week.

Double glazed?

Yes.

New insulation?

Floor and ceiling.

She handed them a copy of the list. Congratulated them on a "bonnie wee cottage," and drove back up the muddy driveway with a professional wave.

For several minutes, Ewan stared at the paper in his hand, then he grinned, pulled out his phone and dialed Ainslie with only slight hope of getting through. But she was in her surgery and her anxious voice came over the speaker.

"Aye, Ewan, what's the word? Tell me it's all okay."

He pointed at the others. "On three," he said. "One, two, three…"

"We passed!" Mairi and Noah called with him, and Ainslie squealed in a way that would have made Ella proud.

Mairi had never seen Noah in such throes of happiness that he danced. He grabbed her into a waltz position and twirled her around the living room. They were giddy and inexpert, but so enthusiastic that stepping on each other's toes didn't matter. After several minutes, he twirled her into Ewan's arms who took a turn, laughing along with his brother.

"Thank God we have a woman," he said. "Otherwise, he'd have tried this with me."

"Aww, we could give it a go," Noah called. "But, dang, where's Bing when we need music?"

"Not all that far off, come to mention it," came the voice from the door.

They all stopped in surprise at the sight of Bing and Bob standing beneath the lintel, black macs dripping, heads bowed a wee bit sheepishly.

"What in the world are you two doing here in this dreich?" Ewan laughed. "You look like the grim reaper's twin sons. Get in out of the rain. Pull off those macs, though."

"We couldnae miss hearin' what the powers 'at be had to say. Not that we had a doubt."

"Aye, not a doubt," Bob echoed.

There's not much you two miss, is there?" Noah asked.

"Try not to," Bing said. "Auld Bob here has ears like a bat. Useful."

Noah laughed again. "I really need to apologize for those nicknames. You don't have to use them, you know. We've just done it so long we barely remember your real ones."

"Nae, we like 'em," Bob said. "Call ourselves by them now even t'home."

"Ooo-kay," Ewan laughed. "Whatever floats your boats. C'mon, you two. Back to the house for tea. We have to share the news with Cat and Innis and Isla, and you two were a big part of this."

"That would be right braw," Bing said. "But d'ya want me to sing first? Finish your dance?"

Ewan clapped the young man's shoulder. "Serenade us up the hill why don't you? We've lit up the dance floor enough."

"'I'm Gonna Be' it is," Bing said, and they all joined in the "walk five hundred miles" chorus as they trooped up the drive.

Everyone clung to the high of success as best they could over the next three days of finishing work, but heaviness crept inexorably into the happiness. Painting started immediately the next day, and since virtually every room was painted with the same pretty, warm-toned tan that blended with the cottage's exposed stone, the task was straightforward. Mairi delighted in the moment, however, when she broke open the can of beautiful, rich coral paint and pointed to the two accent walls that were to receive it, one in the kitchen and one in the loft.

"You traitor," Noah moaned. "You said you'd changed your mind."

"Such a whingeing boy," she countered and patted his arm. "I changed it back and you're going to love it."

He did.

Everyone got to paint, even Ella after school. By Wednesday night, everything in the cottage was finished except kitchen and bathroom tiling. By Thursday night, with only one day left before Noah left Saturday morning, the kitchen was finished, and Ewan declared a holiday from working late. Instead, after dinner, he gathered everyone in the living room.

"There are things besides tiling my brother has to take care of before he leaves," he announced. "And I've called us all together to embarrass the heck out of him in the process."

"Nobody asked me about this," Noah protested.

"Nobody intended to. Nobody being Innis and me. Here's how it's going to go. In all the insanity since you've arrived, we've mentioned very little about the party coming up in December."

"What party?" Ella cried. "Can I come?"

"Darlin', you and Skye are to play big parts," Ainslie said.

"Ewan and Ainslie are gettin' married," Mairi said.

"Married! With a white dress?"

"I'll show you a picture of it later," Ainslie whispered.

"While I've been playing at carpentry, my amazing Ainslie has been pulling triple duty. She, Isla and Cat, and recently Mairi, have been planning all things wedding with zero help from me."

"Aye, you lazy do-nothing," Ainslie said lovingly. "You haven't seen me help with much hammering, have you?"

"Fair enough. But there's one thing even the amazing women can't do—and that's fit the groomsmen with their attire."

Mairi grinned at what she realized was coming when Innis entered the room in the company of another white-bearded man carrying several large boxes and three garment bags.

"This will be my wee baby brother, the one and only Seamus MacFarlane," Innis said. "He has a nicer beard than I do, but I'm much nicer than he is."

"True, that," Seamus said.

"But Seamus has a skill. Though he's long retired, he knows well how to fit and make a bonnie guid kilt. His shop, MacFarlane Kiltery, now belongs to his son and grandsons, but I've bribed him into coming out of retirement to measure these two for their wedding kilts. Our Ainslie thought it would be a proper early hen's party to have a wee fashion show for you, so they can choose the style. What say you, ladies?"

Agreement was unanimous.

Mairi hadn't had such fun ever, nor found anything to take her mind off her real life better than watching a flustered Noah disappear with his brother and Innis to try on his first kilts. Seamus had four different styles, and he had come to make the boys play. He had Innis's sense of humor times ten, and the three men had no choice but to change multiple times.

The first time Noah appeared he wore a casual kilt—one made with only four or five yards of fabric and boasting fewer pleats than a formal kilt—he entered the room with a red face and no idea what to do with his hands and arms as the women made him circle and swish the kilt bottom. All Mairi could do was stare, having never seen Noah in anything but jeans and T-shirts. His sculpted calves in the white knee socks, and his slim hips encased in heavy leather buckles robbed her of words.

"You do that proud, laddie," she called when she found her tongue. "You should never wear jeans again."

His face deepened to the next shade of red.

The next kilt was historic, according to Seamus, with box pleats and less swing, but spectacular, like an old guardsman or an ancient piper.

For the third, all the women heard were loud protests from Noah and guffaws from Innis and Ewan. Finally, Seamus came into the room carrying an armful of fabric. He stretched it out on the floor, a huge pleated piece of tartan half the size of the open space.

"Ainslie, how about having your men dressed like in that famous show…*Outlander* is it?"

"Not a bad thought." Ainslie laughed.

"Have just the one for ye, then. Normally this would be a flat piece of wool and we'd fold it into pleats ourselves. But we've nae time for that. These are cheater pleats. Bring out our groomsman."

This time Noah appeared with a full-fledged scowl—and no pants save his boxers. Mairi covered her mouth with both hands to keep in her squeal of delight. Ella threw her head back and howled.

"Noah's in his underpants!"

"This is not appropriate for children," he growled.

"Totally appropriate for Scottish children," Mairi laughed. "How d'ya think we grow the next generation?"

"Noah gets to lie down on our great kilt," Seamus said. "Now watch this."

With a huge sigh, Noah positioned himself atop the fabric. Seamus did some fancy wrapping, looped a leather belt around Noah's waist, pushed and tucked, and five minutes later he wore a kilt that wrapped his waist and covered his knees, and a fabric top that crossed his shoulder and tucked back into the belt.

Mairi almost jumped off the couch and into his arms.

"I've changed my mind. This is what you wear from now on."

"Who gave *you* too much to drink tonight?" Noah asked. But she didn't miss the smile that tugged up the corner of his mouth.

It was nearly twenty minutes before the three men returned. This time in full Prince Charlie formal splendor. Seamus had brought standard eight-yard kilts with their seemingly infinite number of sharp knife pleats. He'd popped white shirts, bow ties, and black Prince Charlie jackets on each man, added red flashes to their knee socks, white fur sporrans to their belts and, for the complete picture, brought laced-up Ghillie Brogue shoes.

They were all stunning men, Innis like an ancient clan chieftain with his wild white hair and beard, Ewan elegant and model handsome, and Noah like a rugged half-Scots lumberjack, stunning in his dress clothes, ready to outshine any born-and-bred Highlander who dared stand next to him.

Mairi stared like a starstruck teen. She'd never tell a living soul she'd developed a crush as wide and endless as Rannoch Moor on this man, but she knew the picture of him standing before her like this would be permanently burned into her memory. Even after the fun was over and Seamus had measured each man for a bespoke wedding kilt, packed up and said his farewells, Noah changed back into his jeans and even they looked different. In a downright erotic way.

She and Noah had maintained their strict friendship-only pact for the past week, but this was truly was his last full night. Tomorrow night he'd leave by seven in order to catch a midnight plane to Amsterdam. Suddenly, the thought of not touching him one last time left her bold claim of good-byes being part of life tattered like a broken sail. In reality it hurt exactly like he'd claimed it would. He'd been right, but it was too late.

All she could do was pretend she hadn't figured it out.

And then her daughter ruined her grand resolve. When she was ready for bed, Ella went quietly to Noah and stood, eyes searching for his.

"Hi, Ella," he said.

"Do you really have to go tomorrow?" Her little eyes shone.

"For a little while, yeah. I'm sorry. But I'll be back at Christmas."

"Christmas is a hundred years away!"

"Nah. Only fifty."

She crawled onto his lap, and he didn't stop her. Nor did he look at anyone else. She wrapped her fairy-like arms around his neck, snuggled in as close as she could, and there she sat, unmoving, like a protestor who'd chained herself to the tree she wanted to save. He placed his lips against her wild, not-quite-red hair and left them there.

Finally, slowly, he lifted his head and stood with her still in his arms. "Come on. Let's go read a couple of stories, okay? Where's Eachann?"

Without moving her head from his shoulder, she pointed toward the kitchen table. He looked at Mairi.

"Is it okay?" he asked.

She simply nodded.

He came back forty-five minutes later, walked straight to her and took her hand.

"My turn," he said. "Come with me." To his brother, he added. "I'll bring her back in a little bit."

Ewan only shook his head, a smirk marring the smooth curve of his lips. "Don't hurry on my account."

"And thanks for the overly public introduction to kilts. It was rough, man."

"All I can say is you were more gracious about trying them than I was."

"I'm a better man, Ewan. A better man."

It took him six seconds once they were out the front door to haul her into a kiss that literally knocked the shoes off her feet. One floppy clog fell when he lifted her half a foot off the ground. The other stayed on, hanging by her toes. Her head swam, her heart pounded against his chest, her breath hitched as if she grabbed an electric fence over and over.

"I couldn't go without telling you I was wrong. It has to be your way—I have to remember what we've become to each other and that it's good, not sad."

A strangled laugh caught in her throat. "No. I was going to be good, the way *you* wanted. I was going to keep my hands off and make this less painful."

"It's painful either way."

He kissed her again, deeper, harder, thrusting his tongue and then letting her do the same, until their rhythm almost had them swaying their bodies with the kiss, building the tension, strengthening the electricity.

"In a short time, we got pretty darn good at this," he said against her lips.

"We were good from day one."

He chuckled. "We were." Then he sobered. "Mairi, sleep with me tonight. *Sleep* sleep, like last time. No quickie sex. Not at this point."

"No slow sex, either?" She kissed his earlobe.

"We wouldn't have time for slow," he growled against her neck, and shivers burst across her shoulders.

"A man who doesn't want sex. How refreshing."

"I didn't say that. I'm a man who'd give a lot to have sex. But it would be contrived and fast and final. I want to hold you for as long as I can."

"Have you been reading women's pornography books again. Jeezo, Noah."

"Yup, what I read at night. 'Shit girls want you to say'." He kissed her forehead.

"I don't care what gave you the idea. I will sleep with you, Noah Portman."

Her phone buzzed in her pocket, and she frowned. It was close to nine. "What the...? She pulled out the phone. "It's my mother. Could there be a worse time to talk to one's mum?" She ignored the call. "I'll ring her back after you kiss me again."

"Good plan."

The phone buzzed again immediately.

"You'd better get that."

With a nod and a sigh, she put her mother on speaker. "Mum?"

"Mairi—oh Mairi!" Her voice was just short of hysterical.

"Mother, what's happened. Are you all right?"

"You have to come, Mairi. You have to help him!"

"Help who? What's going on?"

"They have him. They took Aiden!"

Her throat closed; her mind flew in five directions. "Who took him?"

"The police. They have your brother."

CHAPTER TWENTY-FIVE

"Got everything?" Noah looked deep into Mairi's eyes as she made to pick up her overnight case. Her gaze was surprisingly clear and steady.

"I do. I'm sorry, everyone. Mum was hysterical; I can't leave her till morning."

"Of course you need to help your mum through this." Catrione went to smooth her hair. "I truly believe this will mean something good for you, too."

"I hope. It remains to be seen what they're holding Aiden for. This might amount to nothing."

"Are you sure I can't come with you?" Ainslie said.

"Thank you, Ains. I know you'd drop everything and I love you for it, but I have to face my family on my own. Mom needs to understand. Aiden *has* to go away."

Noah walked her to her car, nerves still thrumming from the power between them compounded by the shock of the past half hour. He couldn't even be disappointed that their tryst was ruined. He only prayed with all his might this trip would end her nightmare.

"You've got this," he told her. "Go fight like Mairi MacDonald."

"Maybe this time I'll kill them with coolness like Noah Portman."

"Mairi." He pushed the long strands of breeze-blown hair away from her face. "If you can't get back by the time I need to leave tomorrow, it's all right. You'll be fine. I'll be fine. Don't change. You are amazing."

"I don't know how to thank you for that."

"No need."

She straightened and took a fortifying breath. "Whatever happens with Aiden, I'm done hiding."

"See? Mairi MacDonald is pretty smart and cool."

She hugged him tightly. "Not as cool as you. Thank you, Noah. For everything."

"Here's lookin'—"

She put her entire palm over his lips. "Don't quote that. I hated that movie."

"Who hates *Casablanca*?"

"That ending? She's free but sad. Nope."

"Okay then... I'll just leave it with we had a pretty good summer fling."

"Aye. Much better." She kissed him one last time. "Bye, Noah." She offered her version of a breezy grin, but he knew her well enough now to see the effort behind it.

"And I'll take Ella to school tomorrow and pick her up. Our last date."

"She'll love it." The bright smile dimmed. She hesitated, but no words came, and with a sad wave, she was gone.

Noah had driven twice during his visit, and he managed Ewan's right-hand drive Rover more or less gracefully while Ella, buckled in behind him, gave him directions to school.

"You did brilliant," she told him when they arrived.

"Thanks, El. Now show me where to pick you up, then it's your turn to be brilliant all day."

"Right there." Ella pointed to the end of a short brick wall where it met with a wide swinging gate.

"Okie doke. Have a good day, kid."

"Have a good day, grown-up."

And he did. He finished the last of the grouting and, with Ewan, moved the small kitchen island and all the cabinetry into place. By three-fifteen, when it was nearly time to fetch Ella, everything he could do was done, and the little cottage shone like a model home. A wave of melancholy buffeted him, and in that moment he'd have moved in himself.

He went out back to the goat pen, and an unwelcome welling clogged his throat. What was she going to do now? Did a goat feel loss?

"You eejit," he said. "I hated you on day one; now I'd pack you in my duffel if it was allowed." He stretched a hand over the fence, and she rubbed against it with a soft *maaaa*. "You better be good. When I come back at Christmas, I don't want to hear any more Houdini stories. Got it?"

He couldn't stand there any longer. Softly he kissed his fingers and touched her between the ears. Then he turned away and refused to allow a single tear.

He pulled up to the curb at school ten minutes early. Older children already milled around the school grounds, and some headed down the street to catch the city bus that served as transportation for those who lived in town. As he watched them go, jostling each other in good-natured camaraderie, his attention slipped to an adult stopped alongside a wrought-iron gate half a block down the street. The man was nondescript in jeans, a plain brown suede jacket, and a gray newsboy hat that made Noah lift a hand

and adjust his own tartan cap. The man lit a cigarette and shook out the match before dropping it carelessly at his feet, drawing deeply, and exhaling a curl of smoke. Without looking back, he headed toward the bus stop, and a rush of well-being infused Noah at the knowledge that strangers didn't have to worry him anymore. He offered the man a salute of thanks for reminding him he could now leave, secure in knowing Aiden had been caught. Mairi and Ella were free of his threats.

He got out of the car and leaned back against the hood — the *bonnet*. He smiled dryly—watching until the younger children began emerging from the building. At one minute past four, Ella appeared, and when she saw him, she broke into a ground-covering skip that made Noah's trip along in bittersweet pleasure.

"Noah! Noah! You should have been at sharing today when I showed Eachann. Everyone loved him and everyone wants one. You should start a business making Eachanns. Mrs. Cowan said you could be rich."

He laughed at her rapid-fire report, the chatter reminding him of the first day he'd laid eyes on her. Except now, the kid had infiltrated his carefully constructed protective shell, and he'd be as willing to pack her off to the U.S. as he would Juliet.

"Whoa there, missy, take a breath. I'm glad they like Eachann, but he's one-of-a-kind, just for you."

That actually stopped her, and her eyes shone as, without warning, she threw her arms around his waist. "I know. I told them that."

He placed a hand on her head and for that second was as rich as he ever wanted to be. Straightening after a few seconds, he let out his breath. "If we stop for ice cream on the way home, will you promise it won't ruin your dinner?"

She released him and hopped in place with excitement. "I promise!"

"Off we go then. Our last date until Christmas."

Her lower lip jutted out slightly. "When do you have to leave? Do you really have to go?"

"I do," he said gently. "In about two-and-a-half hours."

"That's too soon."

"Yeah."

Melancholy never lasted long around Ella, and by the time they'd finished their treats and Noah pulled onto the long road leading to Craigwarren house, he was fully engaged in the little girl's version of "I Spy" wherein the spied object had to be something they'd passed *outside* the car. It was nearly impossible and yet silly, compelling fun.

"The cow we passed at the Davidson farm before the turn," he guessed.

"No! She was brown not tan."

"We didn't pass anything tan."

"Did."

"I give up then. That was my five-hundredth guess anyway."

Her giggle filled the car. "Nae, 'twasn't, Noah. But it was the hay she was eating!"

"Tan!" He stared at her. "Who taught you your colors?"

Ella's giggling turned into belly laughing, and they reached the house both chuckling simply because they couldn't stop.

"That's strange," Noah said, pulling to a stop at the side of the house. "No cars. I'd think Innis's would be here."

"Hey! What's Juliet doing up here?"

"Juliet?" Noah caught the flash of brown and white as the goat trotted from the far front corner of the house. "I swear that animal is bedeviled."

Bedeviled?

A Mairi word.

He didn't even have time to chastise the ridiculous creature when he climbed out of the car before Juliet gave the loudest call he'd ever heard her make and barreled toward him like a mother bear finding a lost cub. She butted his legs, rubbed her head against him, and all but put her front legs on his chest.

"What in the world?" He pushed her away gently. "What's got into you?"

"She knows you're leaving. She's sad," Ella said.

"No." Noah frowned at the goat. "She's upset but I have no idea why. Wonder if everything's okay inside."

They left the unhappy Juliet at the front door and hurried inside, calling Cat's name and getting no reply except from the three cats. David Tennant was with Ainslie as usual. To Noah's relief, he found a sheet of flowered stationary on the kitchen table covered in Catrione's neat handwriting.

Isla and Skye will be home soon from a baby class. Innis and I ran to get something special for our final supper tonight. Ewan is at the bank. Ainslie will be back by half-six. Fresh shortbread in the oven. Eat at six. Love, Aunt Cat.

"I forget Fridays are always busy here," Noah said. "All right, all's well at least. Come on, let's take Juliet back to the barn. By the time we get her settled, everyone should be home."

Ella led the way back out the front door. The goat hadn't moved. Patting his leg as if summoning a dog, Noah strode across the lawn and smiled in satisfaction when Juliet *maa'd* and trotted along.

"She's a trained goat," Ella laughed.

"She's crazy."

When they drew even with the cottage, however, Juliet stopped and bawled in protest at going further.

"Come on, Juliet!" Ella said. "Come and play with Ailish."

Juliet planted her feet. Noah gave a gentle tug on one horn. "Come on, dopey."

The goat trotted instead to the door of the cottage where she lowered her head at last and made a few agitated nips at the grass. Noah frowned, unsure why his gut suddenly churned in concern rather than annoyance. He didn't believe for a second the animal knew he was leaving, but something had her riled.

Ella bent to hug the goat, and Noah reached to remove his belt to use as a leash, when he noticed the cottage door was open an inch. His pulse raced into double time. He'd closed the door himself and hidden the key in the small nook behind one jamb. Holding his breath, he checked for that key. It was gone.

"Stay with Juliet," he said to Ella, and pushed open the door.

The main living space was just as he'd left it, pristine and new, but then he noticed the sweatshirt draped over one ladderback chair at the refinished table. He knew the gray hoodie well; it belonged to Bob. Apparently, Bob had been by and left it. It wasn't like the boy to leave a door open, however. Bob might have been a goof, but he wasn't a sloppy goof.

The sudden sound of running footsteps from one of the bedrooms approached so quickly he had no time to turn before a painful blow to his lower back sent him sprawling face first to the floor. Gasping, his first thought was for Ella. God keep her from coming in, he prayed, and fought to push up. Another powerful punch between his shoulder blades kept him down. He managed to turn his head and saw a booted foot next to his face. The other foot was on his back.

"Stay down, Yank, if ye don't fancy a clout t' the heid." The voice was heavily accented and smoker raspy.

"Who the hell are you? What do you want?" If Noah's arms hadn't been unevenly splayed over his head and by his side, he'd have grabbed at the man's standing leg, but the more he struggled to gain position, the harder the man stood on his back.

"Go' a message for ye from Aiden Murray. Y'tell that cow of a sister o' his that her wee girlie is with her uncle, aye? He'll be tellin' her where to meet them and how to get her back home."

"Son of a—"

The man stomped. Noah's breath left him again in a whoosh of pain, and as it subsided, he finally understood what was happening.

"Magnus," he wheezed. "Ferguson."

"Shut it."

"There's no point to this," Noah managed. "Aiden Murray is in custody."

"I said shut it," came the sharp reply. "You say what you like to try and stop me, but I'm takin' the girl to him, and he'll sort the lot of you. I only want the money he'll gi' me and I'm awa'. Now if ye' stay here like a guid lad whilst I lock the door, the wee lassie won't be hurt. Hear me, pal?"

"I'm not lying. The police have Aiden in Glasgow. His sister is there now. They're looking for you, too, Magnus. If you give this up, you can still get away."

He didn't care if the man escaped as long as he did it without Ella, but Magnus was evidently done talking. He removed his foot from Noah's back and unleased a quick jab with his toe at Noah's ribcage. For the first time, Noah groaned out loud, and then anger infused him like a wildfire. He lurched to his knees, but a sharp pain forced him to stop and catch his breath. By the time he scrambled to his feet, Magnus was at the door. Noah's eyes went wide and his stomach clenched. Blue jeans. Brown suede jacket. Gray newsboy cap. The man had been right in front of him at the school.

"Stop!" he shouted.

Idiot. As if that was going to halt him.

He stumbled toward the door but Ferguson laughed and held up a key. "I've been watchin' youse. It's well planned," he said. "You're going to sit in here long enough for me to get on my way, because Aiden is lookin' forward to a bit o' time with his niece." His toothy grin was pure, satisfied malice.

Noah's blood ran cold at the thought that this man had been near the house in the past doing the cowardly Aiden's bidding. He charged the door, but Ferguson slammed it in his face and jammed the key in the lock. A sliding scrape at the handle told Noah it had been jammed with something. Seconds later Ella's shout filtered through the walls and jarred Noah to his bones.

"No! Go away! I'm not going with you. Noah!!"

He rattled the handle in desperation, but even after he unlocked the new deadbolt from inside, the inward-opening door held fast. He glanced at all the windows, but they opened like awnings. He'd have to break one to get out. For three seconds he gave into panic. Then his brain cleared. He grabbed Bob's sweatshirt from the chair and took four running strides to the kitchen where he yanked open a cabinet drawer and pulled a screwdriver and hammer from the basic toolkit he'd left there. The wooden door was massive but it had only two hinges. Noah had installed it himself and knew precisely where to pound out the hinge pins.

It took mere minutes, and when he could pull the loose door open half a foot, he was able to remove the metal spike Ferguson had slid through the handle. Noah burst through the opening and followed Ella's calls to the side of the cottage. The front bumper of a car stuck out from the back wall—something he'd completely missed when they'd arrived. He also saw a scene that under any other circumstance would have bent him double with laughter. Ella was not going quietly into the vehicle, and Juliet wasn't having it either.

Ferguson was, for all intents and purposes, trying to hold onto a Tasmanian Devil. Ella twisted and kicked and slapped and hollered, and the harder her captor tried to contain her legs, the more she twisted her top half free and smacked at him. When he wrapped her arms tight, she flailed with her feet. To top it off, Juliet circled him like a crazed billy, butting his legs whenever she found an opening.

"Let her go, Magnus," Noah yelled.

He caught the man off-guard enough that Ella got an opening. She leaned forward in his arms and bit his shoulder. Ferguson yelped and loosened his grip. Ella slipped free.

"Run, Ella. Back to the house! Now. Go somewhere safe," Noah yelled. Ferguson lunged for her, but Ella dodged and sent Noah a fierce look he couldn't decipher. Fear or anger? Both, knowing her. "Go fast. Don't look back. I won't let him follow you."

He turned to Ferguson and hefted the sweatshirt he'd carried with him. Noah was the last person anyone would choose as their fight champion, but if he could throw something over the man's head—

"Oy! What's all this!" Another voice, welcome as sunlight, rang from behind him.

Bob.

"Noah is with the bad man!"

Ella's voice held nervous fear, but Noah had no time to assess whether she was following his directions. Ferguson came at him like a furious dog and caught him in the stomach, sending them both to the ground and the air rushing from Noah's lungs yet again. For several seconds he grappled, wheezing, with the man on top of him, succeeding only in keeping him from punching or kicking anything vital. Ferguson was no bigger than Noah, but he was wiry and tough as a street boxer. Whatever muscle Noah had built climbing ladders and swinging hammers wasn't much of a match against his opponent's pure strength.

And then, with a shout and a grunt, Ferguson was flung to the side. Noah rolled instinctively away before he looked to where the man lay flat on his back with Bob seated on top of him, pinning his wrists to the ground. Since Bob outweighed Ferguson by half, the man's wiry strength was no longer an asset.

"Give off, dobber," Bob said to the struggling man. "If you donnae, I'll have the boss 'ere add his weight." He grinned at Noah. "Came to get my shirt, aye, but saw you were a wee bit busy."

Noah shook his hand, breathing deeply to get his heartbeat under control. "I've never been so happy to hear a voice in my life."

He searched up the lane but Ella, to his relief, was not in sight.

"Got a belt, have you?" Bob asked.

Noah frowned but then snorted as understanding dawned. He undid his belt and yanked the leather through the loops. "You've watched your share of crime shows, I see. Cheesy but smart, I guess. I was going to try using your sweatshirt."

"Might 'ave worked." Bob grinned. "Help me get this round his wrists then you call the police. We'll have to hold him here until they come; these aren't exactly handcuffs, are they?"

Ferguson was surprisingly quiet even though he struggled when Bob and Noah inefficiently but effectively tightened the belt around his wrists behind his back. Noah called 999 and was connected to the Glencoe Police. Once they understood the situation and agreed to come, he called Ewan. Properly upset, his brother promised he, Cat, and Innis were only five minutes from home and they'd check on Ella.

"You're really all right?" Ewan asked.

"As long as there are the two of us here watching Ferguson, we're fine. I don't want to leave Bob alone—"

"No, of course not," Ewan replied. "If Ella's not with you, I'm sure she's fine. Noah?"

"Yeah?"

Silence filled the connection for several seconds before he spoke. "Thank you. I'm..." His voice cracked. "Be careful with that jackass."

"We will be."

Time lost meaning in the long minutes that followed. Magnus Ferguson cursed and berated his captors, especially Bob who delighted in keeping him on the ground, only allowing him to leave his belly-down position as the police arrived. They wasted no time taking Noah's full story and hustling Ferguson into their squad car.

"That should do it, Mr. Portman," the constable who'd taken the details said. "Our sergeant has connected with your DI Donnelly. He sent word that they indeed have Mr. Murray in custody. We'll be calling if we have more questions.

"Thank you," Noah replied. "That's a huge relief."

The constables climbed into the car, but Noah and Bob had no time to congratulate themselves on their success before they caught sight of Ewan jogging toward them, his face a mask of concern.

"Got 'im!" Bob called.

"Good. That's good. But I need to know if Ella came back down here. We've searched the house and she isn't there."

Noah's stomach leapt back into a freefall of panic.

"She has to be there."

"We've searched every room."

He fought to calm his mind. From day one he'd seen Ella was nothing if not resourceful for her age. Just as on the day they'd found her with her bogart, he simply had to find the room she'd locked herself into this time. His breath rushed out in sudden relief.

"The little cottages along the driveway. She's hidden in them before."

At a dead run, Noah, Ewan, and Bob followed the departing police car past the house to the first little building. Noah thrust the door open to find nothing but the familiar ladder and paint cans. No smiling Ella. No friendly bogart.

They searched the other two little houses and found them empty as well.

"Damn," he swore. "Where would she go?"

A rumble of engine and the crunch of tires spinning too quickly over hard-packed gravel made them look up the road. Mairi's Kia came far faster than it should have, and when it drew even with them Mairi put on the brakes and skidded. Noah's heart slid back into his throat. What was he going to tell her? He'd lost her daughter when he'd promised to keep her safe? Mairi jumped from the car almost as it jerked to a halt. Even with her features contorted in worry, and though his own mind reeled wishing he could shield her from pain, relief flooded Noah the instant he saw her. She was the mama bear. Whatever came next, she would deal with it. She was a lighthouse in any storm—in his storms.

"Did you find her?" Mairi asked.

Noah stared. How had she known?

"My brother finally came clean. He told us this afternoon about his buddy already here to take Ella. Magnus carries no phone, so Aiden couldn't reach him, and I couldn't get hold of anybody here. I headed home right then but couldn't get here before school ended. I reached Cat ten minutes ago."

Noah took her upper arms and brought his face close to hers.

"She got away from Magnus because she's brave and amazing. She's gone somewhere she feels safe and we just have to find her. She's fine."

Mairi hung her head, letting it rest a moment against Noah's chest. A second later she snapped it back up.

"If the house was empty, and you were not available, in her mind Diarmid or Eachann would be the next logical protectors."

"I'll go check the barn," Ewan said. "C'mon, Bob."

"The loch," Noah and Mairi said together.

They ran until they reached the narrow path to Loch Warren. Twenty strides in, he saw the colorful figure in the grass and pointed. They stopped beside his carving. "Look at your smart girl," Noah said and let out a breath.

Eachann had not been randomly dropped. His hooves were deliberately poked into the ground, and he faced the water. "Thank, God," Mairi whispered.

It took twenty more minutes of walking and calling before they heard her respond at last. When they saw her, it was in the very spot Mairi had once pointed out as forbidden—across a piece of shoreline made up of large, slippery rocks leading to Eachann's cave.

"Oooh, glad I'm not Ella," Noah joked, his dissipating worry couched in relieved laughter.

"Maybe, just this once, I'll thank Eachann for keeping her safe and let it go." Mairi didn't hide her tears or even bother to wipe them away.

"This is why mothers are superheroes," he said, and kissed the top of her head. "Go meet her. Tell her everything is all right."

He watched mother and daughter embrace halfway across the rocky beach and his breathing hitched while Mairi held Ella's hand until they were back on even ground. Ella ran full tilt into Noah's legs, exactly the way she'd barreled into him the very first day he'd met her. This time he swung her into his arms, engulfing her in a smothering hug. She squeezed him so tightly he could barely breathe, but he didn't loosen her grip one centimeter.

"You stopped the bad man," she said into his shoulder.

"You got away first, my brave girl," he said. "Then I could stop him. And you're safe now."

"I love you, Noah."

His world gave a seismic shift. "I love you, Ella."

By the time the household had settled back to a semblance of normal, Ella had recounted her entire adventure, admitting she'd let herself get so scared she'd kept running until she was almost to Eachann's cave, even though she wasn't supposed to go there. Mairi had confirmed her brother was not leaving police custody anytime soon, and Isla returned and had to hear the entire story again. Nobody even mentioned Noah's impending departure. When he remembered with a sharp pang of panic and checked the time, it was nearly quarter to seven, fifteen minutes before he was supposed to leave.

He didn't question how it had been possible to forget. The little girl he'd lost had become far more important than running home to meet Leonard Frederickson. His decision was easy. Without a word he slipped up to his room.

When he returned, Catrione was the one who put a hand to her mouth.

"Oh, Noah, *mo cridhe*. We have to take you to your plane! And there's been no supper. What's happened to my brain? I'll put some bread and sausages out. And we had Rose McGinty's celebration bread pudding—that's what we went to get..."

"Auntie, Auntie." Noah took the half-distraught Cat into an embrace and rested his cheek on her crown. "You don't need to rush. I'm not leaving."

He stayed five extra days, long enough to be certain Aiden no longer posed a threat and Mairi's life could permanently return to normal. Despite his power to fabricate accusations and palm his bad deeds off on others, Aiden's connection to Magnus Ferguson finally nailed him. The two were aligned with a mid-level drug dealer for whom Aiden was both buying and selling—confirmed by the bonus of finding heroine in his possession—but when Magnus admitted he'd stashed the drugs in Mairi's house and gone after Ella on Aiden's orders, the pair were charged with both drug dealing and attempted kidnapping. They had lawyered up, but nobody believed they were going anywhere but prison for a very long time.

When Catrione insisted Mairi bring her mother to Craigwarren, Noah finally knew Mairi and her daughter could start on the road to healing. Sheila Murray, slender, almost frail, with her pale Celtic skin and salted black hair, clearly struggled with the knowledge that her beloved son was not the sweet reformed lad she'd wanted him to be. For the first two days of her visit, tears fell easily, but Noah watched as Catrione fussed over the broken mother and Ella bewitched her grandmother into finding smiles despite the sadness. On his last day, Noah would have been satisfied if he hadn't been more than a little envious Sheila was staying and he was leaving.

No matter how hard he tried to slow it, time flew inevitably to his last moment at Craigwarren when he stood beside Ewan's car with Mairi. The cottage was completely finished. The famous newlyweds would arrive in three days. Mairi had received good news from Paul Taylor in Glasgow. Aiden's hearings were imminent. Things had been wrapped up far better than Noah had ever imagined. Still, nothing felt settled much less right.

"Last chance." He smiled as brightly as he could manage. "Come with me. You and Ella."

"Last chance," she replied, resting her forehead against his lips. "Stay with us."

"You got your teaching job back," he said. "That'll keep you busy and happy."

"Aye, and it's feast or famine. This afternoon, Christina Sullivan called and said she'd be thrilled to offer me the job back here, too."

"That's wonderful. Have you decided which to take?"

"Nae. It's a hard choice now. Ella likes this school. She has new friends. The uniforms are prettier." She allowed a quiet laugh. "We'll see. And you? Your work starts right away?"

"Pretty much. They want the project finished in time for New Year's."

"And you'll lose a couple of weeks for the wedding here in three months…"

"Admittedly, scheduling needs to be negotiated."

"I hope it all turns out to be perfect, Noah. Whatever happens, that hotel has a very special artist working for them."

"And whatever classroom you end up in will have the best teacher in the school."

"We *are* pretty perfect."

"Hard to argue against that." He wrapped his arms around her. There wasn't anything left to say.

He released her, pressed a soft kiss on her cheek, and a sad wave later he was headed away from Craigwarren. He'd see her for two weeks in December. He'd probably come visit his brother and new sister-in-law off and on in the future. But he'd been right from the beginning. As Ewan guided the Land Rover farther from Mairi, Noah didn't see the future, only the loss.

EPILOGUE

Jetlag overlapped jetlag. Noah gave a huge sigh of relief as he turned off the motor of his rental car in front of Craigwarren house. Arguably, he hadn't been in the best condition for making his first solo drive on the A82, but he'd arrived in one piece.

Two days. That was all he'd been gone. It felt like two years, but he reminded himself the royal cottage guests weren't even here yet, Aiden Murray and Magnus Ferguson were still awaiting sentencing, and it had only been yesterday he'd told Bridget he was turning around and going back.

It had taken a mere hour on the plane heading home to know without a single doubt he'd made a mistake. One hour to have Mairi's lesson finally register for good: that sometimes a person needed to fight for his own path in life rather than go along with other people's wishes. For the first time in thirty-three years Noah knew what he wanted to fight for. Somehow, he'd convince Mairi they could make this love he couldn't walk away from work.

Aunt Catrione had devised the plan. He needed to talk to Mairi alone, she'd insisted—simple as that. Since Mairi's Kia stood by itself in the driveway, Cat had obviously managed her part by spiriting the family away to give him time. His heart drummed against his ribcage as he pushed open the front door without knocking. David Tennant skittered into the room, and Noah bent to fondle his ears before the dog could give him away.

"Help me out here, Davy old boy," he whispered. "We need to surprise her."

The mantel clock ticked, metronome steady; the house creaked in its centuries-old language, familiar now that he was back home. He gave David Tennant a final pat before heading quietly up the stairs.

He saw her through her open bedroom door and stopped short in surprise. A half-filled suitcase lay open on her bed, and she added to it as he watched. Disappointment flared. The packing had to mean she was leaving Craigwarren and going back to Glasgow. He brushed away the feeling. Fine. Then it would be Glasgow. He moved into the doorway.

"Hi there. Going somewhere?"

She screeched and jumped backward, hand at her heart. "Noah?" Her face went white as the sweater she dropped in a heap on the floor and her voice rose in pitch. "Oh, Lord, *Noah?* How are you here?"

He grinned. "A car, a plane, a plane, and a car."

The cry she gave before launching into his arms gratified him as thoroughly as any kiss, and when he wrapped her close, the perfect peace that infused him was all he needed in the world.

"You only just left," she said. "What happened? Did you not get home?"

"I did. I stayed a day—long enough to see Bridget and talk to Leonard Frederickson. I told him I hadn't been quite honest. That I got a unique opportunity overseas I don't want to lose and if he wants me as much as he claims, he'll have to let me split my time."

"You did?" Her eyes shone with disbelief.

"I did. Details to be determined, if you'll help me figure them out."

She placed a hand on each of his cheeks, and giggles erased her incredulity.

"Oh, Noah, this is...you'll never believe..." She gestured toward the suitcase.

"You took your job back. In Glasgow."

"No. I'm packing to come to you."

He stared, stunned. "To the U.S.?"

"Wherever you were, that's where I was going."

"But your job?"

"I've chosen to stay here, but I'll not start until after Christmas."

"Wait. You haven't bought tickets? I'm not screwing up an expensive—"

She placed a finger over his lips and shook her head. "I haven't. I was going to tell everyone tonight and book the flight for day after tomorrow. It would have been a short trip to see if you'd help *me* figure this out. You weren't gone two hours before I knew I'd follow you anywhere."

"Remodeling a hotel ballroom meant nothing the closer I got to it without you. I knew I'd give it up."

"Och, Noah. Look at us! Is this some daftie *Gift of the Magi* thing? I never liked that story."

"Seriously? No Magi? No *Casablanca*? Where's your romance?"

"Turned to fairy tales." She tapped his chest. "I thought I didn't believe in them, but since Ella fell in love with you, and you with her and her kelpie, I want my life to be every Disney movie rolled into one with Eachann and Diarmid thrown in for good measure. That's what I planned to give as my reason for going. It was a lucky break they left at the same time today. Gave me a moment to myself to plan the words…" Her eyes narrowed and she shook her head. "Wait a minute. Oh, bollocks! They *know*?"

He grinned. "I wanted an hour alone with you. They're my family. They'll do anything for me."

"I see. And did *you* know even before you left?"

"No. I genuinely believed leaving for good was best. That lasted an hour—and then I knew the opposite was true. Frederickson's a good man—after I talked to him he wished me luck. I won't get wealthy on the hotel job, but there'll be enough so two things can happen. Ewan won't have to sell his cabin, and I can make several flights to you. When the job is done, things can change. I don't exactly hate it here."

She laughed, joyous and bell-like. "Let's travel back and forth. I want to see where you come from. I want Ella to learn your legends."

He kissed her slowly but then pulled away and held her eyes with his. "I haven't magically changed overnight, Mairi. I'm making this sound easy but it won't be—for either of us. I might not ever fully believe I deserve you and Ella, but I have learned that I trust you to take me faults and all. I promise I will make a proper go of this."

"And haven't you just proven that, my sweet Noah? The only thing you have to change is your doubt. Don't ever doubt this or us. I'll travel to the ends of the Earth with you if that's what we need to do."

"I have a plaid driving cap some pretty girl bought for me. If that'll do for traveling clothes, I'm ready to start out now."

"Will y'add that great kilt Innis's brother kitted you out in?"

"Oh, I don't know. I can't deal with that thing by myself. It would mean committing to traveling straight into the seeing-me-in-my-boxers stage." He quirked a brow suggestively.

"Bugger all, there's a disappointment. I would have hoped no boxers."

"*That* kind of trip? Well then, who needs the hat?"

"Och, nae. There's a great old song says it all, doesn't it? You can leave your hat on."

She initiated their next kiss, one that was immediately different—soul deep, filled with promise and permanence—and Noah knew the real trip had well and truly begun.

THE END

AUTHOR'S NOTE and ACKNOWLEDGEMENTS

To Scotland for Love wasn't the easiest book I've ever written, but in the end, it was worth the struggle. Neither Noah nor Mairi, once I met and got to know them, was anything like I'd first imagined. Noah was so quiet and reluctant to tell his story that I thought I'd have to make something up that wasn't true to him. Mairi, with a failed marriage and a dangerous brother, first struck me as a damsel in distress. I couldn't have been further off-base! Noah was simply the strong, silent type—a little clueless but kind and searching for love. Mairi—oh, this woman! She was strong and feisty and a fierce mama bear who knew when she'd let fear get the best of her and wasn't having it. Together they made this story different and stronger than any I've written, and I adore them both.

Mairi leading us to the Edinburgh Fringe Festival was a joyous treat, where I got to relive the elegant craziness of Scotland's capital in August. I love that Noah brought us all down to earth with his calm and peaceful way. The way he fell in love, not just with his Mairi but with the very special Ella who made everyone (I hope you, too) believe in kelpies and brownies, let me know he deserved the status of hero.

I want to thank two amazing women, Cat Schield and Nan Dixon, without whom I might have turned in my keyboard long ago. They are not only fellow authors of immense talent, but therapists, advisors, imparters of the newest business-of-writing trends, critique partners, but most of all friends.

Thanks, as ever, to Kelli Collins—an editor with so much talent that she can fix even chapters that "go off the rails fairly spectacularly." But her skills don't come close to matching her heart and kindness. To Dana Lamothe of Designs by Dana, thank you for creating covers I adore, this one being absolutely no exception.

Finally, to the readers who keep patiently asking for "the next book," my love and gratitude is boundless for you all.

ABOUT THE AUTHOR

Award-winning and No.1 Bestselling author Lizbeth Selvig writes heartwarming contemporary romance. Whether set in the Scottish Highlands, a huge ranch in Wyoming, a small town in Minnesota, or a Kentucky racetrack, her strong, fun and funny characters will never do the expected while finding their ways home to family and love. Lizbeth turned to fiction writing after working as a newspaper journalist and magazine editor, raising an equine veterinarian daughter (handy, since there are usually too many horses in her stories) and a talented musician son (also handy because she's been known to write about rock stars). She shares life in Minnesota, where her first book series is set, with her best friend (aka her husband, Jan), her two pretty horses, Jedi and Largo, three human grandchildren, and her four-legged grandbabies of which there are nearly thirty (including two alpacas, a couple of small goats, a mammoth-eared donkey, two miniature horses, a pig, and many many dogs, cats and regular-sized horses). In her spare time, she loves to hike, quilt, read, and ride horses. An incorrigible extrovert, she also loves connecting with readers—so please do contact her any time.

www.lizbethselvig.com